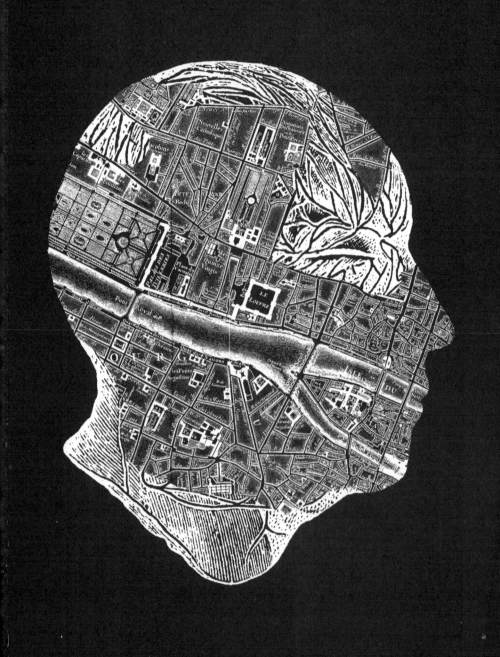

Stephen Volk

UNDER A RAVEN'S WING

Stephen Volk

UNDER A RAVEN'S WING

2021

Cover and book design by Pedro Marques.
Text set in Caslon and Didot.
Endpapers: *Rue de Paris, temps de pluie* (1877)
by Gustave Caillebotte (1848-1894).

Printed in England by the T J Books Limited
on Vancouver Cream Bookwove 80 gsm stock.

PS Publishing Ltd
Grosvenor House
1 New Road
Hornsea, HU18 1PG
England
editor@pspublishing.co.uk
WWW.PSPUBLISHING.CO.UK

CONTENTS

For Kim Newman and David Pirie,
who have also played in this sandbox

Also dedicated to the memory
of two of my own mentors:
Bill Stair (1939-1991)
and
Robin Carroll (1948-2019)

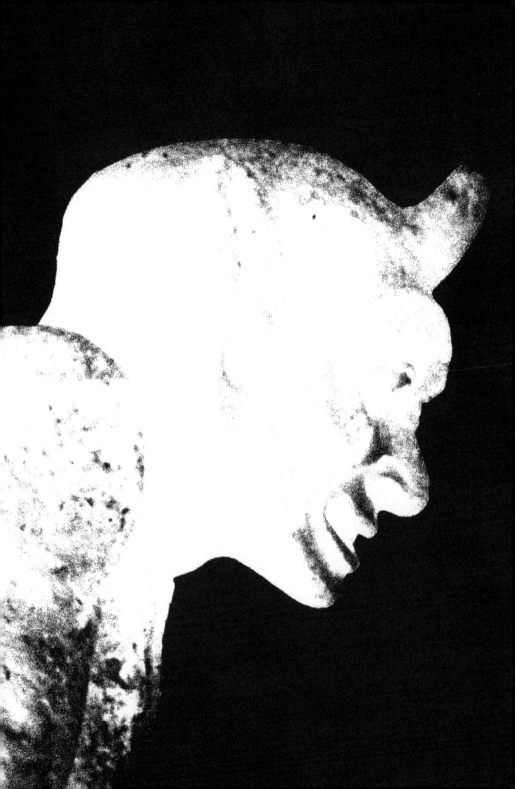

Introduction

CHARLES PREPOLEC

"I was enjoying the twofold luxury of meditation and a meerschaum, in company with my friend C. Auguste Dupin . . ."
Narrator, "The Purloined Letter"

"Now, in my opinion, Dupin was a very inferior fellow. That trick of his of breaking in on his friends' thoughts with an apropos remark after a quarter of an hour's silence is really very showy and superficial. He had some analytical genius, no doubt; but he was by no means such a phenomenon as Poe appeared to imagine."
Sherlock Holmes, *A Study in Scarlet*

"Mediocrity knows nothing higher than itself; but talent instantly recognizes genius . . ."
Dr John Watson, *The Valley of Fear*

"Cut out the poetry, Watson . . ."
Sherlock Holmes, "The Adventure of the Retired Colourman"

Arthur Conan Doyle's Sherlock Holmes stories are quite likely the most often imitated short stories—in terms of characters, style and plotting—in the world today. A veritable cottage industry has sprung up around the doings of the Great Detective and it has exploded exponentially in size since the advent of self-publishing in the digital era. Readers who've finished Doyle's original sixty tales, and yearn for more, can now choose from literally thousands of new Sherlock Holmes stories written by virtually hundreds of writers, who slavishly attempt to replicate the traditional Watsonian voice through a pastiche of Doyle's style, characterizations and story format. Unfortunately, while imitation may be the sincerest form of flattery, it doesn't often result in great art.

While Arthur Conan Doyle's remarkably rich but economical use of language may seem deceptively simple at first glance, it really isn't at all, and while most pastiche writers can nail the format, the language is often out of reach. As a result, the bulk of those thousands of new traditional Sherlock Holmes stories tend to be largely empty, flat, formula fiction and ultimately disappointing to discerning readers. Sometimes simply having more is less, and mediocrity is the norm when quantity, rather than quality, is the goal.

With that scenario in mind, when my co-editor, Jeff Campbell, and I decided to pitch an anthology of new Sherlock Holmes stories to our publisher in 2007, we opted for a somewhat non-traditional approach: Each of the stories would have to blend Sherlock Holmes with elements of fantasy, science fiction or horror, rather than just being straight-up mystery or crime stories, and to that end we invited writers who worked specifically in those genres to contribute. For an added injection of creativity, we told contributors to take any approach to telling their stories. Mimicry of the Watsonian voice was certainly an option, but not a requirement. Our ultimate goal was to present great stories, not necessarily Sherlock Holmes stories, simply stories utilizing Sherlock Holmes and his world. Imitation wasn't the name of the game. We wanted to elevate the nature of the sub-genre. We wanted both talent *and* genius.

Enter Stephen Volk ...

I first met Steve in person at the 2008 World Fantasy Convention in Calgary, while launching that first anthology—*Gaslight Grimoire: Fantastic Tales of Sherlock Holmes*, although we'd had some contact online via *All Hallows*, a newsgroup for members of the Ghost Story Society, and I was familiar with his short stories published in the group's journal and then collected in his 2006 short story collection *Dark Corners*. I was, of course, also well aware that he was the screenwriter of the groundbreaking BBC television production *Ghostwatch*, Ken Russell's *Gothic*, the ITV television series *Afterlife* and a variety of other things, but it was the short stories, some featuring a sort of period occult detective named Venables, as well as the truly stellar "The Chapel of Unrest," that really caught my attention. It was clear that we shared similar influences as the nods to Algernon Blackwood, M. R. James, William Hope Hodgson, Arthur Machen, and, of course, the granddaddy of them all, Edgar Allan Poe, permeate the writing. It was obvious that here was a writer who understood the subtle nuance and beauty of period language, had studied the classic weird fiction form, yet injected it with a uniquely personal and pointed modern insight to the nature of human fears, and how we attempt to understand and rationalize them, with each story.

Needless to say, when we met, we got on like a house on fire.

I asked him for a Sherlock Holmes story, one where Holmes could not "eliminate the impossible". He asked all the right questions about guidelines, what I'd hoped to achieve, what I wanted to avoid, etc. . . . and a short while later "Hounded" landed in my inbox, making it clear that Steve is as well versed in the works of Arthur Conan Doyle as he was with the horror writers, riffing as it does on Doyle's fine séance story "Playing with Fire" and presenting us with an elderly Watson descending into the sort of nervous maelstrom of madness and horror that plagues Poe's narrators in "The Tell-Tale Heart" and "The Black Cat".

I can recall initially reading my print-out of it at the time, reclining on my couch, getting caught up in the wonderful opening and then feeling the rising sense of dread, manifesting as a swirling mass of butterflies taking wing in the pit of my stomach, as I twigged where it was heading, and that I was reading exactly the sort of story I was after. My excitement was such that I practically read the whole thing aloud to my wife as I wanted desperately to share my joy with someone in the moment. It was, and remains (I just re-read it moments ago), a perfect Sherlock Holmes horror story, juxtaposing the rational with the irrational in a manner I had never encountered previously. Here was the elevation of the Sherlock Holmes story—beautifully written, thrilling, moving and loaded with atmosphere. For a taste of the sort of atmosphere present, take a look at the opening scene of the 2011 film *The Awakening*, for which Steve wrote the screenplay.

As a commissioning editor my ship had come in; and as a reader, this was a dream come true. Anyway, in accordance with Watson's self-serving quote above, I must be something of a talent, as I'll say it without hesitation, Stephen Volk is a genius, and I'll take a self-congratulatory pat on the back—thank you very much—for directing his gifts towards the subject of Sherlock Holmes.

But Steve, too, is also a talent, since he recognizes the genius of both Arthur Conan Doyle and Edgar Allan Poe, unlike that ingrate Sherlock Holmes in that other quote above—which brings us to the contents of the book you now hold . . .

"Hounded" duly appeared in our second Holmes/horror anthology—*Gaslight Grotesque: Nightmare Tales of Sherlock Holmes* (2009)—and we went on to planning the third book. Needless to say, Steve was top of the list for prospective contributors. Again, he came through, this time with "The Comfort of the Seine"; the first in this present volume. Once again, he raised the genius stakes and knocked me off my feet.

The twin streams of Doyle and Poe, the student and the master, came crashing together in the most literal, and literate, way yet, with a naively young Sherlock Holmes finding his calling and learning his trade in 1870s Paris from none other than Edgar

Allan Poe's own creation, the original and first great detective, C. Auguste Dupin.

As a concept, it sounds remarkably simple, however the mechanics of making it work, and the levels on which it works, are anything but simple, and a testament to the depth of thought permeating Steve's work. For starters, by setting his story in a largely undocumented period in the fictional life of Holmes he's got free rein to do what he will with the proto-Holmes character. And, in this story, and those that follow, he takes hold of every opportunity to play about with formative experiences that shape and explain elements of the character as we know him.

Over the course of the tales you'll discover the root of Holmes's drug use, his aversion to romantic entanglements, why he did not investigate the Ripper murders, etc. . . . and all of them covered not as a specific focus, but as natural elements of the story. At the heart of it all, there is a delightful reversal of the standard Sherlock Holmes formula, with Holmes taking on the role of Watson, operating as friend, companion, and documenting his own adventures at the side of a Great Detective. Our Master is here both pupil and Boswell. Watching all the elements drop into place as proto-Holmes moves towards the character we all know so well is an incredibly rewarding journey. As is the notion that Holmes's skills come through a handing of the baton from his literary predecessor, Dupin.

Mind you, that's all just one side of the equation, the Sherlock Holmes side. The real element of genius is in what Steve does with Poe's Dupin. He is both the great detective as we know him from "The Murders in the Rue Morgue" (1841), "The Mystery of Marie Rogêt" (1842) and "The Purloined Letter" (1844) and, as contradictory as it may sound, simultaneously a complete reinvention of the character.

How that works is the brilliant central conceit upon which these stories hinge, and it's so deliciously clever that I'll leave you to discover it entirely for yourself in the pages ahead. I will, however, reassure you that the influence and legacy of Poe can be felt, perhaps even more strongly than the Sherlock Holmes elements, in every single page ahead, sometimes even echoing specific story elements from "The Fall of the House of Usher," "The Masque of the Red Death," "The Black Cat," "Hop-Frog," "The Premature Burial," etc. . . . and their underlying themes of madness, corruption and decay.

It's a heady mixture, this literal and literary combination of Doyle's economical rationalism with Poe's fantasist extravagance, but you're in the hands of a master who makes it seem effortless and the most natural and perfect thing in the world.

I probably shouldn't even mention that the author also manages to work in lovely nods to Leroux's *The Phantom of the Opera*, Hugo's *The Hunchback of Notre-Dame* and even a delightful appearance from Jules Verne, but yes, he does, and it all makes for an incredibly rich, textured and thoroughly rewarding reading experience.

Now, I've held you back long enough. Ignore Sherlock's admonition and never cut the Poe from poetry, as it's time for you to engage your talents and discover a bit of genius for yourself. Pour yourself a drink, shutter the windows, leave the woes of the modern world behind as you travel to late 19th century Paris and take shelter under a raven's wing . . .

Calgary, Alberta
March 2020

Charles Prepolec *is a former mystery bookshop owner, currently freelance editor, writer, artist, speaker and reviewer with published contributions in a variety of books and magazines. He is co-editor of four Sherlock Holmes fiction anthologies (with J. R. Campbell) for EDGE SF & F*—Gaslight Grimoire: Fantastic Tales of Sherlock Holmes *(2008),* Gaslight Grotesque: Nightmare Tales of Sherlock Holmes *(2009),* Gaslight Arcanum: Uncanny Tales of Sherlock Holmes *(2011) and* Gaslight Gothic: Strange Tales of Sherlock Holmes *(2018), plus* Professor Challenger: New Worlds, Lost Places *(2015); as well as co-editor (with Paul Kane) of* Beyond Rue Morgue: Further Tales of Edgar Allan Poe's 1st Detective *(2013) for Titan Books. At the turn of the century he served as news editor for actor Christopher Lee's official website. He lives in Calgary, AB, Canada with his wife Kristen and their cat, Karma.*
Twitter: @sherlockeditor
Facebook: facebook.com/cprepolec

*"As a rule, the more bizarre a thing
is the less mysterious it proves to be."*
Sherlock Holmes
"The Red-Headed League"

*"You remind me of Edgar Allan Poe's Dupin.
I had no idea that such individuals
did exist outside of stories."*
Dr John Watson
"A Study in Scarlet"

*"It is only left for us to prove
that these apparent 'impossibilities' are,
in reality, not such."*
C. Auguste Dupin
"The Murders in the Rue Morgue"

The Comfort of the Seine

But in front of these horrible corpses,
In front of whose terror you freeze
The crowd, content and without remorse,
Takes their place as though at the theatre.
Angelin Ruelle, "The Drowned"

My Dear Lestrade

It is not a huge deductive leap to know you are at this moment wondering why this document is presented into your hands, and not those of my friend and chronicler Dr Watson. The truth is, I cannot bear the thought that he might construe my privacy on these matters for so many years as something of a betrayal.

After you have read it, please place the enclosed securely in the files of the Black Museum at Scotland Yard. The reason for my not wanting this "adventure" to come to public attention in my lifetime will become clear in the reading of it.

But now, as the evening light is fading, I feel a heavy debt not to depart carrying an unwritten chapter of history to my grave, and if my arthritic hand will hold this pen long enough, I shall put the record to rights.

Read on, detective. For what could be of more peculiar interest than the solution to a mystery where it seemed no mystery existed?

Holmes

Youth is a country visited fleetingly, at the time with the only intention of reaching another destination, but in which we wish later we had lingered longer, whilst our energy was boundless and our eyesight good, and the colours of the world less grey and circumscribed. One ventures near cliff edges. One climbs branches, unable to conceive that they can snap. And one leaves one's home country on a whim, feeling no more than a sleeve tugged urgently by an eager and fresh-faced friend. Thus, at the age of twenty, I found myself abandoning my studies in chemistry, zoology and botany at Sydney Sussex, Cambridge, to accompany the Scales brothers to Paris.

A fellow science student with whom I shared digs, Peter Scales, had coerced me to tag along with him and his sibling, Olaf, a young painter. They were twins, but beyond the superficial similarities—*identicalities*—the lads could not have been more *dissimilar* in terms of personality. Olaf wore an overcoat like a Prussian cavalry officer, tartan waistcoats and extravagant facial hair. Peter, on the other hand, was quite happy to be the wallpaper in a room. But it was fun to see the pranks they played, teasing the passengers on the cross-channel steamer, being seemingly in two places at once, doffing their hats first inside the cabin, then on deck, as if a single person had transported themselves by magic from the first location to the second. We laughed. Yes, I laughed not infrequently in those days.

Our journey had been prompted when Olaf heard that Renoir, Monet and Degas were exhibiting in the studio of the photographer Nadar. This was the very birth of the era of Impressionism, you understand—when the word was first used by the critic Louis Leroy to ridicule Monet's *Impression, Sunrise*, thereby accidentally naming a movement. "Come on Yorkie!" cried Olaf; I still had quite a pronounced accent from the land of my forebears in those days. "It'll be tremendous! The colours. You have no idea. These painters will be world-famous one day, mark my word. They'll be hanging in museums!" I was by no means certain of that, and had little or no interest in art, but his enthusiasm was infectious. How could I refuse? England had become a bore. Disraeli was Prime Minister at the age of seventy. And we were young.

The other ulterior motive was, frankly: I spoke French. Not well, but enough. I'd learned it at my great-uncle's knee—my grandmother was the sister of Vernet, the French artist, no less— and though I had hardly any memory of him, the old *je suis* ran in my blood. Peter even quipped I had a nose like a Frenchman.

So, whilst the brothers sought out paintings that captured the fall of light, I was content to observe the fall of light itself on the architecture of the great city around me, and the atmosphere of *boulevards* once trodden by revolutionary feet, walls that still echoed with the Communards' bullets and the cries of shop-keepers taken to arms, shockingly, within all-too-recent-memory. It was hard to believe: the streets I saw before me regimented, grand, beautiful, populated by civilised and polite citizens of the modern day, yet behind that beauty lurked a spirit quick to anger and pitiless in its violence.

Having explored the Conciergerie, grisly staging-post before the guillotine, I found myself walking along the Quai de la Corse with the intention of crossing the Pont Notre Dame to delve into Les Halles, the so-called "belly" of Paris, when I heard a female voice behind me:

"Monsieur!"

Instinctively I turned, and to my surprise the unmistakable scent of lilies hit my nostrils. Indeed, a lily itself was being thrust towards me. Equally instinctively, I pushed it aside, glimpsing the vagabond creature in rags and bonnet trying to force it upon me.

"Non! Monsieur. Monsieur . . ." she insisted, following me, in fact blocking my path as I turned away.

"Elle mourra," she said.

I was taken aback. A strange phrase which I instantly translated: *It will die.*

For some reason this gave me pause. *She* gave me pause. What would die? What was she telling me—or warning me of—and why? I felt a prickling sensation of unease across my shoulders, a vestigial memory awakened of the supernatural talents of gypsies . . .

The beggar girl thrust the flower at me again, her arm outstretched.

"Elle mourra," she repeated.

It will die.

What a fool! She meant that if she did not sell the flowers in her basket by the end of the day they would have to be thrown away and wasted. Laughing at my own stupidity, I took the lily and urgently dug into my pocket for change, but by the time I looked up from my palm she was disappearing into the Place Louis-Lépine. She glanced back from under the trees, the sunlight catching the corners of her eyes like the dabs of a paint brush. Then she was gone. Her act—the simple gift of a flower to a complete stranger—done.

That night the boys and I went to the Café Dauphine, not far from our lodgings in the Rue Quincampoix, and sank several nightcaps. They lost themselves happily in their cups, but, intoxicated in quite another sense, I could not concentrate on a word they said.

~~~

The next morning, after dressing, I suggested we walk through the Marché aux Fleurs, the flower market on the Place Louis-Lépine. The twins humoured me, with no idea my stomach was churning at the prospect that I might not see the girl again. But there she was, standing at her stall, in sturdy workman's boots, cardigan tied sloppily round her waist, woollen balaclava under her second-hand bonnet, ruddy cheeks and pink knuckles, full lips spare of the gaud of make-up, nattering in a Parisian dialect incomprehensible even to my ear, giving the uncouth males around her a run for their money.

"All right," said Olaf. "Hi-ho. Go and speak to her, then."

"I have no idea what the devil you mean."

"Do you not?" He laughed, sticking his hand in his waistcoat and making a mime of a beating heart. "I thought he was interested in the botany here," he said, nudging his brother. "But obviously it's the biology he's got his eyes on."

"Rot."

"Own up, Yorkie, old boy. It's not a crime, for Heaven's sake ..."

I turned on my heel, not wanting to show them my cheeks were flushed.

We spent the rest of the day touring the Louvre, but I was beginning to grow sick of their company. Nothing to account for this, other than the fact that their jocular presence prevented me openly seeking the flower seller for fear of incurring their puerile taunts. Yet it was a preoccupation that refused to leave my mind. I was simply unable to banish it.

"My gosh. He really is sickening for something, this lad," said Olaf later, sipping strong black coffee of the kind only considered palatable in France. "I think Cupid's arrow has really struck its target this time ..."

I was tempted to punch him on the chin. As it was, I grabbed my coat and returned to the Marché aux Fleurs, buying her a silly gift along the way in reciprocation for the flower she had given me.

It was late afternoon by now and the working day almost at an end. She did not see me at first. I loitered like a felon, content to observe the way she folded the brown paper to make bouquets and made gay little ribbons of rope or twine. Her grace was an attribute that captivated me. *She* captivated me. The hand upon her hip, the sway of her shoulders, the toss of her head. The ragged edges of her skirts skimming the cobbles. The wisps of reddish hair curling from the soft cleft at the back of her neck. In the end I could not disguise that I was staring at her—and finally our eyes met. I thought suddenly she might find me foolish, but as soon as she laughed and made a little curtsey I felt at ease. I handed her my gift. She looked at it with astonishment bordering on awe, the expression on her face utterly delightful.

"*Je m'appelle Sherlock,*" I stammered, like a schoolboy.

"*Sheeur-loque,*" she attempted, waiting for me to continue the conversation, but I could not. My courage punctured by the stray guffaws of some hefty-looking labourers, I lowered my head with embarrassment. In defiance of their ridicule she kissed my cheek. I can remember the warmth of her lips even now, as if a Lucifer had been struck inside me. I felt all at once weak at the knees and as powerful as a steam train. And, even as I fled stupidly, thought: if my next breath were to be my last, I shouldn't care.

Over breakfast Olaf said there was nothing like someone else's tragedy to raise his spirits. Peter asked if love was a tragedy, then? His brother told him, in a pitying tone, that he'd led a sheltered life. Refusing to enter into their *badinage*, I combed my hair fastidiously in the mirror and sped to the flower market without a word, determined that this time my shyness would not get the better of me.

Now, those who have followed my exploits later in life will know I have been confronted on occasion by scenes of unutterable horror—at the risk of disappointing you, this was not one of them. In fact the sight of her stall bolted up when all the others were open gave me at first only a mild sense of disappointment. She was not there—today—perhaps for good reason. I had no cause, *at first*, to believe anything untoward had happened. No reason at all. And yet . . . my heart told me otherwise.

The longer I conversed with the stall-holders, showering them with inquiries, the more the grip of foreboding took hold. My only response was a series of immensely irritating Gallic shrugs. Nobody knew where she was. Nobody even knew her name. How on earth could that be?

The questions multiplied. By the time I returned to the apartment I was beside myself, fretting visibly, but received no real sympathy from the twins. Yes, Peter could see I was upset, but in his naivety wondered why. Olaf on the other hand could only belittle my concerns.

"Isn't it obvious? She shut up shop to go off with a man. Brazen hussy."

"She wouldn't do that."

"Why not? How do you know? How could you possibly know? You've only just met her."

"She's not a hussy, I know that much."

"Rich men. Tourists. Poverty-stricken women on their own have to make a living in all sorts of ways." He saw me glaring at him, and held up his hands. "I'm just telling you the possibilities."

"I'd really appreciate it if you didn't," I said through tight lips.

The following day I returned to the market, hoping against hope that a different scene would greet me. It did not. The padlock on the sorry-looking flower-stall was firm. A fat knife-sharpener scraped at his stone. The labourers unloading carts joked and whispered, rolling up their sleeves to show off their biceps to giggling waifs. What were they concealing? What did they know? I was determined to return, and return until I saw her—or know the answer why.

Two more days passed before I sat down the brothers and told them my absolute fear that some terrible calamity had befallen her. And that, in order to prove or disprove my conviction, I had resolved to visit the Paris morgue.

～

Now it comes . . . Dear Lord, how I have postponed many times describing this, the most painful part of my narrative. Not that the details are vague—far from it. The images in my mind are pin-sharp and all too hideously indelible. I venture, should all my memories slip away, tumbling like rubble down a slope as my life grows interminably longer and more brittle, this scene alone will remain. I even pull my dressing-gown around my shoulders now, as I feel the icy chill of those walls upon my body . . .

Imagine a gentleman's convenience with the dimensions of a palace. The same white tiles on every surface. The same overwhelming sibilance. The same residual smell of toxic substances masked by acrid disinfectant. We passed under pebbled-glass gratings through which could be seen the feet of Parisians going about their daily work, oblivious to the macabre and poignant scenes below.

Mentally, I urged the line to move faster. A woman up ahead was dabbing her eyes with a handkerchief, her backdrop a haze created by several hoses dousing the bodies. The cadaver of a large, hairy man, with half his head missing, silenced some dandies come for whatever perverse thrill they sought from the experience. If I was not sickened by that, I was sickened by what I saw next. For, amongst the dead, arranged with uniform indignity upon marble slabs, lay the flower girl's corpse.

It knocked the air out of me and Peter caught my elbow. What was most shocking was the exhibition of every inch of her pale, untarnished skin. Skin I had never touched, yet presented here for the entire public to see. Had she been touched? Had they touched her? Rage clouded my vision. But when the callous spout passed over her, spraying water and giving the illusion of movement across her flesh, I could bear it no longer. I dashed forward, plucking the strand of hair thrown into disarray over her face by the hose.

"For pity's sake, Sherlock . . ."

I shook my head vigorously. Lifted her ice-cold hand to my lips.

A moronic attendant shoved me back towards the line, barking that it was forbidden to touch the corpse. *"Ne touchez pas le cadavre! Écartez-vous du cadavre!"*

I felt another harsh prod against my chest and launched at him and would have killed him, had not Olaf's tall frame stood separating us. The man backed away from my fiercely blazing eyes and spat in a drain.

"It's time to go," said Peter softly. "You need to sleep and you need to get out of this damned awful place."

My eyes were red raw and I had no idea how much time— minutes or hours—had passed and what had occupied them but my devastation. I was sitting on the floor near the foot of the slab with the rain from the hoses dripping down the walls.

"My dear fellow," I heard his brother's voice. "Peter's right. There's nothing you can do."

"Go. Go, if you want. Both of you. I'm going to stay."

The next full hour I spent alone with my—how can I use the word? But I shall—*beloved*.

Presently the gas dipped lower and I heard footsteps and the rattle of keys. It became apparent I was the last visitor in the place, and was compelled to tear myself in agony from her side. I walked, leaden, to the stairs, but once there the terrible urge for one final glance overcame me.

There was no doubt, but at first there had been *only* doubt, so unerringly, absolutely *strange* was the picture before me. A man— *was* it a man?—stood over the bier: an elderly man with snow-white hair covering his ears, a pair of tinted *pince-nez* perched on the bridge of his nose, a black cape covering his entire frame, bent over the corpse, owlish head hovering but inches above her, as if smelling the bouquet of a fine wine. Toad-like, barrel-chested and with spindly legs, he made no sound—there *was* no sound but that of the water from the hoses. His hands moved in alacritous gestures, almost those of a mesmerist. As I watched, dumbstruck, he went about his odious theatrics as if I were invisible. Was I invisible, and this a vile construction of my harried mind? If so—what did it *mean*? Why had I not seen him before, or heard his footfall?

Immediately I hurried to the nearest morgue attendant—the one who had manhandled me. But no sooner had I caught his arm and turned to look back than I saw, open-mouthed, that the apparition was gone.

"*Excusez-moi. L'homme aux cheveux blonds,*" I gabbled. "*L'homme qui etait là-bas, habillé en noir. C'est qui?*"

The morgue attendant looked entirely baffled. "*L'homme, monsieur?*"

"*Oui. L'homme. Le vieux avec les lunettes.*"

The attendant looked over a second time then shook his head, opening the iron gate for us both to exit. "*Je n'ai vu personne,*" he said.

I have seen nobody.

⌒▵⌒

The twins tried to placate my anxiety with stiff alcohol and poor explanations, suggesting it was a visiting doctor or anatomist, but nothing they came up with accounted for the *manner* of the figure's intense interest, or the *diligence* being applied to the macabre task. I could see now from their faces their answer was that I had seen something whilst the balance of my mind was unhinged. I laughed bitterly. Olaf said that I must know as a biologist that, when a person suffers a shock, their powers of observation become temporarily unreliable.

"Not mine," I said. "I assure you. Not mine."

Come the morning, Peter reminded me our tickets on the ferry were for noon. He said he and his brother fully intended to return to England at the prescribed time. I said very well, but I was afraid I could not join them. My studies were of scant importance to me now, and my trickle of inheritance would be enough to sustain me. In any case, I wasn't worried if it didn't. The point was: I could not live with the mystery. The mystery of the girl about whom no-one cared, or grieved, but me. The mystery of the girl over whose corpse a vile old man bent in sensual enquiry. The mystery of the girl who, out of nowhere, said to me:

Elle mourra.

It will die. The flower will die ... But also—my God, why had I not thought it before? My stomach knotted as I watched the ferry depart—

She will die.

I returned to the morgue, where the flower girl's corpse still lay naked, nameless and unclaimed, convinced more than ever that this flesh-and-blood ghoul was somehow implicated in her death.

The same odious morgue attendant recognised me, from the night before, and seemed keen to avoid me. Minutes later I saw a few coins placed into his hand by one of the bereaved and he tugged his cap, which told me this rogue's silence could be bought cheaply—and had. I gravitated to the other, slightly more savoury employee at the wooden booth next to the stairs and described the man in *pince-nez*, whilst pointedly pressing coins into his palm. After which he whispered, yes, he *had* seen him, too. Several times.

"*Comment s'appelle-t-il?*" I asked.

The man's eyes darted shiftily right and left. He coughed into his hand, turned the register towards me, and ran a grime-encrusted finger down the line of signatures forming a column on the left.

"*Dupin,*" I read aloud.

It meant nothing to me. The only "Dupin" I knew was a mere fictional character, the brilliant detective in Edgar Allan Poe's story "The Murders in the Rue Morgue"—a supremely far-fetched fantasy in which a devotee of the so-called science of 'ratiocination' works out that the culprit in the gruesome murder of a mother and her daughter (whose throats were cut and bodies mutilated) is in fact, amazingly, the pet Orang-Utan of a sailor, trained to shave its owner with a straight-razor. I recalled the ugly tale only vaguely and dismissed the connection as quickly as it occurred to me.

"Do you know anything about him?" I asked in French. "His profession?"

"*Détective,*" came the terse reply.

I smiled and gave him a few more centimes for his trouble. The old man of the morgue was disguising himself, clearly. Or he *was* a detective named Dupin, the factual basis of Poe's story; or, again, a detective who *took* the name from Poe. All were possibilities, and all unedifying. The words came back to me:

Elle mourra.

In what dreadful capacity could the girl have known that she would die? And if it was her expectation, how could it feasibly be any kind of accident? Did the white-haired man know? Indeed, did he execute the deed? Was this man the murderer? What was his connection to her, if not? And why did he visit this place of the dead with such incessant regularity ... for now I saw *Dupin* in the ledger on page after page, back, long before she met her death, long before I even met her . . .

I was only aware of the footsteps on the stairs when they abruptly stopped. I spun round and saw a shadow cast by gaslight upon the stone wall, hesitating, frozen before descending. I recognised the fall of the cape, the cut of its upturned collar, the spill of the cravat. The very frame was unmistakable, albeit faceless. It ran.

I was up, after it in an instant, but the bats'-wings of the cape flew upwards to the light with supernatural speed for a man of his advanced years. By the time I emerged into the street, breathless and blinking into the sun, I saw only the door of a carriage slamming after him. I hailed another, almost getting myself trampled by hooves as the reins were pulled taut. We gave pursuit, my head in a whirl, my heart pounding as I urged my driver at all costs not to lose our quarry.

After ten or fifteen minutes, to my relief, I pinpointed the distinctive St-Médard church on my right and that gave me my bearings. Leaving behind the medieval-looking streets of Mouffetard, we eventually turned from the Rue Geoffroy Saint-Hilaire into the Rue Cuvier, which I knew to border the famous Jardin des Plantes. My transportation pulled to a halt and I climbed out, paying swiftly in order not to lose sight of the man I pursued.

To my astonishment, at a leisurely pace he entered the Ménagerie, France's largest and oldest public zoo, created during the Revolution for the unhappy survivors of the one at Versailles—those not devoured by the hungry mob—and a new population of animals rounded up by the armies of the Republic from far-flung lands abroad. He walked on an unerring path, seemingly impervious to the hooting calls of jungle birds and the pacing of lions. I followed until he came to a halt, his back to me, looking through the bars of a cage.

I approached him from behind, careful not to surprise him unduly until I was directly upon him, then yanked him round to face me.

The countenance of a handsome black man grinned at me, his smile radiant in a sea of ebony. His curly hair had been covered by the hat and scarf, his age—which explained his athleticism—not much more than my own.

"My name is Adolphe Le Bon," he said in immaculate English, with a pitch as *basso profundo* as I have heard in my life. "At your service, *monsieur.*" He touched the brim of his top hat. "A gentleman said to give you this." He handed me an envelope from his inside pocket. "*Bonjour.* Or should I say; *Au'voir?*"

Whereupon he strolled away, in no particular hurry, and I found myself considering the contents of the letter unwrapped in my fingers—a jumble of proof-readers' symbols and numbers amounting to nonsense—whilst gazing through the bars at the rubbery, wizened visage of an aged and enfeebled Orang-Utan.

～✦～

What game was this? A game I was compelled to play, obviously. Downing coffee at a street café, I stared at the hieroglyphs on the sheet of paper, cursing that if only I had Dupin's deductive power to decipher them—or those of his creator. Then I remembered—of course!—in another of Poe's tales, "The Gold Bug," a code showing the whereabouts of buried treasure is broken by elucidating which character predominates, and relating it to the order of frequency of letters generally in the English language. Even so, how did I know this was in English? I was in Paris. What was the order of frequency of letters of the alphabet in *French?* Then the notion came to me that this was not a code *similar* to that in "The Gold Bug"—it was the *exact same* code as in "The Gold Bug".

I sped to an English book shop I knew in Saint-Germain, purchased their only copy of *Tales of Mystery and Imagination* and secluded myself in a corner. *"As our predominant character is 8, we will commence by assuming it as the e of the natural alphabet . . ."* Within minutes I had translated the cryptograph. What I held now in my hands was an address. But that was not all I had discovered.

In thumbing through the pages, I had naturally alighted upon "The Murders in the Rue Morgue". And by chance my eyes had fallen upon a certain name: that of "Adolphe Le Bon," who was arrested for the extraordinary crime— *"a ferocity brutal, a butchery without motive, a* grotesquerie *in horror absolutely alien from humanity"*—before the real culprit was incarcerated: a large, tawny Orang-Utan of the Burmese species.

~~~

By fading light, I walked to the Pont Neuf, crossing the river to the Île de la Cité, where I sensed the man in the Rue de la Femme-Sans-Tête confidently awaited me.

I struck a flint to read the name-plates of the apartments. All were blank. I saw a handle, which I pulled, presuming that it sounded a bell somewhere within the belly of the old building, though I heard nothing. Laughter came from a lighted window opposite and I wondered if this was a district of ill-repute. It was the kind of shriek which could be interpreted either as extreme pain or extreme pleasure and I preferred to think the latter.

"He expected you an hour ago." The door had been opened by Adolphe Le Bon, now wearing a tail coat and bow tie.

I stepped inside. A matronly woman in a cloth cap stood half-way up the stairs.

"Madame L'Espanaye will show you up."

Madame L'Espanaye? Then I remembered . . .

"EXTRAORDINARY MURDERS—This morning, about three o'clock, the inhabitants of the Quartier Saint-Roch were aroused from sleep by a succession of terrific shrieks issuing, apparently, from the fourth storey of a house in the Rue Morgue, known to be in the sole occupancy of one Madame L'Espanaye . . ."

Another character had stepped out from the pages of fiction . . . Or fact?

I followed her, trailing my hand through the thick dust on the banister rail, dreading with every step I was entering some kind of house of insanity, a realm where the imagined and the real were interchangeable. Where the fabrications of *grotesquerie* took the place of the norm. Where actors—if they were actors—took the place of the killers and the killed. I looked over the parapet of the mezzanine to see Le Bon far below, staring up at me.

Madame L'Espanaye curtseyed and drifted backwards into ash-coloured shadows. I was left alone in front of a door.

I pushed it open to find myself in a Louis XIV room so packed with all manner of artefacts (once my eyes had accustomed themselves to the gloom) it had all the semblance of a fusty and abandoned museum. A museum of clocks was my first impression: pendulums from the Black Forest; cuckoo clocks from Switzerland; automated clocks from America, all blending into a whispering, clacking, clicking chorus of ticks and tocks. But there were other denizens in the shadows. Vast collections of pinned butterflies hung like oils. Not one human skeleton, but several. Stuffed birds of extravagant plumage. I reached out to touch a macaw—quickly to realise, as its beak nipped my finger, it was not stuffed at all. To my greater astonishment, it spoke.

"*Who is it?*"

"Mr Holmes," I replied, announcing myself to my unseen host.

"*Who is it?*"

"Sherlock."

"*Who is it?*"

I hesitated, fumbling for words. "An Englishman. A student . . ."

A laugh came from the darkness as a man poked a fire in the small grate. "There lies the way to madness, *monsieur*. Or enlightenment." In spite of the glow of revivified coals, I could not yet discern his features.

"I disturbed it," I said. "I didn't know it was real."

"Quite possibly the feeling was mutual."

As he held a candle to the flames and set it in a brass holder beside his high-backed leather chair, I saw illuminated the old man who had been arched over the flower girl's corpse. Now, by contrast, settling back, crossing his thin legs, he looked professorial, almost statesmanlike, and I found it hard to envisage him as the insane criminal I imagined, with his high forehead and weak mouth. But common sense also told me the most devious and successful criminals were those who passed for ordinary men and women. And intellect did not preclude a person from committing abominable acts, merely added strength to the possibility of them evading capture.

"You laid a trail for me to follow. Why?"

Dupin shrugged. "I do so admire . . . detection."

"You may not like what I have detected."

He took his time to light a cigar, puffed on it and used it to indicate an empty armchair facing him. I sat down and found his open case of Hoyo de Monterreys offered to me, then shortly afterwards a tray of various cut-glass decanters. I abstained. There were secrets to unveil and I would unveil them.

"I know who you are," I said. "But not why you are here."

"If you applied the science of ratiocination, Mr Holmes, you would."

"The brain is a curious organ and often it needs relaxation, but sometimes it needs to be spurred by fear or anxiety for the pieces of the puzzle to fall into place."

Dupin hazarded a thin smile. "Illuminate me."

"Pieces, shall we say, such as the bust of Pallas, semi-hidden in the darkness over in that corner. Such as the talking bird I encountered upon entering. Such as the cipher I was given. Such as the appropriation of certain names from certain tales. The ape . . ."

"Circumstantial."

"Perhaps. As is no doubt the way you wrote the date in the register at the morgue, which I thought barely notable at the time. The French, like we English, write it for brevity, day, month, year. Alongside the name *Dupin* however, the date reads month, day, year, in that order—much in the manner of an American."

Dupin sat in silence and allowed me to continue.

"You see, *monsieur*, it was not until I left the bookshop with this volume under my arm that the very obvious conclusion occurred to me." I produced *Tales of Mystery and Imagination*. "For, as in 'The Purloined Letter,' it had been in plain sight all along. Yet it was not until I thought of my good friends—the two brothers who so uncannily resemble each other that, to a stranger, they cannot be told apart—that the picture was complete."

"Indeed?"

"Indeed, *monsieur*."

"And will you share with me that . . . conclusion?"

I took another, smaller volume from my pocket. "The prefatory items in the *Tales* were instructive but inadequate. I returned to the bookshop and luckily found upon the shelves a copy of Thomas Holley Chivers' *Life of Poe*, published by Dutton in 1852." I looked into Dupin's eyes but they held no expression—not even, particularly, of interest. "Edgar Poe died on the 7th October 1849, the theory being that he had been the victim of a so-called cooping gang. The congressional elections were in full swing in Baltimore and, because there was no register of voters, bully boys were being employed by candidates to round up derelicts and get them drunk enough to register false votes a number of times in succession." I referred to my notes and underlinings in the Chivers. "He was found by Joseph Walker, a compositor at the Baltimore Sun, lying in the street outside Cooth and Sergeant's Tavern on East Lombard Street, which served as a polling station.

"Dr Snodgrass received a letter from Walker about a gentleman rather the worse for wear at Ryan's 4th ward polls, and found the writer without his customary moustache, haggard, bloated and unkempt, his clothing, I quote: 'a sack-coat of thin and sleazy black alpaca, ripped at intervals, faded and soiled, pants of steel-mixed pattern of cassinett, badly-fitting, *if they could be said to fit at all* . . .'" I put particular emphasis on this last phrase, but it had no effect on the listener.

"Poe was taken to Washington hospital," I continued, "where he experienced exceeding tremors of the limbs, and active delirium. When questioned in reference to his family, his answers were incoherent. When asked where he lived, he could not say. Towards the end, in his stupor and torment, he called out for 'Reynolds! Reynolds!'—which onlookers took to refer to the navigator of the South Seas, an inspiration for *The Narrative of Arthur Gordon Pym*—until his poor soul was finally at rest." I looked up. "But he is not at rest, *monsieur*—is he?"

Dupin had sunk back in his seat, the wings of which served to conceal his face in shadow. He placed his fingertips together in a steeple.

"Yes, a man was found drunk in a gutter," I said. "But he called out 'Reynolds' in his delirium because that was his own name. And nobody would listen. He was identified by the Malacca cane borrowed by Poe from Dr John Carter simply because the object had been placed in his hands by another. On the evidence of witnesses themselves this substitute was more 'haggard' yet more 'bloated' than Poe (perhaps the word 'fatter' would be more accurate); except Dr Snodgrass recognised his friend's clothes, albeit that they *hardly fitted* the occupant. Of course they didn't. Because the man was not Poe. Poe was alive. *Is* alive."

"*Who is it?*" squawked the parrot.

"And the mystery of the missing moustache is self-evident," I said. "For one can dress a double to look like one's self, but one cannot force him to grow facial hair he does not have."

"Bravo!" Dupin laughed and clapped his hands. We had been conversing in French but he spoke English now for the first time, with the musical lilt of a Southern gentleman. "Many have tried but none has got so far! Le Bon, the cognac! This is a cause for celebration! C. Auguste Dupin has met his match!" The dapper black man emerged from the gloom and poured me an ample glassful. "I do not partake myself."

"The stuff can be the death of you."

"I fear water will be the death of me now." Poe grinned, holding up a glass into which he had poured clear liquid from a jug. "A 'way to watery death' is not quite the poetic thing, is it? I quite resist banality, in death as in life."

"And the death of the flower girl?" I made it quite clear in my tone that I had not forgotten the purpose of my visit. "What is the poetry in that, sir?"

He avoided my question.

"Let me first tell you of the last weeks on this earth of Edgar Allan Poe." Whilst he spoke, the manservant, Le Bon, circled the room lighting candles. "It had been a year of wild dullness . . . I was drumming up support for a five-dollar magazine and trying to convert my Philistine countrymen to literature—an impossible task. I came to the conclusion I could only raise money by lecturing again: with tickets at 50c I could clear $100—if sober. So, with the ferocious spirit of the true dipsomaniac, I took the oath of abstinence, prostrated myself at the Sons of Temperance: a solid challenge to my cravings—but, alas, unattainable . . . The word 'teetotal' had hardly wetted my tongue before—I fell, spectacularly . . . My lecture was stolen. I descended further into debt: but these are excuses. The true drinker repels the very idea of his own happiness. We deem the prospect of solace intolerable.

"I had to leave Richmond on business, but the real reason was a desperation to escape. Escape my own shabby dreams, and, ringing like a foul tintinnabulation, the doctor's warning after Philadelphia that one more drop of the hard stuff would see me to the bone yard. Truth was: my life had become all pose and no prose. Fancy-mongering was wearisome now. I was a performing dog wandering the miasmic stars of Eureka. So I propped up the steamer's bar, wishing most the while a maelstrom would suck it down, and me with it.

"As you said, the streets of Baltimore were *en fête* with election fever. I went unnoticed in streets teeming with drunks filthier drunk than me. I was on a spree. Maybe my last. I was determined to put an end to this life, little knowing I would start a new one.

"Outside a tavern a man pestered me for a game of cards. He wanted to win back money he had lost, because he was sailing for Europe the next day and didn't want to arrive penniless. The man was drunk, drunker than me—so drunk he was not even aware that, a little thinner in the girth and thicker in the cheeks, he was my double. I did not even remark upon it and I drank with him until he passed out in an alley. I thought he was dead. I felt his pulse.

"Then, with a thundering heart, I saw an extraordinary opportunity to reinvent my life, if I had the audacity to carry it through. He, being dead, had nothing to lose, and I everything— *everything* to gain. I took a ticket from his inside pocket, made out in the name of 'Reynolds': his passage across the Atlantic. I changed clothes, taking all his identifying belongings and giving him mine, finally leaning the Malacca cane I had borrowed from Dr Carter against his knee: the final piece of evidence that this dishevelled inebriate was Poe.

"I took the ocean crossing, shaving off my moustache and cutting my hair lest someone identify me. No-one did. On arrival I read of my own demise, of poor Reynolds calling out his name again and again: my *doppelgänger*, my *William Wilson*, calling for his own identity to be restored, in life, in death—but, alas, it never was.

"He was interred at the Presbyterian cemetery on Lafayette and Green Street. My premature burial. I read the despicable death notices penned by Griswold, twisting the facts, emphasising my bad points and down-playing my good, but I could hardly react to any attack on my former identity without exposing my new one. As it was, I feared someone might uncover my ploy, the police or the Reynolds family, and come looking for me, so I changed my name again on arrival."

"To *Dupin?*" I said. "Your most famous character?"

Poe shook his head. "Not at first. To begin with, I stayed with my friend Charles Baudelaire, the poet. He had read many of my works before I died. For that reason, and my innate Francophilia, I gravitated to Paris. He'd translated my piece on Mesmeric Revelation in *La Liberté de Penser*. He saw me as a mystic and visionary and the inventor of skilfully engineered tales, and had written to tell me as much, so it was fitting I turned to him in my hour of need. He kept me under lock and key in rooms at the Hôtel Pimodon, always in penury over the years, partly because he kept me afloat too.

"We had certain similarities. His stepfather, General Aupick, he despised, as I despised mine. He endured a life of money troubles, as had I. He was afflicted by bouts of pessimism, as was I. Arrogant, as was I . . . But his *vie libre* was also a *vie libertine*, centred on the taverns of the Latin Quarter. He hated solitude. I welcomed it. To begin with, I ventured outside rarely, if at all. I helped him with his satirical contributions to the *Corsaire-Satan*, and later with *Les Fleurs du Mal*. He in turn brought me the world, by way of the Café Tabourey or the *Théâtre de l'Odéon*.

"After a while he introduced me to his Bohemian cronies as 'Dupin'—his little joke. The name wasn't known in France because in the first translation of *Rue Morgue* the detective was re-named 'Bernier' for some reason unknown to either of us. And 'duping', you see—the pun was deliciously appealing.

"Baudelaire's French versions of my tales appeared in *Le Pays*, and *Adventures d'Arthur Gordon Pym* in *Moniteur Universel*.

I helped him out with some details about compass bearings and such, and acted as his lexicon of the Southern states. But his abominable life style took its toll. As a former imbiber of substances—I had not touched a drop since my resurrection—I saw all the signs of a hopeless addict. He collapsed with a cerebral disorder on the flagstones of l'Église Saint-Loup in Namur, upset by a poem he'd read about happiness." Poe attempted to smile. "They sent a confessor in his last hours, but by then all he was saying was *Bonjour*, like a child."

"I'm sorry."

He waved the sentiment away.

"No more . . . Nevermore . . ." He gazed into his glass of water. "Every day is an act of will. Which is something. To have a toe at the very edge of doom and resist the urge to plummet."

I found myself saying out loud: "I too have dark valleys."

He sipped and placed the glass on the table beside his chair. "Then you and I have similarities too."

"But why use the name 'Dupin' if you didn't want to be found?"

"Who said I didn't want to be found?" He rose, wrapping a woollen shawl round his shoulders. "Perhaps I was waiting for the right person to find me." He walked to the macaw and stroked the back of its neck with a curled forefinger.

"Whilst he was alive Baudelaire kept me reasonably secluded, but to keep me from going mad with inactivity of the mind he would bring me puzzles in the form of stories from the newspapers. Robberies. Murders. Abnormal events. Inexplicable mysteries. I would study them and, if I could, write to the newspapers with solutions, as I had done with 'Marie Rogêt,' always under the inevitable *nom-de-plume*— 'Dupin'. From the moment I set foot on French soil, with that poor sot in my coffin, I found I had no more stomach for writing fiction. Death, madness, my trademark—I'd had enough of that. The raven had croaked itself hoarse. It is one thing to write a detective story. You know the solution and simply confound the reader. But to deduce by the powers of logic in *real life?*... That is *true* art. And I felt it stimulating to accumulate skills to that end. Pretty soon the police got to know the name and would come to me for help. It was no more than a game at first. But a game that kept me alive."

"As the re-naming of your servants is also a game," I interjected. "Le Bon, Madame L'Espanaye ... in the manner of a charade. Surrounding yourself with characters of your own creation to keep the real world at bay. To feel safe."

"But I am safe. Immensely safe, *now*." As he walked to the mantelshelf his eyes gleamed in the sallow light of the candles. "For I am no longer, you see, under the glamour of my pernicious gift: my imagination. Anyone who has ever studied my stories properly knows they are all about one thing: the awful toll of madness, the horror of lost reason ... 'Rue Morgue' says it all, for anyone with eyes to see. That even the most absurd, most abominable crime can be solved by rationality. Well, rationality was my driftwood in the storm. It was my salvation, Mr Holmes—as it can be yours."

I was startled. "Mine?"

He stared at me, dark eyes unblinking with intensity. "We human beings can be the ape—the basest instinct, dumb force of nature—or we can excel, we can elevate ourselves." He tapped his expanse of forehead. "By civilisation. By enlightenment. By perception. By the tireless efforts of eye and brain ..."

He spoke with the utter conviction of a zealot, or lunatic. A chill prickled the hairs on the back of my neck. I asked myself if the "awful toll of madness" had indeed been left behind him, or if I was in the presence of a maniac who had committed one crime by his own admission, and could easily commit another to cover his tracks?

I rose to my feet, frightened now.

"Why am I here? Why did you bring me?"

By way of reply there resounded four brisk knocks at the double-doors to an adjoining chamber—so sudden that it made my heart gallop. Poe had turned away and was adjusting his string tie in the mirror, as if he hadn't even heard my voice, or simply chose to ignore it.

"Entrez." He moved only to deposit the stub of his cigar into the flames.

The double doors yawned open and in silence four men emerged from the dark as if from another realm. They marched in slow formation with their backs erect, the reason for which became hideously clear—they carried a coffin on their shoulders. My chest tightened. I found I could not move, powerless but to watch as they laid it down in the firelight in the centre of the room, resting on two straight-backed chairs arranged by Madame L'Espanaye.

The pallbearers straightened. One I recognised as the morgue attendant who had lied to me, now shuffling back into the shadows whence he came. Another, the elegant Le Bon in his spotless shirt, had procured a screwdriver from somewhere and was proceeding to unscrew the lid of the casket as a continuation of the same odd, balletic ritual.

I looked at Poe. He was idly, at arm's-length, leafing through the pages of the *Life of Poe* I had placed on the side-table, then shut it disinterestedly and tugged at his cuffs. It made my blood run cold to realise that, far from being alarmed by this extraordinary intrusion, he had *designed* it.

Each screw emerged, conveyed by Le Bon like a bullet in the palm of his kid-gloved hand to a kidney-shaped dish. As he circled the coffin to the next, and then extracted it with the lazy precision of a priest performing Eucharist, I was filled with a growing presentiment of what I was about to behold: what I *had to* behold, to make sense of this, if it made any sense at all. After the lid was prised off the loyal servant blended into the darkness of the adjacent chamber, closing the doors as he did so.

I stifled a sob at the inevitable sight of the flower girl's body inside, the bluish-purple shades of *livor mortis* bringing a cruel blush to her ears and nose.

"Dear God. This is obscene . . ."

"No," said Poe. "*Death* is obscene. But death, when all else is removed, is no more than a mystery to be solved."

"Sir . . ." I could hardly spit out the words, so full was I of repulsion. "You have abandoned all that is human, and decent and, and *good* with your *delusion* . . ."

He remained unutterably calm as he gazed into the casket. "If you truly believed that—*sir*—you would have walked away long ago."

"What makes you think I cannot walk away this second?"

"Because you cannot walk away from the mystery. That is your curse."

"You are mad."

Poe smiled and quoted from a familiar source: "True, nervous—very, very dreadfully nervous I have been and am; but why will you say that I am mad?" Then his eyes hardened. "You know I am not."

He fetched a candlestick and set it down closer to the corpse, the better to illuminate the indecent marbling of her once flawless skin.

"Though your powers of deduction are elementary, by now you will have realised the purpose of my clandestine visits to the morgue. The meticulous observation. I was of course undertaking exercises in ratiocination. The building offers me subjects in the purest possible sense. On every slab, every day, a code, a cipher to be unlocked. The application of logic telling the very tale the dead themselves cannot. What better place to perfect my craft?" He chuckled softly.

"This hobby amuses you?"

"Of course. What is there in life, my dear Holmes, if not to be amused?"

"Damn you!" I pushed him away from the coffin.

"You see? Emotion rules you completely. It surges when you should keep it at bay. To what end? If you wish to discover why she died . . . If you want to know the truth of what happened to her, there is only one course open to you: the cold and relentless application of rationality."

"I loved her!" I roared, turning away.

After a few seconds he whispered behind me: "*I also loved one who died.*" His voice was disembodied, sepulchral and totally, alarmingly devoid of self-pity. I felt guilty at my outburst and listened in earnest to the terrible words he uttered: "Her gradual decline . . . From imp to skeletal invalid. Not the loss of love over days, over a glimpse, an idea, but over years. From childhood to womanhood, in a laugh. Over the lengthening of her bones and the plumping of her hips, then to watch it snuffed out by the red death running in her blood. Listening to time, whose hands creep towards midnight. Thinking, what right did I have to sob, to weep, to wish for it to happen, *yes*—to will the chimes and choking to come, when all suffering will cease for all but the living?"

I turned back to him, wiping away tears with the heel of my hand.

He had none.

He said: "I can think of no higher endeavour than to banish hurt and pain from people's lives by the application of logic. I understand your grief, sir. God knows, no man stands my equal in that subject. But one must look upon death and see only that— *Death.* One must stop being victim to the petty frailties of our own conjecture. Instinct. Guessing. Terror. Love. Such fripperies are the sludge which gums up our nerves and dampens our intellect. And self-perpetuates, like a virulent disease. The very king of pests. Like alcohol, emotional supposition is toxic to our system, but our system rebels against being deprived of it. It must be abandoned, and dependence on it shed, lest it rule our lives completely."

Seeing the torture of unanswered questions in my eyes, Poe picked up the candelabrum and circled the coffin, looking down at what lay inside, the tiny, jewel-image of her face glimmering on his black irises.

"I shall proceed as I always do, with general observations, moving on to the nature of the crime. Your friend was raised by devout Catholics, in the city of Nîmes, from which she absconded and became a scullery maid . . ."

I was choked with disbelief. "You can't possibly . . ."

"I assure you, everything I say is arrived at by the painstaking application of my methods. At the morgue I procured her clothing, which had not yet been incinerated, and her petticoats were imprinted with a faded workhouse stamp of Ste-Ursule of Nîmes. The flesh on her back, sad to say, betrayed healed scars which indicated the application of a scourge used specifically by Catholic nuns. And the condition of her hands, ingrained with blacking invisible to the naked eye, presented ample proof of her time in service. But what concerns us here primarily is the manner of her death . . ."

He bent over the corpse, finger tips on the rim of the coffin, exactly as he had done in the morgue, and sniffed, taking the air into his dilating nostrils in short gasps, eyes closed as if savouring its bouquet like a connoisseur of fine wine.

"The scent of putrefaction is repulsive to most individuals, quite naturally: as human beings we have bred ourselves over millennia to abhor decay. Which is a great shame, because its study I've found to be invaluable. Just as a tea-taster can discern subtleties in a blend that the uneducated could not possibly discern, I have trained myself over the years to be able to assess the olfactory distinctions between stages of decay. This, when combined with other observations—visual, tactile—enables me, most often, I would say *invariably*, to be able to pinpoint to the day, sometimes to the *hour*, the time of death. These are not extraordinary talents, my dear Holmes, but ones that most people could apply, given the inclination and training. Foremost, I noticed immediately the corpse had not decomposed as swiftly as it might—always a good indication of immersion in the intense cold of water. This was confirmed by finding none of the customary bruising caused by the effect of gravity on an inert mass on land—*ergo*, she either drowned or was committed to the Seine very soon after dying. Since there were no *pre-mortem* signs of violence on the epidermis, my conclusion was therefore the former.

"The wind that night was unseasonably harsh," he continued. "Coming as it did from a south by southwest direction. The covers of the stalls were flapping and she was the last of the stall holders to leave. She was in high spirits. Perhaps she even contemplated that she might have been in love."

"Do not tease me," I snapped.

"On the contrary. I am delivering the facts, however shocking or unpalatable they may be. Now, do you wish me to carry on?"

I had no alternative but to nod.

"Alone now, she feels a few dots of rain in the air and opens her parasol. A new parasol from her young admirer. In a flash it is caught by a sudden gust of wind, plucked from her hands. She grasps after it, but in vain." This he acted out in spasmodic motions. "She chases it, but it bounces away across the Quai de la Corse, taking flight, this way, that, cart-wheeling down the boat-man's steps and landing in the mud ten, fifteen yards beyond.

"And so she ventures out—but the mud is not as firm as it looks. It acts like glue. It is up to her ankles before she knows it. Frightened, she tries to extract herself, but only sinks deeper. Almost certainly she cries out for help, but nobody hears. The river level rises. Water fills her mouth, her lungs. Soon she is submerged completely."

"This is outrageous . . ." I breathed.

He ignored me. "In time, buoyancy lifts her and carries her away in the predetermined arc of the current to the jetty near the Pont Ste-Beuve. The activity of the morning boats dislodges the submerged corpse once again and it travels, aided by the wash of tourist vessels and commercial traffic, lodging temporarily against

the supports of the Pont Cavaignac on her way to her final port of
call, the Pont Olivier Knost, where the body is spotted by passers-
by and conveyed by the authorities—*requiescat in pace*—to its resting place, the City Morgue."

I shook my head, struggling hard to assimilate all he had
told me. Struggling to believe that such deductions were possible.
Wanting to reject them as fabulous, as fictional—as another of his
fanciful *tales* . . .

My doubt all-too-visible in my features, he explained: "Upon
minute examination, I found slivers of timber in the knots in her
hair. Under the microscope these fragments showed algae matching those upon the vertical struts of the jetty near Pont Ste-Beuve.
I also found fragments of paint and rusted metal in a *post-mortem*
gash on her skull, the shade of blue matching that of the Pont
Cavaignac.

"After my first examination of the body in the morgue, I sent
Le Bon out on a mission with three questions. One, what was
the prevailing wind that night? Two, what was the colour of the
paint used on the Pont Cavaignac? And three: is there a factory
near the Pont Notre Dame, working through the night, producing sufficient noise to cover a drowning girl's cries for help? There
was. A printer's shop, hard at work producing the next day's news.
Upon whose pages, alas, come the morrow, the mystery of a missing flower girl did not merit so much as a single line."

A bitter sadness rose in my throat. I was numb with astonishment, dazzled, uncomprehending, light-headed, on the brink of
alarm. The feeling was not unlike love: I wanted to be seduced, I
wanted to believe, to succumb—yet everything told me to protect
myself from harm, to dismiss that which drew me so compulsively
to it.

Poe placed a hand on my shoulder.

"There was no murder, no murderer, no rhyme nor reason,
no conspiracy, no plan, no suicide . . ." he said. "Just the wind, the

water, the mud, the current . . . Sometimes Nature itself is the most devious criminal of all."

I turned away from him and looked into the crumbling coals of the fire. The heat from it dried and prickled my eyes but I continued to stare without blinking. A piece of coke had fallen out below me and he lifted it back into place with long-handled tongs. He was silent for a while and I was grateful for that. I heard him refill my glass of cognac and place it on the table beside my chair. The other chair creaked as Poe once again occupied it and crossed his spidery legs. I had a sense of a snowy halo in my peripheral vision. The black loops of a string tie. A weak mouth. A massive brow shadowing the eyes of a nocturnal Caesar.

"Your logic is faultless except for one thing," I said, controlling the quaver in my voice. "The parasol. It strikes me as something of a conjecture."

"Not at all. I might *conjecture* that what took her out onto the mud must have been something of meaning to her, something of sentimental value, which is why she felt compelled to retrieve it. I might *conjecture* that, given there has been a parasol seller on the corner of the Rue de Lutece for twenty years, that is what I would have given her as a gift, had I been in love. But my business is not conjecture." He picked a small red parrot feather from his sleeve and examined it between his fingers. "I know she was the last to leave the market simply because, upon enquiry, nobody remembered seeing her leave. I spoke to the knife sharpener and he told me the only unusual thing that day was she had a parasol—one he had never seen before—and an object altogether too *bourgeois* for someone of her status in society. It stuck in his mind, he said, because she walked up and down like a queen, her smile radiant. He said, in fact, he'd never seen her so happy."

Happy. That last word had a devastating effect on me. It immediately drained me of everything but remorse. The feelings I had patently kept submerged for days welled up and overwhelmed me. I could do nothing to stop them. They broke the banks and I wept like a child.

"Now, look at her."

Poe took my hand and wrapped my fingers around a candlestick. It lit my way to the coffin, where the prone, lifeless husk that had once been so vibrant shimmered in its amber glow.

"Géricault, when he was painting his *Raft of the Medusa*, locked himself away with no company but dead bodies and even shaved his hair off to eliminate completely his need for contact with the outside world. All so that he could concentrate completely on the work at hand."

I wondered why he was unrolling a cloth bag of surgical equipment—scalpel, forceps, scissors—but my query was soon answered.

"We are going to stay here, like Géricault, for however many hours it takes until your tears run dry. Then we will be done." He lifted the cloth cover from a microscope on a desk. "You shall grow to know her as only God knows her. And then your wisdom will have outgrown your pain, and you will be free." He walked over to me and placed an object in my hand.

It was a magnifying glass.

⁓

Dawn light began to outline the shutters as the screws were secured once more round the rim of the coffin lid. Poe rolled down his sleeves, buttoned his cuffs, and sent Le Bon with a message for the unscrupulous attendants from the morgue to come and remove the body.

"We shall say no prayers for her," he said. "She goes to the ground and becomes dirt, as we all shall."

⁓

He opened the windows.

The air became fresh and clean. Slowly the noises of ordinary life and work permeated from the cobbled bustle of the street. A gentle bathing of the everyday was welcome after a long and suffocating night of cigar fog and candle wax. By sunlight, the apartment in the Rue de la Femme-Sans-Tête was no longer a prison, no more a threat, a labyrinth with some Minotaur, part god, part monster, at its centre.

"I am not, nor have I ever been, *healthy.*" He pinched my nostrils and drew the razor carefully down the cleft between my nose and mouth. A gobbet of soap hit the water in the bowl. "For my sins, a sedentary existence and the habitual use of alcohol and opiates is now written upon every organ in my body. At sixty-five I am heavy and weary, rheumatic and vulnerable to colds. My stomach is a harsh critic. I take quinine, digitalis and belladonna: one loses track of what produces the symptoms and what treats them. Truth is, I cannot know how many summers I shall endure . . ." He did not look into my eyes, focusing only on brushing more soap into my bristles. "Having no biological offspring, I have long harboured the desire to pass on what I have learnt of the science of ratiocination to someone else in this world before I take to dust. I have sought a pupil. A young adept, of sorts. Foolish perhaps. Vanity, certainly . . ."

"That was the purpose of your test."

"You found me, Holmes, and in so doing, I found you. Even though the clues were abundant, you were the first to show the propensity to solve such puzzles. Perhaps it is arrogance—that has always been my fatal flaw—but I do believe there may be some merit in my methods. I know the young despise the old, quite rightly and *vive la revolution!*—but . . ."

I was stricken with incredulity as I gathered the nature of his proposition.

"*You* would teach *me?*"

"There is a price, of course." He wiped the straight razor in a cloth, both sides. "The price is your heart. Your *tell tale* heart . . . The tale it tells is always a lie, and always leads to pain." His sad eyes turned to mine. "Is it a cost you are prepared to pay, Sherlock?"

I took the cloth from his hands and wiped the residue of soap off my face as he waited for my answer.

We played four hundred games of chess, and a thousand games of cards. He taught me every intricacy of luck and chance, and every statistic that disproves every superstition. He dissected every belief like a pinned-out frog, occasionally making it kick for demonstration purposes, then revealing how the effect was achieved. He knew the machineries of life and mind and held them in his head like railway timetables. He revealed to me the foolishness of crowds and the absurdities of love, the fallacies of poor thinking, and the whirring cogs of the criminal mind. My old education was over and my real education had begun: my training to be the outsider. Observing life, but not being in its thrall.

We argued over Hegel's *Logik*, perused by the beady eye of a parrot named Griswold. We pored over Giovanni Battista Morgagni, and Taylor's seminal work on pathology and toxicology— the first in the English language.

We read by lamplight. We slept on the floor or in our chairs, but more often talked through the night.

When we were busy, and the doors bolted so we would not be disturbed, food and drink was lowered on a rope through a trap door from upstairs by the loyal servant Le Bon.

I was made to memorize a hundred imprints of soles of shoes. And a hundred types of house brick. Coins. Coral. Types of dentition. Birds' eggs. Navigational equipment. Moths.

Blindfolded, I learned how to identify cigarette brands by smell alone.

The nature of breeds of dog—not to mention their owners.

He would show me a hundred Daguerrotypes and direct me to deduce the maladies from the patients' photographs alone. And more. *More, more,* he taunted me. *What more do you see?*

Hour after hour, day after day, the room became clearer, as if a veil were lifted. As if my eyes had been put through a pencil sharpener. As if the world, muddy and intangible, were slowly being made clean and whole.

<hr />

Habitually we would visit the aforementioned Ménagerie, and always pay a special pilgrimage to the old Orang-Utan named—I remember it clearly—'Bobo'.

Sometimes, after supper, as we walked beside the Seine, Poe took my arm. He liked a stroll, but sometimes his vanity meant he left his walking cane at home. He would tell me not to nag him when I reminded him of the fact. Often we sat on a certain bench and gazed at the Moon reflected on the water.

Watson spoke in derogatory fashion of my lack of knowledge in the field of astronomy. The truth is, I know not too little, but too much.

Poe taught me to listen to the music of the spheres.

Giordano Bruno said there is no absolute up or down, as Aristotle taught; no absolute position in space; but the position of a body is relative to that of other bodies. Everywhere there is incessant relative change in position throughout the universe, and the observer is always at the centre of things.

The observer. The detective.

I spent six, almost seven, years with Poe before he died, and he taught me—not "all I know" (such a claim would be absurd)—but *how* to know. He was no less than a father to me, and the only thing he ever asked in return was that I keep his secret from the world.

We were sometimes seen around Paris: C. Auguste Dupin, with his white hair, black cape and yellow sunglasses, and his young English assistant.

Some mysteries were solved.

The affair of the so-called "phantom" of the Paris Opera. The case of the *horla* and its tragically afflicted seer. The 'crying spider' of Odilon Redon.

We applied arithmetic to decadence and catacombs.

I never resumed my studies at Cambridge. My university was that of Poe: of detection, and of life.

As he became frail, I cared for him in that apartment, when his world shrank to that of a single room.

He observed life from that tiny bedroom. We tested each other in deducing the characteristics of passers-by. The butcher with blood on his hands and the baker with flour on his. The misanthrope and the ne'er-do-well. The blue stocking and the lady of the night: sometimes more difficult to tell apart than you might think. He'd bemoan my pipe tobacco. I'd call him a pious ex-drunk.

When he could no longer make it to the window sill, it pained him to walk, and his eyesight had grown cloudy, I read to him aloud, as a mother might her infant, and never thought anything of the task. His company fed me as much as the other way around. And it was not without its amusements. I remember all too well his reaction to *Notre Dame de Paris* by Victor Hugo. The tragic fate of Quasimodo making him grimace. I stupidly thought he'd been moved by the fates of the hunchback and Esmeralda, but he quickly disabused me of that, mumbling that it was obviously influenced by his own work, "Hop-Frog"—and vastly inferior.

Would have been far better in verse, he declared . . . and *shorter.*

The man was cantankerous and conceited, vain as a poodle and unmelodious to the ear. But I have never known a more intelligent or *electric* individual, which almost always excused his inveterate rudeness and dire fluctuations of mood.

Most of all, I owe him my vocation. Sherlock Holmes—*detective.* What would I have become, else?

It will be a surprise to no-one that my friend had a fear of being buried alive, and therefore stipulated in his will that the examining doctor open a vein in his neck to ensure no such ghastly mistake could be made. In the event the medic was all thumbs and I had to perform his final wish myself.

Thinking of that grave in far-off Baltimore and its false incumbent, I watched the smoke rise from the Paris crematorium in a black plume.

The bird of death was silent at last, the black ink fading to the white of an empty page, the book of awe and wonder closed, the coffin breath exhaled, the great, unfathomable mind becalmed, the weight of his torment lifted at last. He exists now only on every bookshelf in England, and in my final thoughts.

For, as I now lie close to death myself, I know more clearly than ever what my master—*the* master—knew: that Nature is chaos. Chaos is truth. Death is the final mystery. And our only defence is knowledge.

Infinite knowledge. Infinite, and futile, knowledge . . .

The Purloined Face

My Dear Lestrade,

I doubt you expected a further package from me for Scotland Yard's Black Museum, given that last time you heard from me I was at death's door. But the chill in my bones has passed and my doctor, a brusque devil, with none of the bedside manner of Watson, has told me to get air in my lungs and sun on my face. Whilst in that endeavour this afternoon, I experienced to my alarm something which brought back vividly to life one of the strange cases I investigated with the remarkable C. Auguste Dupin, long cloistered in fusty memory.

The local cinema is not a place I frequent often. I simply wanted somewhere to rest my feet, and can't say I even took note of the film that was playing before I entered the gloom. What unfolded on screen I found both sordid and spectacular, at times a turgid melodrama, but punctuated with moments of the most lurid terror.

It slowly dawned on me as I saw that wretched underground lake, the abducted girl swept away in a gondola by the Phantom to his lair, that this was an adaptation of a novel I knew all too well. A beautiful soprano in love with a disfigured madman, a tepid variation on "Beauty and the Beast": if only the truth, I thought, were as comforting in its roles of monster and victim. And when, in the Bal Masqué scene, the Phantom appeared as the Red Death from Poe's story of that name, the irony tore an involuntary laugh from my throat, somewhat distracting some members of the audience, who hushed me with frowning hisses of irritation.

The gross travesty of what really happened in the Paris Opera first appeared in the pages of Le Gaulois *back in the first decade of this century, but now this motion picture, starring the renowned "Man of a*

Thousand Faces," was spreading that fallacy to the world, projecting it in huge images, with organ accompaniment, for all to see. As I sat there watching the audience squirm and shriek at the monster's unmasking, I thought: "If only they knew the truth . . ."

You hold it in your hand, Inspector. Unmask it, if you dare. But I warn you, a decent man will be shaken by what he reads.

Holmes

Many mysteries came to the door of the man in the Rue de la Femme-Sans-Tête. The district we lived in, known as the Île de la Cité, once thronged with thieves, whores and murderers, but was now hemmed in by the grey edifice of the *Préfecture de Police,* law courts, and offices of civil servants, a bastion against the unrestrained and malevolent. He and I often yearned to stray into areas of the dissolute, vulgar and unpredictable. At other times tales of the aberrant and profane beat a path, unbidden, to our door.

To relieve his inveterate boredom—and for the purpose of my further instruction in the science of "ratiocination"—Poe had set up a mirror at the window by which to observe the street below. When the brass bell rang unexpectedly at the *porte-cochère* on that particular April morning, echoing through the apartment, he asked me to report my observations in the short time it took for Le Bon to descend the stairs and return with our visitors.

"A man and a woman," I began, squinting down at our guests. "She seems nervous, delicate, uncertain . . ."

"'Seems' is not a fact," Poe interjected.

"Very well. I'd say from their relative ages he is her father. She wears a coat from Le Bon Marché and a black veil over her face, which indicates she is in mourning. I deduce, therefore, it is her husband who has died, mysteriously, and it is for that reason they have come. The man is around fifty-five years of age, rotund, and bears an uncanny resemblance to Balzac. Well-fed, and well-off, by the cut of his jib. Overcoat worn over his shoulders in the manner of a Hussar. A definite military man. From his sallow skin tone and black hair there is Indian blood in his family tree, or Eurasian, possibly. And—hello?—a dash of red on his cravat. Blood? Good grief, perhaps the perpetrator of the deed is presenting himself to us with all the brazen aplomb of a murderer who thinks he is beyond the powers of detection . . ."

"Brilliant! That was truly instructive." Poe jumped from his chair and combed his thin, paper-white hair in the mirror. "Instructive in how to arrive at an entirely erroneous conclusion. Remind me not to ask you to fetch me black peppercorns in a field of rabbit droppings." I tried not to affect the disgruntlement of a schoolboy handed back homework that fell ruefully short of the mark. "That is not blood on his cuff, but strawberry conserve. To be exact, the one served with a *kipferl* at the *bijou boulangerie* on the Rue Bertrand Sluizer. Furthermore, he uses moustache wax by Marie Helene Rogeon, is a Corsican, has three brothers, lived in Avignon, the son of a shoe-mender, ran a ballet company, married a woman called Mathilde, and has five children. All girls. None married. Though one is the fiancée of a locomotive driver."

"Heavens above!" My head was spinning. "How on earth . . ."

Poe's laugh was high and shrill as he slapped me on the shoulder. "My dear Holmes, forgive an old Southern gentleman his petty amusement! How could I resist teasing you when such an opportunity presented itself? I saw from the reflection that the man is Olivier Guédiguian, manager of the Opéra de Paris. The reason I know is very simply I have met him before, at the very *boulangerie* I mentioned: his habitual haunt for *petit dejeuner*. During our conversation he imparted a good deal about his life. At the time he was worried about a malignant superstition having a grip on his stage workers that some kind of, ahem—*spectre* was causing damage and maladies of all description. I was able to convince him that it was nothing but a series of accidents and coincidences, each perfectly explicable in its own right, but overall signifying nothing. And certainly nothing *supernatural*—the very word being a contradiction in terms. Metaphysics and philosophy! Why will people waste my time with trivialities!" We heard footsteps on the stair. "And by the way, the dress is from La Samaritaine, not Le Bon Marché."

I was speechless in the briefest pause before Poe's black servant opened the double doors and ushered M. Guédiguian and his female companion—*veiled* companion—into our presence. Griswold squawked a few bars of the "Marseillaise" before chewing on a ball of nuts. There is no brass name-plate with *Dupin* etched on it down below, but it is curious that those who need his assistance always find him, one way or another.

Guédiguian untied his scarf and rolled it in a ball.

"Monsieur Dupin?"

I have described elsewhere how Edgar Poe lived beyond the date chiselled on his gravestone in Baltimore. Far from being, as is popularly believed, the drunken victim of a "cooping" gang at the elections in October 1849, he encountered that night, by remarkable coincidence, his *doppelgänger,* complete with a one-way ticket to Europe, and sensing escape from the rigours of his former life, swapped clothes with the dying inebriate, abandoning his old identity for an unknown future. He made Paris his secret home, at first in self-imposed exile at the Hôtel Pimedon, aided by his friend and translator Charles Baudelaire, assuming—with typical playfulness and black humour—the name of his famous detective of "Rue Morgue" fame: Dupin, and occasionally, under that appellation, helping the French police with their more baffling investigations, as food for a brain no longer with an appetite for mere fiction.

"Monsieur Guédiguian. My pleasure, yet again." As he shook his hand Poe saw our guest eyeing the thin young man standing at the window—myself. "This is my assistant, Mr Holmes. He speaks

French like an Englishman, but is a master of discretion, as are all his countrymen. You may talk freely."

I met Poe in the guise of "Dupin" when I first came to Paris in my early twenties, and once within the penumbra of his intellect, having succumbed to his alluring devotion to his science, was unwilling—*unable*—to leave until I had learned all I could from the great man's unparalleled talent for deduction. Little did I know how that learning—or that friendship—would change my life forever.

"Allow me first to introduce Madame Anaïs Jolivet." Guédiguian touched the woman in the veil lightly on the elbow as he led her gently forward. She shuddered with every step as if treading on broken glass, so much so that, had she not possessed a curvaceous and upright frame, I might have taken her for an old crone.

Poe, as was his custom, took her hand to kiss it, and I saw instantly that the hand was not only shivering, but bandaged. She quickly inserted it in her fur muff as Guédiguian guided her to a seat, puffing up a cushion before she settled in it.

Sitting on the arm of her chair, the man seemed exhausted merely from being in her presence, and I feared he would not find the wherewithal to speak. She certainly showed no willingness to do so. It seemed as though all her physical effort went into holding herself in one piece, and a gust of wind might make her tumble down before our eyes. I also realised that the dress I took to be black was in fact navy blue, with tiny embossed fleurs-de-lys that sparkled like stars in a summer night. And who, I asked myself, dresses in navy blue whilst in mourning?

"Tea?" enquired Poe as Madame L'Espanaye, the maid, entered with a pot of Darjeeling. "Or something stronger? A glass of Virville? Pernod?" He was a teetotaller since his resurrection, but did not begrudge the pleasures of others, and kept a moderate cellar.

The woman looked up at Guédiguian like a frightened puppy.

"Water," he said. "And a drinking straw. If you please." He took her other hand gently in his own as the maidservant quietly exited, closing the doors after her. "I don't recall precisely how much you know about opera . . ."

"I know," said Poe, "by a certain deportment and an assessment of the capacity of the lungs that I am in the company of a *prima donna.*"

I could not tell if the woman blushed behind her veil, but her chin sank slightly and she let go of the manager's hand in order to avail herself of a handkerchief.

"But, monsieur, that term only puts her within a category of greatness," said Guédiguian. "Madame Jolivet is beyond that. Madame Jolivet is immortal. We are blessed that she walks the streets of this fair city and does not sit in heaven making the saints weep. When she played Gounod's Juliette she raised the roof of the Théâtre-Lyrique. Her Marguerite in *Faust* was outstanding. Those who missed her Pamina in *Die Zauberflöte* or the Countess in *The Marriage of Figaro* missed the supreme roles of the supreme soprano of her generation." I could see my elderly friend sinking in his armchair, his forearms making a bridge and his fingertips touching and separating with patient regularity as he listened. "She is a monument, sir. A monument! To both *coloratura* and dramatic intensity. There is . . . not another lyric singer alive who is . . . who can rise to the demands of . . ." The *impresario's* shoulders sank and he pressed his fingers to the corners of his eyes. "I'm sorry . . . I'm sorry . . ."

"Not at all," I offered, sitting at the nearby bureau and opening my notebook.

Poe leapt from his chair the moment Madame L'Espanaye knocked and snatched the tray from her. He knelt in front of the veiled woman's chair and placed it on a foot stool. The glass filled, he inserted the straw and held it out to her. The merest croak of thanks—not even that—emerged from her lips. I would not have credited it as a woman's voice, had you pressed me. And possibly not even human.

She lifted the veil an inch and put the straw in her mouth.

"No," said Guédiguian as he saw Poe reach out his hand, but it was too late to stop him.

"I must."

The veil was raised, in the manner of a groom lifting the veil of his bride on their wedding day to plant a kiss on the lips of his betrothed—nothing can be more grotesque or appalling an idea in view of what actually greeted our eyes.

I beheld the face of a rotting corpse. No. Half a face. Which, far from diluting the impact, only served to throw it into heightened obscenity by contrast. One eye was lustrous, that of a poor, frightened doe, the other lidless, shrivelled and blistered. The skin on one side flawless and pure, that of a beautiful woman, yet on the other— pitiful thing!—almost non-existent. She was eaten to the bone. I can only describe it, absurdly, as resembling the surface of a burnt sausage. Even that is inadequate. Her right cheek was gone, a flayed cavern in which I could count the teeth in her jaw and see her pink tongue wriggling, her right ear nothing more than a gristly stump. All this absorbed in an instant, and not forgotten in a lifetime.

I heard a death rattle, which was Madame Jolivet breathing with the horrid restriction her injuries compelled. Yet she held Poe's eyes without self-pity. And to his credit, he did not avert his gaze.

"Who did this?"

"We do not know." Guédiguian whimpered and sandwiched his hands between his thighs. "That is why we are here. It happened three weeks ago. Madame has not been well enough to move until today."

"You've spoken to the police?"

"We told them everything."

"Tell *me* everything."

"We had just begun rehearsing *La Traviata*. I had fired the conductor for being a drunk." Guédiguian began to pace back and forth behind her chair, occasionally tweaking it with his fingers as if to steady himself on a rolling sea. "I was calling in favours from old friends to ensure the production didn't run off the rails, but everybody was excited about Madame playing the part of Violetta. I knew it would be a complete triumph."

"How many of the cast had worked with Madame before?"

"That is not vital at this moment." Poe cut me off, his eyes never leaving the *diva*. "Please describe the incident as clearly as you can remember it."

"I must speak for her," said Guédiguian. "The merest exertion of the vocal cords causes her unbearable agony. She will never sing an aria again."

"Madame, not only has your body been cruelly abused," said Poe, "but so too has your soul. In that regard, justice is your only balm and my expertise—my *considerable* expertise—is at your service. Are you happy for M. Guédiguian to continue on your behalf?"

Now self-conscious, the woman lowered the veil before nodding. Her face covered, she became perfection once more. And I could breathe freely.

Poe turned to the manager. "Pray continue."

"One day during rehearsals, at about four in the afternoon, Madame retired to her dressing room for a nap. She gave her boy a swift instruction that she was not to be disturbed. She undressed, put on her dressing gown and lay on the day bed while upstairs the new conductor, Francesco Mazzini, put the orchestra through their paces. Half-dozing some minutes later—but not too much later because the music had not changed, it was still *Sempre libera*—she remembers hearing the door open, thinking nothing much of it— perhaps it was the boy again, with flowers from an admirer, after all, a day did not pass without her receiving some token or other. Suddenly, but not with horror, she felt liquid on her face. It had no obvious odour. Though momentarily startled, she presumed it was water—though why anybody would splash water on her face mystified her. She could only think it was a silly prank. Hardly had that thought begun to materialise when the substance began to burn. And when it did not stop burning, and when she felt the cheeks under her fingers turning to mud, she screamed. Screamed till her lungs burst. Horribly, for a few seconds the singers next door took the high notes to be her practising, then the truth . . ." The man's thick hair hung lank. "I'm—sorry . . ."

"Please, monsieur," Poe urged. "For Madame."

"There is little more to tell." Guédiguian waved a hand spuriously. "The hospital did what they could. They still are doing. But her face is a ruin. Her life is a ruin. They can rebuild neither. If she had a husband . . . but now . . ." He swallowed the thought, shaking his head, regretting he had even given it form. "Who would do such a thing? Who?"

"The police conducted interviews?"

"Endlessly. The chorus were becoming hoarse from repeating where they were and with whom. I think the paperwork must be longer than *La Comédie Humaine*."

"Word count is only an illusion of achievement," said Poe. "Over time, and with increasing desperation, the core, the essence, becomes obscured like a diamond lost in a bush of thorns. What is the name of the officer in charge?"

"Bermutier."

"Henri Bermutier. Not the sharpest bayonet in the army, but count yourself lucky you didn't get that lazy pig Malandain."

"It was he who pointed us in your direction, *Maestro*. He said if any man in Paris could find the solution to the mystery, it was C. Auguste Dupin."

"*Naturellement*." Poe explained that his method demanded he have unfettered access to the scene of the crime, and our new client assured us of his every co-operation, together with that of his numerous employees, whether performers or artisans. "The tea is stewed to the consistency of an Alabama swamp. I shall get us a fresh pot."

"We—we shall decline your kind offer, monsieur..."
Guédiguian accurately read the signal of his companion tugging
his sleeve. "We have to go. Madame, you see—she is tired ... the
slightest exertion ..."

Speaking for Poe and myself, I said we understood completely
and any other questions could be answered in the fullness of time.

Neither had removed their coats. Guédiguian offered La
Jolivet his arm. Once more Poe took the lady's hand and kissed
it, and I sensed she was thankful that he did. Charm sometimes
trumped his insensitivity. Otherwise life in his company, frankly,
would have been intolerable.

"There is something else I should say, which I fear will shock
and displease you." Guédiguian turned back, knotting his scarf.
"This incident has rekindled backstage rumours of a *Fantôme*.
Tongues are wagging that the production is cursed, that the opera
house is haunted, that this is merely the beginning of a concerted
spree of malevolence from beyond the grave ..."

"It always displeases me," sneered Poe, lighting a cigarette
from a candle, "when I have it confirmed that the imaginative
excesses of the poorly educated know no bounds. But shock? No. I
would have been shocked had they not."

"But—beyond the grave? M. Dupin, I confess to you, I was
brought up in fear of the Church and in fear of God ..."

"Then good luck to you." Poe jangled the bell-pull to sum-
mon Le Bon. "But there is no *beyond* in matters of the grave. There
is only—the *grave*. The Conqueror Worm and all his wriggling
allies in decomposition. If this abominable act tells us anything, it
is that the creature we seek is flesh and blood."

"I wish I could be so certain."

Behind Guédiguian, the woman's back was turned, like a silhouette cut from black paper. A long curl of fair hair, colourless as
flax, lay on the night-blue of her shoulder. The man placed his hand
against her back, and they were gone, like phantoms themselves.

⌒ℝ

"The quantity used was small, so the assailant must have been close. Very close." Our carriage took us at speed down the Avenue de l'Opéra. To Poe, the imposing five-storey buildings either side, which had eradicated the medieval city at the mercy of Hauss-man's modernization, were invisible. "Sulphuric acid, by the lack of odour. Used to pickle silver by jewellers. Readily dissolves human tissue, prolonged exposure causing pulmonary incapacity and tooth erosion. Severely corrosive to most metals, and shows an unquenchable thirst. If a flask of it is allowed to stand uncovered, it'll absorb water from the air until the container overflows, so must be handled with the utmost care. In highly diluted form it is available as a medical laxative. Used in horticulture to eradicate weeds and moss. Also as a drain cleaner . . ."

"Paris has good need for drain cleaner, I'll give you that. It out-stinks London."

"London has a perfume by comparison." He blinked languor-ously, acknowledging my presence for the first time in minutes. "Paris was born in filth and blood and other liquids, my dear Hol-mes. Violence is its beating heart. Violence and freedom."

The Opéra Garnier was not to my taste, but had to be admired. A triumph of engineering, indeed of artistic will, it cap-tured something, if not everything, of its era. Completed only a few years before, the neo-Baroque masterpiece had been commis-sioned by Napoleon III as part of his grandiloquent and massive reshaping of Paris, designed unashamedly as a flamboyant riposte to the established opera houses of Italy. Over its fifteen-year gesta-tion, construction had been held up by multifarious incidents and set-backs, from mundane lack of funds to upheavals such as the Franco-Prussian War and the demise of the Empire in favour of a new Republic. As a visual statement, its Imperial glory suddenly spoke only of the former regime in all its dubious splendour, and the politicians, freshly warming their rumps in the seats of office, were inherently ill-disposed towards its existence. The most that was done, in the end, was to change the Opéra's official name on the entablature fronting the loggia from "Acadamie Imperiale de Musique" to "Academie *Nationale* de Musique". Happily, for the craftsmen involved, a difference of only five letters.

Personally I saw the edifice before me as a resplendent example of grandeur and folly in roughly equal measure. With sunlight gilding the figures of Music and Dance on the façade and Apollo atop the dome, it was almost impossible to conceive that such an odious crime could have happened under the aegis of such gods and noble virtues.

As we climbed the steps to the entrance, Poe pointed out Carpeaux's sculpture—which had so shocked the Puritans of Paris in its erotic depiction of *La Dance* that ink had been thrown over its marble thighs. "Another disfigurement. Almost a prediction, if you believe such nonsense . . . Ink. Acid. I know some critics where the two are synonymous."

If we had doubted the atmosphere of superstitious dread permeating the company, we soon found it illustrated when the doorman almost leapt out of his skin at the sound of our rapping. Poe introduced himself—as "Dupin" naturally—and proceeded to interrogate the individual, a *sapeur-pompier* with a wooden leg, about his actions on the afternoon in question. The fellow was adamant that nobody had entered or left the theatre on his watch and he himself never strayed from his post until the doors were locked.

We ascended the Grand Staircase, with its balustrade of red and green marble and two bronze female *torchières,* in the direction of the foyers. Poe sniffed like an eager bloodhound as we were surrounded by immense mirrors and parquet, more coloured marble, moulded stucco and sculptures.

"These are the mirrors in which the audience watch the show *before* the show." He looked at the vast room in reflection, and at his own. "This is where they see each other, and themselves. And find themselves on the upper step, or the lower. The inane dance of the socially-inclined and the artistically disinterested. I'd wager, by law of averages, that of the myriad citizens crammed in here on opening night, at least five are murderers."

"A sobering thought."

"On the contrary, a thought to turn one to drink," said Poe. "I should know."

We had lied to the doorman. Our appointment with Guédiguian was at three. It gave us a full hour to explore unhindered; an opportunity my colleague took to with relish. He had been given extensive floor plans of the Opéra, but nothing, he said, was a substitute for the application of the senses. If there were gods that deserved statuary, Poe declared, it was Sight, Smell, Touch, Taste, and Hearing.

And so we roamed the interweaving corridors, stairwells, alcoves and landings. Before long it was not hard to imagine a clever infiltrator scampering from floor to floor, or room to room, unseen. Skulking round the Romano-Byzantine labyrinth, several times I wished for Ariadne's ball of twine, fearful that we had lost our way, while Poe counted his footsteps into hundreds, storing myriad calculations of I-knew-not-what. But then, I seldom did.

A swell of music rose up and I was momentarily reminded of the old adage of a dying man hearing a choir of angels. The gas-lit passageway gave the notes a dull, eerie resonance making it tricky to know whether the source was near or far. But when Poe opened a door and we stepped into a fourth-level box overlooking the stage, the voices and orchestra took on voluminous proportions.

The tiny figures before us were dwarfed in a five-tier auditorium resplendent in red velvet, plaster cherubs and gold leaf. The magnificent house curtain with gold braid and pom-poms was raised above the proscenium. And presiding over all—in fact partly obscuring our view—hung the magnificent seven-ton crystal and bronze chandelier; which alone, if you are to believe the controversy, cost thirty thousand gold francs.

I am marginally more familiar with *La Traviata* now than I was then, and could not have told you in those days they were rehearsing Act Two, Scene Two—the *soirée* at Flora's house, in which Alfredo, here a beefy man with the build of a prize-fighter, sees his love, the former courtesan Violetta, with Baron Douphol. After winning a small fortune from the Baron, he bitterly rounds up the guests to witness her humiliation—*Questa donna conoscete?*—before hurling his winnings at her feet in payment for her 'services'—whereupon she faints to the floor.

"She faints in Act One, too," said Poe, paying less attention to the stage than he did to the fixtures and fittings of the box. "Never a good sign."

"More to the point, Guédiguian hasn't wasted any time in finding a new Violetta. I presume that's her understudy."

Poe arched an eyebrow.

As we listened to the guests turn on Alfredo—singing *Di donne ignobile insultatore, di qua allontanati, ne desti orror!*—Poe could no longer bear the pain and left the box, muttering that high art was invariably highly dull. The art of the street, the Penny Dreadful and barrel-organ, he found more rewarding, he said—and more honest. "I don't know about you, but I have seldom been accompanied by an orchestra in my moments of intimate passion."

"But is there a clue in the play?" I caught up with him in the corridor.

"Why would there be?"

"I don't know. Do you? I've never stepped in an opera house before. I don't even know what *La Traviata* means."

"*The Fallen Woman.* It is based on *La Dame aux Camélias*, a play in turn based on a novel by Dumas *fils*—in turn based, some say, on a lady of his own acquaintance. The play was a big success when I first arrived in Paris, especially after it was vilified by the censors."

"For what reason?"

"A high living prostitute depicted as a victim of society? Especially when she never sees the light? In London, I believe they tried to put an injunction to stop it. But then, it is never entirely a bad thing for a work of art to be pilloried by the Church. In America they say the plot is immoral, though no worse than *Don Giovanni*. Here, it was first performed at the Théâtre Lyrique on the Place de Chatelet with Christine Nilsson in the title role. Too chaste-looking for a harlot, if you ask me."

"You saw it?"

"Yes, which is why I abhor opera with every fibre of my being. Rarely does an art form offend all the senses at once, and the buttocks more than any. Nothing less than the crucifixion of Christ should last more than forty minutes. And God forbid that Judas should sing about it. Though, given time, I'm sure he shall." Keeping up his sprightly pace, he turned a corner. "The truth is, my dear Holmes, I endured this mellifluous obscenity once and did not care for it. In fact, I walked out."

He strode on several yards before replying to my unspoken question, but did not turn to face me.

"You see . . . the soprano was too old, too obese, almost to the point of being flabby, to play—to *conceivably* play—the part of a young woman dying of consumption." His face creased and twitched with the most intense inner agitation. "That she sang with such—abnormal gusto. With superhuman energy—with such buoyant, lustrous, glowing *health*. And the fact that she was— applauded. That people *cheered* . . ."

He had told me before of Virginia, his cousin and child bride. Her icy pallor, cheeks rubbed with plum juice to fake a ruddy complexion. Her dry lips enlivened briefly with the colour of cherries. The coughing of blood onto a pure white handkerchief. He had also, once, intimated that the disease gave spells of excitement, even desire. That there was an aphrodisiac quality to the fading bloom. I think it was this that haunted him most of all. I cannot imagine what he had suffered. To bear helpless witness to a death so inevitable yet so gradual. To see loveliness—one's very reason for living—wither on the vine, and all around feel harangued by the prejudice of others, not knowing whether to blame habits or heredity or himself. Then to be there as the leaf takes to the wind, leaving its heavy load behind . . .

"From the opening music we are in the presence of death. Eight first and eight second violins portray the frail consumptive. Curtain up on a party scene. We are told the hostess is seeing her doctor. I know that feeling well. I have been in that scene, that room, many times. She wants to enjoy life fully because it is fleeting. Parties will be the drug to kill her pain. I understand that too. They drink a toast because love is life. *Fervido. Fervido . . .* A fever . . . A passion . . ."

The female voice rose again, distant as the angels.

"It is a lie, as all Art lies. There is no aria at the end. There is only the incessant coughs, the swelling of joints, the loss of weight, the cadaverous emaciation, delirium, torment—and, if one is lucky, the uttering of a lover's name."

Straightening his back he walked on, anxious not to meet my eyes, though he would never have admitted it. No more was said on the subject. He had closed a heavy door and I knew I could not open it. Only he could do that, when—and if—he wished.

We found a staircase. Narrow. Badly-lit. And descended.

I made to speak, but Poe raised a finger to his lips. We entered the auditorium and the music swelled louder.

We crept nearer to the stage, where Laurent Loubatierre, the tenor playing Alfredo, stood delivering an aria. We settled into a couple of seats off the central aisle, far enough back not to be noticed by the several people with their backs to us who formed a meagre audience—costumier, copyist, dramaturge, dance-manager and so on. Or so we thought.

Poe sank in his chair, thin neck disappearing into his collar, long white hair sitting on his shoulders and eyes heavy-lidded like those of a slumbering owl. I had placed my note book on my knee, when I was aware that the tenor's notes were falling flat, and looked up to see Loubatierre pinching the bridge of his nose, blinking furiously, then shading his eyes with his hand as he advanced to the footlights.

"I am sorry, Maestro! But this is impossible! I cannot work with such distractions!" He peered out, pointing in our exact direction, straight past the hapless conductor. "Who are these people? You! Yes, you sir! Both of you! Who invited you here? On what authority?" He became apoplectic. "Somebody fetch Guédiguian! Fetch him *immediately!*" The assorted lackeys threw looks at each other and one, by some mute agreement, ran out to do his bidding. "I cannot continue—I *refuse* to continue—until you reveal yourselves!"

"I shall, gladly." Poe spoke calmly, examining his fingernails. "When the cast of this opera reveal themselves and give a true account of their movements on the day Madame Jolivet was attacked."

"How dare you! This is outrageous!"

"The ravaging of a beautiful woman's face is outrageous, M. Loubatierre. Your indignation merely ludicrous." A couple of ballerinas in the background looked at each other, open-mouthed. And if Loubatierre was already red-faced with anger, he was now virtually foaming at the mouth. "You told the police you visited M. Rodin, the sculptor, at his *atelier* on the Left Bank to sit for him, but according to my enquiries M. Rodin has been in Italy and only returned yesterday, for the unveiling of his *L'Âge d'Airain* at the Paris Salon."

"I don't have to account for my whereabouts to you!"

"You might find that you do."

"Who is this man? That is an unspeakable accusation! I have a good mind to thrash him within an inch of his life!"

"I would very much prefer an answer," said Poe with lugubrious contempt. "Need I point out the truism that a man who has recourse to violence usually has something to hide?"

"Beckstein!" Loubatierre, supremely flustered, addressed the most smartly-dressed and rotund of the assembled, whom we later came to understand was the opera house's dramaturge. "Throw him out this instant! I insist! *I insist!*"

The singer turned his back sharply, appealing with extravagant gestures to the gods. Other members of the cast hurried on in their tights, bustles and blouses, trying their best to placate him, though he shrugged off, equally extravagantly, any attempt to do so. Poe, to my amazement, started to applaud and shout "Bravo! Bravo!" which served only to agitate the performer further. The poor man was incandescent to the point of immobility.

"Monsieur!" Guédiguian arrived, puffing. "What is the cause of all this—?"

"Exactly." Poe rose to his feet and shot his cuffs. "M. Loubatierre's behaviour is inexcusable."

The tenor rounded on him now, head down and ready to charge off the stage, had he not been held back.

"M. Dupin! Really!" blubbered Guédiguian, whose own cheeks were reddening. "Perhaps you can explain—"

Poe cut in before he could finish, with his habitual air of distraction. "Perhaps *you* can explain, monsieur, why we were able to wander every floor of this building with impunity, not once being asked our identity or purpose of our visit till now. But to wander with impunity is one thing, to escape the building without being seen by the watchmen at every exit, quite another. If we solve that conundrum, we solve the crime. Now, I should like to question the understudy. What is her name?"

Bamboozled, Guédiguian could do nothing better than to answer the question directly. "Marie-Claire Chanaud."

"Excellent. Where is she?"

Guédiguian appealed to his staff for an answer.

"She—she is not here, monsieur," said Beckstein, in a thick German accent.

"Not here?" Poe approached the orchestra pit, and I with him. "Then where? Back-stage? Bring her out. It is imperative."

"No, monsieur. She has been working very hard. She complained of a dry throat. With nerves, as you know, the throat tightens. And a singer is an athlete. They must take care of their most delicate instrument. We thought it best she went to the dressing room to rest . . ."

"You left her *alone*? Unprotected?"

I barely had time to register the ferocity in Poe's face as a clatter of footsteps drew my eyes with a whiplash to the wings, where a small boy ran onto the boards, almost tripping over his clogs in his haste. The entrance was so dramatic that for a split-second I took it for a part of the rehearsal, until I saw his blanched face and the tiny hand pressed to his chest as he tried to catch breath, ripping the cloth cap from his tousled head as he cried out to Guédiguian:

"Monsieur! *Monsieur!* He's struck again, sir! The Phantom!" His eyes were unblinking and his lip quivering. "He's struck *again!*"

Alarm taking hold in the auditorium, Poe and I wasted not an instant in thundering down stairs and through coffin-narrow corridors in pursuit of the lad, who moments later stood aside in terror of seeing what revolting scene might confront him in the dressing room.

Inside, we saw what he had seen—a large bunch of flowers tied in a red bow propped against the mirror, shrivelling on bending, blackening stalks as we stared at them—a sickening picture of decay seen through some kaleidoscope free of the strictures of time, speeding towards dissolution. Beside it, the open pages of a poetry book lay sizzling, Gérard de Nerval's *Les Chimères* turning to acrid vapour in the air. Poe coughed into his handkerchief. I moved forward to enter but he extended an arm across my body to block the way.

The chair was overturned.

The dressing room—*empty*.

With a terrible, rising certainty that the understudy had been abducted, I ran to the Stage Door, only to find it bolted.

"Here!"

Returning, I saw that Poe had whisked aside the curtain of an alcove to reveal the trembling singer standing there in nothing but her underwear, having narrowly escaped having her face ravaged by the same demon who had attacked Madame Jolivet. He picked up a cloak and wrapped it round her shoulders.

"Did any of it touch you? Madame? Are you hurt in any way?" She shook her head. "Are you sure? If it fell on your skin—or eyes . . ." He turned to the loons congregated at the door. "Water! Get water! Now!" She stepped forward, but sagged into his arms.

I grabbed the chair to prop it under her before she fell. "Stand back! She needs air, can't you see? Clear the way. We need to get her out of here." The two of us lifted her under the armpits and knees and deposited her gently on a wicker basket in the corridor. She was light as a feather.

"Open the Stage Door and let the fumes out. And nobody go in that room. Be careful how you touch anything."

In a few moments water came, and a sponge, and I ran it over her forehead and cheeks. "Did you breathe it in?"

Again the young soprano shook her head, her blue-black curls, which fell below her shoulders, shining. In this semi-swoon, with her almost painted eyebrows and porcelain skin, extreme thinness and long neck, I suddenly thought her the perfect picture of the phthisic beauty of consumption. Uncomfortably, it made me look over at Poe, who was glaring at her.

"There was no note with the flowers. Who sent them?"

"Dupin!" I protested.

"Allow her to answer, Holmes, please."

"In truth, I do not know," Marie-Claire said. "I simply came to my dressing room and there they were."

"From an admirer," I suggested.

"Precisely," said Poe, crouching at her side, resting the flats of his hands on the silver wolf's head of his walking cane.

"The door was bolted!" snapped the Stage Doorman, Christophe. "You saw it yourself, Monsieur. Nobody could have left without me seeing them, I stake my life on it! Nobody living!"

"Tell me what happened," said Poe to the young woman.

"My dresser, Rosa, helped me change out of my costume." Marie-Claire regained her composure admirably, perhaps because her leading man, Loubatierre, now held her hand. "The girls took it away to do some alterations. I ate some fruit and felt a little better, but didn't want to sleep anymore, so I read my book and combed my hair. It's foolish, but that has always calmed me, ever since *Maman* used to do it when I was little. I think the motion is soothing; it clears the mind. Well, I was gazing at my own reflection, not especially thinking about anything. Perhaps I was wondering who sent the flowers. Many things. Or perhaps nothing. Sometimes nothing at all goes through this head of mine." A smile flickered, accompanying the most nervous of giggles. "Then . . ."

"You monster," snarled Loubatierre. "Is it really necessary to put Madame through such torture?"

"It is," insisted Poe. "Continue."

"Then I dropped my bookmark and bent to pick it up. I heard a splash and I sat up straight again wondering what it was, and saw this most horrible sight, of the flowers dying, evaporating, right before my eyes. Something prevented me from touching them. Thanks be to Jesus, Mary and Joseph. And in the mirror I saw behind me, perched on my reflection's shoulder, such a face—indescribable! With holes for eyes. Empty sockets, and . . . and a *beak*, like some storybook witch, not even human at all, more like a bird—

a bird with green scales and no eyes. I don't know what it was, but it was the face of some kind of devil, of—of pure darkness . . ."

Loubatierre kissed her tiny fist.

"I dare not even think what might have happened if I wasn't wearing this." Marie-Claire touched the crucifix on a chain around her neck, then kissed it. "It saved me."

Loubatierre, the bear, embraced her.

"In the name of Pity," said Poe. "Please do not burst into song." He turned to me. "The flowers were not from an actor. To an actor, flowers before a performance mean bad luck. But they're from someone who knows *this* opera enough to send camellias. So he is someone already in the building. But that is not our culprit. Come with me." He strode to Christophe, the Stage Doorman, and addressed him: "Look directly into my eyes and tell me, what colour are the buttons on my assistant's waistcoat?"

"Brown."

"And how many are buttoned? Keep looking into my eyes."

"Two."

"There is nothing wrong with your vision. Where were you standing? Or sitting?" The man shuffled into his position behind the shelf of his booth. "And you did not leave? Nothing distracted you?" The man screwed up his beret in his fists and shook his head. "Then if someone entered you would have seen them."

"Madame saw nobody. I saw nobody. The thing cannot be seen. Doors and walls are nothing to the Phantom. That much is certain."

"Nothing is certain," said Poe.

An hour later we were in the Opéra manager's office. His hand shook as he poured brandies, and to my astonishment expressed concern that the production would be ready for opening night in a few days' time.

"Monsieur." I stepped forward to stand beside the chair in which Marie-Claire sat. "You cannot seriously be considering that can happen, even as the remotest possibility, while this criminal is at large and his intent against Madame could hardly be more clear."

"Please, M. Holmes, do not impugn my sensitivity. No man could be more appalled than I, but my position here means I have to think of the Palais Garnier."

"You value the fortunes of the Palais Garnier above a *life?*"

"Of course not. I nevertheless have to bear in mind that if opening night is cancelled, people will ask why. The natural consequence of that is the future of the Opéra may be called into question. The government is all too eagerly looking for the appropriate excuse to shut us down. I have to think not only of Madame—with the greatest respect—but of every soul working under this roof."

"In any case . . ." Marie-Claire rose to her feet. "I'm sorry gentlemen, but there is no question of my *not* playing Violetta on opening night. M. Dupin, I appreciate your efforts as a detective, and those of M. Holmes today, but I have waited my entire life for the opportunity to sing this part." Her back ramrod-straight, from a frail, *petite* girl she took on the aspect of an Amazon. "As I see it, if we let the fiend stop us, whoever or whatever he might be, then the fiend has won."

"Admirable," said Poe, resisting a smile as well as the brandy snifter. "Foolish, but admirable."

"But be under no illusion regarding our gratitude, M. Dupin, nor our desperation. Our safety—Madame's safety—is now entirely in your hands." Guédiguian let the import sink in as the golden liquid trailed down his throat, and my own. Marie-Claire had downed hers in one gulp and returned the glass to its tray before we did.

"My father taught me that."

"My father taught me Shakespeare," said Poe. "He was an actor, but a bad one. You should always have enough gum on your beard when you play Lear, or hilarity ensues. Not what the Bard of

Avon had in mind. Though entertaining enough to a four-year-old standing in the wings."

Marie-Claire smiled, but I thought of Poe's mother, an actress too, he'd once told me. I didn't know why I hadn't thought before of his obvious connection to the world of theatre. It was in his blood: literally so. She too had died of consumption—his 'Red Death' to be—coughing up blood on stage as little Eddie watched, mouthing her lines, the audience not even knowing something was wrong as she slumped in agony, thinking the acting peculiarly good that night in Richmond during *Romeo and Juliet*. Inconceivable to think of it other than as a ghastly foretaste of Virginia and the tragedy to come. The first of a catalogue of losses that were to blight Poe's life, and to this mind, the anvil that forged him. The reward being a great writer. But what a price. Too, too much a price, for any man.

C. Auguste Dupin took the fingers of Marie-Claire Chanaud and pressed his lips to them. Her arm was barely bone in her sleeve, the hand itself as fragile as the skeleton of a bird. Her skin white and untarnished, the perfection of a tombstone freshly carved. Her eyes lustrous with the burning of night.

"The curtain will rise," said Guédiguian.

"The curtain *has* risen," corrected my friend the detective with an expression I could not decide was one of fear or of singular anticipation. "Our characters are on stage. Our villain is waiting in the wings. After the interval, we shall begin Act Three. I simply hope we have not paid to watch a tragedy."

～

I knew things were amiss whenever he asked me to talk rather than listen, and that night as the gliding Le Bon lit candles and Madame L'Espanaye served us a supper of oven-warm bread and Normandy camembert so ripe it ran from its skin, he demanded to hear my theory.

"Theory?"

"Yes, Holmes. Theory. Of this elusive Phantom. You have been silent. I hope you have been thinking, but possibly I'm in for a disappointment."

"Well . . ." I had been caught on the hop. Again the schoolmaster and pupil. I lit a pipe of Altadis Caporal, an earthy *tabac gris*. "I think there's a productive line of enquiry in the fact that Guédiguian, the manager, comes from Corsica. From what I have read, certain Corsican families who get money by extortion and intimidation operate within a secret code called *vendetta*—members are obliged to kill not only anyone who besmirches the family honour but anyone in *their* family, too. Slights and grievances go back decades. There have been four thousand murders—"

"Mostly garrottings and stabbings, with the odd blinding." Poe took the pipe from my mouth, filled his cheeks and handed it back without a word. "The Corsicans are a predictable bunch. They like the victim, or the family of the victim, to know precisely why they're doing it. Rarely cultivate a sense of mystery. Quite the opposite. But well done. We can now rule that out. Anything else?" He descended low into his armchair, crossed his legs and put his hands behind his head before expelling the smoke, which rose in an undulating cloud to the ceiling.

"I noticed a proliferation of tattoos amongst the men working behind the scenes. Also the swaying gait common to seamen. According to my researches, many of the stage crew are traditionally hired from ships in port. If a seafarer was seeking revenge against somebody—a captain perhaps, responsible for the loss of a ship. We could look at the records of shipwrecks, the names . . ."

"And entirely waste our time."

"Forgive me, but why ask for my deductions, if you seek only to dismiss them?"

"I seek only to arrive at the truth. And they are not deductions, Holmes, they are *suppositions*. Flights of fancy. I have told you before that guesswork is the recourse of the buffoon or the police inspector. When we use my methods, we build our house on sound foundations or not at all."

Poe flicked the tails of his coat and sat on the piano stool at his writing desk with his back to me. He lifted a candle-stick to his elbow, unscrewed an ink pot and started to scratch with his pen, but the real purpose, I knew, was just that—to have his back to me.

I tapped my pipe bowl against the fire surround but did not take myself off to bed as he perhaps wished. Stubbornly, I stayed. I hoped he might, as a clever man, draw some conclusion from that. But his pride excelled his wisdom that night.

"This Phantom . . ."

"Phantoms. Demons. Ghosts!" He rubbed the back of his neck without turning. "Do not desert C. Auguste Dupin for the realm of actors and unreason. If that is your desire, Holmes, I tell you now—go home to London. I have no more to teach you."

A lump came to my throat. He was goading me but I refused to rise to the bait. I would not be his mental punch bag.

"I intend to stay."

Poe did not reply. He remained sitting with hunched shoulders and the sound of his scribbling nib in the candle-light. I intuited however—intuition being only a hop and a skip from guesswork, as he might say—that his change in mood was not about me, and not entirely about the nature of the mystery that was testing us so sorely, either.

He crossed the room and yanked the servant cord. When Le Bon came, Poe asked him to deliver a message by hand the following day. "To Colonel Guy Follenvie, postmaster at the Place de Ravaillac. Tell him to meet me on opening night of *La Traviata* at the Palais Garnier on Friday. The details are enclosed. And remember to tell him to bring Madame Lop-Lop."

"Madame Lop-Lop?" I sniggered, perplexed.

He ignored me. "Are my instructions clear, or are they not?"

Le Bon said they were.

"I have an appointment tomorrow with a saddle maker, name of Hermès," Poe continued, this incongruous piece of information as mystifying to me as the first. "Do not let me sleep after nine. I shall take coffee but no toast. Holmes can do as he pleases."

His tetchiness with the man confirmed what I had begun to suspect: from what Poe had said in the shadowy corridors of the Opéra Garnier, I knew he had turned over old soil, and that the bones of the most painful recollections imaginable, that of his long lost love, his first and only love, Virginia, had been unearthed. To my dismay, far from being a hero of vast intelligence and inde-fatigable vigour, the figure in the semi-gloom—Dupin, Poe—now looked like a husk of humanity. Not a god of the dark imagination, or giant of literature, but a brittle insect crushable under foot.

I stepped closer. "Can I get you—?"

"No."

Reluctantly, I left the room and went to my bed, but did not sleep.

Lying awake I pondered whether, for all his absolute faith in the appliance of 'ratiocination' and his unwavering dedication to that skill in his latter years, the Socrates to my Plato had increas-ingly built a dam to keep the vast lake of his inner feelings at bay, had done this at no inconsiderable cost. After the sudden ill temper I'd witnessed, I wondered whether one day, if unchecked or unheeded, that dam might burst.

⌖

My private concerns over my mentor's well-being only contributed to my further unease as opening night drew closer. I slept badly, drank excessively, and by the time we arrived at the Opéra Gar-nier, my nerves were so jangled that the gas-lights of the boulevards swam in my field of vision like Montgolfier balloons, the conflux of so many carriages dispensing their chattering cargo so overwhelming I felt palpitations. My grip on my senses was so unsteady, I swear I saw a man in a peaked cap taking a pig for a walk.

"Lo! 'tis a gala night . . ."

In the cab, Poe lifted a mahogany box onto his knees, unclipped the brass catches and opened it. Wrapped in red satin lay two flintlocks I recognised immediately as Denix French duelling pistols.

"Our difference of opinion has come to this?" I mused, not entirely seriously.

Poe—po-faced—handed me one. "I can think of no man I would rather trust when cogent thinking runs aground and the only logical recourse is to a lead ball and gunpowder." This was as much as I could expect as an apology for his recent behaviour, and rather more than I was accustomed to. "My home country is big on these things. I hear they often use them in lieu of democratic debate." He blew down one barrel, then squinted along the length of the other. "I'd have picked up a gun in the Civil War, had I been on the right continent."

"No you wouldn't."

He pouted indignantly. "I went to West Point Academy, I'll have you know."

"Don't be ridiculous."

"Kicked out for insubordination."

"Now I'm starting to believe you."

Dressed for the opera in top hats and capes, we joined the milling throng and were carried by the flow of the crowd up the Grand Staircase. Mildly ironic to think all these theatre-goers done up to the nines were coming to see a tale about disease, death and prostitution, but such is the wonder of art—or of beautiful music, anyway—to make anything palatable.

We met Bermutier in Box C, as planned, from which we could watch the seats filling below. If the policeman had nerves half as frayed as I did, he concealed it well. He reported that, according to Dupin's explicit instructions, there were thirty men in plain clothes placed in strategic positions around the building. Poe repeated his insistence that they were in sight or earshot of each other and Bermutier confirmed that they were, several with *Garde du Corps de Roi* firearms secreted about their persons, and all with batons and whistles. The one thing they lacked, he said, was any rough description of what this malefactor might look like.

"M. Holmes will tell you," said Poe, to my evident surprise.

"Me?"

"Yes, my friend. I guarantee that within the minute you will be telling Bermutier here exactly what our criminal looks like." He looked down upon the audience as he spoke. "What manner of man could hide in a room unnoticed? Hide under the dressing room table, perhaps, invisible? Slip under the Stage Door shelf, unseen by an eagle-eyed doorman? And slip away again, below the eye-line of you or me?"

"Someone of exceptionally, I don't know—small stature . . ." An idea went off in my mind like a struck match. "Good God! You can't mean—a *dwarf!*"

"Yes. A dwarf. When you remove the impossible . . . What was your phrase, Holmes? I thought it was rather good . . ." Poe unfolded a large sheet of paper from his inside pocket and thrust it at Bermutier. "Holmes and I are going to take up position outside the dressing rooms. Your men are covering the back-stage areas and front of house. I've marked this architectural plan with red crosses where I've seen trapdoors or manholes down to the under-world. That's where he will make his escape."

"Underworld?" I was shocked.

"There is a subterranean lake under this building. A laby-rinth of canals and vaults almost the equal of that which is above ground. His hiding-place, if not his habitation."

"The Phantom was under our feet all the time!" I said.

Bermutier folded the plans and stuffed them in his pocket, tugging the brim of his hat as he headed to the door.

"Take the utmost care, Bermutier," said Poe. "He does not want Violetta to sing tonight. He intends his desecration of beauty to be complete."

The dressing rooms were busy as we took up our positions near the Stage Door. Loubatierre, in his wig as Alfredo, emerged to make his way upstairs, taken aback to see C. Auguste Dupin, detective, walking towards him.

"Merde," said Poe. The traditional 'break a leg' of French actors.

"Merde," repeated the *primo tenore* grudgingly, and was gone.

Dressers and wardrobe-mistresses with peacock-feathers and robes flitted to and fro. A man in a waistcoat continually checked his watch. Christophe was ensconced at his position. I casually asked after the small boy. "We never saw him again. His mother sent a letter saying he was too afraid to come back." Neither of us found that wholly surprising.

"We would do best to split up," Poe said to me. "You stay here, outside the door. I shall position myself in the dressing room with Madame Chanaud." He checked the hammer action of his pistol, turning to go, but I caught his arm.

"You do not believe in demonic forces, and neither do I. But these acts are no less than atrocities. Mindless atrocities. Is it conceivable that pure evil can manifest in a human being?"

"Evil is a convenient label invented by the sanctimonious to describe the unfathomable." He walked to the dressing room door and knocked. "There are only *deeds*, which we may define as good or bad according to our nursery training and the books we read. The deeds human beings commit upon each other, and the infinitely complex, or infinitesimally simple, reasons they commit them." He knocked a second time and entered.

I felt strangely alone. As if by magic the corridor was deserted. The chaotic movement of figures all round us had abated: they had all flown to their posts. Actors waiting in the wings for the action to begin—as were we all. Nervous—as were we all. Fearful—as were we all.

Now the man checking his pocket-watch was me.

Above, muffled by distance and woodwork, I heard the orchestra practising in short, unpredictable bursts. Discordant notes seeped through the building and into my bones.

Walking to the Stage Door to test the bolt, I passed the dressing room door but could hear no voices within. Christophe's chalky pallor matched my own.

I heard a clatter of footsteps from the dark. I caught a rake of a man by the wrist and asked his name. He said, "Rennedon," and stuttered that he had to give Madame her fifteen minute call. I told him to do so quickly and go.

When he came a second time, he looked frightened of me and retreated a step or two. He held up the five fingers of one hand. I jerked my head with approval. He rapped on the door and delivered his message.

"Five minutes on stage, Madame Chanaud!"

Again, I heard no voices from within.

I wondered whether the two were talking in the dressing room or sitting in silence, Edgar Allan Poe and his new dark maiden, the uncanny mirror of his beloved. He could not save his sick wife, and now another young woman played a dying consumptive. Could *she* be saved? And if not—if he failed . . . if his old enemy, Death, took *her*, as well . . .

The strings, having tuned up, fell into a chasm of silence.

At that point my concern became acute. Minutes had elapsed since the rake-like man had rattled off. Why did Marie-Claire not emerge? Surely she would be late for her all-impor-tant entrance. What was delaying her? It was then that I heard, as if in answer to my unspoken query, the loud *bang!* of the Stage Door.

I spun round. Saw it swing back into place. The chill draught of night hit me. In the same instant, paralysed, I saw that the bolt had been lifted.

My hand pulled out my flintlock and held it at arm's-length. My mind was racing. Had they not been speaking because *the fiendish assailant was already in the room?* Had I been pacing, stupidly, and checking my watch while—God in Heaven, *was I already too late?*

"Holmes! *Holmes!*"

Poe's cry was one of—what?

I ran to the door, pistol outstretched, and kicked it wide—

The sight that confronted me shocked me to my core. Never, in the many cases I have encountered over the years as a consulting detective in London, Sussex, or on Dartmoor, was I more stricken by utter horror.

Marie Claire stood facing me, immobile. I recognised the lilac 'courtesan' gown worn by Violetta in Act One, the bell-like shape of the crinoline, the tight-fitting lavender bodice with pagoda sleeves buttoned to the pit of the throat in a white collar, the leghorn hat beribboned in silver-grey tilted off her braided sausage curls. But it was not the lack of movement that pinned me to the spot, for she stared at me from a face not merely painted with the stark white of grease paint, but a face that bubbled and collapsed, the hissing of a deadly steam rising not only from the cheeks and withering locks, but from the breast of the bodice itself, swathing the entire head in a pall of vapour.

No sooner had I absorbed the nightmare image than her hands tore the front of the bodice asunder, popping the buttons and ripping away the collar.

Pulling my cuffs over one hand, I reached out to help—but the swing of her arm knocked mine away.

The features were falling asunder. Nose. Chin. One eye, a hollow, *slid* . . . Then to my amazement Marie-Claire's gloved hands—no, *gauntleted* hands—tore off her face and flung it aside.

Fizzing, it broke apart against the wall and fell to the floor. A plaster of Paris mask made by any of a dozen workshops along the Seine. The wig of sausage curls came off next, hurled after it, sizzling on the floorboards like a cut of beef on a griddle.

The figure hastily disrobed a leather balaclava to reveal a thin mop of snowy white hair. Even the leather, extending as it did over the shoulders, was blackened and burning in patches where the acid had eaten through the clothing, and Poe wasted no time in divesting himself of it, and the thick brown gloves with it. Last to be thrown aside in a heap were the goggles as he stepped out of the hoops of the crinoline cage.

He ran to a bowl of water and up-ended it over his head. Shook the water out of his hair and flattened it back with his hands.

"Did you see it? What did you see?"

"Nothing!"

We were in the corridor. I still brandished my pistol. Christophe the doorman looked like a startled sheep.

"Tell M. Bermutier, the policeman, that the Phantom is in the building," said Poe. "Tell him M. Dupin says the devil has been foiled, but he has escaped underground. It is imperative he send all his men in that direction. *All* his men. You understand?" The man nodded. "Tell him they must descend to the lake. Immediately! Or he will get away. Go. *Go!*"

The man shot off. I followed him—but Poe caught my arm.

"No. We go this way—"

He swept out of the Stage Door entrance into the dark, not pausing to answer any of the questions rushing through my mind. Not least: if the *prima donna* was not in the dressing room—*where was she?* In the hands of a terrible abductor? And if the monster was secreted, as he had just said, in the Opéra, or *under* it—why on earth were we running *away* from the place as if our lives depended on it?

As we took to the street I kept up with the detective, an incongruous if not ludicrous sight in his flapping skirts and petticoats.

Even with trousers and boots underneath, his long white hair and jagged elbows gave him the appearance of a spirited old maid.

Poe dropped to one knee, and I almost fell over him.

He picked up an object from the ground. A theatrical mask with green feather-like marks, eye holes and a large, hooked beak.

"*Papa guinea!* Onward!" Poe cried, inexplicably. "Keep up with the pig!"

At first, I thought that this was some strange colloquial expression in the French vernacular to which I had not previously been exposed, but no. What we had to keep up with was indeed just that—*a pig*. A very fat, very *pink* pig whose curl of a tail and rear end I now could make out wobbling in and out of the shadows cast by the street lamps ahead.

I was convinced I was going mad. No, that I *had* gone mad. The process was complete and unequivocal. But it was there, in front of me. A pig on a leash, no less—with a man in a peaked cap in tow, keeping up a brisk walking pace with the animal, its ears flapping and its snout rubbing along the pavement like a bloodhound. Poe, following—in the billowing dress of a courtesan. Me, following him.

On the boulevards people were laughing and drinking in the harsh, false glare of the cafés as if the garish reds and golds of the theatre were bleeding out after us. The signs were phosphorescent—names like *La Barbarie, Sans Soleil* or *La Bataille*—the eerie glow of absinthe and folly, of love affairs not yet begun and those long ended. And not a single soul batted an eyelid at three men hastening past with a pig at the end of a rope.

Then I glimpsed him.

The dwarf!

Far ahead—almost out of sight. Scurrying along low to the ground, head down, swathed in a scarlet hood and cape. And soon just that—a *swirl* of red, lost into the crepuscular haze as the Boulevard des Italiens became the Rue St Marc.

Soon we had left the bright lights of the cafés behind, and lost sight of the hooded blood-stain to whom we were giving chase. Solitary women now lingered in the shadows, hands extending for money, but we hurried past them, interested only in where this path, and this misshapen gnome, clothed in his Red Death cowl, was taking us, and if, in some nether-region of Poe's 'ratiocination,' this insanity—this unparalleled *absurdity*—made sense.

Whatever trail the beast was following, and clearly the scent was still in its nostrils, took us to the grim environs of the Rue St Denis, of notorious repute, den of vice since medieval times, and the expectation of such did not fall short. Almost every doorway was adorned with a streetwalker showing a leg or sometimes a bare, grubby breast to advertise her wares, with the shamelessness of the desperate and misbegotten. I shuddered at the rough brush-strokes of rouge that were intended to rouse passion, but instead only invoked, to this young observer at least, an overwhelming disgust, tinged with pity. But these specimens—variously termed *comediennes, lorettes, grisettes, les codettes* or (most dismissively of all) *les horizontals*—did not crave my pity, and likely would have bitten my fingers off if I had offered a helping hand.

Our four-legged companion, moving at great speed, spurred only by the occasional *"Allez!"* or *"Vite!"* from its master, led us via a murky alleyway to the Rue Blondel.

Its snout dragged us to a doorway with red *faience* tiles on its façade. Snorting, it tugged the man in the peaked cap through into an ill-lit stairwell, where he was unceremoniously grabbed by a bald, nattering Chinaman with rolled up sleeves and the girth of a pannier-horse. Poe thrust his arm against the ogre's chest but one might as well have tried to keep a mastiff at bay with a pipe cleaner. The thug pawed it away effortlessly, and was about to punch him in the nose and quite possibly take the head from his shoulders in the process when, registering that his assailant wore a flouncy pastel-coloured dress, simply burst into laughter. The hearty guffaw was cut short when the barrel of my pistol made a cold circle against his temple.

A wrought iron staircase led upwards.

The pig was first up it. The man second. Poe third—"Don't touch it!"—and I came close after, backwards, making sure I did not step on the empty bottle of Sulphuric Acid lying there, still hissing. I kept the oriental giant in my sights the whole way. Even with his animal intellect he knew better than to follow, and I fear I would have put a bullet in him with not a vast amount of provocation.

I pulled aside a red curtain sticky with grime and heard screams ahead. Shrill, girlish screams, and those of men—and of a dwarf, for all I knew.

A cigar-smoking man hastened to pull up his trousers, probably convinced I was a policeman. He stood with his hands in the air and just as quickly his trousers fell.

In another room a fat woman, suddenly shrieking as she saw me, rolled her doughy frame off the bed, revealing a skinny old man secreted in the pillows under her.

My cheeks did not blush so much as burn.

As I followed Poe and pig, each doorway I passed was a window into debauchery. If this was where so-called gentlemen came for their treats, then their play was beyond anything I would have credited, had I not seen it with my own eyes. My education with Poe had been extensive, but this was tantamount to setting foot on another world—not unlike his fantastical account of a trip to the Moon.

Pistol in hand, I gaped into unexpectedly grand, if faded, salons with walls adorned with voluptuous nymphs lolling on clouds and men—or gods—endowed with the envy of Priapus. Through another open door I saw a man biting the cloth off sumptuous bosoms while a second woman wore a strapped-on phallus in lurid pink. Then there were the *tableaux vivants*—The Crazed

Nun, The Naval Officer's Homecoming, The Naughtiest Boy in School—which added theatricality to ardour, setting copulation and flagellation in a variety of frankly highly unlikely settings for the purpose of pepping up the proceedings. I will not dwell on the proliferation of nakedness or the contortions exhibited, but will remark only that the excitement of the physical organs of both genders was not only evident, but, in the main, exposed to view with little attempt to recover dignity.

So this—*this?*—was the dwarf's abode?

One of the *maisons d'abattage* or "slaughterhouses" I had heard about, where a man took a number and waited in line for a woman who had up to sixty passes a day? Where adulterers from the mansions of the Champs-Élysées, or off-duty soldiers with a franc in their pockets, came to roll their clothes into a ball?

A door slammed and the pig squealed. I elbowed past a square-shouldered female sucking an opium pipe.

Ahead of me, the man in the peaked cap was yanking the leash so hard that the pig was standing on two legs, its corkscrew tail vibrating excitedly. He slapped its ears as if admonishing a disobedient infant. In front of him, Poe was holding open a door, the room beyond him thick with darkness.

I snatched a candle from the pipe smoker. Holding it aloft, I joined my friend, who had now lowered to his knees. I shone it over his shoulder. Its glow made a halo of his cloud-white hair, and fell beyond, picking out a shape in the far corner of the room.

A shape I immediately recognised as the dwarf's all-encompassing scarlet cape. A tiny human being was under it, knees tucked up to its chest, trembling, its lungs clearly gasping for air after the exertion of running through the streets and a kind of throaty sobbing emitting from it in bursts. As my candle entered the room the hooded head sunk down so that its face was even more completely hidden in shadow.

Poe crept towards the huddled figure on his hands and knees.

I caught his shoulder with my free hand. "Be careful. He might be armed." I drew my duelling pistol, but he placed a hand on the barrel and pushed it away.

"Stand back," he whispered. "As far back as possible."

Reluctantly, I obeyed. The candle went with me, and the pistol went back in my coat.

The retreating amber glow threw Poe's shadow longer over the filthy floorboards and onto a grim, stripped bed, its mattress a continent of stains and mildew. The shape, the scarlet bundle, sat sandwiched between it and the peeling wall. The dwarf did not move as Poe edged closer. It merely continued to shudder.

My hand slid into my waistcoat and derived some small comfort from the butt of the Denix.

He moved closer still. I wished I could be sure that this wasn't some damn foolish action of a madman I was watching. The death—the second and *final* death of Edgar Allan Poe, more than worthy of his outlandish fiction: at the hands of a lunatic dwarf.

"Don't be frightened." The master of the macabre spoke so softly now I could hardly hear him. "We are not here to harm you . . ."

He rested back on his heels and reached out one hand. A slender hand, a womanly hand, with the long fingers of a pianist. Or so he had been told, he once said, by a gypsy reading palms in Philadelphia.

My finger dug down for the trigger.

I expected the dwarf to galvanise as the hand grew closer, but it did not. I expected the Phantom to jump forward, to grab, to bite, to resist, to run in sudden desperation to escape—but it did none of these things. Somehow satiated, repentant, inactive, or resigned to its fate, it only breathed. And its breath was a thin kind of mewling.

I imagined the grotesque mockery of human physiognomy that would be revealed under the hood, but what I did not—*could not*—imagine was that, when it was pulled back, the face was that of a little girl no more than eleven years of age.

The gentle mewling continued as she rocked back and forth, the candle-light picking out in silver the pearls of tears coursing down her pretty cheeks as I stepped into the room.

When we left the building at dawn a battalion of street-sweepers had begun their daily grind, moving as a mechanical phalanx down the width of the cobbles, brooms sweeping the dirt in front of them in semicircles, pushing all the rubbish into the gutter with the same rhythmic motion of reapers in the field. We saw them on every road on our way home, working like puppets. But all I could think of was the dingy room that lit up as I walked in to it, a faded sampler and a map of the world on the walls, furnished as it was with a rocking-horse, an abacus, a wooden Noah's Ark and a family of china-headed dolls, in a vile parody of a nursery.

"The pig is a much maligned species." Poe took a curl of sugared orange peel from the tray proffered by Le Bon and dropped it into his open mouth, the sunlight from the window making it a curling sliver of gold. "Just because it lives in its own faeces, people presume it is dirty. Nothing could be further from the truth. In fact it is very clean, and highly intelligent. More intelligent than a dog, and it has a more acute sense of smell than a dog, which is why I have undertaken experiments in their relative use to the police. Unfortunately they are not as loyal and obedient as dogs, but once on track are far more reliable than an average black-and-tan Beauceron—though perhaps not as manly-looking at a law-enforcer's heel. However, because of their poor eyesight they can detect food with astonishing precision: the reason for centuries they have been employed to forage for truffles up to three feet underground. The female is used because the smell resembles the male reproductive organs. Dogs, I've found, are, by and large, not sexually excited by fungus."

"Madame Lop-Lop ..." I elaborated for the benefit of Guédiguian, who perched his coffee cup on the arm of his chair as I added cream to mine.

"Madame Lop-Lop, indeed." Poe sipped his own. "She was used to great effect in uncovering explosives being shipped via Marseilles by a gang of anarchists. They can be trained, you see. In this case, with a reward of food over several weeks, trained to sniff out explosives. Soon afterwards she retired, as did Colonel Follenvie who received a bullet in the leg and took on the old sow as a pet. But her usefulness as a bloodhound was proven. The best snout in Paris. Reason enough to lure her out of retirement for one last case. I devised a concoction of chemicals, tactile enough to stick to the sole of a shoe. Then I knew we could trace our Phantom wherever he, or she, fled ..."

Guédiguian shook his black locks with their sheen of macassar oil. Poe's racing intellect and breathless reasoning often left people bewildered bystanders. Today was no exception.

"There were distractions. There always are. The wasteful detritus of any investigation. The tenor Loubatierre being absent and refusing to give an explanation: that confounded me until I had Le Bon follow him, and found he was visiting his ailing father at the mad house in Bicêtre. He simply wished to keep the stigma of insanity in his family a private affair. The other being the dramaturge Beckstein's unrequited love for Madame Chanaud. It was he who sent the mysterious flowers with no card: camellias in symbolic celebration of her role on stage. On our first visit to the theatre I noted he wore a pale pink camellia flower in his buttonhole—Lady Hume's Blush, if I'm not mistaken—a secret signal to our *ingénue* that he was in love with her. If she did but care, or even notice ...

"Anyway, unimportant! The crucial fact, as Holmes now knows, was Marie-Claire saying that the intruder's face was level with her shoulder. Common sense dictated that only three possibilities existed: the figure was on its knees (unlikely in the extreme); it was a dwarf (which I considered *highly* fanciful)—or else a child. From her description I had no doubt the infiltrator wore the traditional mask of Papageno, the bird-catcher, birdlike itself. Confirmed when we were told the name of the previous production at the Garnier: *The Magic Flute.*

"The problem of the bolt on the Stage Door then presented itself. Yes, a wire from outside poked through the crack could yank up the bolt to allow entry—any pickpocket in Pigalle could show you that trick in five minutes—but why and how was the bolt *shut immediately afterwards?* At that stage I could not dismiss the notion that Christophe might be an accomplice. Which is why I could not tell you, my dear Holmes, of my plan on opening night. Your most minute gesture or reaction might have betrayed to the doorman the fact that the *prima donna* was not in her dressing room, and as a direct result our elusive Phantom may have been alerted and the chance of capture jeopardised." Poe saw my displeasure. I could not disguise it. "Don't sulk. You thereby give the evidence that my decision was correct. It is not a fault, my good friend, but an observation and an accurate one: you wear your heart on your sleeve, and could no easier lie or deceive than you could remove the beating heart of a starving orphan. Where was I?"

"The bolt," said Guédiguian. "Which was locked."

"Which was locked because Christophe locked it. The man had not seen the *Fantôme* enter or leave—or rather he *did* see it leave, in that he saw the door open and close. Mystified, and thinking he would be blamed for being inattentive, when the screams went up, he simply threw the bolt himself and claimed, because he had to, that the door had been closed the whole time. Self-protection being the most powerful of motives.

"My plan then was simplicity itself. The first priority was to remove Madame Chanaud from any possibility of danger. To that end, I arranged that she be secreted in your office with two armed guards on opening night. I then went to a saddler to acquire protective clothing, impenetrable to the acid, and a plaster mask lest the perpetrator see me in the mirror.

"That the criminal was a child I was certain, but a child is not a natural aggressor, it is a natural victim. What was the catalyst for such monstrous acts as these? I needed to know and my fear was that the clod-hopping police force would get in the way. It was imperative to misdirect them, and so I invented the ruse of the underground 'lake'—a fabrication. The most cursory investigation into the building of the Opéra revealed that when Garnier first cleared the ground, water constantly bubbled up from the swamp below. All attempts to pump the site dry failed miserably. Wells were sunk. Eight steam pumps were put into operation to no avail. The only solution was construct an enormous concrete tank—called the '*cuve*'—to relieve the pressure of the external ground-water and to stop any of it rising up through the foundations. But there is no *lake*, no labyrinth—"

"And no Phantom," I added. "Just an insane and frightened child."

"Do you want cream?" Poe addressed our guest. "Sometimes the bitterness of black is too much for some people to take. I confess to having no such qualm. It's the sweetness that I often cannot take. The universe is black. Blackness is reality. It's a flavour I prefer untarnished."

I had no idea if he thought he was being amusing, but Guedigian gave a polite smile as if he was.

"Well, the main thing is, thanks to you and M. Holmes, Madame Chanaud sang Violetta on opening night."

"So I believe," said Poe. "That was the precise intention."

"And I have to say she was magnificent." Guédiguian puffed his chest. "You can never be sure with the *claque*, but the whole of Paris was enraptured by her. I've never seen a success like it. She said to tell you her dream had come true after all. And to say when she sang her final aria, M. Dupin, she sang it for you."

Poe tilted his head in the most miniscule acknowledgement, his eyes a little shinier than they were before. He shifted in his chair and examined his cuffs.

"I feel I have endured an earthquake, or a volcano," said Guédiguian, standing. "I felt at times the lava might consume me. But now all is well. The threat has passed. The mystery solved. And what a mystery! It remains only for me to thank you for saving my business." He extended a hand to Poe but the writer only stared at it.

"A pity I cannot save your soul, monsieur."

The opera director took a faltering step backwards.

"M. Guédiguian, if I were truly covering my tracks, I should enquire as to the motive for the crime. That would be the thought and action of an innocent man. Though I doubt you would know too intimately the actions of an innocent man, would you?"

Guédiguian retreated to his seat, ashen, and sat with his hands between his knees. "I swear. It is not—*not* what you imagine . . ."

"I am not prepared to imagine, monsieur." Poe stood and buttoned his jacket. "I am only prepared to *know*. And I know I am right in thinking you have bedded both Madame Jolivet and Marie-Claire Chanaud, her former understudy. As well as many singers before them, probably. Perhaps they see it as no less than their duty, and you as no more than your privilege."

"Please . . ." Guédiguian began sweating profusely and took out a handkerchief to stem the tide.

"'Please'? It is not a question of *please* . . ." Poe refused to back off. "What I also *know* is that you regularly frequented the premises of Madame Floch on the Rue Blondel, known as 'Tante Berthe' to her girls. I'm afraid she was very illuminating when I said she might be implicated in some exceedingly violent crimes. Extremely eloquent and forthcoming."

"Don't . . ." The opera manager cringed, holding his skull in torment. I could only stare as the Master rounded on him, unabated.

"She would not normally divulge the names of her clientele, but to me she made an exception. She said you were amongst that fine coterie of men who have certain proclivities. That is, an insatiable longing for young flesh. To use the untouched and the unknowing for your gratification and . . ."

Guédiguian shot to his feet. "You can prove none of this! This is preposterous! I am not listening to another word! Who said such—?"

"I heard it from the lips of a child."

Guédiguian stammered. "A child? What *child?*"

"The child whose bed you took, whose chastity you took, whose childhood you took, for the price of a few francs."

Afraid the opera manager might become aggressive, I got up and stood between them, holding him by the upper arms. He barely made a show to get past me as soon as he saw in my eyes that everything M. Dupin the detective knew, I knew. I think he saw the plain disgust there. As Poe had said earlier, I was fairly inept at masking my emotions. And didn't care if he did.

"I do not sit in moral judgement. That is between you and your Maker, if you are foolish enough to believe in one." Poe stood at the window, the profile of his supercilious nose against the sunlit panes. "Over weeks and months you visited this child. You knew her in every carnal and intimate fashion. Sometimes you took a toy or doll. She didn't understand she was the merest plaything to you, an object to satisfy your lust. To her, you became special. She looked forward to your visits. I will not say you hurt her, though many others did. On the contrary, perhaps you were the first to show her the illusion of love. Perhaps that was your downfall. You thought nothing of her, but *she* loved *you*. And, in time, came to be sad when you left, and one afternoon followed you.

"That day, having crept into the opera house, invisible, she espied you with Madame Jolivet in all her finery. A beautiful woman adored by the gentleman she thought was hers. She thought, 'Why not me? Would he truly love *me* if not for *her?*' The hatred and envy festered in her. She was an orphan. She had not known love. All her young life she had only known those who wanted to use her as a commodity. She saw prettiness and wanted to make it ugly. She wanted those bright, successful women who lit up the stage, and your life, to feel as mutilated and destroyed as she herself was by the countless men who passed through her room. She wanted—"

"Stop!" Guédiguian wrapped his arms around his head. "Stop! In the name of heaven and all its saints—must you torture me? I am not a criminal!"

"You took what was not yours."

"As a hundred men do in Paris every day!" He scowled. "And worse!"

"I say again: your morality, or lack of it, does not interest me. You can discuss that with a priest, or some other confessor. I am, however, interested in your culpability. In respect of your . . . addiction—and I am far from able to pronounce of anyone's *addiction* to anything—setting in train the events that have generated such pain and anguish."

"Then I *am* culpable. There. You have said it. Could I have known? No! Could I have stopped it, had I known—perhaps! But I did not know! I did—*not*—know! How could I? She—"

"Say her name."

"Don't tell me what to—"

"What was her name?"

Guédiguian crumbled. His shoulders heaved and he let out a strangled moan. I helped him to his chair. He slumped in it like a sack.

"Édith."

"Édith Dufranoux," said Poe. "She came with it, according to Madame Floch. But if you ask me, her real name, like her true family, is lost on the winds of time."

Guédiguian wiped a slime of spittle from his lower lip. His eyes could no longer meet ours. I wished I felt an ounce of pity for him.

"You see, monsters come in all shapes and sizes, Holmes," said Poe. "They do not all wear wolf-skins. Some wear the utmost fashion in respectability. You do not need to open the covers of a book of horror stories by Poe. You need only look in the mirrors of the Opéra Garnier."

"You are not privy to my mind, Dupin," Guédiguian spat.

"I very nearly am. Do not be sure about that. I am the Man of the Crowd. I walk in many shoes. That is my business. To under-stand pure logic, one must understand its opposite, perversion, when pure instinct is unleashed, unrestrained. The tragedy is, you could not have known the harvest your libidinous appetite would reap." Poe's words took on a melancholy tone as he stared out of the window at a passing world blissfully unaware of the dark, imp-ish secrets we discussed. "You were haunted by the phantom of all kisses: obsessive love."

The opera manager covered his face with his hands.

"What will happen to her? The police . . ."

"The police know nothing," said Poe. "About you, or about her. As far as Bermutier is concerned, the Phantom of the Opéra Garnier escaped from their clutches, disappearing forever. A mys-tery unsolved. I bade him persuade his *gendarmes* not to divulge any details of the crime to the press, but that may be a vain hope that some juice does not seep out of the apple barrel . . .

"As for the girl, earlier this morning I took her to a woman I know at the Hôtel Dieu, the last bastion of *'La Couche'* as it is known, the old Hôpital des Enfants-Trouvés, created as a refuge for the abandoned waifs of the city, amongst other things to pre-vent them being purposefully maimed and sold as beggars. I have no idea whether she has a chance there of a 'proper' or 'decent' future—whatever that is. She may end up a wastrel or die of cold and hunger on the streets, or drowned in the sewers, or be sold to peddlers and mountebanks for money-making purposes. Or become an opera singer. I can only say that for now she has food and water, the prospect of friends and even adults who do not despise her. For a while, at least, she will be safe. Beyond that, her life is her own."

"Can I see her?"

"If you do, I will see to it that everyone in Paris knows what I know."

The opera manager choked and swallowed. "Did she . . . did she say anything about me?"

Poe glared at the man. "She asked if she would go to the guillotine for her crimes. She said she wouldn't mind if she did. She said she had no fear of dying because she was dead already."

Guédiguian closed his eyes. I cannot remember clearly what he said after that, but he was a man diminished, and the conversation over. In a fatuous gesture to make amends, he proposed, mumbling and almost incoherent, that he would donate some of the opera's profits to the poor, to the workhouse, perhaps expecting us to cry "Bravo!" Poe greeted it with the silent disdain it deserved, and I think thereafter Guédiguian found it difficult to sit much longer in our presence. It took every atom of politeness I could muster to shake his hand, but for all his insistence that he had no morality, Poe did not.

I attempted to give back the gift he had brought us—people often did, as C. Auguste Dupin accepted no fee for his services— but Guédiguian showed me his palms. He did not want it and was now eager to go. When the door closed after him I was left with it in my hands.

"Stradivarius," Poe commented. "You should take it up. There is a power in music to soothe the savage breast."

He took the rolled-up playbill Guédiguian had brought advertising *La Traviata*—a memento of our adventure, he had

said—unfurled it briefly, glimpsing the name of Marie-Claire
Chanaud as Violetta, then placed it next to the violin case.

"I apologise if I gave vent to a modicum of anger. It brings it
back, you see. Some used to say my bride was a child, and said it
as if it was the foulest perversion imaginable. Imaginable to *them*,
perhaps. The accusation stings, even now. And hurt her, terribly.
Though it made our love not just stronger but unconquerable. That
anyone could think . . ." He shut his eyes, as if to rid himself of the
completion of the sentence.

"You knew it was a child all along," I said, gazing into the
fire to stop my own upset from showing, not concerned about his.
"Poe, I am constantly amazed at your capacity for casual cruelty.
You were prepared for me to . . . to ridicule myself by talk of a . . . a
maniacal *dwarf?*"

"To feel ridiculous is a very small price to pay, my dear Holmes." He had shed the disturbance of past slights. "It was necessary for you to *appear* to deduce that fact convincingly, in order to
send Bermutier on a hunt for the proverbial wild goose. Before
condemning a child to the punitive forces of law and order, I
needed to know why it had chosen such vehement and intractable
actions."

"Then you see yourself above the law?"

"Not above. Parallel. Let us debate this on another day. Today
I find it tiresome. It has stirred the murk. Let us just say, I wanted
the whole picture to be complete. I am sorry I allowed you to feel
foolish—*je suis désolé!*—but it was to that end, I promise. I would
never be cruel unless it was for the greater good. Well . . . *almost*
never." And my anger could almost never sustain itself when I saw
that dark twinkle in his eye.

Without calling Le Bon, he fetched our coats from their pegs.

"Will he live with his shame?" I asked, inserting my arms in
the one he held up for me.

"Of course he will," said Poe, doing the same in reverse.

"I shall never be able to listen to opera again, after this vile business."

"Crime is vile in all its manifestations. Mysteries abound. We are adrift in an ocean of unknowing. The only respite is to solve them. And until we conquer the great question of un-dimensional creation, the seeking of those solutions will be the essence and eternal vexation of Man. Come, let us go to the Rue du Faubourg Montmartre, to the Restaurant Morot, and talk about the rigours of decapitation. There's a murder in *Le Figaro* today and I'm convinced they have the wrong man. You remember? With its dark fittings and the hat racks above the tables it's like dining in a railway carriage. Vidal will always find a table for me, and he serves the best pig's ears in Paris. You can drink, and I shall watch."

"Amontillado?"

"Please. That is beneath you."

He took my arm. His own was thin. He was a skeleton in a suit by sunlight. It brings a tear to my eye now, but I hardly noticed then a creeping frailty that was increasing with the passing of years. Years all too few.

We were, of course, too late. Out of gossip and half-truths the myth was born. If accidents happened at the theatre, the stage hands would still ascribe it to their *Fantôme.* He had escaped, but not into the non-existent lake—into stories. Descending with his disfigured face and mask to his watery home. And coming to haunt us from the pages of a book, and the flickering screen.

In the months and years that followed we had other cases, including that of an extraordinary patient of Dr Charcot at Salpêtrière, the "Gates of Hell" affair, and the nefarious spirit photography of the despicable M. Buguet, but none pierced my heart quite as much as the strange and sorry tale of Olivier Guédiguian, whose mask disguised a monster, and little Édith Dufranoux, the true Phantom of the *Opéra de Paris.*

The Lunacy of Celestine Blot

To Whom It May Concern

I entrust this package to your care in the knowledge that, like the others, it will be kept from the public eye until the appropriate time. While the unwashed multitude's appetite for sensation is insatiable, I need not emphasise the peril of these pages coming into unscrupulous hands while certain parties are still alive and could be hurt by such revelations.

Furthermore, the literary world would be rocked (as well as my word broken) if it learned that Edgar Allan Poe did not die in an American gutter in 1849 as popular belief would have it, but rather fled to Paris, where he applied his considerable intellect to criminal inquiry under the nom de guerre *C. Auguste Dupin—his fictional hero of "Rue Morgue" fame. As you will remember from the previous manuscripts, now in the Black Museum's safe keeping, it was in this guise he crossed paths with Sherlock Holmes, at that time in his twenties, resulting in the young man's tutelage in the art of "ratiocination" before his return to London.*

The enclosed investigation is no less "grotesque and arabesque" (as Poe might say) than the others you have under lock and key. If not for the corroborative evidence, I confess, as a policeman to my boots, I might reject it as fiction—and if not for the fact that this account was penned by the greatest mind, and man, I ever knew.

Signed,
Geo. Lestrade
Dep. Commissioner (ret'd),
Metropolitan Police

Hearing the keys rattling in the locks behind us, we found ourselves in the Versailles of Pain. A large and well-kept garden lay before us, which under any other circumstances may have been delightful, even uplifting—but not today, in spite of the warm stillness in the air and the cloudless sky above. Male figures circled the paths, seeming supernaturally mobile in contrast to the females, who stood immobile as statues, only giving sudden and unpredictable spasms as we passed, rolling their eyes or jutting out their chins with the dull, uncomprehending interest of ungulates in a field. By far the most animated was a woman who sat on a swing with her legs sticking out, twirling an umbrella. The rest of the inmates however, were as stiff and indifferent as the Talrich waxworks on the Boulevard des Capucines. We were entering Salpêtrière Hospital—the so-called "feminine inferno"—an asylum for the sick of mind in the midst of Paris's colourful Belle Époque. But nothing could have prepared me for the reality as we stepped inside the run-down Sainte-Laure building where epileptics and hysterics were indiscriminately housed with madwomen.

Here, swarming residents gesticulated with bizarre contortions, dragged themselves, hurried with indecipherable urgency, scuffled—old women, poor women, some stoically awaiting death on a bench, others howling their fury or weeping their sorrow—none reprimanded or given redress by the sub-warder escorting us, who presumably accepted this as the standard behaviour he saw in his work on a daily basis. Yes, the walls I saw around me in their solemn dilapidation retained the majestic qualities of the capital under Louis XIV, but only as a most disturbing and tragic backdrop to the shattered souls who resided there.

"Entre, qui que tu sois, et laisse l'espérance," said Poe out of the corner of his mouth. *Abandon hope all ye who enter here.* Never has the expression been more apposite.

On entering the consulting room of the great man who had summoned us—a man who was later to earn the somewhat unflattering nickname of "The Napoleon of Neurology"—I was immediately drawn to the painting dominating one wall: Robert-Fleury's *Pinel Liberating the Madwomen of Salpêtrière from their Chains.* Fetters lay in the foreground, telling the age-old story. Pinel had been chief doctor at the hospital, responsible for instituting a new, progressive regime, enabling the dawn of the benevolent rather than punitive care of the mad. With the focus on science and curability, he had instituted a revolution of sorts, liberating the deranged from confinement and allowing them to co-exist with a degree of autonomy. Nevertheless, on the day we visited, so called "debauched women" rubbed shoulders with convulsionaries and "women of abnormal constitution." I could not avoid the conclusion that all the female dregs of society rejected elsewhere in the city, whatever their malady, ended up here.

"M. Dupin, M. Holmes . . ."

Jean-Martin Charcot was not the kind of man to thank us for coming at his urgent bequest. In fact, he made it seem as though he were doing us a great favour by seeing us. Middle-aged, with rounded shoulders and slicked-back, slightly-greying hair, he resembled nothing so much as an otter. But clearly saw himself as somewhere between Socrates and the Emperor Augustus.

"Doctor." Poe, fifteen or so years his senior, gave a polite but imperious nod. "Or should we address you as Monsieur le Professeur?" He knew, as did I, that Charcot had been made Professor of Anatomical Pathology by the Paris Faculty of Medicine, being the foremost expert in *les maladies du système nerveux.*

"I prefer the latter. Many of my patients think a doctor is there to cut them up."

"When in fact you want to study them."

"Our purpose here is cure. But study is as important to that end as day-to-day treatment. The intellectual pursuit and the medical cannot, and should not, be unconjoined."

He stuck his hand in his waistcoat, Napoleon-like, with all the grandiosity of a man deeply sure of his own judgement. Yet we, two detectives, were here because of a problem he could not solve. So he was not nearly as all-knowing as he might wish.

I felt the need to offer some blatant flattery to ingratiate ourselves. "I hear that students at Oxford have to read Charcot now as they read Hippocrates and Celsus for their degrees in Bachelor of Medicine."

He shrugged. An equally blatant display of mock humility. "If I have advanced medical science in any way by distinguishing hysteria from epilepsy in particular . . ." He waved his hands, as if to imply he desired no personal credit for the achievement.

"Especially as one cannot get under the skin of a nervous patient to see how the illness works," said Poe.

"Even less can one pathologise a deranged mind without putting that life to an end. One must restrain one's actions to observing, without so much as touching or, often, even communicating. The rigour of my process, my methodology, may seem counter-intuitive, unjustified, a kind of madness of its own to those outside the discipline, and far-fetched . . . But my research needs a clinical eye and the eye is as important a tool as psychomotor experiments and psychological diagrams."

Poe nodded gently.

I could tell he felt he was in the presence of a man after his own heart—a fellow devotee of cold *ratiocination*, and that pleased him. As for myself, I was unsure about this dapper gentleman who reigned over his domain at Salpêtrière—this pensive brow, this sombre visage with searching eyes set deep in the shadow of sockets, and lips accustomed to silence. Whereas Poe now cast him as a fellow investigator, in my mind I likened him to Dante: the Dante who descended into *Purgatorio*, where sinners are kept in punishment, where penance is done before judgement is made, and the unfortunates are deemed holy enough to pass to Paradise or else consigned to Hell.

I found myself staring at such "sinners" in the ghostly grey images on the wall of the study, and was reminded of Balzac's remark that bodies, insofar as when they are photographed, become spectres. In stark detail and under unmerciful lighting, here were faces like those we had witnessed *en route*: distorted, startled, grimacing, eyes rolling heavenward, or with hands gripped in an attitude of prayer. Portraits not of royalty or military heroes but of twisted musculature, the impossible distortion of limbs—yet, as Charcot soon told us in answer to my evident curiosity, his patients seemed to suffer no physical injury, no apparent discomfort from these poses, attacks—"*attitudes passionelles*, crucifixions, ecstasy"—all the postures of delirium, all caught by the miracle of the lens. "Photography is invaluable in the examination of neurological cases."

"As it will prove to be in the detection of crime," said Poe. "Which is our area of examination."

"The photographic plate is the true retina of the scientist," agreed Charcot. "Human sight combined with memory is endlessly flawed and endlessly open to misinterpretation. You cannot really claim to have seen something unless it is photographed."

An intriguing concept. We are used to the faces of the corporeal betraying the soul within, yet this art was at the service of a strange and territorial science, like that of Gall's phrenology. But instead of Gall's caressing fingertips on a woman's face, all we saw here was the fall of brutal light on the convulsions of overheated minds. All detail was clear, but all meaning tenuous. To me, these snapshots of the mad, while they appeared to show all, showed nothing—except for the physicians' insatiable desire for imagery of hysterics who willingly participated with their increasingly theatricalised body shapes.

"The gestures are so grand and unnatural," I could not resist saying, "they seem to be acting."

"Monsieur Holmes, performance is a part of the condition," said Charcot. "Do we know for certain any action, mad or sane, is not committed for an audience, to elicit sympathy, or even shock? For punishment? Even self-punishment?"

"And what is the root cause of such exhibitions?"

"That," interjected Poe, "as M. le Professeur will agree, is the greatest mystery in medicine."

"Indeed so. All the efforts of pathological anatomy through the century have been directed at discerning the configuration of such illnesses by their symptoms . . . and localizing the essence of them."

"Yet the autopsies of hysterics have so far revealed nothing palpable," said Poe. "In other words, hysteria seems to escape the anatomical doctrine of *localization* entirely."

"Until we find it."

"Unless you do *not* find it."

"Which would be a great blow to medical orthodoxy."

"Medical orthodoxy is not the goal. The sickness is a paradox and medicine does not like to confront paradoxes. Perhaps the truth is it has no locality at all, in biological terms."

Charcot grunted. "Are you saying then that it is a disorder of the soul? Or *humours?* Or a malady of *passion?* You may be an educated man, but with deep respect, this is my area of expertise. And those are concepts from the Dark Ages."

"I am saying we are possibly living in the Dark Ages now, as far as hysteria is concerned, if we but knew it. Landouzy defined it as 'neurosis of the woman's generative apparatus'—yet when Voisin opened up hysterics found nothing in pelvic cavities . . . A few years later Briquet said, 'no, it's neurosis of the encephalon' . . . They have looked in the ovaries. Nothing. They have looked in the skull. Nothing . . ."

"Nevertheless, if you had worked here, as I have, you would have seen that hysterical women are often tormented by a feeling of heat and acridity in their generative organs. That their menses are irregular. If the disposition is not genital, then is it the effect of a special mode of sensibility?"

"*Feminine* sensibility?" I enquired.

"Because a female endures the suffering," snapped Poe, "it does not mean that the suffering is somehow female. Even on a semantic level, such a concept is—appropriately—quite insane and deluded. Perhaps the fantasy here is provided as much by the practitioners as the inmates."

"Dupin. Please." I tried to calm my friend's flow of abuse, but to my surprise Charcot simply laughed, allowing Poe to continue unabated, as if he had heard similar attacks many times and was immune to them.

"You yourself, M. le Professeur, seem to have assembled a rag-bag of causes into predisposing factors—moral impressions, fears, the marvellous, exaggerated religious practices, rheumatism, masturbation, tobacco, certain professions, certain races, Israelites . . ."

"There may be any number of *causes*—the cause is in many ways irrelevant—because the essential *mechanism* of hysteria is heredity. It is a condition hidden until prised out by circumstance. And that circumstance, from person to person, might vary. M. Holmes, your companion is an extremely rude man."

"I am afraid so, monsieur." I blushed.

"And if you were not here for an important purpose I would have him ejected immediately."

"I would not blame you for a second, M. le Professeur, if you locked him in a padded cell. But indulge him his vice—which is extreme contrariness—and I am sure in time, if you have need of his services, his presence will reap dividends."

"How delightful to be discussed as if a patient," trilled Poe, prowling the room in a distracted fashion. "Likewise, I have no more power over my outbursts than the dispossessed in your care. For which I apologise deeply. Consider it my 'supranervous expressionism'. Add the term to your bag of tricks, if you wish."

"Dupin."

Turning back, he fell silent, seeing as I did that the learned doctor was pressing his fingertips to his forehead in a gesture of the utmost perturbation. In the hallowed halls of the perturbed, this was a disarming sight.

"Messieurs." Now Charcot spoke in a small, fragile voice. "I can only say I am determined to try any and every method to illuminate these conditions. Sadly, they cannot be dissected, stitched up, repaired like a cracked shin or cut on the epidermis. These illnesses are far deeper than flesh and bone."

"And that troubles you," I ventured.

"One case in particular troubles you," said Poe. "Her name is Celestine and her photograph is under your right elbow, with her name clear to read even upside-down."

Charcot looked at it. "As a detective, Dupin, you know one cannot observe a brain, but we can observe behaviour—reaction, cause, effect—and usually reach a conclusion. But this woman has eluded my classification. I cannot file her as the 'venomous' woman, the 'chlorotic', the 'menorrhagic', the 'feverish', the 'visceral' or the 'libidinosa' . . . She evades the grammar of the visible."

Poe took the photograph and examined it intently. It was titled: "HYSTÉRO-ÉPILEPSIE—ÉTAT NORMAL" and showed a handsome, square-shouldered girl with a strong, defiant jaw and black eyes staring with an intense air of suspicion into the camera.

"Our patients are generally incapable of giving reports of themselves," said Charcot. "Communication runs dry, leaving gaps unfilled and riddles unanswered. The connective tissue of information is mostly incoherent, even the sequence of events uncertain . . ."

"And she?" Poe did not look up.

"Quite the opposite. Her symptoms are only a minute element in a grand narrative tableau."

My friend's nose was almost touching the photographic paper. "Intriguing . . ."

"At the very least."

Thus we were introduced, by proxy, to Mademoiselle Celestine Blot (pronounced *blow* for the edification of the English ear), who had been subject to the immense distress of an attack of monomania, incapacitated with ataxia, disorder and confusion, and whose life had changed radically as a result.

"She attacked a man of exceptional repute and good character. It was only by a fluke she avoided trial for attempted murder. Luckily, her family saw that she was unable to return to society and entrusted her to the care of this institution five years ago, during which time her state of delusion has, if anything, worsened."

"And that state of delusion takes what form?"

"Everything related to the Moon. She will not have any lunar imagery in her presence. Even a crescent design on a napkin or wallpaper will set her off in a paroxysm . . ."

"How often do these 'paroxysms' occur?"

"It varies. Sometimes she has two or three a week. At times of the full moon, as many as a hundred a day."

A hundred! I could scarcely believe that was humanly possible, but the doctor had no need to lie. As if to provide evidence he furnished us with a second photograph, titled: "DEDUT D'UNE ATTAQUE: CRI"—in this Celestine's face was massively disfigured, her tongue extended, hanging out.

"Before this we see the tremors, like hiccups, sometimes growing to the extent of suffocation, and apparent distress. It's preceded by some sharp guttural exclamations, laryngeal noises that resemble a cock's crow, then when it comes, the cry she utters has a unique quality, piercing as a train whistle."

Another photograph showed Celestine curled up in her bed, twisted and alert. In another she was madly crossing her legs, writhing in her straitjacket. In yet another, wriggling like an ignoble and ridiculous worm. It occurred to me that her cry was the last place to hide, or lose herself from the pain. But I was not a doctor, of either the body or the mind, and was quite sure at that moment I never wanted to be. And I am not sure whether I admired or found loathsome the cold, dispassionate way Charcot described her anguish.

"After the apparent pain and cries come the spontaneous convulsions." He gave every impression the attending doctors might do little more than adjust their spectacles as they witnessed such a scene. "Then, just as quickly, after the *coup de theatre*, she will invariably return to her relative normality prior to the attack."

He proceeded to tell us that the word "Moon" itself would strike her like a wound, in the belly, or lower generative organs, to the extent that it would have to be banned in her presence. At times of heightened agitation, even a word starting with the same sound—that *might become* "Moon"—could engender a significant grimace or spastic movement. Her jaw would lock, her eyes roll, her body jerk, arms stiffly outstretched, legs twisting and locking round each other like a corkscrew, as if fending off a physical attack. None of the above seeming to be under her conscious control.

Which prompted me to ask a question.

"What is her attitude to such frightful and disabling displays on a regular basis?"

"She is hardly aware of them having happened. They pass like the wind in the trees. In fact, when questioned on her beliefs, she is convinced her anxiety is entirely justified and cannot understand why we, her carers, are not similarly imbued with her own level of terror and concern. Sometimes this rouses her to a point of anger which tips over into volcanic explosions of violence. To her, the guards represent attackers—she does not even believe their authenticity as humans. This is allied to a wilful obsession over the phases of the Moon, 'the Orb' as she calls it to avoid the offending word. Needless to add, the full moon is when we see her at her worst—she curls into a ball, insists on being tied to her bed and observed until the crisis period has passed."

"It is not, of course, uncommon for the mad to be affected by phases of the Moon." Poe placed the photographs side by side on Charcot's desk. "They are not called lunatics for nothing."

"She insists on all drapes to be pulled at night time, as she intensely fears moonshine might fall on her skin, with some kind of elemental toxicity . . ."

"Excuse me, monsieur." Poe became more animated. I could almost feel the crackle of electricity from his skull when he became hooked by a mystery. "You said she believes her fears to be justified. Kindly elaborate on that."

Charcot sat back at his desk and took out a hefty batch of paperwork, but did not need to consult it.

"The origin of her mania would seem to be an episode in which, horse-riding in the Bois de Vincennes, she was overcome by strange sensations—prickling skin, headache, giddiness. She fell from her steed and says that she saw a light in the sky grow larger. This, she is adamant, took form in a craft like a ship, but metallic and shimmering. She then described figures of the most remarkable kind making their way relentlessly towards her, wearing tight-fitting clothes, or skin—she is not sure which. She is positive she is going to be captured by these 'little men' she calls *farfadets* . . ." (Goblins, in English.) ". . . or sometimes *lutins* . . ." (Night imps.) ". . . with their mushroom-white heads and absence of noses. She describes their teardrop-shaped eyes as brown and mottled 'like of leaves beginning to wither', and she says they emitted guttural squawks from what looked like the mouths of fish. With absolute clarity she knew she was being assessed for a purpose. She felt they were intrigued by her skin colour and began to undress her. She then felt a knitting needle inserted into her navel and soon afterwards some sort of cold, glassy object attempted to extract her vital fluids or to deposit some seed— she is unsure which—via her generative passage."

My mouth was incredibly dry. A jug of water sat on a side table and I helped myself to a glass. Poe, in contrast, was by no means unsettled by these revelations, for all their monstrousness, and remained sedate and attentive throughout.

"Go on."

"In short, she insisted these lunar creatures had raped her—though, medically, there was no evidence of sexual infiltration. Thereafter she felt her mind 'raked' by their thoughts, and was shown a vision of earth's future ruin. When she awoke, there was no craft, no *farfadets*, dawn was breaking and she had lost twelve hours in what had seemed merely minutes."

"She remembers the incident in detail?" asked Poe.

"Uncommon detail, yes. Some hysterics exhibit amnesia, but most are in slavish thrall to memory—their dynamic outbursts, I believe, are a violent reflux of the 'first scene'—the birth scene of the ailment, if you will, which demands a restaging. Many hysterics spout their 'first scene' in simple, honest words, with a wealth of detail. To the listener, the delirium seems too precise to be mere delirium."

Was he implying that he believed her incredible story? I could not credit that he did.

But Poe's focus of interest was elsewhere. "Have you considered the symbolic interpretation of her descriptions?"

Charcot turned down the corners of his mouth. "Symbols are everywhere. Symbols solve nothing. A patient tries to coyly cover her modesty as a woman, and simultaneously attack her sexual organs like a man . . ." Again, the esteemed doctor waved his hands, letting the thought drift away on the air.

"Then, forgive me—your view of the role of this event in her mental history is what?"

"As I have said before, hysteria is, I believe, the result of a weak neurological system which is *hereditary*. Yes, it can be ignited by the trigger of an act of violence, or an accident, or an imaginary assault such as this clearly is—but after that it is progressive and irreversible. The exact catalyst is unimportant."

"So, excuse me, why have we been brought here?" I asked. "If the mystery of her condition is unimportant to you?"

"Her condition is not the mystery I wish you to solve." Charcot leaned back in his chair. "I never said it was. That is not a criminal matter, but a medical one."

"Then I confess I too am perplexed," said Poe, not without irritation.

"The story is incomplete. If you will grant me the good grace ..."

"By all means."

Charcot stood.

"Shortly after the strange episode in the Bois de Vincennes, the nature of which Celestine eagerly shared with her deeply concerned family, her mania took the form of an obsession with the author Jules Verne, who has written, as you know, extensively about an imagined expedition to the Moon. Believing him to harbour secrets that would account for her vile encounter and the *farfadets'* obscene intentions upon her, Celestine fired a pistol at him, thinking him in collusion with her inter-planetary beings."

"Good grief." I was taken aback.

Poe said nothing.

"Incarcerated here five years later, she has only persisted in her conviction of a conspiracy of Verne with the Moon Men. She reads his work—two novels a year—avidly, as soon as they are published, in search of corroborative signs and clues ..."

"Fascinating," said my friend, restless now. "But M. Verne, if I am not mistaken, is alive and well. And it seems the cause of the crime is locked in the lady's cranium, from whence we will have great difficulty extracting it."

"Exactly so. But the reason I was so desperate to call upon your special talent, M. Dupin, is that Celestine had a recurrence of her 'Moon Men' experience two nights ago, whilst here on these premises. The guard on duty found her in a state of rare and aggressive agitation. She claimed immediately that her other-worldly *far-*

fadets had entered the building by means of their craft and she, frozen in horror, had watched helplessly as one of her follow internees was bundled away and abducted by the savages from space."

I frowned. "Obviously no more than another hallucination."

"Surely this, and nothing more …" whispered Poe, and I noticed a slight smile on his face, even a twinkle in his eye.

"But you see M. Holmes, the point is this," said Charcot with the utmost gravity. "Gertrude Socha is still missing. We have no explanation for her whereabouts. There was no way out of that room two days ago. The staff and nurses saw no one enter or leave. There is no possible way she could have left the building, given the extensive security in place. And yet she has totally and completely disappeared—you might say, into thin air."

After ascertaining that the police had searched the building to no avail, and showed little interest or alacrity in pursuing the case, Poe requested to see the room where the 'abduction' had taken place.

We were guided there past an avenue of women, treated to the sight of drooping breasts and open gowns, the occasional one prone and writhing on the floor, to which the attendants seemed oblivious. This was indeed "a great emporium of human misery" as Charcot called it, whose aim was to make this quasi-city with its seedy areas, secret dens, playrooms and laboratories "the centre of truly theoretical and technical teaching". But I could only think of Dante again: *In truth I found myself upon the brink of an abyss, the melancholy valley containing thundering, unending wailings …*

Poe had taught me above all else to be distant, cold and rational: to preserve the scalpel of intellect from being blunted by emotional distractions, but in these circumstances I found it impossible. I realised my distress at my surroundings was due to a memory in my formative years of my brother Mycroft being sent away to an Aunt for the summer—even then knowing it was a lie, and being robbed of his company feeling like a punishment. Later I learnt that his summer had been spent at the Middlesex County Asylum Colney Hatch, an alienist having pronounced that his mind was "too active for its own good"—as indeed we, his family, could testify. He returned not greatly changed, and told me only of the aviary where they bred canaries. Yet it inculcated unnameable fears in my young mind, which re-emerged as I watched one woman, whose fingers crawled like spider-legs round her neck and through the curls of her hair, and another, with a torn dress and bony legs, bursting out laughing like a hyena.

Poe was asking if Celestine had any personal connection with the missing woman, before or after incarceration.

"No. They have rooms in separate parts of the building, and none of my staff have seen them communicate in any way."

"What can you tell us about Gertrude Socha?"

Charcot kept his steady pace. "Ordinary. Unimportant. The wife of a bartender in Montmartre. He left her and she took to drink—and I don't mean the occasional glass of Aÿ . . . I mean the green fairy, in quantity. She is afflicted by the most profound delusions. I suspect she was mentally defective from early age, and the absinthe did her no favours."

As we approached double doors, I asked: "Were you able to categorize her madness?"

"She was what we define as an *écritomaniac*—her every waking moment obsessed with making marks on paper."

"I've heard of such people," said Poe laconically. "They are also known as writers."

The room we were shown was large but with no decorative niceties except for a constellation of randomly-placed open-armchairs, a bare mahogany dining table and, incongruously, a harpsichord. We were introduced to the guard, name of Hennetier—the sole cogent witness to what had transpired—who sported the face and moustache of a weathered old *grognard*. He confirmed that on the night in question he had kept the keys to the doors and windows on his person at all times, fastened securely to his leather belt. French windows opened onto a small balcony in front of us. Poe asked for the double doors to be opened, and stepped out into the fresh air, as Charcot added that his staff had reported to him that every possible exit was found locked. I stood on the balcony briefly, after Poe returned inside, and registered the considerable drop to the courtyard below.

"You saw nothing?" Poe addressed Hennetier, who stood to attention.

"Yes, monsieur—I mean no, monsieur..."

"Tell me what you *did* see."

"I don't remember. That is, I *do* remember—though it will not be much use to you ..."

"We shall see about that. Stand where you stood. Do as you did. And be as exact as humanly possible in your description."

Hennetier did as he was bidden.

"This is the point from which I can see every corner of the room, if the sparrows are behaving themselves. And if they're not, I will suppress them in the requisite manner, and if that is not enough, blow my whistle for assistance."

"Did you blow your whistle that night?" I asked.

"No, sir. Not until afterwards. After she was gone, I mean."

"At which moment you were here, facing the French windows?"

"That is correct, sir."

"And where were Madame Gertrude and Mademoiselle Celestine?" asked Poe.

"Gertrude was there, sir, in the rocking chair next to the French windows, facing into the room, and Celestine, here, between the two of us, facing the fireplace. With a candle beside her. You have to watch them regarding candles."

"Anything unusual about their temperaments or demeanour?"

Hennetier shook his head. "If anything they were both unusually calm, sir. I am not used to Celestine being quite so calm. Normally wound up like a twisted wire, that one. Gertrude, on the other hand, is never any trouble. Long as you give her pencil and paper, she's the most contented sow in the farmyard." He scratched his cheek and grinned, until our own seriousness made his smile slide away. "And all ... all was fine until the clock struck seven and the 'Moon' book fell to the floor with a thud, and I perceived Celestine gasping and jumping to her feet and backing towards me, shaking her head. I caught her by the shoulders to stop her crashing into me, but this only made her turn on me with arms thrashing, so I wrapped her in a bear hug and struggled to..."

"... blow your whistle," Poe completed, impatiently.

"Aye, sir. It was only when Sazzarin and Goyon ran to my aid and were able to apply the strait-waistcoat did I see that poor Gertrude was gone. The rocking chair was still rocking. Her manic scribblings were scattered on the floorboards. I searched the room, as we all did, even yanking up the floorboards when the police arrived, but ..."

Poe turned to Charcot. "Pertinent information reported from other inmates on the night?"

"They can tell us nothing. Remember, one thinks she is the Empress Josephine. Another, Mary Magdalene. Their fantasies are as many and varied as human imagining can provide. Reality is not their strong suit."

I voiced my frustration. "Then how can we ever discover the facts?"

"By talking to the only other witness we have," said Poe, turning again to the Professor of Anatomy. "Is Celestine capable of being questioned on the subject?"

Charcot blanched. "She is not capable of recalling the incident without the greatest distress. As you can imagine ..."

"I cannot imagine, monsieur—and neither can you. But I do wish to find Madame Gertrude—and not because this is an idle Sunday afternoon puzzle: experience informs me that every minute she is away from Salpêtrière the potential danger to her mortal being increases."

"That's as may be, but as Celestine's physician I cannot condone the idea of interrogating her about something so disturbing to her consciousness . . ."

"Then we shall have to bypass her consciousness altogether." My Southern gentleman chose not to look at the incipient horror rising on the doctor's face and consulted his pocket watch. "By a method that offers us far more than mere recollection. Hypnosis can enable a subject to recall the smallest detail with vivid clarity, free of the hubbub of our natural, waking existence. And I am not unaccomplished in the art."

Charcot almost choked on his laugh. "This is not a place for art, but for science."

"You yourself use the technique."

"Yes, indeed. But to induce and study the symptoms." The doctor felt the sceptical glare of black, lantern eyes. "I'd go as far as to say the ability to be hypnotised is a clinical feature of hysteria. Both are concomitant abnormalities . . ."

"But its usefulness is only to demonstrate? Preposterous. Forty years ago Professor John Elliotson publicly mesmerised the Irish O'Key sisters and it contained their convulsive symptoms. According to my own extensive researches, if used properly, the practise seems not only to sedate but to *reveal*—in extraordinary fashion."

"That may or may not be so, M. Dupin—but I will not be responsible for the harm such an undertaking might do to my already vulnerable patient." Charcot's paleness became mitigated by a ruddy glow of anger. "I refuse to inflict upon Celestine a potential resurrection of her most abhorred possible fantasy. It goes against my vows as a surgeon and my discipline as a theoretician. I simply will not do it."

"Very well, then," said Edgar Allan Poe. "I shall."

⟡

Charcot's silence as he escorted us to his *salle d'examen* let us know he was caught between a rock and a hard place. Though his expression made his misgivings plain, he nevertheless wanted to find his missing inmate, and was perhaps aware that his intellectual stubbornness, or even pride, might stand in the way of that outcome. Still, he was by no means happy. And if he was at all human under that icy, pompous exterior, part of him was fearful. Fearful he was handing over control of his patient to—what? A *detective?* But a detective was exactly what he needed.

Tension locked my shoulders and the dream-like character of our environs was made more peculiar still by the echo of a disturbed woman's cries: "Where's the lion? The lion? The giant lion? Where is it? I'm concerned. It needs to be fed ..." I was selfish enough to be relieved when the closing door of the examination room shut her ravings out.

Within seconds, Celestine was brought in, and the first thing that struck me was Charcot's manner in the way he greeted her, which was that he barely acknowledged her presence at all. When he did, the merest turn of his hand directed her to a chair, which she sat in like an obedient child.

As for Celestine herself, I saw no face of madness, or even of nervous illness. She was taller than I imagined, by no means filthy or ill-kempt, and had taken great care in her *toilette*. Dressed in a plain, coarse shift not unlike that worn by mill workers, she did not act with servility in any way, but conveyed an admirable self-assuredness. None of the inmates wore their hair in chignons, but rather cut raggedly and unadorned with pins or clasps that might, I concluded, be used to do ill to themselves or others. The only thing that betrayed her maladjustment was that her hands were bunched tightly in fists, making her knuckles white. This made me smile at her, in an effort to help her relax. It had no effect whatsoever.

The fact we were strangers did not bother her, though. Rather, it excited her, and she stumbled over her words, asking us if we were astronomers with news of discoveries, as she had written to several, and did so on a weekly basis. She then alluded to the regimen that imprisoned her, but with only the mildest rancour, murmuring: "They keep all news of discoveries from me . . ."

I said: "I'm sure that's because they do not wish you to be upset by such matters."

"Why? What would upset me?" For the first time a flicker of panic in her eyes indicated the scale of terror lurking under the surface.

"Nothing." Poe had immersed himself in a strange activity, using a ruler to tear up the blotting paper from Charcot's desk into a rectangle, punching a hole in it with a pen nib, then holding it up to his eye. "Nothing at all, my dear . . ." He rolled it into a scroll, slid it over the chimney of an oil lamp, affixing it with red wax used for sealing letters. "Nothing will upset you, I promise. Nothing . . ."

The American slowly knelt on one knee in front of her, old bones creaking, one hand steadying himself on the arm of her chair. His sudden proximity made her flinch slightly. Though he did not touch her, his face was level with hers, and closer than a gentleman was accustomed to get.

"Your eye. I really think there is something in your eye. Is there? Do you mind if I look? Try and be still. That's it. Perfect. Just look straight forward. Don't move. Don't blink. Just relax . . ."

He held the lamp with its pinprick of light off to the side, at arm's length, in her peripheral vision, and gave several passes, which I could see reflected as glimmers like tiny comets on her irises. He told her repeatedly that her eyelids were heavy. Within seconds they closed.

"Just feel completely relaxed and safe ..." The detective's voice was low, almost tender. "And whatever you say and whatever you see or feel, remember, no harm can befall you ..."

I side-glanced at Charcot, head half-buried in shadow. His fingers were splayed in a flying buttress at his temple, but his eyes were fixed on Celestine.

If she harboured any anxiety about our identities or why we were there, it no longer showed on her features. The somnambulistic trance had acted like an extraordinary potion.

She had been mesmerised—or 'hypnotised', to use the verb invented to separate it from the hucksterism of fairground quackery and mysticism. Though mysticism is not a hundred miles from what it looked like to these eyes. It did not look like medicine. It looked like fakery—though I knew it was not. It was some occult process that disrupted and pried into the functioning of the brain, or the soul, or both. Though Mesmer himself always denied any supernatural element, espousing his skill to be a "peculiarity of observing," I found it incredibly hard to retain control of the idea that what I was watching was entirely scientific and not a peephole to the uncanny. No wonder that Poe, in his former incarnation as Master of the Macabre, had written about it several times. His "Facts in the Case of M. Valdemar" is, of course, about a mesmerist who uses his specialism to halt death—and fails in the most gruesome fashion. But here we were not toying with characters on a page, but the mental life of a living young woman. And the trepidation of so doing created a knot of dread in my stomach.

"You are in the day room two nights ago, Celestine. Hennetier is standing in his usual place by the door. Why are you smiling?"

"He has an egg stain on his tunic. He is always so fastidious in his shiny shoes. He had an egg for breakfast." She tittered.

"He did. And look around. The sunlight is fading. It is evening. Gertude is in the rocking chair, scribbling away. Do you see her?"

Celestine nodded. Her eyes were still closed. Her head lolled slightly. Her hands lay palm-upwards on the arm rests. Poe placed the oil lamp on a drop-leaf table where its pallid flame flickered. I could still not be sure whether this was science or hocus pocus. A treatment, or a showman's dexterity.

"The clock strikes seven." He counted out the numbers at regular intervals. "Does anything happen?"

"No. It is quiet. Quiet as the grave. Mathurine isn't shouting and that's a surprise."

"How do you feel?"

"I feel bored. My book is boring."

"Why is it boring?"

"It tells me nothing new. Nothing important. Verne irritates me so much. Why won't he tell me what he *knows?*"

"And Gertrude?"

"Gertrude is boring too. Scratch, scratch, scratch with her charcoal and crayons. Nothing but scratch, scratch, scratch . . ."

I had seen a corpse on a slab, even a dissected one, and this was much more unpalatable. It had a weird theatricality in its aspect, and in her lack of resistance, her subjugation, a rendering naked that made me uncomfortable.

"But I look over at her and I see it." Celestine twitched. "I see it again. The craft."

"Where do you see it?"

"Out . . . outside the French windows. Shimmering. There." Her eyes remained shut, but she pointed, almost striking Poe's cheek with her hand. A hand we all saw was trembling.

"What happened next?"

"No . . ."

"You are relaxed, so relaxed you are almost asleep, but you remember everything. What happened next?"

"No. They are coming. They . . . No!"

"Remember, you will not come to harm or pain while you are talking to me. Celestine, what happened next?"

"I see them. Just like before. They are outside the glass, clinging like bats. Then inside in their tight suits. Standing. Unsteady. Because this is not the earth they normally stand on. This is not their world, but ours!" She thrust both hands between her legs, locking them there with her thighs and tilting forward and back. "They look at me. They see me!" She began panting and her expressions changed with astonishing rapidity. "It's happening again! Oh God! Oh God! They're coming *again!*"

I was sorely tempted to look around me and check that the Moon Men were not in the room with us.

"Coming for whom, Celestine? For whom?"

"They have come for me! For *me!*" Her breathing was irregular, the oppression of her lungs obvious. Charcot rose to his feet, feeling an attack was imminent, but Poe held him back with the flat of his hand. "Ah! I feel sick . . . *Nnnn* . . ." Her belly heaved. She made intermittent chewing motions, her forehead etched into a frown, the eyelids fluttered rapidly...

I could hardly bear to continue watching the extravagant agony of a body in the throes of its symptoms, but Poe presided over this hideous pantomime with utter calm, as if to him the seeing and knowing was all, and the suffering invisible.

"You are in a safe place now. No-one can touch you. No-one can hurt you."

"*Chchchch* . . ." She ground her teeth. "Get away, sprites! Damned things! Go back to the stars!"

"Celestine, listen to me . . ."

"Leave me in—*ahhhhh*—*sssss!* No! Put away the tube! Not the tube!" I had an awful foreboding that the drawn-out moan she then emitted was escalating towards the despicable '*cri*'.

"You see a tube. Where is the tube?"

"*Gggggg . . . !*"

I recalled the phase of tonic immobility or tetanism I had seen in her photographs, and feared that I would be subjected to the sight of a human being abandoned to contractures that were both fantastic and inevitable—a tensing of the shoulders, the tongue withdrawn, almost swallowed, wrists touching each other on the dorsal side, acute mydriasis—jolts, quakes, cramps, throes . . . but no.

"They have it. They have it. They suck on it. They are like bees with nectar. And they touch. They *touch*."

"Who do they touch, Celestine?"

She froze, perplexed, with an air of abandonment—even disappointment. Her eyes still not open. Or were open only to her internal, persecutory universe.

"Celestine?"

"They touch . . . her." The tone in her breath of a question. Or disbelief. Or relief. Or wonder. "They touch *her*. And embrace her. And wrap her up, so quickly she has no time to protest, or even cry out. And lift her . . ." Her cheeks shone with perspiration and her lower lip quivered. "And—take her."

In my mind's eye I saw the empty rocking chair, the sheets of paper strewn across the room. The French windows—locked.

"And now?"

"Now their arms are around me and I'm struggling to get free and it's as if I wake from a dream and I'm in the arms of Hennetier and I am screaming, screaming until my throat is on fire. And my head is bursting and my legs feel cut off at the knees. And—as they strap me into the jacket and gag me, when I look over to the French windows I see the craft hanging in the night sky beyond the panes of glass. And I am laughing, laughing, laughing because they have returned to the Orb once more."

Indeed, she was laughing now. Not with pleasure or amusement but with the kind of animal prattle that accompanies an inhalation of nitrous oxide. The manic gibber of something unchained and unchecked.

"And the more I laugh, the more they tighten the straps . . ." I saw her teeth gnash and the pearl of a tear glisten in the corner of one eye. "Tighten . . . Tighten . . ."

"And before the warders take you away, what do you see?"

"The room is empty."

"What does that tell you?"

"It tells me the inhabitants of—*that place*—are no longer on our soil."

"That's correct. Which means what?"

Celestine did not answer.

"It means they can no longer threaten you," said Poe. "While you hear my voice they are powerless, and you are free, and you are sleeping, the deepest and most comforting sleep you have ever known . . ."

Within less than a minute she was becalmed.

"And when I tap the arm of the chair you will rouse from that slumber without remembering any bad thoughts you might have had or emotions you might have felt. You shall be refreshed and as gay as you were as a child in the most beautiful meadow under the warmest sunshine."

He did so, and her eyes opened.

She looked at each of us in turn, with a bewilderment, as if she had just lifted her head from her pillow.

"Celestine, that will be all." Charcot walked to the door and opened it. The two guards who had brought her stood waiting.

Celestine gave a light laugh. A laugh that would not have been out of place at a respectable *soirée*. Not at all like the chattering she had displayed to us only minutes earlier.

"But, monsieur. I have just this second sat down."

Charcot merely turned his hand towards the door. Without questioning his authority she rose, gave Poe and myself the most rudimentary curtsey, and obeyed.

"Remarkable." The Socrates of Salpêtrière closed the door after her. "Perfectly remarkable."

My friend was unmoved by his praise. "She is calm because I willed her to be calm. She is sick because you will her to remain sick. You imprison her with your misbegotten quest for a biological cure." At sixty-nine, age had not tempered Poe's ability to speak as he felt. The barbs he once wielded as a literary critic now flew at plentiful targets, invariably making me cringe.

"How dare you, monsieur!" Charcot was flabbergasted at his effrontery. "You—you are not a medical mind ..."

"No, but I am a mind. And I hope you will think on what you have seen. You have eyes to observe, and I pray they have done their duty." Poe tidied his cuffs and tugged his sleeves. "Now please direct us out of this labyrinth. We have seen enough."

Thus we bade an ambivalent farewell to the "Cathedral of the Sent-Mad," where a system of measuring and cataloguing souls seemed no less absurd than the fantasia of "Doctor Tarr and Professor Fether". I could not wait to get to the far side of the gates.

Crossing the courtyard, past the fountain, I saw an elderly woman pressing her hands into a pile of sand with all the absorption of an infant. I looked back at the high window, behind which a stern visage looked down, his hand gripping one dark lapel. Doctor Charcot was clearly master over all he surveyed, but I wondered how much his patients' survival depended in some fundamental way on pleasing him? I wondered even if, on both sides, there existed something of an invisible, unknowing pact?

⌁

"And much of Madness, and more of Sin, and Horror the soul of the plot ..."

Madness, of course, was Poe's quintessential subject. His writing told us not to look in the madhouse for such ideas, but within us all. That evening, with pipe smoke thick in the air, we discussed whether a mad person had lost their truth or found it, in grasping something beyond the stifling realm of the incurably sane. "Perhaps the *coup de theatre* results in a lifting of the veil and seeing reality, in all its dreadfulness, the falsehood being the *entr'acte* of so-called 'normality'..."

"A romantic notion," I opined. "There is no romance in diseases of the mind."

"And yet can we fail to see in the mad a failed version of ourselves? Why not a different being, but equal? As one sail may be battered by a storm, but one more tightly bound stays unmoved?"

Madame L'Espanaye served cardamom-flavoured Réunion coffee as Le Bon closed the curtains across a silver disc hanging in the sky. The manservant was not our gaoler, but after what we had seen I had difficulty shaking the notion that our rooms in the Rue de la Femme-Sans-Tête were a kind of confinement.

Poe crossed the room in his Persian slippers, pipe locked in his teeth, and slid open a plans chest, removing faded manuscripts I had never seen before in spite of living there for years. Proctor's *Chart of the Visible Stars*, the *Globi Coelestis in Tabulas Planas* and, lastly, the 1742 *Tabula Selenographica* of Homann and Doppelmayr, created in full colour to illustrate the lunar mapping of Johannes Hevelius and Giovanni Battista Riccioli. Astonishing me in both detail and beauty, here the Moon was seen as it never could be from earth—at greater than 360 degrees and with all visible features given equal weight.

"What is a lie? Merely what we cannot see?"

"Are all things possible, then?" I said with heavy sarcasm. "Surely not, in scientific terms."

"But science has to change, to adapt to what is perceived." He fetched a candelabrum, the better to peruse the surface of the Moon, whose whiteness mirrored his thinning hair.

"And what *is* perceived?" The implication of his words stunned me. "Poe, you cannot possibly consider that Celestine's story is true?"

"I have not had it disproven," he said disinterestedly—and provocatively.

"Then let me oblige." I eagerly seized the gauntlet. "There are trees in the Bois de Vincennes. One can postulate, and an experiment might easily demonstrate, that as she galloped through the park in bright sunshine, a stroboscopic effect was created between a low evening sun and the space between the tree trunks, at a certain frequency inducing a seizure in the brain. Or else this: the attack was real, by real men intent on rape, and as a defence mechanism she has retreated into fantasy. To blank it out."

"But, *mon brave,* she has *not* blanked it out. It haunts and plagues her. It gives her no respite. Why would memory do that in an attempt to salve the psychic wound?"

"Because the brain knows not what it does," I said, trying not to flounder. "And pain cannot be eradicated. So the malicious act is transformed into a malevolent fantasy."

"But what of the actual disappearance of Gertrude? That is not a mental aberration but a physical one."

"Then Celestine saw men from the Moon?"

"You think it a ludicrous concept?"

"I do!"

"Recall, then, the indigenous Aztecs of Mexico who saw the first sailing ships from Spain on their shores and could not conceive of their reality." He circled the esoteric charts. "They thought *Conquistadores* on horseback to be exotic centaurs—not two animals but one monstrous hybrid . . ."

I laughed. "Which is only to say those very implements of observation and knowledge—our eyes—can sometimes lie. To protect us from the truth."

"And the truth is what?" He tossed book after book onto the maps. They thudded with the heft of their contents. "Greater minds than mine have found the idea of non-terrestrial life not only credible but likely. The astronomer Flammarion espouses the belief in his *La Plurité des Mondes Habités*—" One of the volumes before me. "—and Gottfried Liebnitz, Newton's rival in the creation of calculus, said it must be acknowledged that 'an infinite number of globes have as much right as ours' to hold rational inhabitants—'though it follows not at all that they are human.'"

"But recent calculations show the Moon to be too small, its gravity too feeble, to hold an atmosphere. And Julian Schmidt has shown there are no cities or artificial structures."

"My dear Holmes! You are dangerously close to thinking our planet is the centre of the Universe! Giordano Bruno disputed that back in *De l'Infinito, Universo e Mondi*, and was burned at the stake for it. For declaring 'Countless suns and countless earths all rotate around their suns in exactly the same way as the seven planets of our system'. And that these worlds must be no less inhabited than our Earth."

"And if they did exist, these imps or *farfadets*, on the Moon or Venus or Mars—what possible desire or inclination would they have to visit us and for what purpose? To abuse us, to examine us with their instruments, to assess our biology, the better to understand?"

Poe shrugged and watched a circle of pipe smoke rise to the ceiling. "Or to play, as we would dangle a ball of wool for a kitten? Which we would just as swiftly drown."

"Human beings also have a capacity for affection."

"Ah, but we are not considering human beings."

Now I sensed the kitten he was playing with was me. Could he really be serious in his assertions? Or, like a dutiful defence lawyer, was he simply stating a case which he privately disavowed?

"Please. For these many months your intelligence has impressed me, overwhelmed me—no, transformed me." I could not disguise that I was upset. "I beg of you, do not destroy that gargantuan monument by telling me you believe we are being visited by other worlds."

His hooded eyes looked away from me with supreme non-chalance. "Let me just say, my dear Holmes, that as regards life within our Solar System or beyond, I follow the precept of Tertullian: *Credo quia absurdum*. I believe it *because* it is absurd."

I returned the books to the shelves. "All fancies aside, what we have here on earth is a room from which a person vanished without trace."

"You are right." He closed the plans chest. "Our satellite exerts an eternal fascination in its confluence with madness, even a mythological power—was it not Aristotle who suggested that the brain was the 'moistest' organ in the body and thereby most susceptible to the pernicious influences of the Moon, which triggers the tides? The sun is Helios, giver of life—but what does the Moon offer? It is the light by which the nocturnal hunt and their prey cower . . . But we cannot travel there to solve this puzzle."

"We agree at last," I said. "But if the key to unlock the mystery is not in the high heavens, where is it?"

"In Celestine. In her crime of attempted murder." He blew out all the candles save one. "Come, let us take to our beds. Tomorrow we shall need all our wits about us, and more. We are going to seek out the madwoman's nemesis . . . And find indeed if he has secrets to hide."

～

The next morning we hastened to catch the first train to Amiens, a two-hour journey via Abbeville. I expected, and found, a sleepy provincial town, near enough to feel a reflection of Paris but without its insufferable racket and agitation. The honeysuckle scent of bougainvilleas drifted on the air from the floating *Hortillonnages* amongst the canals—or *rieux* as they were called in the dialect of Picardy. Willow, alder and the sight of wildfowl combined to give a welcome sense of Eden.

The house at 44 Boulevard Longueville was severe-looking but spacious, and we were quickly greeted by its owner—ruddy tan from striding the jetty at Le Crotoy, hair like an undulating sea frothy with waves, a nautical beard and slightly heavy-lidded eyes that nevertheless sparkled with intense vigour. At the age of fifty, not a line marred Jules Verne's features other than around his eyes: more the product of laughter than frowning.

"Dupin! My friend!" he boomed as he shook my companion's hand. "I feel I know you intimately, even if it was a name only used in the American editions! Honestly, there is not a greater devotee of Poe in France than the man before you!" I now thought his handshake might break bones. "I confess, when I read of his death, I wept like a baby. In mourning a great writer, even one you never met, you mourn a friend."

"Indeed," said Poe, extracting his paw. I could tell he was flattered, even if he dared not show it for fear of revealing his true identity.

"Did you know him, then? I detect the trace of an American accent."

"We were acquainted." Poe coughed. "In Richmond. Briefly. He was good company but a difficult man. Hard to like. Drove away friends as others would swat away bees."

"But had a sting of his own." Verne grinned. "Albeit delivered with his critical nib."

"Which made him more enemies than friends. I was one of the few."

"And to die by *delirium tremens*. Awful way to go. Dreadful to think of his febrile life, wracked as it was by madness . . ."

"Relieved by periods of horrible sanity," said Poe without inflection.

Verne laughed like a bear, if a bear can laugh. He slapped our shoulders and led us down the hall.

However, the conversation had made me consider Poe's "madness"—which I had cause to consider, oftentimes. *Was* he mad? I remember him once imagining the fate of an individual gifted, or rather cursed, with an intellect far superior to those around him. Surely, he said, that person's opinions and speculations would differ so widely from the rest of Mankind that he would be considered mad? *And how horribly painful such a condition. Hell could invent no greater torture than being charged with abnormal weakness on account of being abnormally strong.* I had no doubt at the time that the individual he was ruminating upon was himself.

At the door to Verne's study we were intercepted by his wife, Honorine, not a great beauty, but a pleasant if homely woman. She offered us soup made from local produce from the market gardens—carrots, turnips, leeks—but we declined.

"My dear, these men have come to discuss business." (Indeed, our pantelegraph message had said—falsely—as much.) Honorine curtseyed and absented herself to elsewhere in the house. Verne shut the door of the study. "Poor darling, she does not understand the writer's life. She complained her husband 'was forever in his balloon', but that same balloon was to make her a wealthy woman."

Poe and I glanced at each other.

I saw one table to write on, another piled with reference books, a comfortable arm chair and a camp bed—at peak intensity, Verne desired to be no more than five paces from his work—a pipe rack, and beyond it all, a library. I half-expected the riveted metal of the hull of the *Nautilus*, but no. The only concession to his yarns, and his upbringing in the sea port of Nantes with its Cape-Horners docked with exotic cargo from across the world, was a large propeller mounted on one wall. Now his mind was full of the "Cape-Horners" of space, of the future—as attested to by framed illustrations from *Five Weeks in a Balloon*, Verne as Professor Aronnax from *20,000 Leagues Under the Sea* and two scenes depicting Captain Nemo at the helm and the battle with the giant squid.

"Ah, this is my '62 edition of Poe's works." Verne took a volume from his shelves. "But I first read it close to '48 when it first came out in translation. I devoured it! Of course the 'Balloon Hoax' and 'Hans Pfall' gave me the idea for *Un Voyage en Ballon,* but neither of his stories is particularly convincing. 'Pfall' is nothing but a humorous fantasy . . . clearly a flaw."

Flaw? I looked at Poe, but Poe remained mute.

"What I do, you see, is to make the fantastic seem *convincing.* What's annoying, as I said in my essay on Poe for *Le Musée des Familles,* is that he could so easily have made his tales more *plausible* had he just respected a few elementary laws of physics."

Poe's mouth twitched into a fixed grin, but Verne was in full flood.

"You see, over the years, I have compiled thousands of data cards, the better to educate a general public who know little of what is happening in the world of science—but you cannot drag a horse to water and expect it to drink! Reading Poe I immediately saw what could be done if you mix fantasy and *facts.* But in Poe science plays a secondary role, a pretext, a frame for the writer's own anguish by depicting human behaviour in abnormal situations—the *bizarre* for its own sake. Moral deviation was his way of showing his crushing scorn for progress in American society. I wanted to do the opposite! Show that man can achieve fulfilment by tackling the environment, nature, which is both real and hostile—not the escapist cults of Truth, Imagination or Beauty."

"But Poe created a new form of literature, a form coming from the sensitivity of his excessive mental processes." I spoke up on behalf of my friend, to avoid him having to do so himself. "I see in his stories a relentless scrutiny of his own morbid traits, a discussion of obscure facts, sometimes through satire, yes, but with no whiff of the supernatural. Poe saw the fantastic in the real."

The corporeal Poe appreciated my defence.

"But without *science* . . ." Verne gesticulated. "A manuscript in a bottle, a descent into a maelstrom—what is it worth? Where is the excitement? Where is the *commerciality?*"

Now, Poe had to sit down. But he also had to take it on the chin. He was, after all, not 'Edgar Poe' but 'C. Auguste Dupin'—and we had a job to do.

"I do not deny," said Verne, "that he is the undisputed leader of the school of the strange."

"And his characters are eminently human." Poe now spoke. "Endowed often with a supercharged sensitivity. Exceptional individuals, galvanised as if by air with more oxygen than it should have, and whose lives are one long combustion. If they are not mad, they most inevitably *become* mad through the abuse of their minds. They push self-reflection and deduction to the limit. They are fearsome analysts. Starting from the merest trifle, they reach absolute truth."

Far from contradicting him, Verne's face became enraptured with glee.

"Don't misunderstand me! I owe him everything! Look at me!" He gave an expansive gesture, encompassing the room. "He wrote a little concoction about a cosmological oddity called 'Three Sundays in the Week' and I turned the idea into *Around the World in Eighty Days!* The popular edition sold over a hundred thousand copies and the illustrated three times that! It was the novel that made me famous!" He kissed the book squarely on the cover.

Poe's lips tried hard not to tighten. "Then you owe old Edgar quite a lot. And not just in terms of plagiarism."

Verne guffawed. "Novelty of situation. Little known facts. The drama of nature and destruction . . . But my heroes are never unhealthy or nervous of temperament."

"God forbid . . ."

"If only Poe could have gloried in human energy. In the positive!"

"And have Man defeat death, perhaps? In what way does that reflect any life actually lived?"

"But to strive, M. Dupin—to *strive!* That is what Man does. And so I push my characters to the extreme—outwards . . ."

"Perhaps the real exploration is inwards."

Verne made a face. "I took literature in a different direction."

"Yet at times," I chipped in, "it feels you had to make an effort not to step in his footsteps."

"Ah, you're an Englishman. My apologies for not detecting it earlier."

"My name is Sherlock Holmes."

"I saw the Blackwall Tunnel and the Great Eastern being built in Greenwich. Most impressive! More impressive than the *Macbeth* I saw at the Princess Royal." Verne's smile twisted. "But I also saw children in rags and beggars holding out hats beneath the tall London house fronts."

"Alas, that dichotomy is not unique to my homeland."

In a room above I could hear somebody playing the piano. Perhaps one of Verne's married step-daughters, Valentine or Suzanne, or his son by this marriage, Michel, still a schoolboy.

"Now, the reason for your visit. I understand you have a business proposition."

"If you'll indulge me just a moment longer, monsieur," said Poe. "I'm such a fan of your work . . ." Remarkably, the words did not stick in his craw. "Can I just ask where the inspiration came from for your astounding books about the voyage to the Moon?" He had slyly opened the door to our investigation.

"I was at the height of my popularity, but still dividing my time between the capital and the coast. Sailing round Cotentin and Finistere in the *Saint-Michel*, while travelling to the stars here." Verne tapped the side of his head. "*De la Terre à la Lune* drew on all my accumulated knowledge, in exactly the way I've talked about. I even got my cousin, a cosmologist and mathematician, to establish the correct trajectories. There were problems of excessive initial velocity, overheating due to friction in the atmosphere, the design of the breaking rockets, and so on. But I was determined to make the project ballistically feasible."

Like most of France, I had read his story of the Baltimore Gun Club, a post-Civil War society of weapons aficionados, building a sky-facing cannon in Florida to launch a projectile containing three people (their president Impey Barbicane, his plate armour-making rival, Nicholl, and a French poet) at the Moon—and land on it.

"Yet they failed," I said.

Verne shrugged. "That is the cost of realism. After a series of misadventures they fall short of their target. But I couldn't let them revolve in orbit forever or go crashing into the surface below, so in my sequel, *Autour de Lune*, I had Ardan get the idea of using auxiliary rockets, planned to buffer the landing, to steer Barbicane and his companions back within the gravitational pull of Earth."

"The three men discuss the possibility of life on the Moon," I said. "If I remember correctly, they conclude it is barren."

"Absolutely! None of 'Hans Pfall's' ridiculous two foot tall Lunarians!"

"And that is the view you maintain, given the current scientific knowledge with which you are at great pains to keep up to date?"

For the first time, Verne sensed he was being interrogated. "Most definitely and emphatically." His mood darkened. "Forgive me . . . What is the exact purpose of this conversation?"

Poe remained unruffled. "Please answer the question, monsieur."

"I am not sure I shall. At all. I don't like your tone of voice, whoever-you-are. And who *are* you? I had thought from the telegram your interest was a 'business venture'—a theatrical one. In my stupidity I'd assumed the signature, *Dupin*—obviously a pseudonym—was a wry way of informing me you wanted my services to adapt a story or stories by Poe for the stage."

"And if we had told you anything else, would you have admitted us?"

"Almost certainly not, without suitable credentials. I am— well, astonished. You—you have found your way into my home by—by gross deception, messieurs . . ."

"Deception was the only way open to us, because of the utmost gravity of the situation," I explained. "A life is in peril, and . . ."

"And I would like an answer to Holmes's question," Poe cut in. "Do you believe inhabitants of the Moon visit this planet?"

Verne's demeanour, formerly relaxed and free of airs and graces, now became taciturn and formidable.

"I'm afraid I must ask you to leave." He rang a bell-pull.

"Not an unpredictable request," said Poe, "but we are undertaking an enquiry on behalf of Salpêtrière Hospital. And though we are not the police, that enquiry is a criminal one."

"Salpêtrière?" Verne could hardly have looked less horrified if told one of his children had been maimed. "That woman? That harridan! *Mon Dieu!* I vowed never to discuss that event again."

"If there is a prosecution for murder, you may have to. And in a glare of publicity you could do without."

A servant appeared, but with sudden irritation Verne waved him away. When the man was gone, he spoke again, through beetle brows: "I have nothing whatsoever to hide. What do you want of me?"

"Firstly and foremost, a simple account of Celestine's attack on you."

Verne wiped his face with meaty hands, took up his pen and held it, as if the object gave him some kind of comfort. "I was in the Paris offices of my editor, Hetzel, in the Rue Jacob. We were revising the final proofs of *Une Fantasie du Docteur Ox*. A woman burst in. She waved a book—*my* book, *The Moon Voyage*—and blathered without pause or breath that I was conspiring with creatures from the Moon in their invasion of our planet. That I was deliberately disseminating information to the population of the world that life on the Moon was impossible in order to trick us all, to disguise the horrific truth! Before I could even laugh, she fired a pistol at me. Luckily, the bullet only grazed my shoulder, but she was aiming for my head. Then she came at me violently, as if possessed, kicking and screaming, but, having heard the gunshot, Hetzel's assistants rushed in and pinned her to the ground."

"You are shaking, even now," I observed.

"I was rattled. So was Hetzel. It is rare to encounter the mad. Michel, I know—my boy has his problems—he can be sullen, odious, charming—full of selfish actions, stubborn, impulsive—his mother and I don't know what shall become of him—but this . . ." Forlorn, he looked a different person from the one who had greeted us with such *bonhomie.* "The next day I was numb and couldn't write a word. I told Honorine I felt I should contact this woman, help her if I could, but she wisely counselled me it was better not to. The girl plainly cannot be shaken in her convictions, and it is better she is left to the care of experts."

"Can you tell us anything more about her temperament or demeanour?"

"Her eyes were glassy, lacking in focus. She had the determination of an animal fixed on its prey."

"You did not report the incident to the police or the press?"

"Strange as this may seem, I did not want to bring undue unpleasantness to her family. My fame brings unwarranted consequences."

Poe examined his lapel distractedly.

"Tell me about Hetzel."

"I would trust the man with my life. He is my literary and spiritual father. He took me in when other publishers rejected me. He had faith in me when others didn't. He created me."

I could not help but look at the reclining Poe with his crossed legs—my wonderful, supercilious *Dupin*—and think the same.

"As for his character," Verne continued, "he was a revolutionary. I came to Paris as a student cheering a republic he had helped create." He picked up a sheet of paper full of crossings-out. "From the beginning, he helped me rewrite, to change a sad ending to a happy one, tone down any political messages, to get rid of the pessimism and add sentiment—which always goes down well with the public."

Poe made what I can only call a grimace.

"I never knew a good editor whose instinct was superior to that of a good writer."

Verne shook his head. "I wanted Nemo to be a vengeful Pole sinking Russian ships. Hetzel persuaded me it would be a mistake. So I made him a more general rebel against tyranny."

"Diminishing your character in the process."

"Not according to the sales figures."

"And his death in *L'Ile Mystèrieuse* was somewhat tardy." Poe's nostrils flared.

"You sound like a critic."

"Perhaps I was. In another life."

Verne could never have realised the infinite truth behind such a remark. We sat in the lap of luxury, with servants and surrounded by domestic bliss. Verne had been given the Légion d'honneur, had recently enjoyed a private audience with the Pope, had been embraced by Venice where they put up bunting saying "Eviva Giulio Verne!" and let off fireworks. Poe in his lifetime had never had even a glimmer of such success or adoration. His was the struggle of a troubled genius, a narrative of starvation, setbacks and ill-health, a reputation, yes—but never reputation enough to keep the wolf from the door.

"I suppose she will now be under lock and key for the rest of her days," said the Frenchman. "I presume she has killed one of the other inmates."

"Presumption is a dangerous thing." Poe stood. "And certainly not scientific. I would think you would have learned that in your years of research." The two writers shook hands. "Now, we shall take up no more of your time."

Verne accompanied us back through the hall, decorated as it was by illustrations from his *Voyages Extraordinaires*, a painting of the aeronaut Tissandier and an advertisement for a *"Panorama de Paris"* ride up into the air in a *"Grand Ballon Captif a Vapeur!"*— *"Tous Les Jours Ascensions Captives de 500 à 600 mètres D'Altitude!"*

"One last thing, M. Dupin. Before you go . . ." Verne hovered on his doorstep. "Did you really know Edgar Poe?"

Poe revolved on his heel, turning back to him. I wondered what he would say.

"Intimately."

"Then put me out of my misery, please. Ever since I read it I have been obsessed by the inconclusive ending of *The Narrative of Arthur Gordon Pym*. The giant white female figure barring his way to the South Pole . . . Is she some mythic eternal mother? The symbol of the cosmic breast? An angel? Or some white race superior even to *homo sapiens?*"

"I think I am safe in saying, nothing was further from the author's intention."

"But he implies it is not of this earth. Did he believe such things possible? What does it mean?"

"To a poet, meaning is a very over-rated commodity."

"But the public do not love poetry, they love a good story!" cried Verne. "And the ending is so vexatious, it leaves us perplexed and dissatisfied."

Poe's face was both haughty and pained. "Perhaps that was the intention."

"But surely, had he lived, he would have changed it? To satisfy, rather than baffle the reader?"

"He may have changed nothing," said Poe wearily. "Perhaps he got tired of writing marvel after marvel. The temptation constantly hovers, when to write 'The End'. As we must end this conversation, monsieur. *Au revoir.*"

After stating that the visit had been entirely wasted, Poe spent the entire sprightly walk to the station—and he could be sprightly when required—grumbling about Verne, thanking the

Lord that he had not trapped us into discussing the problem of the Newfoundland dog that conveniently vanishes, or whether the crewmates were 'scientific' in their cannibalisation of the unfortunate seaman Parker.

I asked if he was by any chance riled by the man. "Not at all!" Yet still he wittered on about the novelist's egregious faults, specifically and generally, arriving at the dismissive summation: "He devises his plots as a bricklayer builds a wall. And the worst of it is that in listening to his self-aggrandising drivel, we are no closer to solving the mystery of Gertrude Socha's disappearance."

"That may not be true." I saw a plume of steam announcing our train was shortly to pull into the platform. "I think I have the answer. As we left the house, the final piece of the puzzle fell into place ..."

Poe looked at me with the delight and astonishment of a proud parent.

His features brightened from his previous all-pervading gloom, but then, just as somebody barged past behind him, became pale, then quizzical, his neck straightening.

"That is most curious ..." He blinked, leaning with one hand against my chest. "I always wondered what the sensation would be like, and now I know. It is like being hit by a mallet. Now a coldness is spreading through my body ... Take note of this for future reference, my dear Holmes. I feel extremely—yes—*faint* ..."

Frighteningly, his eyes became totally blank and fixed, corpse-like. His head fell forward but his legs had given way, and he sank to the platform before I was able to catch him.

He lay in a heap, limbs splayed, passengers hurrying by in blissful ignorance, as I fell to my knees beside him. Behind his head and neck, I saw blood pumping out of him, forming a thick, viscous pool to which strands of his long white hair stuck.

The life was leaving his body, as the light had already left his eyes.

"Dupin! Dupin!" I yelled, then, without thinking, blurted out his real name. *"Edgar!"*

Even as his skin turned from parchment to grey, he lifted a weak hand, feebly, and covered my mouth.

⤙⤚

We rushed him, soaked in blood, to Amiens Hospital Infirmary in one of the *barque à cornets*, resembling nothing so much—to my horrified heart—as a funeral barge. He was unconscious when I left him to the mercy of the surgeons. I could not take in what the nurse was telling me, then heard my friend telling me to snap out of it and concentrate on the valuable information. He had been stabbed in the back. A downward swipe at his shoulder blade. I damned myself for not pushing aside the crowd on the platform, for not having the instinct to search for his attacker—but it had all been a blur.

I asked if the wound might be fatal. She said they didn't know yet. I thought: "They will not know until the person dies: then it's fatal all right." I was ungrateful to her, hated her, in fact, though she didn't deserve it. My rage had to target somebody. Again I heard Poe telling me I must keep my feelings in check. I remembered the first few days and weeks training in 'ratiocination', spent learning that emotion is an enemy to logic, that it lures us further and further from the truth. If I succumbed now, all my education would have been in vain.

I caught the next train back to Paris. I knew I had to act swiftly or the Master would never forgive me. Also, sickeningly, there was a possibility I was now seeking the murderer of Edgar Allan Poe, and while the world had mourned the writer many years before, I would have to mourn my friend alone.

Sitting in that railway carriage, I wept far more than when I heard of the loss of my father. But I had to steel my nerves. Apply all the lessons he had given me, crack the crime and apprehend the criminal. And I had to remember not only was Poe's life in the balance, but that of Gertrude Socha. And the clock was ticking on both counts.

I raced to Salpêtrière. Demanded to see Charcot. With no time for his objections, I demanded to see Hennetier, threatening him with the police if he didn't let me. As soon as I saw the guard, and he saw the devastation in my face, and a smirk arose, I lost all reason and grabbed him by the throat, driving him hard against the wall. It was all too obvious he thought 'Dupin' was dead. He shoved me away and blew his whistle deafeningly—a woman inmate in our vicinity covered her ears and shrieked like a pig at slaughter—and by the time I got my breath back two gigantic warders were fastened onto my arms.

"He is the one you should be apprehending!" I screamed, as I saw a third gaoler carrying a strait jacket. "*He* is the one instrumental in the kidnapping of Gertrude Socha!"

Hennetier tried to cover his fear with an air of bravado, showing Charcot the palms of his hands. His colleagues held me firmer still, but I found some of Poe's arrogance and fearlessness had rubbed off on me.

"You can lock me up or throw me out, but you would do well to listen unless you want this institution to descend into extreme disrepute." Now I was certain I had Charcot's undivided attention. "My deductions have led me to the inevitable conclusion. Hennetier 'saw nothing' yet was the sole person responsible for the locks on all the doors and windows—so, eliminating all other possibilities, he *must* be involved. In 'seeing nothing' he sought to divert attention to Celestine's delusion, in order to buy him and his accomplices time. And what he is too stupid to realise is that if they do something reckless, he will go to the guillotine with them."

Hennetier seemed to physically diminish in stature. Open-mouthed, he darted his eyes from me to Charcot and back again, as furtive as a rat in a trap.

"I—I never knew it would come to this. I am a simple man . . ."

Charcot signalled for the men to let me go.

"What are their names?" I rubbed the bruises on my elbows. "Quickly, damn you!"

"Corcoran."

"And the other. One above, one below. I'm not an imbecile."

"Lamiche."

"Where are they holding her?"

"A house in the Rue Maillard, monsieur. But they will not be there now. Please . . ."

"Where will I find them?"

"Tonight? In the Bois de Vincennes."

How could mention of that place not chill me like ice? It was the very location of Celestine Blot's first encounter with her denizens of the Moon.

⤙

The Bois de Vincennes.

Royal hunting ground, neglected by one King Louis, restored by another, donated to the city by Napoleon III to be made into an 'English-style' park: it almost made me feel patriotic. But in the dark of night, with a pounding heart, I had room for no such warm thoughts. Unless to keep my teeth from chattering.

The design was by Housemann's landscape architect Jean-Charles Alphand. As I waited, I imagined them as teacher and pupil, like Poe and myself. Probably a fantasy. The purpose had been to give green space for leisure to the working class of East Paris— colourful splendour, picturesque landscapes, lawns, groves, flower beds and lakes: though there was precious little colour to be seen now under bleak evening cloud. The site had its problems, which Alphand solved by annexing sections of land and creating three smaller parks, each with its own artificial lake and surroundings.

Lac des Minimes to the north encompassed the original medieval monastery that once stood there, and the Lac de Saint-Mandé in the southwest, while Lake Daumesnil was created as a setting out of a romantic painting, with two islands and sloping lawns. Alphand also planned it to have popular attractions such as a horse-racing track, similar to the Longchamps hippodrome at the Bois de Boulogne, and there were café-restaurants, a bandstand, buildings for vendors and game concessions—all eerily silent, for now.

Through my telescope I could see the Temple of Love: a round Doric edifice placed on a promontory on the Isle de Reuilly, above an artificial grotto. We were stationed facing it.

I had sped immediately from Salpêtrière to the *Préfecture* at 36 Quai des Orfèvres, home of the police *judiciaire,* as had been the Rue de Jérusalem in the days of Balzac. Albert Gigot, the current *Préfet,* had been helped in many cases by "Dupin" and listened attentively to my story once he knew there had been an attempt on his life—possibly a successful one. Without hesitation he appointed Claude Bident to be officer in charge—formerly of the *Sûreté nationale*—an Englishman's idea of a Frenchman; a little, bearded man in bowler hat and morning coat. The police in those days were both bureaucratic and sabre rattling, monitoring a city still moody and dangerous, operating amidst enmities and grievances born of the recent struggle resulting in the creation of a new political order.

And so we waited, hidden by shrubbery, under the great orb of a full moon. It seemed inevitable.

The only sound was the water from the ornamental cascades, and the waves splashing the pleasure boats tied inertly to their docks.

Bident, in the shadows, tapped my shoulder. Pointed.

I saw motion on the lake. My lens enlarged it.

A rowing boat, its oars being silently heaved. Two men— the taller one, who would turn out to be Corcoran, sitting at the stern, the other, Lamiche, using the brute force of muscled arms to power it. Between them sat what I first took to be a bundle and

then concluded from its shifting movement was the huddled figure of Gertrude Socha, a sack over her head, arms tied behind her
back, with a noose round her neck.

They were heading for the island.

I had discussed this eventuality with Bident. I'd told him we
could not risk hitting Gertrude if there was gunfire, so we'd initi-
ated a plan for Hennetier to call his fellow miscreants to shore
before we pounced. This Hennetier readily agreed to do, in return
for a good word in court from the police—anything to diminish
the full force of the law, and possible decapitation. As Bident said,
it focuses the mind, decapitation.

So, true to his word, once his partners in crime were in sight,
Hennetier walked to the waterline and waved his arms in the air.
They soon caught sight of his lantern and stopped rowing. The two
men looked at each other. Hennetier imitated the hoot of an owl
and we watched as the boat slowly changed direction, only one oar
spooning the waves, and it made towards him—and, little by little,
nearer to us . . .

Suddenly, only yards from running aground, Corcoran made
a stirring motion in the air with his hand. Lamiche, startled, looked
right and left, and paddled furiously. The boat turned in a sharp
curve, pointing once more to the island. Corcoran stood up—but
only to fire a pistol directly at Hennetier's head, killing the man
outright. The gang leader knew somehow, by the oddity of Hennetier's unexpected arrival, that he had been betrayed.

It was then the police opened fire. Lamiche dived into the
belly of the boat and in so doing almost capsized it. Gertrude,
being masked and incapacitated by her bonds, could do nothing
to re-balance herself, and was thrown into the lake, even as dozens
of bullets tore splinters out of wood, and punctured the watery
surface in a flotilla of splashes.

I threw myself in after her, hearing Poe in my ear telling me
that it was absurd to risk my own life when the chances of sav-

ing her were slim, but some part of me equated saving her with bringing the case to a conclusion. Though if I was thinking this, I wasn't aware of it. I simply did it. Submerged myself, and swam out, knowing that if I didn't the sack-cloth would clog her mouth in seconds, and with her hands tied, she would drown. She had already sunk like a stone.

If it was night above, it was ten times night below the waves. My blood protested as if it were the Arctic, but I went down at the spot where I'd seen her entering the water, and nothing, *nothing* could I find but branches, weeds, everything that could be a barrier to me—not least my own pathetic lungs. I emerged, gasped, descended again, combed and snatched at those hellish fronds. Where was she? *There!* I felt her. I had her. I grabbed her. *What part of her?* Her shoulders. Chin. I hooked her with my elbow, bobbed myself to the surface, and swam.

Legs surrounded me as I hauled the object onto the lawn, face-down in the moonlight. Bident slashed her bonds with a bayonet. I turned her onto her back, trying desperately to eject any water she had swallowed. I saw no movement under the coarse material covering her face, other than the spastic jerks caused by my frenetic beating of her chest. To better see if she was breathing or not, I tore off the hood.

I did not want to believe she was already dead. I did not want to see that her eyes, gluey with pond water, were fixed half-open. I did not want, above anything, to behold that her face was a mass of bruises and contusions caused by incessant and heartless torture. But that is what I saw. I groaned and rocked back, realising that my actions were futile.

I closed her lids with my fingertips. Perhaps now, at least, she had peace from her madness. Amen, if anything, to that.

The night air was still after the flurry of gunshots. On my knees in the mud I saw that one of the thuggish individuals had been shot dead by the trigger-happy police. The other struggled in the grip of uniforms, a knife shaken from his fist. This was Lamiche—short to the point of being pygmy-like, shaven-headed and well-muscled, stripped to the waist like a boxer. I immediately knew he was Celestine's night-imp, her *farfadet*—and Poe's intended murderer.

As they bundled him off, I picked up the weapon and hurled it far into the lake. When I turned back, Bident had extracted something from the dead Corcoran's pocket. He unfolded it and held it up to me. Even by the light of the moon, there was no mistaking it was a treasure map.

⌒⌁

"The Gold Bug," Poe croaked. "The deadly bug that infects all men—greed." He was sitting up in the hospital bed, bandaged, with pillows supporting his lower back, but was now out of danger. The sawbones had sewn him up, and to his deep regret he now had to pronounce that he and Verne had *something* in common—if only attempted murder.

"I asked myself, why would Gertrude be abducted?" I said. "As you taught me, I asked, who had the opportunity and who stood to gain? It transpires that her entire time at Salpêtrière she insisted 'Gertrude Socha' was an expedient alias: she was in fact 'The Contessa de Calvi'—of course a delusion. But Hennetier must have overheard her speaking of her fortune, her ramblings about having millions of francs squirreled away, that she was rich beyond the dreams of avarice . . . and took her at her word. He imagined bank notes hoarded under floorboards, chests of doubloons on a desert island . . . If only he could get the exact location out of the patient. So that is what he planned, by secreting her away and interrogating her until she gave the information up. He couldn't carry this off alone, he knew that—but there was enough money to go round, the way she was talking. So, he approached his acquaintance, Titus Corcoran, an aeronaut who organized balloon rides at the *Exposition Universelle* last year in a craft called 'Le Géant' after Nadar's contraption. Corcoran's background was in the American use of balloons in combat. In the Civil War, armies fighting for the Union flag were helped in the Virginia campaign by Thaddeus Rowe and eight military balloons of the Military Aeronautics Corps—flying hydrogen balloons for reconnaissance—powered by a portable hydrogen generator. They were known as 'Mr Lincoln's Air Force' and here Corcoran learned his skills.

"Their plan was to kidnap Gertrude by rising above the cloud line. A third party, Lamiche, an acrobat friend of Corcoran from the *Cirque Fernando*, would scurry down a rope and enter via the window opened by Hennetier, scoop up the 'Countess' in his arms, then speak through a tube—the tube featured so vividly in Celestine's account—signalling for Corcoran to whisk him skyward.

"When the latter turned on the air burner, the roar was heard by one patient who imagined it was a giant lion. And the sand in the courtyard, too incongruous to be a sand pit, was the deposited ballast to let the balloon make its escape. What Hennetier did not allow for, though, was the other inmate in the room . . . Celestine.

"What *she* saw entering and abducting Gertrude was not Lamiche in his goggles, helmet, straps and leather, but one of the bug-like space-imps from her damaged mind. She immediately conceived it as evidence her Moon Men had returned. Consequently, it was the only possible explanation for the magical vanishing of her fellow inmate. That is what she saw; *literally*—even, as the cloud cleared and the balloon dropped, an enigmatic sphere disappearing into the distance. You see, we were diverted when you insisted that the answer was in Celestine's madness, and crime—but that was a dead end. The true key was the mania of *Gertrude*."

Poe leaned forward to clap his hands, but agony seared across his shoulders, and he sank back in the pillow.

"Excellent work, Holmes." His voice was constrained by a tightness of breath. "Perhaps I should tussle with the Grim Reaper more often. Not only is my method in safe hands, I should say now, having solved a case entirely by your own diligence—*elle avoit vû le loup!*" Literally, she has seen the wolf. He used the old French saying for losing one's virginity.

My cheeks reddened. He laughed, but once again twinges of pain inhibited him from persisting with it, like a censorious Puritan.

"The next morning I returned to Salpêtrière with a heavy heart to give Dr Charcot the news. He was delighted with the arrest of Lamiche, shocked by the death of both Corcoran and Hennetier—I think he still harboured the idea that his warder was an honest man. I told him to sit down before telling him we had lost Gertrude too. He sighed. I showed him the treasure map. He gave a thin little laugh.

"He took me to Gertrude's room. It was full of such maps, from floor to ceiling, none of them the same or even similar. He told me she spent her days drawing diagrams of where her mythical fortune lay buried. This explained the beating the gang had given her in their increasing frustration, thinking she was keeping the truth from them. The truth was, there was no fortune. How many maps had she drawn for them, like these I saw before me? How many places had they searched before the island in the Lac Daumesnil? They would never find it, because the 'Contessa' did not exist, apart from in the head of a poor, abandoned woman wrapped in a fantasy.

"I asked if I could appraise Celestine Blot of the situation, hoping it might be some relief to the woman to know that the invaders were flesh and blood, and human flesh and blood at that. She listened patiently as I spoke of hot air balloons and the three men ..."

"But staunchly refused to believe it." Poe's reasoning went ahead of me. Naturally it did. But he was absolutely correct. "She still chose to believe in the Moon Men. Although, I should not say 'chose' because choice is nothing to do with it. She clings to her belief because it is all she has. Sane or mad, we all cling to what we know, or think we know, in order to protect ourselves. To Celestine, the unpalatable thing she cannot face is that there is no truth in Moon Men—only in madness."

He gestured to a jug of water. I poured a glass and pressed it to his lips. His eyes thanked me in a way that words could not. I sat and could only listen as he stared at the ceiling.

"In a future written by Jules Verne there may be a Captain Cook who strides amongst the mysteries of the heavens, conquering our deepest fears and wonder. We may discover non-human things, or they may discover us. But the most frightening voyage is always inside the mind."

His sunken eyes shifted in the dark hollows of his skull, fighting sleep. I wanted to take his hand, and perhaps he knew I did, because he moved it to shield a cough, then lay it flat across his chest.

"We are by nature unstable," he wheezed. "Sanity is not *de rigeur* but a condition of immense irrationality and perverse achievement. It is not our natural state. Our natural state is madness, greed, violence, sexual urges, inner distress. And that is a terrible geography few dare to explore." I did not know then, but I know now, that he was giving me, as near as I ever heard it, the root of his fascination with crime.

"Your friend was lucky, Mr Holmes." The lanky young doctor who entered was, to my surprise, an Englishman. "The knife struck a glancing blow on the infraspinous fossa of his left scapula. Fortunately, the blade missed the lung on that side, and the aorta. The muscle's taken a bit of a pounding, which accounts for the rather dramatic loss of blood . . ."

"With a complex anastomosis of arteries running over it," said Poe, "that would hardly be unexpected."

The doctor smiled. "But he's on the road to recovery, and he'll be right as rain if he takes care, a good deal of rest, and most importantly, if he leaves those stitches alone. I used silk rather than catgut, by the way, so they won't dissolve. You'll need a doctor to take them out when you're back in Paris."

His name was Tom Stamford, and I shortly learned he was on his way back to London to work at Bart's. I made him promise to allow me to take him to dinner, by way of thanks for saving my good friend's life, the minute I returned to England.

"*If* he returns," mumbled Poe.

Stamford replied he would be delighted to renew acquaintance on our home shore. That was, of course, not to happen for another two years, at which time I had rented rooms in Montague Street, round the corner from the British Museum, and had just begun to embark on my solo career as a consulting detective. It was Stamford who not only gave me use of the chemical laboratory at Bart's, but also introduced me to a certain doctor, with whom he had served at the battle of Maiwand.

Within weeks, as a direct consequence of the case of Celestine Blot, *Monsieur le Professeur* put hypnosis on his teaching programme at Salpêtrière. But not until six years later did an ambitious young doctor join the hospital, attracted by the great name of Charcot. Sigmund Freud had done a nice job on brain sections in Vienna, but wanted to show them to the Master, little realising that at Salpêtrière the madwomen were always centre stage, and he would be the disoriented witness of the hysteria of hysteria. Besotted, then critical of Charcot's theories, he went on to devise a markedly different concept of the condition. Hypnosis solidified the relationship between authority and patient: the love affair between madness and medicine was consummated at last. It seemed only fitting that Poe, whose tales foreshadowed psychoanalysis, had a hand in making it the universal idea of the century to come.

I often remember my last picture of Charcot with Celestine, and that last glimpse of her expression, so like a child pleasing her father. He had domesticated this wild beast, this idea of Baroque abandon, this whirlwind. Celestine was his star, his pearl, his masterpiece of exquisite porcelain, taken away to be wrapped up again, until his gaze required her. Perhaps in such unusual circumstances the attention a patient gets due to her illness is all? And the loss of it unthinkable?

By uncanny coincidence, years later, out of the blue and "in a fit of madness," Jules Verne's twenty-five year old nephew Gaston—an intelligent and hardworking young man with a job in the Ministry of Foreign Affairs—fired at him twice with a revolver. Luckily, only one shot hit Verne, in the foot, but the wound festered and the bullet could not be extracted, giving him a permanent limp. I could not help wondering, peculiarly, if Gaston too had believed in Moon Men—and what Celestine might conclude from the occurrence if she knew. Needless to say the attack, like hers, was hushed up in the press. Meanwhile Gaston was taken away for observation, certified insane and spent the rest of his life in a succession of clinics, finally dying in Luxembourg during WWI.

I next heard of the author when I was investigating "The Dancing Men," and he achieved what he had threatened long before, namely a new, improved version of *The Narrative of Arthur Gordon Pym* in the form of *Le Sphinx des Glaces (The Sphinx of the Ice Realm)*. As I expected and feared, Verne set out to make it "more true to life and more interesting" by rendering mundane everything Poe left in suspense, scrubbing the fantasy elements and laying on his dread realism with a trowel, even explaining away the vast, shrouded giant as an iceberg—and the rest as Pym's hallucinations. The man might have been a prophet to some and a literary hero to many, but I could not help feeling the vast unknowable was reduced immeasurably by his pen.

"It all ends in a mystery, because it has to," Poe told me of his supposedly-unfinished novel during our last months together. "Doesn't our own narrative always end in Death? Who is to say that it ends not in darkness but in whiteness?" The whiteness of the blank page, perhaps.

I was quite sure that his tale—*Pym's* tale—is about a journey into Mystery itself. Poe's journey. Always. Unerringly.

"The ending did not evade me," he'd said on the station platform at Amiens. "It presented itself as inevitable."

Poe was the failed romantic. Verne the idealist. The Frenchman's life had been a full one. He'd written millions upon millions of words, enchanting generations. With no more than pen and ink he could transport the reader to the slopes of Popocatépetl or the sands of Timbuktu—yet at the end he became disillusioned, fearful of the fate of his beloved science and knowledge against the rise in power of industry and that dark, tentacled creature from the depths—finance.

Thankfully, the Frenchman died before seeing the monumental horrors that were to consume Europe—machines as a perversion of scientific progress, created for carnage; not for enlightening and liberating Mankind, as he dreamed, but providing ever more ingenious methods of self-destruction.

Now, Lestrade, old fellow, sentimentality has blurred my vision, or the light bulb has—I am not sure which, but it is time I gathered these arthritic bones and took them to bed. When I wake it will be another day, alas, without the company of that formidable brain, that gracious and insufferable poet and detective whose prodigious brilliance moulded me, and whose secret life I have carried as a burden all these years. Hard as it has been, it is but a feather when I think of what he gave me.

You will see appended to this file a letter I received shortly after the case of the missing patient at Salpêtrière. The handwriting and signature will confirm that everything you have read is true.

~~~

A Sh. Holmes

Amiens, 26 9ème. 1879

Cher Monsieur

 You will forgive me for undertaking my own "detective work" to find your address.

 I have just read in the press of the remarkable arrest of Lamiche and the fatal shooting of Corcoran in the Bois de Vincennes—and am deeply saddened that the patient from Salpêtrière, Gertrude Socha, was not saved. However my purpose in writing is not to offer my condolences, or congratulate yourself, M. Holmes, or your partner, 'Auguste Dupin' in solving the mystery. The article only served as catalyst to express what has been raging in my heart like a tempest.

 Moments after I closed the door at the end of our meeting at my home, I was overcome by the idea that either I had been in the company of a doppelgänger *of miraculous accuracy or the gentleman who had stood before me was Edgar Poe himself. Yes, older—twenty or more years older than the famous Daguerrotype that now graces every frontispiece of his* Tales of Mystery and Imagination. *Yes, without the customary moustache—but the physiognomy, the great forehead, the creased brow, the straight nose, the small lips—and not least, the* soupçon *of an American accent, almost inaudible but emphatically* there—*was incontrovertible! I almost fainted from the shock! I stumbled. My servants gathered round me—but no, I said nothing of what I knew to be true.*

 And I shall say nothing—*much as I wish to visit Paris, or rather Olympus, now, and embrace my literary god*—I shall not, *and though it wounds me,* never will!

 If there is some reason Poe seeks anonymity, let him enjoy it. If he flees from the limelight, or debtors, or aggrieved women, or aggrieved men—*let him. I owe him worlds and it is the least I can do to keep my*

*mouth shut on the matter—even if I cry into my pillow, not that there
will be no more stories, but tears of joy that he* lives!

*And so, it is with astonished excitement but the deepest respect
for him, I tell you that no soul will hear of this from my lips. He would
cringe at the cliché, and no doubt castigate me for it, but his secret is safe
with me.*

'Dupin' is on his own Voyage Extraordinaire *now. He is 'Nemo'—
he has no name. But he shall always have my love.*

Votre bien Dévoué
Jules Verne

The Three Hunchbacks

MY MIND IS A CORNUCOPIA. It houses libraries. But this morning I cannot remember where I put my slippers. How the mighty are fallen.

The only conversation I ever hear is the hum of the hives. Loneliness, to me, has never been a villain to be thwarted. Befuddlement is. I pray that the work of my pen will keep the slow creep of fragility at bay, but I am under no illusion: old age is a one-way street. There is no heroic about-turn. No derring-do. Yesterday might be an empty hole, a confusion—yet, paradoxically, my early days grow more vivid day by day. However, science and a life of observation tell me that distinction may not last. My greatest fear is that my memory will let me down before I have had time to recount these exploits, and then they shall be gone forever.

I have heard a rat in the attic. Its scampering gives me broken sleep, which is why I am here at my desk before dawn breaks. I saw a large, bearded man standing in my bedroom, berating me. "You have done nothing of worth in your lifetime." But my father was neither large nor bearded. It was a dream, I know, but I cannot dispel, even now, as the window pane brightens with the rising sun, the dire feelings his intrusion evoked.

In the past, dreams did not perturb me. Or I used to say as much. Such secrets I kept imprisoned within me. The time has come to let them out.

Once upon a time, dreams and bizarre reality were indistinguishable. Sometimes I faced them with a steely eye and a soldier at my side. And before that—a dream within a dream—in the company of an American whose mental prowess dwarfed my own.

I loved them both.

If you believe nothing else as you read these pages, Lestrade—
believe that.

Holmes

⌒

"I have been anticipating your arrival," said Edgar Allan Poe, "ever since the bells of Notre Dame chimed thirteen."

It had been an unaccountably sultry autumn, that of 1875, a rare humidity conjuring the *eau de toilette* of Paris from the sewers, a reminder that civilisation could not hold back every type of nastiness. If, indeed, any nastiness at all.

My mentor in the art of ratiocination had investigated two extraordinary cases back to back. The first had concerned a locomotive stoker who had disposed of his father's body parts in the furnace of his engine, and might have succeeded in getting away with his crime, had not his own guilt manifested into the most tenacious insanity, taking the form of a belief that the monstrous vehicle now desired to consume more human flesh, having acquired a distinct taste for it. Five more disappearances transpired as the fireman tried to satiate the hunger of "La Bête," finally realising the only way he could break its grip on his soul was to crash the train at high speed. Luckily, Poe and I were able to intervene in time to avoid the loss of hundreds of Parisian lives. Our other investigation was the notorious theft of *The Languishing Venus* from the Grand Musée Pierre Spitzner in the Pavilion de la Ruche—a life-size wax anatomical sleeping beauty whose uncannily realistic body opened up like a cabinet to reveal all manner of obstetric and biological delights. Within days Poe had enabled the baffled *Préfecture de Police* to find the stolen exhibit in a private collection and return her to her rightful owner. Said to have been based on Louis XV's mistress Madame du Barry, she reclined on white silk, her expression approximating that of religious ecstasy, with lustrous hair, glass eyes, a string of pearls round her exposed neck symbolising the passing vanity of human life, and a bosom gently heaving by dint of a clockwork mechanism hidden inside. I couldn't help wondering if my tutor, who had once declared famously that there is nothing so poetic as the death of a beautiful woman, would have liked to keep the somnolent nude for himself. Perhaps in assuming the whimsical but entirely serious disguise of "C. Auguste Dupin"—master of deduction and logical extrapolation—he had, of necessity, relegated his perverse side, which so informed his fiction, to the past. Nevertheless, it was inevitable that E. A. Poe took an interest in E. A. Poe in the years subsequent to his death.

Twenty-six had passed since he had been buried in an unmarked plot—on a "dark and gloomy day, not raining, but just kind of raw and threatening" as the sexton put it—and in this month, October, the original site overgrown and sorely untended, his bones had been disinterred and relocated close to the front of the church. One witness present wrote they had seen "all that was mortal of Poe when the coffin was opened at the second burial" and reported the unmistakable forehead "easily discerned."

Poe grunted in his armchair as he read those words in the *New York Tribune*, knowing, as I did, that the man in the grave was not himself at all but an accidental double. He then quoted aloud for my benefit, in a voice heavy with sarcasm, that his cousin, Neilson Poe, at the graveside, had called him "one of the best-hearted men that ever lived." Perhaps, in spite of his sometimes breathtaking arrogance, on a deeper level Poe could never accept his own worth in the eyes of others. Or perhaps (using the art of deduction myself) the news item only brought back a haunting and unpleasurable memory: that he had used the fortuitous death of a stranger to enable his escape from a turbulent old life in America to a *tabula rasa* in Europe. Yet, even he, surely, could not have been unmoved by the thought that Miss Sara Sigourney

Rice and countless benefactors had raised funds for a new and proper monument to Baltimore's neglected poet? Though it must be strange to see your tomb in all its splendour in an etching when you are still very much alive on the other side of the world.

At the sound of the unexpected knock on our apartment door, Poe let the *Tribune* drop into his lap with a sigh of inconvenience and sipped the dregs of his coffee. I knew by now it was almost pointless to ask rhetorically who this could be, but thought he might have been so immersed in reports of his own re-interment that his sensory acuity might be momentarily diminished.

Nothing of the sort.

"Get a madeleine and a glass of milk for the altar boy at the door, my dear Holmes," he said, as I rose from my seat. When speaking English, as we invariably did in private, his accent was a strange, unique hybrid of French and an effete Maryland drawl. "He has come with an important message from the Cathedral. He'll surely need a chair, too, as he is severely out of breath."

As I gripped the door handle I frowned in puzzlement.

"Come along! We have five senses, not just sight! Sound, when properly observed, can be a universe, a revelation!" He folded the newspaper and flung it aside. "You have lived in this building for months and your lack of basic observation is astonishing. There is a loose tread on the stairs halfway up that makes a distinctive creak when a weight is put upon it, and having calibrated this for some time, I have come to the conclusion a heavy adult male makes a noise of quite a different pitch from a woman, or indeed a small child. Only a child, used to being unobtrusively polite, would knock on the panel of the door so lightly. Practice enables one to decode such signals with ease. Oh, and he is out of breath because I can hear him panting quite clearly, which means his message is important. A child does not consult a detective unless on behalf of an adult, and it is self-evident that something is amiss at God's House that God, in all his omnipotence, cannot resolve."

My master's deductive flourish was confirmed as I opened the door to a chubby *enfant de choeur* with flushed cheeks grasping an envelope as if his mortal soul depended upon its safe delivery. And, yes, he was panting. It was then that Poe, almost distractedly, pronounced he had heard the bells strike thirteen, and drew up a chair for our visitor, who handed the letter to me. It was addressed with one word—*Dupin*. I passed it straight to Poe, who ran each of its four edges under his nose, inhaling.

"Who sent you?" I enquired.

"Smoke. Incense . . ." Poe touched his index finger to the ink and dabbed it to the tip of his tongue. I had no doubt he could tell not only the brand of ink, but from which proprietor it had been purchased. But he said nothing: his brain, as ever, had caught fire with innumerable analyses, not all of which were verbalised. "It is evident from his hesitation that he has been sworn to secrecy by the Archbishop, weren't you, *mon petit ami?*"

"Not the Archbishop, *monsieur*. The Dean."

"Ah! Yet this is the seal of Archbishop Joseph-Hippolyte Guibert. So, the Archbishop has delegated to a lesser mortal, and he to an even lesser one. Quick with the cake and milk, Holmes, I beg you. The boy is near to expiring." Poe plucked an Algerian dagger from the wall, sliced open the envelope, and read the contents whilst I fetched sustenance for our emissary. "Shocking . . . Utmost need of . . . Depends on your . . . *tum-tee-tum* . . ." I returned and watched the glass of milk empty and the boy wipe his lips with the back of his wrist. "Faithful in Christ . . ." Poe looked up and met my eyes. His own now shone with the spark of intellectual excitement. At moments like this he transformed from a sixty-six-year-old man with thinning hair into someone nearer my own age of twenty-one. It was not every day we were summoned to the aid of the Catholic Church or by the most important religious figure in the *Archdiocèse de Paris*, perhaps in the whole of France, to solve the mystery of—what? "*Au nom de Dieu, venez vite* . . . In the name of God, come with haste."

"In the name of God, Montresor," I whispered with a smile. "Indeed. And if God calls, who am I to dawdle?"

⁓

I dreaded to think when Poe had last stepped inside a place of worship; even his marriage to Virginia Clemm had taken place at a boarding house. It was certainly not his natural habitat. When instructing me on types of madness, he had made it plain that only centuries of social habit had prevented devout religious observance being catalogued alongside other definitions of loss of reason. Faith could neither be measured nor tested, and as such warranted no place in his science of perceptual rigour, other than as an aberrant side effect of being human. Therefore, Notre Dame, for all its resplendent glory of stained glass, gothic arches and flying buttresses, which simply as an expression of creative endeavour took my breath away, was of no more potent interest to him than the Zoological Gardens, its denizens an alien species about whom he exhibited no interest or curiosity *per se* other than in relation to the matter in hand. To say that this made him an innately aloof figure as we strode into the high-vaulted nave would be an understatement.

"I hear they have a fragment of the True Cross here," I said, as the altar boy's footsteps scuttled away.

"And one of the Holy Nails from the Crucifixion. So too have roughly two thousand churches across the world. It's remarkable. Our poor Lord and Saviour must have looked like a porcupine."

In those early years of my education Poe's atheism rankled. He never tired of telling me that in 1677 a mob of righteous Christian Londoners burned live cats in a wicker pope, to mimic the pontiff's cries of agony in hell. Yet standing in that building, I remembered that during the French Revolution Notre Dame had been rededicated to the so-called Cult of Reason, its treasures destroyed and plundered; statues of Biblical kings beheaded; its thirteenth-century spire torn down—and wondered if that was what Poe wanted. Even the Virgin Mary had been replaced by "Lady Liberty". Surely that was merely replacing one dogma with another?

Poe rotated, wasting none of his time appreciating the beauty of the light falling through the rose window in the West Front, instead eyeing like a hawk the movements of priests in their soutanes, whispering and congregating in gossipy clusters around the aisles. He asked me what I deduced. I said it was clear that something was up. They were observing daily practice, but I felt an abiding sense that something was wrong.

"Not untrue, but imprecise," he added. "I noticed at least three of the clergy in their perambulations glancing in the direction of the crypt."

"I want to know why they have called upon us, and not the police."

"The Catholic Church, like many hermetically-sealed organizations, prefers to keep its affairs very close to its chest. Some of its secrets will never see the light of day, if they have their way. Perhaps this will be one of them."

The boy summarily returned with the *Doyen de la Cathédrale*, head of the canons of *Le Chapitre* appointed by the Archbishop, wearing choir dress: cassock, white rochet trimmed with lace, a violet mozzetta and biretta fitting to his role as apostolic administrator, and pectoral cross on a chain round his neck. His stole indicated he had either finished, or was about to begin, the midmorning Liturgy of the Hours. He chose not to shake our hands. Perhaps we were required to kiss his.

"Dupin," he said, with a brusqueness indicating he didn't warm to the idea of accepting outsiders into his realm.

"At your service."

"I trust so." Dewlaps gave him the impression of a disgruntled hound. "Your expertise precedes you. The horrific affair of 'La Bête' reached even the ears of His Excellency. I fear we can present to you a mystery its equal in abnormal ghastliness. One not even the most grotesque of imaginations could conjure."

"Mystery. Imagination . . ." said Poe. "I am definitely your man."

The cleric gave no further word of explanation, merely passing a large, rusty key nervously from hand to hand, his face as bloodless as those of the two priests who obediently flanked him, each carrying a candle lantern.

"Please accompany me, gentlemen."

"Where are you taking us?" I asked, as we followed.

"To the crypt," said Poe.

He was absolutely right. Soon we faced an iron-barred gate, beyond which stone steps led steeply down into darkness. The priests looked behind us furtively, as if our task was illicit or obscene. The *Doyen's* key rattled in the ancient lock. His fingers trembled uncontrollably, so much so that I began to think it was a symptom of a medical ailment. But no, it was only a symptom of extreme agitation.

Centuries gave way as the door wailed open and, for a moment, I thought I heard a more sonorous, more human wail—like that of a lost and pitiful soul. But that was, of course, impossible.

As we descended an age-old stench, redolent of tombs and mortality, hit our nostrils. We stepped through another arch and gateway, more sibilant than the first. Its shrieking echo multiplied. I kept my head bowed. Our shadows sloped ahead of us, flickering and eager. The walls, spongy with damp, were layered in a slimy sheen of black algae and hydrophilic mould. I was aware that we had entered the very underbelly of the magnificence above—yet I could hardly have known this was merely the prelude to my terrible adventure. One that would almost cost me my sanity. And my life.

There it was again—the *wail.* And not a ghostly illusion, but one belonging to a living creature all too real. And all too *close* . . .

Poe's eyes narrowed to slits.

The *Doyen* paused too, and looked back, as one of the lanterns yellowed his already wan features. "Come. Not far now. We had to put him here, away from the congregation. You will know why when you see him."

I heard chains rattling, and something shifting its mass and limbs in the gloom—something bulky and inelegant and constrained. Malformed jaws made a kind of bovine moan. Stiff with terror, I was nonetheless desperate to see whatever it was they were keeping away from the eyes of good Christian folk, and what had necessitated an alarum call to the most celebrated detective in Paris.

The young priests aligned themselves either side of the next archway, lanterns aloft.

Within the hefty grille was a door and, beyond the door, a vault. Our guide beckoned Poe and me forward and the lanterns were lowered to illuminate what lay within. Poe gazed without hesitation. *Fear is the enemy,* he had taught me. *Dark imagination, the enemy. It will destroy you, if you let it. What is* true *is your only saint. See. Observe. Ratiocinate.* I knew I must look, but before I did, I saw the *Doyen* shut his eyes tightly and make the sign of the cross.

A ball of flesh and rags rolled into the shallow pool of light. A mouth opened slackly. Silvery spittle hung like a martingale between lower lip and chest. The knuckles of one hairy hand dragged on the dirt of the flagstones, then a twisted elbow locked in position to lift its hulk painfully into view.

The thing was barely human. It had the constituent parts of a human being, yes—but thrown together as if by a vindictive and uncaring God. One eye was blind. One ear missing: a twisted bud of flesh all that appeared in its stead. The left leg seemed boneless, dragged along under him. I suspected unilateral lower limb shortening and pelvic tilt due to contraction of the hip. Most notable of all, as he scuttled, beetle-like, head bowed in bewilderment, I saw an excessive curvature of the thoracic spine.

"Holmes." The master demanded of his pupil.

"Kyphosis," I elaborated my prognosis in a whisper. "With an abnormally raised scapula accompanied by scoliosis with lateral convexity on the left side, severely limiting shoulder movement. His limbs appear atrophic, but normal joint creases and skin condition rule out *arthrogryposis multiplex congenital*. Such extreme musculoskeletal deformity could have been embryonal, osteopathic, myopathic, due to a miscellaneous group of connective tissue distresses, fracture, or indeed, as is more likely, familial." I wished Poe had not educated me so well on the subject of human pathology. The fact was, Notre Dame had its *chimières*—its gargoyles—on the outside, yet this one was within. And not carved in stone, but a living being in flesh and blood.

"He was found this morning before Matins, in the bell tower, swinging on the rope of the great bourdon bell," said the *Doyen*. "It took five men to subdue him. He bit one and broke the nose of another with a crack of his skull."

"Some people take badly to being subdued," said Poe. "Often it depends on those doing the subduing."

"We had no choice. Imagine if the story were to get out."

"The hunchback of Notre Dame. A figure from between the covers of a book. Not unlike Jesus Christ."

Too weary to show he was offended by the remark, the cleric sighed. It struck me the man was both out of his depth and not necessarily unkind of temperament. Poe, on the other hand, refused to countenance that religion could be responsible for anything but the ills of dominance, cruelty and narrow-mindedness. In some instances, to my mind, the narrow-mindedness was his own.

"One jester from the chorale named him Quasimodo. Which comes from the Introit at Mass: '*Quasi modo geniti infantes, rationabile, sine dolo lac concupiscite*'— used with special reference to the newly baptised."

"And from Victor Hugo," Poe added.

"My poor, poor fellow . . ." I crouched down and addressed the cripple before us, softly. "Pray, what is your name?"

The wretch only gurgled and shunned my approach as if I intended to beat him.

"He cannot answer," said the *Doyen*. "He has no tongue. We gave him paper and graphite but he cannot write, or has refused to."

While these words were spoken Poe had walked into the darkness and in the dim penumbra of the lanterns stood behind the captive, whose pathetic and swollen eyes were still fixed on me with an animal distrust. Poe gently lifted aside a strand of the wretch's torn shirt, in order to get a better look at his neck and upper back. Bare skin was exposed for an instant before the figure exploded, snarling, lashing out with its good arm, and a finely-muscled one at that—Poe back-stepped swiftly, chin tucked in his cravat, only narrowly avoiding a hefty blow because of the manacles hindering his attacker—but his heel spilled a bowl of water surrounded by crusts of bread. The hunchback wrapped his limbs around himself and crabbed back into the solace of gloom. The two priests began to move but they were already too late to be of use. Their superior gestured at them to keep their distance.

"This is the mystery, then," I thought aloud. "Who is he?"

"I cannot yet answer that," said Poe, rejoining us. "But I do know this is a crime. And I also know who is responsible." He straightened his collar and examined his cuffs. "Holmes, send our red-headed choirboy back to the Rue de la Femme-Sans-Tête. Ask him to tell Le Bon to return with a blunderbuss and stay here day and night until I give the order to stand down. We need to keep this gentleman safe from those who might do him harm." He was heading for the exit, the bobbing lanterns trying to keep up with him.

"I don't understand."

"You shall."

"Where are we going?"
"To the Catacombs! Without a moment's delay!"

⌒✕

It was enough to have one fictional character—Dupin—made manifest; to have another, the famed Hunchback of Notre Dame, defied all reason. Not for the first time, nor the last, I glued myself to Poe's heels like a gun dog as we found the former city gate, the insensitively named Barrière d'Enfer and gained access to the *Catacombes* from a building in the Place Denfert-Rochereau. The first visits to the renovated mausoleum had begun after the 1814-15 war, only a few times a year, but after too many instances of vandalism and thievery it limited its access to 'permission-only'—then closed completely due to ecclesiastical opposition to sacred remains, as they put it, being on public display. Eventually bowing to public pressure, the government had only within the last year allowed it to reopen bi-weekly, on the first and third Saturday of each month. I did not even have time to point out to Poe it was a Wednesday. He had already picked the padlock and swung open the entrance gate.

We procured a couple of whale-oil lamps the tour guides used, lit them, and took to the three hundred steps spiralling down to the pitch-black subterranean realm. In contravention of his advancing years, Poe flew ahead of me.

"Have you read Hugo?" His high-pitched lilt echoed.

"Not every word."

"Good! *Les Misèrables* is a potboiler, beloved of the masses—never a good recommendation. Social misery invariably causes misery in the reader. 'Demain, Dès L'Aube' and 'Torquemada' have something to be admired as poems, but his novels are as heavy as house bricks, and half as subtle. And *Notre-Dame de Paris* did little more than shame the city into restoring a much-neglected edifice. Not exactly the prime purpose of literature." I was used to Poe's disdain for any author who had achieved more acclaim in their lifetime than he had—not counting Dickens, whom he had met in the United States Hotel in Philadelphia in 1842, and held in high esteem, later calling his ghost story "The Signal Man" an immaculate and faultless example of the form. With this notable exception, he turned bitterness into an art form, albeit a spasmodically entertaining one.

I could hear the gurgling of spring water travelling along a hidden aqueduct.

We entered a long, narrow hallway without any succour of light, save that which we carried ourselves. The concave walls of mortared stone seemed to be bending in around us, an illusion exacerbated by the flickering of our lamps.

"Yet Hugo is the key . . ."

"Poe. Slow down." I struggled to keep up, both physically and mentally. "Quasimodo was a foundling raised by the Church, a grotesquely deformed bell ringer who died at the gibbet in the 1400s, if I recall correctly. Years afterwards his bones were found conjoined with Esmeralda's in death, but that was in the book. He never existed as a *real person*—not then, and certainly not now!"

"I said Hugo was the key. I didn't say his work was. At least, not *that* work." He kept moving without pause. "One of his more obscure stories is far more relevant—*L'Homme Qui Rit*. You've read it? Of course not." He didn't let up his pace. "I'll spare you his endless descriptions, but it is set in seventeenth-century England. The plot revolves around Gwynplaine, the titular 'Man Who Laughs', who, as a boy, had his mouth carved into a terrible, ineradicable grin by *Comprachicos*—a group of villains who get their income by abducting children, disfiguring them, and putting them on the street to work as beggars.

"Keep up! Hugo describes these *Comprachicos*—based on the Spanish word for 'child-buyers'—as having not only a specific history but deep and arcane knowledge regarding how to achieve their vile effects—an art as occult and brutal as the Chinese *lingchi* so beloved of the Hongwu Emperors. And to these, mutilation *was* an art—the snapping of limbs, the dislocation of joints, the removals of organs and bones—all to create the wonders and freaks that would evoke the utmost horror and the utmost pity in more fortunate passers-by. According to the novel, these heartless brigands are not limited to England or Spain, but meet regularly at secret locations throughout Europe to conspire and barter their infant wares."

"You're talking about the pages of fiction . . ."

"It was a persuasive work, and many horrified readers believed in it wholeheartedly, even as they found the idea repellent."

"Exactly! *Believed.* Superstitions around child-snatching have held sway for years—Good Lord, centuries!—usually directed at gypsies and Jews. A tribe frightened of strangers accuses another tribe of eating their babies. It's fantastical, but a small leap of imagination from seeing a growing population of cripples in the slums of Valencia to saying there must be a cripple factory hidden away somewhere."

"Which is exactly what was reported by newspapers in London within the last three years—a house in Highgate, behind the doors of which, quote: 'the mangling was done'—infants of tender years having their limbs subjected to unnatural twisting in a fashion likely to prepare them for a life on the streets of pecuniary benefit to their overlords."

"Newspapers!"

"There have been even those who opined that the creation of some of these perverse, artificial monstrosities was undertaken for the sake of art alone. Indeed, even before the publication of *L'Homme Qui Rit* in 1869, a man was accused in Troyes of trying to grow the wings of a swan on the back of a two-year-old child."

"Poe. What are you saying?"

"I'm saying, my dear Holmes, that just because fiction and rumour abound does not mean the subject has no glimmer of truth. The quality of hoax or canard may merely add to its cloak of invisibility, and suit those who practice it."

I was losing my bearings, and he could see it.

He turned to face me. Lantern to lantern.

"The hunchback we saw in the crypt did not exhibit congenital deformities. A cursory examination provided proof of that at the outset. His state was caused not by divine but by physical intervention."

Appalled, my mind raced to take this in.

"You were close when you said 'fractures'," Poe continued. "These malformations were inflicted with deliberate intent. I noted barely-healed incisions and sutures across his upper back, where a false hump had been inserted. My dear friend, I knew within seconds our *Monsieur Le Bossu* was not a biological aberration but a *man-made* monster."

I resisted the notion, and simultaneously realised I was resisting to protect my own sensibilities. The very idea of such inhuman manufacture was too abhorrent to be true—*but was it?*

"Come!" Poe had disappeared once again into the dark.

If he had a map, it was in his head. And if he knew this maze like the back of his hand—with all its twists and turns—why on earth would that be so? Had he been here *before*? And if so—*why?*

My brain was reeling.

We found ourselves before a stone portal. The entry point to the great ossuary. Poe raised his lamp and read the inscription before us, carved into its lintel.

"*Arrête! C'est ici l'empire de la Mort!*"

"Halt," I translated. "This is the Empire of the Dead."

We both stopped for breath. In the Empire of the Dead, breath was everything—and yet an obscenity. A taunt to the occupants. An insult. This was their country, not ours. We were visiting.

Our breath was visiting. And I couldn't shake the feeling that it was not wanted.

Poe showed no such alienation. He absorbed the dark with quiet relish, as a normal man might stand on a cliff-top and pause to take in the freshness of the air and sea breeze. It was noxious air that filled his nostrils, however—and yet he did not blanch. The atmosphere was chill, yet he did not shiver. I would almost say that for a brief moment he *basked*.

This *was* his natural habitat. The Necropolis. The bone yard. The restaurant of the Worm. The destiny we all await—but all deny. And when I'd thought earlier he knew that place . . . of course he did. It had been present with every stroke of his nib. It was his home.

"Our hunchback is the work of people in Paris whose sorry and despicable trade is to create beggars from kidnapped children: the unfortunates we look away from as we walk past, or toss a *sou* in their direction to salve our consciences—little knowing those coins go into the coffers of a criminal gang who run most of the pickpockets, forgers, touts, racketeers, tricksters, slave-runners, women of the night and assorted ne'er-do-wells in the city." His voice rebounded from the walls. "Like many a gang it is difficult to dig out. You can cut back every stalk, but its roots are like those of a virulent weed. The *Préfecture* have given up on the task, turning a blind eye, happy for the underworld to police itself. And so it persists, and flourishes. Sometimes I think if the truth were known it would shake Paris more than any revolution."

We stepped through the portal.

Thence began the halls and caverns of *L'Ossuaire* proper.

A thousand Grim Reapers stared out at me. The gathered ranks of the Dead, peering from their orbits into the depths of my soul, the motion of my passing illumination almost giving them the semblance of turning their heads. We were surrounded by shelf upon shelf of them, impeccably stacked. Occupying every inch of the walls and every corner of every alcove as far as the eye could see. Femur, skull, femur, skull . . . like the layers of a macabre cake.

I was unprepared for the grotesque beauty of the patterns, which almost, in sheer repetition of motif, resembled more a Moorish palace than a Christian sepulchre. Some were undoubtedly artistic in composition: a heart shape in one expanse created out of specially arranged crania and tibia. But this had not always been the case. In former years the quarry workings had been a haphazard and disrespectful depository for such objects, until de Thury, head of the Paris Mine Inspection Service, dedicated himself to improvements that would transform it into the renovated catacombs we now saw before us. The notion of using these newly renovated passageways for the Parisian dead had been born of the need to remedy overflowing cemeteries at the end of the previous century. It was also, pragmatically, born of the need for mine renovation, and human bones were utilised to reinforce the treacherously unstable tunnels of the extensive network—the 186-mile-long *carrières de Paris*—of which the Catacombs were but a small part.

It was not hard for me to picture the nocturnal processions along the route from Les Innocents and the Close de la Tombe-Issoire, with their black covered wagons carrying mounds of chalky sticks and globes, the grim decanting of those mortal remains from Saint-Étienne-des-Grès, Madeleine Cemetery, Errancis and Notre-Dame-des-Blancs-Manteaux . . .

We entered a round vestibule with a central pillar decorated with more skeletal artefacts, resembling something tribal, an Egyptian column where the language of mere hieroglyphics had been replaced by the remains of actual human beings.

Along the way we encountered other monuments, older than the present renovations, such as a fountain dubbed La Samaritaine. My lamp picked out its engravings as we moved through into another chamber full of headstones, memorials, funerary statues and other items liberated from their former locations.

All around us we saw marble tablets cut with Romanesque lettering, archways bearing inscriptions ... *PULVIS ET UMBRA SUMUS* ... *MORS ULTIMUM VITA BREVIS* ... *HOMO EX HUMO* ... or light poetic verse about the nature of our surroundings, some of it in dubious taste. My upbringing had taught me that death should be treated with decorum, however my sensitivity in such matters was another thing that Poe insisted be stamped out. Distractions got in the way of ratiocination, and were not to be tolerated. In short, I had to grow up. I wasn't that Yorkshire schoolboy with feelings inculcated by pulpit and parents anymore. It was fundamental to my progress as a scientific mind to leave such things behind me.

Poe removed the wooden barriers and ducked under dripping chains, entering a dark passage off the main drag to the inaccessible parts of the Catacombs, where the public were forbidden. He forged ahead, blind to warning signs that described such deviations from the path as dangerous. True to character, he ignored any such instructions from authority.

"Dear God, where are you taking us?"

"Fear not, dear boy," he said. "I have had occasion to come here before, though with the barrel of a pistol in the small of my back, and blindfolded. Still, my other senses provided an extremely accurate record of the route we followed ..."

"With such an aptitude you should have worked for the Sheriff of Nottingham. You would have flushed out Robin Hood and his Merrie Men in a week."

"In a day," Poe corrected me without a flicker of a smile, his eyes darting. "But these are not Merrie Men and their leader is not Robin Hood. He calls himself L'Eminence, and he holds the puppet strings of virtually all the crimes of Paris."

L'Eminence ...

I wondered what kind of ogre we were about to encounter if this was his lair. I did not have long to wait for an answer. It came all too abruptly as I felt the sharp edge of a dagger against the underside of my chin.

A thumb clicked back a pistol hammer. I saw the barrel of a flintlock pressed against the centre of Poe's forehead. It was held by a man in a coachman's cape, a sack-cloth hood shielding his face, save for an ugly slash of mouth.

"I have business with your master," declared Poe, as if the matter of having his brains blown out were tiresome. "If you pull the trigger you will not only destroy my most attractive feature, but have a seventy-five per cent chance of causing a cave-in that will obliterate us all. Possibly eighty." The monkish figure, clearly a dullard, took long seconds to comprehend his flow of words. Poe sighed with impatience and thrust his walking cane, surmounted as it was with a silver skull, at the fellow's chest. "Give him this."

Whoever it was behind me with the blade at my throat now patted my pockets with his free hand. Coming across a bulge in my waistcoat, he divested me of my Remington Derringer .41 calibre with pearl grips—a gift from a satisfied client, and my constant companion. The dagger tightened. My chin jerked higher.

"We are suitably intimidated," said Poe. "Now please proceed."

I think they were too bewildered to argue. My captor bustled me roughly into the dark. I could not see, but nevertheless heard the monk and Poe follow us closely. The knife digging into my gizzard made any thought of escape redundant. I simply had to bide my time, and observe what I could—which was absolutely nothing, just murk and damp. Moments later, a canvas sheet lifted where until then had been shadows, they bowed our heads, and we were obliged to bend double as they forced us through a wet, gullet-like passageway, opening into a vast cavern.

The dark did not yet reveal its secrets. A sound I had begun to hear in the passage suddenly became a loud and echoing cacophony of squealing, barking, growling, jabbering, and laughter. It stretched my powers of perception to their limit in trying to unravel the separate noises to identify them, and I failed miserably, such was the overwhelming impression that we had entered some fully-orchestrated hell. I almost did not want my eyes to become accustomed to the gloom, for fear of what might be revealed. Succumbing to my imagination, I fancied that vast, coiled creatures were floating, cobra-like, ready to strike. Their pairs of baleful eyes hovered and blinked, but as I gathered my senses I realised that these were not eyes turned towards us at all, rather scores of candles, naked or ensconced in lanterns, held in the grip of the manifold denizens of this place, filling a voluminous, domed space like a dripping, rough-hewn St Paul's, moving in a steady, shuffling rabble, towards us.

Most were in ragged dress, as far as I could discern. Others gave the appearance of threadbare dandies. One or two wore the tricorn hat and stockings of a bygone era, as you might expect of ghosts. Skinny, sorry souls stood shoulder to shoulder with thugs, hirsute mendicants, and hoary nautical types. I saw rogues and punch-up merchants beyond number, in all shapes and sizes, decorated with eye-patches, scars, grubby scarves, stained cuffs and cobwebby pompadours; rings on their fingers, blood under their fingernails, glee vying with suspicion in their gimlet eyes. I knew I was at the hub of the wheel, in the *Caverne des Voleurs* that Poe had been aware of for years—a veritable Parliament of villains, gathered en masse. The criminal underbelly of Paris made manifest.

The throng parted like the Red Sea, allowing a giant, bearded figure, enlarged by multiple layers of fur and clothing, to step forward. He held the silver-topped cane that had been handed him. From behind, a raucous cheer went up, an object sailed through the air and landed at our feet. At first, I had difficulty reconciling the inert lump of meat and bloodstained fur before me as a Jack Russell, its ribs still rising and falling in a desperate attempt to cling to life. The brown, wriggling things that had been dangling from it shot away into the darkness seconds before I'd identified their species.

Before the gap in the crowd closed up again I saw a circle of men hunched over a drum-like, circular enclosure, about waist-height. A grimy long-hair counted money into the outstretched palm of another. A third held a pocket watch. The clues led me to one inevitable conclusion: it was a pen constructed expressly for dog-fighting and ratting, and the base fraternity in our company were as avid in that pursuit as any gentleman in Soho.

The giant, whose flourishing beard was indistinguishable from his fur collar, placed his boot upon the dying terrier's head and put it out of its misery. I should like to say silence fell, but the act was met with complete indifference by the assembled as the Falstaff-like figure sat on a throne made out of bones. He gestured loosely, conferring his benediction and simultaneously ordering us to step nearer. Seeing him at close range, I was not sure he more resembled a pirate king or a Norse god: an Odin of the odious.

"Little man." His slit eyes were on Poe.

"You remember me?"

"I remember your bare-faced effrontery."

"The ransom was paid. The necklace returned. The benefit, mutual."

"You were lucky to escape with your tongue."

"On the contrary, Eminence, as I remember it, my tongue saved the rest of me."

Our gargantuan host emitted a grunt of a laugh—no more than that. It was neither friendly nor prolonged and I detected in its weariness an explosive and brittle temperament held barely in check.

He leaned forward. The yellowy flicker of candlelight picked out a wide head with temporal hollows well marked and strong cheekbones, pronounced brow ridges and a prominent glabella, with a sloping forehead reminiscent of William King's Neander-thal. More remarkable were periorbital crescents, the subcutaneous blood vessels bluish under his eyes, indicative either of dark pigmentation in his ancestry or a series of sleepless nights.

"You are not welcome here, long-nose." His upper lip curled. "I did you a favour last time, out of the goodness of my heart. Now the goodness has run dry. I have no heart."

"Evidently."

I'd had it confirmed time and again that Poe had no concept of holding back from antagonising those who might do us harm. If not his most abiding fault, it was his most dangerous. Especially as he jeopardised the life of a vulnerable young man in the process. Namely, myself. Yet the substantial brow of L'Eminence did not so much as furrow.

"Explain yourself. With your last breath."

"Oh, I had my last breath long ago," said Poe. "These breaths I take are all the more fulfilling for being *post mortem*."

I prayed for my companion to realise these people had neither the time nor the appreciation for wit. Our burly regent was the least receptive audience to humour imaginable, his simmering so unambiguous I could virtually feel the heat against my cheeks.

"You, in your arrogance, choose to venture here, where even the police in their numbers do not dare to tread? And you expect *me* to take your insults without retaliation?" Saliva glistened on his lower lip. "You are insane!"

"So they tell me," said Poe. "But I do not carve living human beings the way Michelangelo carved his marble."

Now a hush did descend. Horribly. Like a *piene forte et dure*.

I dreaded, as I often did, that Poe, whom people think to be made of fear itself, had no fear at all—not amongst human beings anyway: perhaps only within his own soul. I sometimes thought that the experience of watching his dear Virginia die in his arms sapped from him every ounce of the ability to care, even about himself. In so many ways he skirted self-destruction as if he felt the world owed him that, if nothing else. But I wished that urge, at that point, didn't happen to encompass my fate as well. In short, if terror had not rendered me mute, I should have pleaded with him to keep his mouth shut.

"Kill them," said L'Eminence, sinking back in his filthy furs. "I have no time for this. Take them in a sack and drop them in the Seine like unwanted kittens."

"You will not," said Poe, ignoring the gun barrel still at his temple. "I have been engaged to solve a mystery. A hunchback has been found in Notre Dame, with all the hallmarks of your work. Your *craft*. I will not leave until you have given up the man responsible. Or, I guarantee, your entire business enterprise will be shared with the citizens of Paris—and every one of you will be apprehended the minute you show your faces in daylight."

L'Eminence rose to his feet and hurtled towards us, his roar bouncing off the stones of the Catacombs.

"You dare? You *dare* to—?"

I saw Poe's head jerk back as the leonine figure's butcher hand grabbed him by the hair and held a straight-razor to his jugular.

Then the chant went up as the crowd of felons began jostling and hissing. Some jeered. Some shook their fists. Poe and I remained held steadfastly by the criminals either side of us.

"Kill him, kill him, kill him . . . !"

I am not sure to this day if L'Eminence hesitated in cutting my friend's throat, or whether he was halted in that desire by the sharp, bestial cry from the dark. Not a word. Not an entire word, in French, English, or any language I understood—it was simply a *cry*. But I did understand the plaintive distress buried within it.

The sound had an effect so immediate as to be alarming. The mob was immobilized. Some heads sank. Others turned. Some seemed startled and shuffled aside, poking their cohorts in the ribs to do likewise as the Red Sea parted a second time.

A silhouette—human, but barely so—shambled from the shadows into the half-light and I was convinced I had lost my mind.

It was a hunchback.

But not *any* hunchback. Straight away, to my astonishment, I recognised the lank straw-like hair. The blind orb. The fallen shoulder. The missing ear. The dragging foot. How could it be possible that the poor unfortunate we had seen in the crypt of Notre Dame could have been spirited to this place, clad differently, and was now before us? My brain clamoured to find reason in what I beheld.

The hunchback mewled a second time.

Without breaking eye contact with Poe, L'Eminence backed away from the detective, hot air gushing from his nostrils. His fat fingers fell to his side and he tossed the open-razor across the ground.

The hunchback groaned in two lilting, plaintive syllables, his lips roving like a cow chewing the cud.

"Brother . . ." Poe translated in a whisper.

Barely able to turn my head for the dagger under my chin, I stared at him.

L'Eminence walked away from us, bent over, shoulders rounded. The impulse to violence stillborn within him.

"By the stars and heavens . . ." Poe's words were directed at me, as he slowly came to realise the scale of his error: "They are brothers. They are his sons!"

L'Eminence turned. "And you accuse me of doing this to my own flesh and blood?" His face was wracked with the most fearsome pity I have seen in a man. One gnome, with dust-begrimed spectacles, picked up the straight-razor and came at Poe to finish the job.

"Stop!" I yelled, pointing at the hunchback before us. "Did you not hear him? He told you to stop! He has good reason. He knows this man can help you—even if you can't see it yourself."

The guttersnipe with the razor backed down.

"His name is Michel." L'Eminence gazed into the hunchback's doleful, watery eyes. Then he turned back to us, ferocious eyes unblinking. "Speak!"

I looked at Poe and hoped he had something to say. I knew for an absolute certainty that if he didn't, we were dead men.

"This son of yours was found in the streets of Paris several weeks ago. Your other son, more recently—that is, today, to be exact. Evidently you had no idea of his whereabouts until I just mentioned Notre Dame. You are already beside yourself with rage. You are a father and a leader. You cannot rule out the possibility that the perpetrator is amongst your own clan, since they have developed this abominable expertise, but you cannot countenance such betrayal and you keep that fear to yourself. Meanwhile you send word of a substantial reward to the wider criminal community. You know as well as any man that thieves will sell their own grandmother for the right pecuniary incentive—was it a rival gang, or person or persons unknown? You didn't know. And you still don't."

"Raoul. Where is he?" L'Eminence demanded, now like a prowling bear. "I want him here!"

"Raoul is being protected. For now."

"The *police?*"

"No, sir," said Poe. "He is a victim in this. I see no benefit in his being locked up behind bars. Not for the present, anyway. Tell me the other measures you are taking to find the individual who performed these horrors. It's your turn to speak. Do so."

L'Eminence was not used to being told what to do. But needs must, in this case, he must have thought, and complied, such was his desperation.

"Cyprien and his lieutenants have been scouring the boulevards, trying to find any scrap of information that might lead to the pervert responsible. They have been at it for weeks, working day and night, but . . ."

"Cyprien?"

L'Eminence nodded. "My eldest."

"*Shipp-rehh-ehh . . .*"

The name struggled with baleful musicality to escape from the tongueless mouth of his brother Michel.

"Excuse me," said Poe. "You have a *third* son? And you last saw him, when?"

"Last Thursday."

"And received a communication from him?"

"The same."

"Where was he? Quickly."

"The Marais."

"And since?"

No answer. "He is searching for the—"

Poe brushed away the gun barrel at the side of his head. "No. I fear your eldest son is in the hands of the mutilator as we speak. The same fate at this moment is being exacted upon him as upon your other two progeny. Unless we stop it."

His basic nature returning, L'Eminence grabbed Poe by the sleeve and then by the shirt collar.

"Tell me what you know!"

"I know nothing, but I shall find out what you and your brigands and brute force will not—and *can* not. If you value your son's wellbeing, let me go. Time is not on our side. With every instant the blade cuts skin." Poe pawed off the man's fists, marched over to one of the thieves, and snatched back his skull-topped cane.

"How do I know this isn't an elaborate ruse to get yourself out of our clutches?" said L'Eminence.

"Oh, clutches. I was forgetting men like you have *clutches* to be extracted from. But you must hang on to the quaint little eccentricities of your *milieu*."

"You ridicule me!"

"Not in the slightest. I ridicule your language. Which could be more creative. I do long for the more *creative* criminal." It was with intense ribaldry that Poe coped with an anxious situation. It was one of his many maddening contradictions. "Now, I apologise for my hellish mistake. My accusations were misplaced, but self-flagellation is useless. I can only make amends by finding the true *Creator Spiritus* behind these acts."

"My men are doing that very thing."

"They are self-evidently not, because they do not know who they are looking for. Because they have not perfected the art of deduction. Their actions are, at best, random and futile. You will not find Cyprien, but I can. Not by use of force, or violence, but by ratiocination."

The circle of ruffians chorused in a peal of derisive laughter at this claim, or at the manner in which it was delivered.

Poe spoke only to L'Eminence, directly. "You plan to laugh at your son's graveside? So be it."

Silence fell as L'Eminence thrust himself forward. "We have our own justice here, and our own laws, and they are not those of overground-dwellers."

"Very well. You would see your eldest crippled and maimed like your other two? Out of pride? That is not any kind of father I have experience of. And I have experience of two who leave much to be desired."

L'Eminence lunged forward at Poe. I stepped between them. But as quickly as I had evaded the dagger to my throat, my arm was twisted behind my back, almost to breaking point.

"Kill them both," growled the ogre, turning away. "I am bored with this prattle."

"Severin!" cried Poe. "Severin Écuyer! I know your name. As you know mine—C. Auguste Dupin. We obey different laws, but we are both men of principle. Of integrity. So, please. Understand this: I *will* succeed. I stake my reputation on it—and while that means nothing to you, admittedly, it means a great deal to me. And you will never know, unless you give me the chance. Yes, you will have two corpses to your credit—Dupin and Holmes, *magnifique!*—and that may give you some small passing glow of satisfaction, but the possibility that I was right will haunt you to your deathbed."

That simple fact hit its target, hard. Thank the Lord.

"If I let you go, how do I know you won't go straight to the *Préfecture* and the next thing we know they'll be swarming down here to arrest us?"

"You do not," answered Poe bluntly. "That is a fact. I deal in facts—which is why I shall solve this crime." He could see my arms were being held stiffly at my side by two thugs. "It is entirely in your gift whether we stay or go, and, as I point out again, the clock is ticking. That is what clocks do. They tick."

Poe walked over to me, to take me with him, but now it was the turn of L'Eminence to step between us two. I could see only the back of his head, which masked Poe from my line of vision.

"You have until dawn to bring my son back to me." L'Eminence took Poe's cheeks between his thumb and forefinger and drew him towards his eyes. "Or your young friend's death will be on your head. And it'll be a slow one, I promise you. And when it is over, I will deliver his skin to your doorstep. Neatly folded, like a delivery of laundry. And his skull and bones will become part of the walls of these Catacombs forever. For the tourists to see for years to come." He held his other hand aloft like a commanding general at Waterloo. "Take him!"

A jab of knuckles hit the side of my face and my feet were kicked from under me. I felt myself dragged away into the shadows, beefy arms hooked round my elbows and someone's forearm across my windpipe. I kicked to get a grip on the floor but my ankles trailed ineffectively. I could hardly get air in my lungs but knew my comfort was not these creatures' priority. Probably the reverse. A boot cracked into my side. I wondered, half-choking, if I might hear Poe cry out in sympathy or alarm, with some message of comfort, but I heard nothing. He had mastered his feelings, and I was a mere novice. Whereas he would have seen stark terror etched in my countenance, if I could have seen his own, I feared I may have seen no emotion at all.

⤙

"Bonne nuit et fais des beaux rêves!" Good night and sweet dreams.

Cackling laughter faded. Blinking, I could make out the thin lines of the edges of the trap door that had slammed over my head. Then it too had gone, they had gone, and I was alone. Abandoned to the dark.

The direction in which I had been dragged, and the distance involved, provided no doubt in my mind that I had been deposited into the empty rat pit, which had since been sealed over with a substantial cover.

I twisted onto my knees. To my discomfort I found myself unable to sit up. The nearest approximation necessitated a head bent forward and a painfully twisted neck. I resolved therefore to lie on my back, knees bent, with my hands flat against the wooden slab above me.

I tried not to think of the horrid nature of the sport the criminals had enjoyed minutes earlier. My extensive studies into crime had informed me that, years ago, at the Westminster Pit in Duck Lane, a dog called Billy the Raticide had set a record by killing twenty rats in seventy-one seconds—and lost one of his eyes in the process. Soon it was being wagered for twenty sovereigns to kill a hundred rats in less than twelve minutes, which Billy dutifully did, a record held until Jemmy Shaw's black-and-tan Bull Terrier Jacko became the star of the Haymarket rat pits. Even as I thought of it, the residual stench of the dead creatures seemed to get all the more powerful.

I turned over and put my shoulders against the trap door, but it was impossible to shift. Bolts and hinges had been secured in place, so I busied myself to see if there might be some other means of escape, running my fingers along the floor and corners of my confines, groping around the edges hand over hand until I had come full circle, discovering nothing of worth except an approximation of the size of my prison.

I retraced my route, this time sliding my fingers over the walls of the pen, finding them to be cold, hard and made up of slabs of stone, many ground to a fine finish—in fact, a remarkably smooth aspect. I paused and let my fingertips explore more detail and found deep indentations, horizontal, vertical, curved, all of the same shallowness. Like a blind person reading Braille, I discerned chiselled Roman letters—"ICI REPOSE"…"REGRETS ETERNELS"…"PERPÉTUITÉ"—Gradually it became clear to me that they had been constructed with the shards of discarded headstones.

Truly, I was amongst the dead now.

They surrounded me. Their families, their marriages. The dates of their births and deaths. "MARIE BOUCHER FILLE DE GEORGE BOUCHER"…"ALBERT TEXIER PRIEZ POUR LUI"…"MORIN"…"MALOUN"…"CHOVET"…My breath had become a whisper and I almost fancied I heard their whispers in return, telling me this was not only their tomb but my own.

With a shudder I huddled, elbows on knees, and went through my times tables to keep such thoughts at bay. This would have pleased my mathematics teacher no end. After that I recited the atomic weights of the sixty-two elements of Mendeleev's periodic table as published in *Zeitschrift für Chemie*. The various symptoms of poisoning, from arsenic to strychnine. The tell-tale physiognomy of various professions. The personality traits to be gleaned from handwriting. Common flaws in the counterfeiting of bank notes. The aliases of criminals still at large … To an outsider it might have seemed as though I was praying. Which, in a way, I might have been. But the stifling lack of air, thick with rodent urine and dog blood swiftly brought me back to the here and now.

Yet again the thought of the poor animals' suffering turned my stomach and I tried to focus back upon the 'homework' Poe had given me over the months of schooling I'd experienced.

It didn't work. I cursed my inability to apply my mind as he applied his. Or did he? What did I know for certain? Only that he blinded me with his arrogance most of the time. Perhaps that was my real purpose to him—as a fool and underdog, and not an apprentice at all.

And that gnawed at me. What if my master Poe—the celebrated detective "Dupin"—was not a master at all? What if ours was not an intellectual pursuit so much as a dependency, or wish-fulfilment? Nothing more genuine than actors prancing on a stage?

What if—and this was the nub—he should *fail?*

Bile ravaged my throat, hot as lava. I tried to resist images of my becoming an *écorché*, as L'Eminence promised, flayed alive like St Bartholomew, my tanned skin being used to bind a pocketbook. At least Burke, the bodysnatcher, had been granted more of a hereafter . . .

Wait, I reassured myself. As it was, my skin was still attached to my anatomy, correct? Though an unbidden spasm told me a rib on my left side was probably broken, and I could feel a black eye incrementally bulging like a balloon and becoming more sore by the second, I tried to remain positive. I would see a doctor soon, wouldn't I? Well, wouldn't I?

The sudden thought that my captors might never return became palpable, along with it the idea that Poe would never again return to the Catacombs, because he had not found the Mutilator, as he swore he would.

Much as I tried to fight the conclusion, I became convinced I would die here of loss of breath. Consequently, my breathing quickened immeasurably—even as it did, and unstoppable though it was, I clearly recognised the symptoms of panic. But I didn't wish to analyse it: I wanted to be rid of it, and so I told myself to breathe in deeply through my nose and exhale slowly through my mouth, thinking of nothing else.

Gradually a calm reasserted itself.

I forced myself to think back to Sundays walking in the Bois de Boulogne, my arm interlocked with Poe's, a young man and old, both of us *flâneurs*, giddy at the pleasure of demonstrating our powers of ratiocination as the trees came to blossom. He would point out a typesetter by seeing the ink on his cuff. I would say a little boy in a sailor suit is English because it only became fashionable after Queen Victoria clad little Prince Edward in the same, as a gesture to the Royal Navy. He would beam with pride at my incremental progress, then call my attention to a youth and a pretty girl enjoying *déjeuner sur l'herbe* and tell me at a distance of a hundred yards that they had recently enjoyed carnal bliss. I would laugh out loud and question that he could possibly be certain of such a thing. "Elementary," he would say. *Élémentaire . . .*

Suddenly the trap door opened. I recoiled.

In the flickering light a shoal of objects rained down on my legs. Instinctively I wrapped my arms around my calves, but the things were already all over me. The noise they made, deafeningly shrill, was amplified by the drum incarcerating me. The trap banged shut but not before I glimpsed what they were, cuffing furry bodies off my knees and away from my ankles, shuffling my feet even as I shrank into a foetal position, making myself as small as possible, covering my face with my hands—but they were already biting me through my trouser legs and at my wrists. I brushed them off my legs as best I could and kicked at them spastically, but they didn't seem in the least impaired by my aggression. I gnashed my jaws as one of them sank their tiny teeth into my finger, right to the bone. I shook it off, but shook a good chunk of my finger off with it. The pain shot though me. My heart hammered fit to burst.

Though small, their force of numbers more than compensated for their size, and the *unseeing* made the experience worse.

In the dark I could only sense them by touch—and *awful* touch it was. Indescribably so. I retaliated as best I could. When the wiry claws cut into me, needle-like, I swiped them with the back of my hand. But it seemed they flew away and returned in seconds to bite and snap and gnaw and burrow elsewhere, anywhere, nosing into my trouser legs where I'd lash at them with a fist, or skittering over my hips and thighs, trying to gain access to my clothing. Their long, slimy tails stroked my cheeks. Their whiskers brushed against my ears.

I could only try to keep on the move constantly—twisting, squirming and thrashing from one end of the rat pit to the other. Yet if I got away from them for a second, they would swarm towards me, their scuttling feet going *scritch-scritch-scratch* until they found a softer surface. They climbed over me, an undaunted army, an undulating blanket reeking of the sewers. And I didn't have gamblers' cigars to keep the pungent stink of the rodents at bay.

My instinct was to constantly swivel, onto my front, pressing down to kill them—lashing out with my fists, hearing their spines break, and their hideous squeals. I had no idea of their number—the calculation in the dark was impossible—but they seemed to multiply.

Knowing that I would be their victim unless I found a weapon of some sort, I tried to think desperately what I had on me. I wore no belt, no buckle I could use to thrash them, and my Derringer had been taken. I had buttons—useless. A handkerchief—pointless. Wallet, money. Nothing. But I wore a voluminously-knotted plastron, held with a tie pin, and plucked it off, clutching it between my fingers like an Apache knuckle-duster.

I went at the rats now in a berserk frenzy, shouting, flailing, slashing at them with my miniscule blade as if I was fencing with a rapier. Some of them were cut and bled. I heard the piercing sounds they made, and I don't know if it was as a result of that, but they fell away in a wave and congregated, as best I could tell, at the far end of the pit, chirruping as if communicating, mind to disgusting mind.

I fell back, panting. In a rat match, the dog's second was allowed to blow on a conglomeration of rats to get them to disperse. My motive was exactly the opposite. I wanted them to stay together—and as far away from me as possible.

To protect myself from further assaults, I knotted my plastron round my throat like a cowboy's neckerchief.

"For pity's sake! Let me out!" I banged my fist on the roof.

The action was futile. Worse, I found that in doing so my tie pin was lost, though I spidered my fingers across the floor to try to find it. Ridiculously, this filled me with as much alarm as if I'd been robbed of a battle-axe. Needless to say, I did not receive a response to my cries. My torturers had long disappeared, and even if they hadn't, I doubt they would have done anything but taken a great deal of pleasure from my horror. I don't know why I thought otherwise. I was alone in the dark with my enemies. The nightmare was mine and mine alone.

Breathing steadily, I felt the wetness of blood on my wrists and cheek. I knew my bleeding was in danger of attracting the rats all the more, so resolved quickly to move around the perimeter, brushing my bleeding hand against the carved tombstones in an attempt to give the creatures a scent trail that might, temporarily at least, distract them from me. However, my movement served only to agitate them, in force. They were upon me yet again. Two hung from the underside of my hand. Another burrowed up my sleeve. I tugged it out by the tail. He was not eager to come. Another sank his fangs into the small of my back where my waistcoat rode up. Two others dived in to gorge on the same spot. Their teeth cut into my flesh. The sudden notion of disease conspired with the lack of oxygen to make me nauseous. I told myself I needed to block out such thoughts. My terror was an encumbrance—as Poe had always insisted. I had to concentrate—concentrate and *observe*—and that was something, thankfully, he had taught me how to do in abundance. But what could I observe in pitch darkness?

Of course! As he had demonstrated that very morning, I had other senses, not just sight. I had hearing, touch, smell . . .

With renewed vigour I shifted my body round the circumference of the pit.

The Pit and the Pendulum . . .

Indeed. With immense irony I saw similarities between Poe's famous tale and my predicament. It made me bark a mirthless laugh. Did the protagonist not feel his way around his prison as I had done, and was doing now once more? I knew only that rats in this case would not be my saviour, as they had been—with utter implausibility—for him. No such plot contrivance—*sorry, Edgar*—was going to come to my aid. Though the author's famous ratiocination, transcended from fiction to reality, might.

Use my methods, Holmes . . .

"I shall," I thought. "I *must!*"

Shutting my eyes tightly (they were no use to me, and their struggle to discern light a distraction), I applied myself to the cover above me—solid, and held fast by ironwork. Inescapable. A very fast deduction indeed.

Underneath, then? My hands explored maniacally.

Floorboards, unpainted, oak or larch; aged, possibly of maritime origin. I sniffed my fingertips. Teak oil. Faint. Irrelevant. What was important was that the planks of wood were weathered and rotten from endless buckets of water used to swill away the blood—the salty sweetness of it unmistakable—and the action of stiff brooms, the hairs of which stuck to my skin like splinters. But between this 'decking'—now my heart beat even faster—*cracks*. Cracks that had opened minutely as the boards had swelled and shrunk.

I extended my right leg, delved deep into my trouser pocket, and pulled out a coin. I pressed it into the widest of the cracks, forcing it through with my thumb.

Half a second transpired before it hit water. Thus I calculated, with some excitement, that below me extended a well shaft with a drop of forty to fifty feet.

I shifted my mass onto my back and swiftly began hitting the planks with my heels. With little room to manoeuvre, it was hellish hard to get force behind the blows, and the immediate result was that the rats became agitated. Not to say frenzied. Again they flowed across my body, nipping at my throat and hands. I tried to keep momentum with the heel-kicks but by now I was exhausted, and had to sink, flat-out, covering my face with my arms in between swiping them away from me to conserve any strength at all. I cried out, hoping that it might inhibit them, but this failed to have the desired result. My lungs anyway were debilitated by the rank stench of faeces and urine, and my morale depleted by the endless crisscross of rat tails over my face.

I sobbed.

In my mind The Pit yawned. Darkness. Death. The Pendulum swung. Time passed inexorably. Inescapably. I saw the illustration accompanying Poe's story. I saw myself strapped to that table, the blade descending inch by inch.

The hideous song of the pests did not abate. I was terrified if I gave in to fatigue, or fell unconscious for an instant, that would be the end of me. The vermin would consume my body from head to toe, and feast, whether I was alive or dead. Perhaps in their animal cunning they were waiting for me to succumb to exhaustion, knowing that then their banquet would begin. I had to deny them that pleasure. I cranked myself up on my elbow, pressing with my free arm against the wooden slab above me, trying to get the rotten plank below me to give. They tore at my clothes, their small feet scratching me all over, their squeals deafening.

I got up on all fours, my back against the roof of the pen, arms outstretched against the sodden floorboard beneath me.

It bent, cracked, gave way, splintered. My hand went through—I had created a hole bigger than my fist—and with an inner *hurrah* I felt the emptiness of air on my skin. The aroma of the spring below rose to my nostrils, the freshness of the Garden of Eden in a cesspit.

My fingers went wild, tearing at the hole, enlarging it until it was twice its former size. Then my plan could come to fruition . . .

I splayed my arms wide across the floor, scooping rats into the hole. They resisted, some clambering out, some on the backs of others, but I was unrelenting in shoving them back in. Some clung to my sleeve and ran up to my neck; I plucked them off and deposited them into the orifice, hearing them fall and plop into the water below—their shrieks amplified by the tubular construction of the well as the rushing water of the spring carried them away.

With replenished energy I lashed out with my legs, scissoring, forcing the rodents into the Pit. They scratched and clung and hopped and skittered away from me—but ultimately fell, in great tangled blobs, tails thrashing. A dozen gone, then a dozen more. Until there were only a few odd ones left. Ten. Five. Three. I grasped them one by one from my jacket and consigned them to the depths.

Eventually they were gone. All of them.

Too drained to enjoy my victory, I lay flat out on my stomach, spent.

Yet I could still feel them scampering over my flesh—and still batted them away, pawed them from my body in spastic motions. I still trembled, though they were invisible. I yelled, though no-one was there but myself to hear. The smell hit me again, and I retched but nothing escaped me. I was a husk.

Shivering, I tried to feel an imaginary carnation petal between my thumb and forefinger. The scent would not come, and I wept.

Devoid of the comfort of light, I thought again of the sunlit child in the sailor suit in the Bois de Boulogne. The boy turned to look at me. He had a rat in his mouth, with its tail and back feet dangling.

A moan tore from my breast and I hammered the back of my head against a slate headstone until I felt the wound seep wetly.

My fingertips crawled over the carved lettering on the headstone beside me, spelling out a new name ... "SHERLOCK HOLMES" ...

I wept, my lips dry and my eye swollen almost shut. The other had been lost in darkness so long it was blinded too.

I realised, in the miasma of battle and the frenzy of survival, I had lost all sense of time. Had an hour passed, or three, or six? It felt like a week or more. An eternity ... "ÉTERNITÉ" ... But all I had to do now was to wait, and breathe, and keep on breathing, and time would pass, and if time passed, eventually I would be released.

As if in answer, the trapdoor scraped open above me. I flinched away from the searing lamplight.

Another sack full of rats emptied into the pen, an avalanche spewing onto my back, a cascade of the vile things scattering in all directions, seeming to fill the entire space around me like a squirming, writhing cloud. Human laughter cut through the turbulent ocean of squeals. Whimpering, I kept my eyes resolutely shut as a second bag disgorged its loathsome contents. This time there were more: *hundreds* more, in an endless flow—and I didn't know how many to come.

I screamed and at the end of the scream my breath and will was knocked out of me. I could not move. All was lost. My mind, my soul, lost. The denizens of The Pit had won. They covered me in a writhing carpet, not an inch of me unclothed with their endlessly wriggling and nipping shapes.

"*Non! NON!*"

I recognised the cry of a familiar voice before the trapdoor was shut. Then it just as suddenly reopened. Candlelight blinded me like the summer sun at its height. One torture upon another.

"*Libérer le prisonnier!*"

I could see nothing, but felt pairs of arms reach in and lift me up. Out of The Pit. Out of reach of the cruel, unrelenting Pendulum. Away from the surging sea of rodents, even as they dropped from my legs and body.

A man put his arms around me and held me close to his heart. I clung to his sleeve, sobbing, but could not part my eyelids. I had been freed, at last.

The Inquisition, I thought, *was in the hands of its enemies . . .*

⌒⤫

Back in our apartment in the Île de la Cité I oscillated between nervous waking and terrible, feverish dreams. When my eyes were able to focus on the wall opposite the foot of my bed, I could see a *vanitas* oil painting depicting a woman beautiful in life, half as a skeletal angel of death bearing a scythe. Other than her, my only company throughout my erratic delirium was a small copy of Bernini's sculpture *The Rape of Proserpina by Pluto*—a strange subject for Poe to choose to own. Perhaps he looked upon it as a terse reminder that not all crimes could be guaranteed to see the culprit brought to justice.

Over the ensuing weeks I was nursed by our landlady, "Madame L'Espanaye"—real name Alicia D'Hont: a rich widow and aficionado of Poe's *oeuvre* only too happy to allow us to dwell permanently in her rooms. Such was her adoration of the poet she had long dedicated herself to serving him, even as far as borrowing a name from one of his most famous stories, "The Murders in the Rue Morgue" and demanding her employee "Le Bon" did the same. Poe, of course, was only too complicit in the game, having chosen "Dupin" as his new identity in a new country.

It was two weeks before I could eat her *pain perdu*. Three before I could taste a tot of *verjus*. Shortly thereafter I was just about well enough to sit up and converse. The room still swam about me and I remarked on the strangeness of the affair we had become entangled in. So strange I could barely credit it to be true.

"Did not Herodotus record his marvels?" said Poe, a pot of broth on his knee. "And Livy his prodigies?" He blew upon the spoon.

"Poe . . ." I supped from it. Even that exhausted me. "I thought I would die."

"My dear boy, I had no such fear. In the popular tradition, does not touching a hunchback bring one good luck?"

"I never touched him, though."

"Luckily, I did." He adjusted the napkin lain on my chest. "Superstition, of course, has no place in our work. But I confess, in those hours between sunset and dawn it was the nearest I've come to praying to the Almighty for His intervention since Virginia lay with the life ebbing out of her." Of course he did not meet my eyes.

"You found who was responsible?" My very existence was proof that he had. "How?"

"That can wait until . . ."

"No. Please. Tell me now. The not-knowing is driving me insane."

Poe smiled. "A born detective. You cannot rest until you have the solution. But open your mouth and eat your soup while I talk, or Madame L'Espanaye will whip me within an inch of my life."

I did as he bade me.

"I knew as I emerged from the Catacombs my task was an almost impossible one. I had mere hours to find the mysterious creator of monsters and precious little information by which to do so. I had to begin with what I *did* have, and that was 'Quasimodo' himself—Raoul Écuyer. I returned with haste to the crypt of Notre Dame and availed Le Bon of my urgency. We stripped the hunchback and by candlelight, I rolled up my sleeves and determined to extract every ounce of evidence from the human being in front of me, knowing each minute that passed was a step nearer the scaffold for you.

"First of all, I discerned these horrific interventions were not cruel, haphazard hackings but complex surgical procedures. Whoever was responsible had considerable medical expertise, a knowledge of narcotic drugs sufficient to know how to overpower their victims, and intelligence enough to meticulously plan and execute such an abduction without being apprehended.

"Even with the most cursory examination I could tell from the location of the scar that the shortened leg was achieved by an incision along the lateral aspect of the thigh, by the parting of the muscles, the dislocation of the hip joint and the excising of the femoral head. This is normally a doctor's solution to a judgement of Solomon—you'd have a limp, but that is preferable to excruciating pain. I then examined the man's ruined eye as Le Bon held his head in a lock. I suspected phenol had been used to blind him. The substance passes through the epidermis and dissolves in the tissue beneath, resulting in the kind of hideous burns that confronted me. The ear? It is just cartilage, so I presumed it was cut off with scissors or sliced with a scalpel.

"Your initial presumption of scoliosis was, of course, wrong. As we now know, there had been no congenital deformity of the spine pushing the ribs out of shape. This 'hump' was man-made—but how? Under my magnifying lens, as Le Bon held the hunchback down, I could see an incision had been made down the line of the vertebrae with the purpose of detaching the origin of the latissimus dorsi on one side. What had been inserted to create the false 'hump' I could only surmise—perhaps a pig's bladder filled with macerated pig fat in a semi-solid porridge—then the muscle had been stitched back to the bone with wire, and the skin closed.

"I allowed a picture to form in my mind of a hasty lancet and bloody clamps. In time, and with diligence, it should be possible to discern from the marks made by such instruments the identity of the user, as from handwriting on paper. But time was not on my side. On the contrary, it was more of a crow on my back. I had to think quickly but not at the expense of accuracy.

"I only had what was before me in the flesh and had to read it as I might some occult personal narrative encoded in a tattoo. Fortunately, I had the means to do so, having catalogued medical tools in encyclopaedic detail—the better to provide the history of a cadaver from the clues apparent—from tonsil guillotines to syringes of mercury to treat the Spanish disease. The nouns and verbs shouted out to me: forceps; probe; hook retractor; weals where leather restraints had cut into the wrists, similarly the ankles; a cloud of tiny dots—broken blood vessels at the temples where the head had been held immobile—yet, of singular interest, these areas were not circular, as might be expected of English or French instruments, but kidney-shaped, a variant popular in the Low Countries. This alerted me to the way the suture along the man's thoracic spine had been stitched, which was highly unusual, evenly spaced as if mechanized, indicative that a stapler or a type of sewing machine had been used. I had seen only one example of this, in a report in the *Bulletin of the Medical Society of Ghent* by the Liège physician Midavaine. No such article even remotely similar had appeared in the *Archives Générales de Médicine* of France. My immediate conclusion was that our perpetrator was both a surgeon and Belgian.

"Wasting not a second, I tracked down, through various persons of my acquaintance in civic office, a supervisor of the *Assistance Publique*—the Parisian hospital administration responsible for creating specialist wards, and demanded to see a list of physicians and specialists currently working in the capital. The man was shocked by my demeanour, and did not question it when I said that lives were at stake. Frankly, I did not care if he was trembling in his socks as long as I got what I wanted. And there it was: . . . a Belgian surgeon-anatomist with experience in field amputations, a lecturer at the teaching hospital with lodgings and a laboratory for private research near Les Invalides. His name was Melchior Vilvoorde.

"I had no idea what I would be up against, but realised it would be foolish to confront him alone, since I had ordered Le Bon, of necessity, to stay with the hunchback in the crypt. To that end, my carriage halted to pick up Aristide Gembloux, a carthorse of a man I once saved from the guillotine. Sometimes brute force is needed in place of a sharp mind, and ex-legionnaire Gembloux was indebted to me. He leapt on board without asking the reason why. I thought the vehicle might capsize.

"A chilling reminder of our quest, the bells of Notre Dame tolled midnight as we arrived at the address I had acquired. A dingy glow flickered behind a shuttered basement window. I could not risk our quarry fleeing, so Gembloux applied his considerable shoulder to the door. The lock flew off as we burst inside. With the naked blade of my sword-stick preceding me, and Gembloux's pistol close behind, I descended the short flight of stairs and threw open the door to the cellar.

"It would have been impossible for Vilvoorde not to hear us enter. In frock coat and leather apron, a halo of oil lamps suspended above his head, he stood calmly with his back to us, surrounded by equipment one might expect in an operating theatre, but there was more the air of an abattoir than a dispensary here, with blood a decorative tincture washed over with acrid disinfectant, each odour fighting the other for the distinction of disabling our olfactory senses—an assault to which the resident seemed extraordinarily immune.

"'Melchior Vilvoorde.'

"Hearing my voice he was evidently in no hurry to turn, but when he did he dropped his scalpel in a kidney dish with a sense of finality, wiped his hands in a filthy cloth, and, presumably mistaking us for police officers, offered his wrists to us as if for handcuffs.

"'Look after my boy,' the Belgian surgeon said quietly, showing the utmost complacency regarding his own fate. 'That is all I ask.'"

"I had no idea what he meant.

"Gembloux, once wrongly accused of murder, had his outstretched Perrin Frères next to my ear, aiming it squarely between the man's eyes. Its barrel was shaking. Then I realised why. The misshapen mass next to Vilvoorde was a human being—or more precisely, the bare back of a human being, hunched over a crude H-shaped frame, its head slumped forward and inert. I spotted a dispenser of Lister's carbolic spray and a cylinder with an elastic tube leading to a face piece for the administration of chloroform. I had no doubt this was Cyprien Écuyer—his spinal musculature having been opened up, the disgusting false 'hump' inserted, and the wound closed using the stapling contraption I saw on the work bench nearby.

"'It is done,' Vilvoorde said.

"I sheathed my sword in my walking cane, turned to my trusty Gembloux, lowered his arm, and was about to tell him to apprehend our foe when a gush of bright red liquid splattered against the ceiling as if a pipe had burst. A pipe *had* burst—but it was Vilvoorde's jugular vein, severed by the slash of the scalpel now wielded in Cyprien Écuyer's hand. The Belgian looked momentarily startled, bewildered, then finally resigned with disinterest to what had occurred as the lifeblood pumped out of his body and his face drained of colour. The claggy blocking of his oesophagus produced a gurgling rattle as he sank to his knees, a scarlet sash staining his otherwise immaculate attire.

"He fell forward, too late for us to act. You did not have to be a doctor to see that the loss of blood was unstoppable, and fatality the certain outcome. Cyprien had freed himself from his bonds. Either the dosage of his anaesthetic had been inadequately calculated or our unscheduled entry had roused him, or both—either way, somehow he had prised one hand loose and cut the leather strap on the other. Now he stood, swaying, dizzy, one eye bandaged, one leg rendered useless, with his abductor at his feet. Gembloux had his pistol up again and forced him into a chair. Cyprien slumped, half-dozing and stippled with blood, raising his hands in mute surrender. Knowing instinctively we must have come from his father, and were not about to kill him, he allowed himself a peal of tittering, abominable laughter before lolling into semi-consciousness.

"We had presumed Melchior Vilvoorde dead. We were wrong. Now he twitched and moved across the floor on his elbows, leaving a livid stain under him as he crawled to the stairs. With immense effort he hauled himself up to the next floor, and as I watched impotently he began the next flight to the upper landing. By now he was flopping and rolling like an oily, crimson slug. I silently urged him to go no further, to ride the Pale Horse and be done with suffering. As if he'd heard my thoughts, the whites of his eyes rolled back and he moved no more. The mad chirurgeon lay with his arm reaching above him, twisted fingers in an unknowing mimic of Adam's hand reaching to God on the ceiling of the Sistine Chapel."

Poe used the napkin to dab the corners of my mouth.

"And in the minute of silence that followed, I heard a cry I first thought imaginary, for it had all the semblance of a distressed fawn trapped in a bush of thorns. Compelled, I stepped over Vilvoorde's body and went up into the attic bedroom from which it was emanating." His large, limpid eyes clouded at the recollection and his voice wavered. "That was where I found the ten-year-old boy. You see, he was pointing. Upwards. To his son . . . Léopold."

Poe stared down into the soup bowl. He raised the spoon, but I could eat no more. Drained of colour, he stood and placed the tureen on the dressing table, where he propped himself and gathered his senses.

"How do you know his name?"

"I know more than that." His reflection in the cheval glass straightened its collar and cravat. "Melchior Vilvoorde's obituary has appeared in the press, but with no explanation for the murder of this distinguished and beloved medical man. Gembloux and I left the place so that it looked like a random intruder, probably a thief, had killed Vilvoorde. Many times have I aided the police in illuminating the causes of murder: in this instance I had to use the self-same skills to make them opaque. The door had been forced. The surgeon's throat had been cut. That was all anyone need know. However, for our purposes, the biographical details in the newspapers amply fill in the gaps in a seamless narrative leading to the motivation for his crimes.

"The obituary points out that Vilvoorde first visited Paris a decade ago as a young doctor full of optimism. His career lay before him. A successful marriage to a beautiful wife he adored. The arrival of a child made his life complete. Then horrible tragedy struck as Léopold was stolen from his baby carriage in Les Halles. In spite of extensive searches the boy was never seen again. As a double blow, Vilvoorde's wife never recovered. He returned to work in Belgium, but it is not a wild supposition that a pall fell over the marriage, the loss too much for either parent to bear. I know no medical term for a broken heart, but undoubtedly, in colloquial terms, that was the true cause of her early death: an inability to carry on living." Poe surely knew that feeling more than most, I thought to myself, but did not interject. "After that, Vilvoorde buried himself in clinical work, at which he excelled, but no accolade of success, or act of compassion from his circle of friends, could have provided sufficient light to ameliorate his darkness. Despair was his only companion. The obituary concludes, he never revisited Paris until a year ago—so from here on I can only extrapolate backwards from what we now know ... One day he passes a ragged and forlorn beggar—only ten years of age, hunchbacked, with a limp and one good eye, rattling his pitiful tin ... and to his horror finds himself looking down at *his own son*.

"Perhaps at first he doubted his conclusion, but the birth-mark I saw on the child's neck would have made identification unmistakable. He took the boy in his arms and sped away to install him in his rooms at Les Invalides, caring for him as best he could. While doing so, he must have cultivated a need to make the people who had done this pay, for he knew his son to be able-bodied when he had been kidnapped. Through his own detective work he must have found out how L'Eminence presided over the creation of such monsters for profit, and that he had three sons of his own. Immediately, in his madness, or perhaps the most lucid sanity, Vilvoorde knew the only possible vengeance he could exact.

"By means we can only inadequately guess, he was finally able to identify the three men who were his target. Michel was the first brother to vanish. The first abducted to his squalid den and operated on, over days, weeks, then taken, incapacitated by one of his somniferous potions, to somewhere where word must have reached L'Eminence swiftly, for the mangled and half-demented youth was soon spirited to the Catacombs with no undue public alarm.

"Vilvoorde's second victim was Raoul, who somehow crawled from wherever he was deposited to Notre Dame and somehow gained access, perhaps mistaken for a poor unfortunate seeking alms. The third brother, Cyprien, by then, was out looking for the perpetrator. He was the brother we found in Vilvoorde's laboratory, under the knife. Before he turned that same knife on Vilvoorde himself."

I had been silent for so long my voice was barely a croak.

"What did you do with Léopold, the child?"

"The sight of . . ." Poe's words crumbled. He crossed the room to the window, as if needing the promise of the sunlight outside, but also in order not to show me any emotion that may cross his features. My most peculiar and most brilliant friend. However adept I became at deduction, I would never get to the bottom of the mystery that was you. Nor would I want to.

"I was not prepared to let him return to a life on the streets," said Poe. "Gembloux said he had a brother in La Forêt de Landes in Gascony. Simple folk who own a small farm miles from the nearest village. They'd not been blessed with offspring of their own and it had always been their dearest wish. 'God is cruel,' he said. 'Then we must be kind,' I replied. He said, 'They will care for him as if he were their own.' I had no doubt he told the truth."

"And Cyprien?" I asked. "The third hunchback?"

"We released him from his bonds, patched up his wounds, and returned him to his father."

I was flabbergasted. "He was a *murderer!*"

"That was the bargain I had struck. In the criminal mind when a bargain is made it cannot be broken. Duty amongst thieves is the only thing that puts them on a higher moral step than savages." He did not remind me that if he had not done so, I would be dead, and this conversation would not be happening. Furthermore my skin would, by now, have been separated from my body. It was beyond Poe's commitment to Reason to admit that he might have done it because he wanted me to live. To desire such a thing, to him, would have been perceived as an intellectual defect.

"And the hunchback we found in Notre Dame?"

"Raoul? I returned him also. And saw tears streaming down Severin Écuyer's cheeks into his beard as he cradled him."

I felt faint. I don't know if my morphine was wearing off or if the thoughts were simply dizzying. "Three brothers, three hunchbacks, reunited. I cannot picture the sight."

"Picture *The Three Graces* of Canova, but where misshapen ugliness replaces beauty." He lit a cigarette from a silver, niello enamel and turquoise case. "Picture a monstrous trio welcomed back to the embrace of the labyrinth by King Minos of Knossos. Or is he King Lear? I daresay, like many a criminal, he considers himself 'more sinned against than sinning'. And a criminal is no more likely to change his ways than the Bishop of Paris. Both are entrenched in

defining who they are by what they do. The Bishop worships a crea-
tor he thinks has moulded us imperfectly from his clay. Meanwhile,
L'Eminence goes on creating cripples to provide a steady income.
Stealing babies. Setting dog against rat, and rat against dog . . ."

"You could almost call him the Napoleon of Crime," I suggested.

Poe looked down his nose. "That hyperbole might appeal to
you, my dear Holmes, but it's as far from the truth as might be imagined. He has no grand plan. He is not born of revolutionary fervour.
He reigns over an empire of beggars. The ones we overlook or are
repulsed by: the disenfranchised, the poor. I have been poor in my
time, stale-bread-and-no-buttons poor, and it is only through some
work I did in avoiding a scandal for one of the true Napoleons, in
that Bismarck business, that an annual stipend from the government
keeps me afloat. But often I think, as we have the luxury of comfort
and leisure, and food and a warm bed, the poor are the only worthy
amongst us. But now . . . rest, recover . . ." He walked over to pick
up the half-empty tureen. "I daresay you will have bad dreams, but
you will wake from them in time, unlike others, who sleep the final
sleep. Pain has a biological function. It tells you you are alive. Which,
though arduous, is preferable to the alternative."

"Poe . . ." The croak of my voice gave him pause at the door.
An eyebrow arched. "You saved my life."

"I did. Now it is incumbent on you to make it a life worth
having saved. By becoming the great detective I know you have the
potential to be." He returned to my sick bed and placed the back
of his fingers against my brow. "And that would be more easily
achieved if you did not die first."

I did not die, self-evidently—though at times during my
recovery over the following weeks it sorely felt as though it would
have been a blessing.

Like an attendant physician, Poe sat at my bedside every day,
and often through the night, his character providing a constant
balm to my ills. As I felt barely a grip on this realm by the fin-

gertips, he would help by apprising me of his progress in a case, for instance the extraordinary affair of the secret, exclusive dining group known as "The Life Boat Club" who drew lots to see which of their membership would be the next *moussaillon* on the menu. Or else he would read to me from recently published examples of American poetry, which he guaranteed would render me into the deepest slumber.

His many readers think Poe dark and dreary of temperament, but here, I must say, his effect was the reverse. His very presence, and the loyalty of that presence, buoyed me up between bleak fevers and raving nightmares during which I feared I could never escape the memory of that all-consuming darkness I experienced in the Catacombs—that unrelenting Pit and its writhing populace of squealing, invisible demons.

Morphine combated my physical, then psychological, pain. It did its job, dulling the senses, but in payment my need for it increased, even after I was back on my feet. Whether my dysfunction was real or imaginary, I was utterly convinced I needed the substance in my veins to face the world without fear—perhaps some mirror-image of Poe's own thrall to drink in his previous incarnation. Entirely with my long-term welfare at heart, Poe gave me cocaine to aid my withdrawal from the morphine—first in the form of lozenges or Vin Mariani, a tonic wine made from coca leaves.

In time, this addiction slept but never died, and my preferred application became by way of a needle and a rolled-up sleeve. A seven per cent solution, three times daily.

In Paris, at my most delirious, I dreamt of being in the impenetrable jungles of Sumatra, pursued by a giant rat. Subsequently, when the cravings returned, as they did with regularity, Poe would call my affliction "The Giant Rat of Sumatra" or say I was yet again on "a voyage on the *Matilda Briggs*"—his euphemism for the time given over to my recuperation: the *Matilda Briggs* being a playful variant he concocted from the name of the daughter of the captain of the *Mary Celeste*, a mystery which he informed me he had solved one afternoon in 1873, between naps.

Sadly, after my dear friend had departed this world, that other friend—cocaine—remained, and, I confess, sometimes took hold. Thereafter, at times of boredom or idleness, when the ghost of Poe emerged to castigate me, or berate my ineptitude, I would take a syringe to fortify my brain. And to shut him up.

Watson, of course, did his fair share to warn me of the dangers of my "weakness"—but I was ever a bad listener. Oh, that I could today hear his voice of old. Warm. Startled. Baffled. Brave. Stalwart, and indefatigably good. That I could tell him, at last, the true meaning of "The Giant Rat of Sumatra," and why it was a story for which the world is not yet prepared: for then I would have had to reveal that my great tutor in detection, Edgar Poe, far from dying ignominiously in a gutter in Baltimore in 1849, lived into a ripe and recalcitrant old age in Paris, and practiced ratiocination to his dying day.

But even now I know I could never have shared with my dearest, most loyal companion the fact that, every time I pricked my skin with the hypodermic needle, it reminded me of the nip of that pernicious tide of vermin in the belly of the Catacombs, and of that endless night when I was lost in darkness, saved from horror by the Shakespeare of horror—the only human being who ever told me I had a place on this earth, and a job to do.

Father of the Man

Lestrade,

I am aware of the very great burden of responsibility you take on, dear friend, when I entrust to you yet another sheaf of scrawled pages with the express wish, as before, that they shall not see the light of day in my lifetime. Furthermore, the document I enclose herewith for safe-keeping in the vaults of Scotland Yard's Black Museum contains a secret so alarming and so incredible that it may cause your steady hand to waver from the loyalty I have demanded. I can only say it caused mine to tremble, too, in the writing of it.

You cannot imagine—nor would wish to—how it felt to stare down at a grave by lamp light, my cheeks chilled by the night air, knowing that my friend Edgar Allan Poe, whose body lay beneath me in the earth, had been committed to a premature burial. Further that I, Sherlock Holmes, was entirely responsible for his ghastly fate.

But I must wind my mind backwards, as one might re-set the hands of a clock, the better to help you understand the events that had led me to that moment, to that spot, and that awful, unimaginable deed . . .

H.

IT BEGAN IN THE YEAR 1878, soon after Easter: I can be exact, for reasons that will become apparent. I was alone, furthering my research into tobacco cuts—Ribbon, Navy, Flake—that late afternoon in our rooms in the Rue de la Femme-sans-Tête. Since his clandestine arrival in France, many years previously, Poe had effectively maintained a false identity; that of C. Auguste Dupin, his great *ratiocinator* in fiction, leaving his problematic life and apparent death behind him, much like a snake sheds its skin. He was his own invention now, and it was the best of him: applying logic to extraordinary cases where the methodology of the police proved sorely lacking. Thus, long having decried poetry and prose as outlets for his intellect, his obsession and preoccupation had turned to crime in all its guises, and some years earlier he had, by peculiar happenstance, taken me under his wing.

The case taking the lion's share of Poe's attention at this time was a singularly brutal murder that had taken place in the Rue Beaugé, a notorious neighbourhood of brothels and seedy lodging-houses. Fabienne Gagnon, a late riser, had not been seen all day Easter Sunday, but by the following day her friends came knocking. They found her prone across her bed, throat slashed open, nose cut off and the contents of her abdomen dispersed around her like a flower in bloom. A bowl of ruby red water indicated that the murderer had washed his hands. The police could find no weapon, but upon the dressing table was an apple with a bite taken out. Poe insisted a cast be made to ensure the clue was not lost as the fruit rotted. His inevitable but gruesome deduction, since the indentations did not match the victim's teeth, was that the killer had taken pause to admire his handiwork. Given the savagery of the attack, the event had swiftly attracted the hyperbole of the press, who variously dubbed it "La Maison Maudite" or "La Maison Sanglante" (translated in *Lloyd's News*—literally, but without subtlety—as "The House of Blood").

Our door bell tinkled and I heard our manservant answer it. No doubt a caller had come to consult Dupin, and was being furnished with the information that, in the absence of the great mind, a lesser mind would have to suffice. Myself.

I closed the book on my knee, stepped into the vestibule, politely dismissed Le Bon, and invited the tall man—I'd say slim, even skinny, if not for square, athletic shoulders—to join me in the study.

"I presume, as an American, you would prefer to speak English?" I said with my back to him, observing his figure via the mantelpiece mirror, a simple trick, the better to visually assess a stranger whilst making them unaware of scrutiny.

"I'd prefer to speak American," he said in a drawling accent that proved my deduction correct.

"I'm afraid that is a little beyond me." I smiled.

"In that case, go ahead. I'll do my best to decipher."

As he removed his gloves to shake my hand I discerned nicotine stains on his fingers, and immediately proffered an open cigarette case.

"You wear a felt US slouch hat, the enlisted version—two rows of stitching as against the officer's slouch which has ribbon round the brim. That and your ankle-length duster sets you apart from current Parisian fashions." I struck a match and he raised an impressed eyebrow. "I also note you are preoccupied. Preoccupied enough to cut your right cheek shaving. And you are a Pinkerton, since you wear a badge under your left lapel, lifting it slightly, but noticeably, away from your Anderson tartan waistcoat—excuse me, *vest*."

The man inhaled and blew smoke, flipping back one side of his coat to reveal a silver shield with the eye emblem of the national detective agency on it, together with its motto: *We never sleep*.

A quick hack of a laugh followed.

"I thought I was the damned detective."

He produced his letter of credentials and certificate of membership from an inside pocket. I checked the information against the man in front of me. I'd have estimated his age at around thirty—a few years older than myself: jaw clean-shaven, moustache dark, skin so free of blemishes as to seem almost feminine.

The female sex would no doubt find him strikingly handsome: on the one hand boyish, on the other stern, somewhat aloof and impenetrable.

"Ezra P. Dugdale."

"So I see. What does the P stand for?"

"Patience. Persistence." As deadpan as they come, if humour was intended. Perhaps it wasn't.

"Excellent qualities. My name is Sherlock Holmes. I must say, I've paid great interest in your organization's role in the fight against crime over the past few years. Especially its pursuit of the Younger Brothers, which I've followed avidly from afar. I detect a small reaction. Were you by any chance involved in that activity?"

"No, sir. But my good friend Orion Hodge was shot and killed by those miscreants." A dark cloud passed over his demeanour, and his eyes did not let me in.

"I'm sorry. That was inept of me, and inexcusable."

Dugdale waved away my apology. "Goes with the shield. Job can be tough, and it can be dirty. Like the Molly Maguires business. Not my kind of trade, drumming up goon squads and infiltrating unions, being duplicitous amongst salt of the earth working men. You ask me, miners deserve an honest wage just like every other bag of bones. I don't take kindly to being used as muscle by folks just 'cause they can pay for it. Workers ain't the enemy. The enemy's the likes of Jesse James and the Reno Gang."

I could only agree. "What brings you to Paris? Not the Reno Gang, I trust."

"No, sir." He settled in his armchair, expelling more cigarette smoke from the side of his mouth. "Missing person. One who seems to have vanished into thin air, over twenty-five years ago. And it's my obligation to find him. I know it sounds like what it is—a nigh-on, gold-plated and polished-so-you-can-see-your-face-in-it Impossible Task, but from what I hear, well . . .

C. Auguste Dupin relishes impossible tasks. The more impossible the better, by my reckoning."

It transpired that the lawman had come across Dupin's name recently when Poe had solved a sensational and bizarre crime from halfway across the world simply by reading about it in the US dailies. The baffling mystery came to light when mariners cutting and bailing a sperm whale off the Azores came to an alarming discovery: inside they found a dead man. Even more alarmingly, the corpse showed obvious signs of a violent attack, leading the police to conclude he had been murdered before being consigned to the sea, subsequently being imbibed by the giant of the ocean, its capacious maw trawling for plankton. Poe had pointed out the error of their ways. Calling his response "A Nantucket Murder," he argued that gouges on the lining of the whale's stomach indicated that the man had been swallowed *alive*, and, starving over a period of days, had satiated his hunger by feeding off the "plum pudding" as pike-and-gaff men call it (parts of the flesh adhering to the blubber; rich, mottled and as edible as royal venison). The shape of the wound in the man's head, shown by diagrams in the original report, further led Poe to deduce that the murder weapon was arrow-shaped and barbed, the exact shape of a whaling harpoon which had pierced the Leviathan's epidermis. In short, he meticulously demonstrated that the sailor, Jonah-like, had been *alive* in the whale's belly when, tragically, a harpoon had penetrated and—by a cruel quirk of fate—struck him through the left temple, killing him outright. My friend and mentor had signed the letter in *Le Figaro* simply: *Dupin*.

The Pinkerton extracted a battered Daguerrotype from his coat pocket and handed it me.

"You will acquire some semblance of my difficulty when I tell you the object of my search is an American man who went missing in October 1849. Last seen in Baltimore, on October 3rd at Ryan's Tavern, sometimes known as Gunner's Hall, where he lost a game of poker."

The year 1849 triggered something in my brain, but it wasn't until I examined the photograph that the reason for its familiarity set off a mental explosion. At that point, it took every ounce of effort to stop my hands from shaking uncontrollably and giving the game away. But *what* game? What *exactly* was I looking at? What I saw was surely impossible.

But C. Auguste Dupin relishes impossible tasks . . .

I tried to focus my eyes upon the man in the Daguerrotype, smiling, seated as he was next to his wife or fiancée in a deeply unremarkable pose. Ah, but so—*so* remarkable! For, I could hardly credit it; the face that looked out at me, and stilled the very breath in my throat, was the face of *Edgar Allan Poe.*

"His name is Julius Jack Reynolds," said Dugdale.

Of course. Of *course* it was! I almost tittered with glee, for it began to make some kind of sense. Some kind.

This was the man Poe had *replaced* on his last day in America, as he had told me innumerable times: the unfortunate fellow, almost his exact *double*, whom Perversity or Destiny had introduced to the plot during a day mad with electioneering and free booze. Poe had stolen his identity as the drunkard lay expired in an alley, thinking it a bizarre act of providence—divine or otherwise.

I was beginning to think "otherwise."

"Reynolds," I repeated blankly, knowing that Poe had felt his doppelganger's pulse and found none, taking thenceforward the courageous or foolhardy opportunity to reconstruct his life thousands of miles away, by the good grace of a ticket for a transatlantic voyage. One way.

Laying his doctor's distinctive Malacca cane across the reprobate, and furnishing him with other items to identify him as a dissolute version of Poe in a state of "beastly intoxication", the real Poe had escaped across the seas to a fresh start in Paris. Meanwhile, back in Maryland, a delirious and incoherent Reynolds, salvaged by a printer called Walker and a doctor called Snodgrass, called out his own name to futile effect as he breathed his last at 5 a.m. on 7th October, in Washington College Hospital. And Edgar Allan Poe was pronounced dead by the attending physician. In short, the man in the Dageurrotype—the man the Pinkerton sought—was the man with whom Poe had swapped identities all those years earlier. The poor man who now lay in Poe's grave.

"Tell me what you know," I said quietly, not offering the fact that I undoubtedly knew more than my guest. But I needed Dugdale to talk for a bit, if for no other reason than to gather my racing thoughts and enable me to keep my sense of incipient panic in check.

Without hesitation the Pinkerton apprised me of the extent of his inquiries to date. At the outset, I could tell he had been thorough, diligent, indefatigable, and I estimated months of dogged questions and foot-slogging had preceded his eventual arrival at our door.

He'd had it confirmed that Reynolds had purchased a cabin passage ticket on the *Gloria Scott*, a steam packet ship due to sail from New York to Liverpool, a trip that would take roughly ten days and sixteen hours. He showed me an etching of a two-hundred-and-eighty foot vessel, single stacked, with three square rigged masts. He'd further discovered that a "Julius J. Reynolds" was ticked off the list upon boarding.

I almost felt sorry for his ignorance. This had evidently been Poe.

"He was seen drinking heavily."

Yes, this was *definitely* Poe.

"I obtained a copy of the passenger manifest from the Collins Line. I then took it upon myself to visit each of those I could track down, in the hope of any clue to his present whereabouts. Tantamount to seeking a needle in a haystack, I know. There was no record of who might have shared his cabin, but at least he was not sequestered in steerage and lost amongst the rabble. By my reck-

oning, over the course of ten days he *must* have had contact with
someone. Someone who might remember him. It was an arduous job,
granted. Some had died in the intervening twenty-five years, not
surprisingly. Others' memories failed them. Others turned out to be
untraceable. And every name I crossed off the list took time, weeks,
months, and as tenacious as I am when I get my teeth into a case ..."

"You reached a dead end."

He sighed and leaned forward. "Luckily, not. As a last resort
I placed an advertisement in several newspapers, in both New
York and Liverpool, citing the *Gloria Scott* and the date of the voyage, offering a substantial reward for any information arising. The
Purser, Irishman name of Muldoon, came forward. Remembered
clearly a man of Reynolds' description being a drunk and a boor
towards diners." That sounded more than credible, I mused. "Later
he saw the same man on deck, staring out to sea, and feared he was
contemplating jumping in. Muldoon talked him out of it, persuad-
ing him instead to commit to the waves the empty bottle he was
nursing. The man said, 'Should I put a message inside it? And if so,
what would it say?' He confided in the Purser that the only friend
he now had in the world lived in Paris, and that was all he dared
desire: 'A new life, leaving my old one behind. The failures, the
disappointments, the paltry and meaningless successes. And those
I have hurt too much.'"

The words brought a lump to my throat. For a moment I could
not speak. The thought of Poe considering suicide was unbearable,
albeit in the past. It nevertheless felt, just the idea of it, an obscene
and pitiful waste.

"And so the trail leads to Paris."

He nodded. "Where it runs dry. And here I am. Begging
bowl in hand."

"Not much to go on."

"Almost nothing."

"How much time have you spent ... ?"

"On a wild goose chase? I dread to contemplate. But I tell you this, Mr Holmes: I won't let go of it. They say certain dogs have jaws that lock when they sink teeth into their prey, so much so that they can't let go even if they want to. I think I'm bred from that stock."

"But you don't even have your prey. Let alone your teeth in it."

He consigned the last half-inch of his cigarette to the open fire. "I am cognisant of that detail. What can I say? My heart drives my head. You get the picture." I did. The Pinkerton Agency did not easily embrace failure, and this gentleman would rather sever his left arm without a tot of rum than return to his superiors with his tail between his legs.

I wanted to end the conversation rapidly. I was not even thinking of how we could help him. Quite the contrary. I wished he had never darkened our door and I couldn't wait to get him out of it. I certainly was not minded to aid his investigation in any way. How could I, when the solution would only point to the criminal subterfuge of my dearest friend?

"It seems your options are few," I said.

"I'd like to know *your* options. That's why I'm here."

"Let me ask the obvious question. What if Reynolds is dead?"

"My client is emphatic on that matter. I must go back to him with incontrovertible proof, either way. Dead or alive, as they say on those outlaw posters out west. He wants to know the truth. That's what's important to him. That's why he pays our daily rate. Money no object. Those are my orders. To stay until I have solved the mystery of what happened to Julius Jack Reynolds, and, should my beard grow long and grey in the process, I will. But Lord knows, I am a stranger in this city, it's not my native tongue, my enquiries have fallen on fallow ground, and I need eyes and ears, and a fresh brain, and a good one, which I will reward accordingly."

He mistook my silence for deep contemplation and did not interrupt it, and I was glad of that. I did not want to arouse suspicion by rejecting his plea out of hand, though I sorely wanted to.

Instead, I decided it was better for him to believe we might aid his search, then for us to reveal at some later stage that our efforts too had been inadequate.

"I can promise nothing, but we shall do what we can. Leave it with me. Rest assured I shall discuss the case fully with Dupin on his return." I stood. He stood, and we shook hands. "May I keep this?"

The Daguerrotype.

He said I could, then gave me his address, the Hôtel de Laâge, and said he would await any illumination. That was his word—*illumination*.

The tragic truth was, I could have given him it there and then. But what would have been the hellish consequences?

As I saw my guest to the door, and the noises of the street drifted up from the courtyard, he paused thoughtfully and turned to shake my hand yet again, this time making sure he held my eyes with his.

"I must impress upon you, Mr Holmes, that the son, now a grown man, is at his wit's end over this sorry business. He has become a wealthy merchant, wealthy enough to enable him to pay for my unlimited endeavours. Anonymity is the deal, but I see no reason for secrecy if it sways you and your partner in your commitment to my goal." He blinked and nodded slightly as if to provide a full stop at the end of a sentence he was loath to have spoken, but of which he was now unburdened. His eyes drifted off me. "My father died when I was ten years old. It leaves a chasm. And not to know? Well, that is unrighteous cruel." After hesitating, he tweaked the brim of his slouch. "I'll bid you good evening, sir."

I bade him the same, more grateful to see him gone than he could ever imagine.

⁓

Unlike Barnaby Rudge, we had no pet raven, only a parrot named Griswold, who welcomed his master home with a habitual squawk of "*Vive la France!*" I knew immediately he was in a sullen mood— Poe, that is, not the parrot—as always when a case was proving opaque, let alone when there was a dangerous murderer on the loose. Though it would be incendiary, I could waste no time in recounting to him the conversation I'd had earlier, and did so as soon as we sat down to dinner.

To my surprise, he seemed to absorb the information with admirable restraint—that is to say, complete silence and utter stillness for several seconds. Whereupon he stopped eating, declared the lamb chops so raw as to be "gambolling in the fields" and pushed the plate away from him, pressing his index fingers to his temples and shutting his eyes.

When he opened them, it was to see the Daguerrotype I had placed in front of him.

I feared what might happen next. Since an element of the legendary "boorishness"—as recounted by the Purser of the *Gloria Scott*—had never entirely left Poe, I was terrified he was within a hair's breadth of smashing said dinner plate against the wall and possibly laying waste to the entire room.

Instead, to my alarm, he erupted in the most uncontrollable fit of giggles, for all the world as if he had inhaled a gigantic lungful of nitrous oxide. He positively rocked in his chair. And I almost rocked back in mine, dumbstruck.

"*Touché!*" he cried, raising his glass of *citron pressé* heavenwards. "What a master stroke! If I were inclined to prostrate myself to a deity, which thankfully I am not—*you*, sir, have proven yourself the court jester to end all court jesters! Indeed, it could be said," (he continued addressing the ceiling) "—it *shall* be said; you have had the last laugh! Or rather *I* have, at this very moment! *Ha ha ha ha!*"

Superfluous to point out, this reaction could not have been further from my expectation.

"Why, Holmes, your countenance is grave, not to say bereft, or bee-stung. You cannot see the *humour* in the situation?"

"Frankly, no. I find the predicament horrible. But the more so for you, being in the eye of the storm, and the one clearly to suffer from it."

"There is that."

"'There is that,' he says!"

Poe rose, strands of white hair combed across the great dome with unsurpassable vanity even at the age of sixty-nine, searched for his clay pipe, and gouged the contents of Henry VIII's head into the coal scuttle.

"What is there to do?"

I was astonished. "What would you *propose* to do? Give in to your fate? Embrace the scandal and ridicule over your deception coming to light, your selfish utilisation of a dying man lying in a back street of Baltimore? What do you imagine the public's response to this fraud will be? This imposture you have perpetuated for nearly thirty years?"

"It may be the perfect end to a perfect charade." His theatrical indifference annoyed me intensely.

"Well, I'm not having it," I declared.

"*You?* Of what interest is it to *you?*" He talked as if I was a complete stranger, and I was enraged almost to the point of tears.

"How dare you! It is of *every* interest to me. I simply cannot—*will* not let you go back to face the music. It would be an act of . . . of blatant self-destruction."

"On the contrary, the critics might approve wholeheartedly. Some might pronounce my transportation of C. Auguste Dupin from the printed page to reality quite the most creative thing I've ever done."

"You think it fitting to *joke* about this?"

"Certainly," said Poe calmly. "What is the alternative?"

"To *do* something. Do *anything* to get this relentless bloodhound off your tracks. Anything, everything in our power to send him packing, with some kind of explanation that satisfies him and draws a line under the whole so-called mystery."

"And how, my dear Holmes, do you suggest we do that?" He blew through the Gambier, clearing its airway. "It's a singular conundrum, and I would posit, an impossible one."

But C. Auguste Dupin relishes impossible tasks...

Now it was my turn to laugh.

"Vive la France!"

"Shut your beak, Griswold!" I left my chair and swiftly covered the parrot's cage with its blackout cloth. I almost wanted to do the same to Poe. Instead I raided the decanter of Tiffon, emptying the balloon snifter in one gulp, then dumped my body into the fireside chair, elbows on knees.

"Damnation."

"Very likely," Poe confirmed, with disarming nonchalance. Except the fact that he turned away indicated to me that under that veneer there resided a palpable degree of terror. This was a mask. Certainly. A supremely irritating one at that. But I had no doubt that beneath the haughty bluster there churned a sea of turmoil. One he couldn't allow to be seen, even by his closest friend.

In any case, if he was not ashen, I am sure I was. "Look. If we could prove Reynolds dead, the story would go away. We could forge a death certificate ..."

"You really think that would pass muster under the Pinkerton's eagle eye?"

"No. No, I don't. I don't, at all. It's a stupid idea." I drew my hands down my face. "So, all right, what if we forge a *man?* We forge a duplicate of Reynolds. We get an actor. We pay him handsomely to play the part. One night only. The performance of a lifetime."

"An actor? How could we be sure he could be even remotely convincing? And what if this *actor* smells a bigger reward from the National Detective Agency and spills the beans? Furthermore, in case it has escaped your notice, there exists a *Daguerrotype.* An

exact representation. Do you truly believe we can drag someone
off the street and create a silk purse from a sow's ... Even if we *did*
perform a miracle on him, the best actor in Paris couldn't pull it off
being interrogated by a trained Pinkerton. The accent alone would
be beyond a Garrick. And, consider this; what if he *did* convince?
Would he be happy being hauled back to Baltimore to face Reynolds Jr.—or a judge? At that point he'd be sure to give the game
away. I certainly would."

"Very well, Poe. Very well! I admit I haven't thought this
out ..."

"To put it mildly."

"And you have a better idea? Other than to roll belly-up and
let this house of cards of your ingenious fabrication fall about our
ears?" I was shouting now, and I didn't care. If the whole world
would soon be privy to this mad façade, what did it matter if the
servants knew? Then, like a blinding flash, it came to me.

"My dear Holmes, I appreciate the mental dexterity you are
applying to this problem, but there is no solution, other than me
telling the truth, or waiting for the hand of the law to clamp down
on my—"

"Wait. Wait a minute and listen. The answer has been staring us in the face. There *is* an actor who can do it. Who resembles
Reynolds exactly, who has impersonated him once, and who can
do so again. Faultlessly."

I gripped my friend by the shoulders and spun him round so
that he could see himself in the mantelshelf mirror.

I watched as his perplexed expression gave way to dawning
horror.

"I thank the Lord that neither Dugdale nor his client are
readers," I said from his shoulder. "Had either of them opened up
a volume of *Tales of Mystery and Imagination* they would have been
greeted by a facsimile of the face of Julius Jack Reynolds looking
straight back at them."

And there it was. Who else could possibly stand in for the man who was Poe's double—*other than Poe himself?*

"No, it's preposterous. I couldn't pretend to be a man I know next to nothing about. I'd be found out within seconds of opening my mouth."

"But that's the beauty of it! You don't need to open your mouth. Don't you see? Because you are dead!"

Poe turned to face me, backing away as if I were a madman, when in fact I was certifiably sane. I gripped him by the sleeves.

"This is the story we tell. We report to Ezra Dugdale that we have tracked down Reynolds, yes. But not alive. We take him to a grave. We show him the body. We convince him, utterly and completely. It will work. I know it will."

"All it needs is for me to be dead."

"To *appear* dead."

"Ah! We create a tableau. We commandeer a photographer's studio. I lie in a coffin. Post mortem photography is all the—"

"No. That won't hold water. It's too risky. Photographs can be faked. And isn't it so, *so* convenient that Reynolds got his corpse photographed? And by whom? Dugdale will smell a rat in an instant. What's more, it will arouse his suspicions that we are hiding something; as good as an admission of guilt writ large."

"Then—my brain is exploding . . . pray tell, what *will* convince him?"

"Why, the real thing of course! Your dead body. Dug up from six feet underground. Your corpse. *Reynolds'* corpse. He'll only believe what he can see with his own eyes. He said as much."

The cogs turned. The eyes shone. The breath quickened.

"I will have to be buried alive," pronounced Poe, ". . . and exhumed."

"It is the only—"

He raised a single finger to his lips. His countenance took on the aspect of an ancient philosopher deep in the rumination of some occult algebraic calculation. On such occasions he went I knew not where.

"It *will* work," I whispered, not knowing if he heard me. He gave no indication at all that he had.

He walked over and replaced his pipe in its rack.

Returning, he pondered the fire dogs. Then looked at me as if I had appeared in a room in which he had previously been alone. But I was grateful to see his dark eyes now twinkled, reflecting the firelight, and his mouth curled into that mischievous, if not wicked, smile I recognised so well as he stated:

"The absurdity alone makes it irresistible."

Paris was now called the City of Lights. Fifty-six thousand gas lamps illuminated streets and monuments all over the capital, making our task all the more difficult: to find a cemetery (or churchyard, as the English have it) hidden from the public eye, ill-lit, and far from a general thoroughfare, in a location where the surrounding buildings had little or no vantage over the graves below. Luckily, I eventually found one in a district with a sparse and sedentary population, blocked from prying eyes by aged cypresses, and a day, or rather evening, when the light of the moon was forecast to be the mere slice of a crescent. I also found a gravedigger compliant to our needs—for the appropriate remuneration.

"There is something satisfying to a hand-dug grave," the old man wheezed, admiring his handiwork as he leaned on the handle of his spade.

"Not if you are the occupant," said Poe, uncoiling the thick woollen scarf from his neck.

It was now three weeks after my meeting with Ezra Dugdale, since our investigation could not be seen to have advanced at too fast a pace, and the bone yard we stood in dated from the Middle

Ages, not a modern-day park or pleasure garden offering respite to a stroller or a museum of the famous. On my first visit and on this, I saw no promise that Nature's beauty would assuage the mourner's pain. It was embellished with no green spaces, just a sense of grim stone and haphazard infinity. Unforgiving and inevitable.

The one statue that by happenchance presided over us, Death, held its ubiquitous hourglass, not a macabre icon but a plain agent of destiny. Ideas once diffuse and vague embodied in a single remorseless figure who, as Poe always showed in various guises, from Prince Prospero to King Pest, holds ultimate reign over us all. The rest of the sober landscape, picked out by our lanterns, lay strewn with disc-shaped stelae of the Merovingian type, and Cathar crosses inscribed with the insignia of the Company of Jesus, popular in the days of the Counter-Reformation. Other headstones sported symbols of baroque vocabulary— scythe, ploughshare, the snake eating itself, symbol of resurrection—while family tombs sat surmounted by religious scenes, praying figures, grieving angels, sometimes a patron saint. Their grandeur all the more pronounced in contrast to the simple wooden cross before us, reduced to its plain four arms, topped with a little roof. No name attached.

Poe stared down into the bleakness of the empty grave, then circled it with all the casual scrutiny of a man buying a chaise longue. He handed his scarf to me and buttoned the breast of his greatcoat.

"Holmes, you have excelled yourself. It is perfect. *Horribly* perfect. I feel as though my entire work and life has led to this act. Almost as if it were pre-ordained."

He must have then seen the expression I wore; that a preoccupation with mortality had seeped into my bones, together with an unshakable worry about the enterprise upon which we had embarked.

"Your heart is beating too fast," he whispered.

My face tried to make him believe that deduction to be false.

Notwithstanding, he laid his hand upon the centre of my chest, and smiled for some seconds without removing it.

"That's better." He patted my shoulder, chuckling lightly. "My dear fellow, hold your nerve. You are more trepidatious about this adventure than I am."

I could not smile back.

He took the scarf and wrapped it about my cheeks, the way a doting mother might for her schoolboy son, and moved closer to me, sufficient that the gravedigger would not hear, as he looked at the frayed cuff of his greatcoat. It had belonged to Reynolds and was the same one the man wore in the Daguerrotype the Pinkerton brought—perhaps his favourite, or only, heavy coat. Poe had worn it during his voyage from America and hours earlier I had watched him remove it from the bottom drawer of a wardrobe where it had lain folded, in mothballs, ever since. I wondered whether he'd held onto it as a nostalgic talisman or a guilty reminder of the man whose life he'd usurped.

"I have not told you this before, but when I was crossing the vast Atlantic on the *Gloria Scott*," he said softly, "I lapsed for days into the most volcanic, debilitating fever. Nothing I have experienced before or since compares to the onset of that *delirium tremens*. My very body did not want to be free of drink, and my reason, my sanity, had no hold over its plight and desperation. So much did it resist my will to sobriety that it took my sickness to the very point of death. My powers to fight it diminished with terrifying rapidity. There seemed little or nothing worth clinging to. Facing what I thought could only be the end, I was nursed in my cabin by an American Spiritualist. She held my hand, saying: *'I will see you in the morning, either way.'* But, Holmes—I did not die. I arrived. In a new land. Life had not done with me yet. Nor has it."

I nodded my understanding, for the benefit of settling his mind. If it failed to have the same result upon my own, I tried not to show it.

By now our friend *le fossoyeur*, filthy and toothless, had positioned a weathered oak coffin next to the hole. He wore the habit of a Franciscan friar and I didn't wish to inquire how he came by such apparel, as he was as far from a Holy man as could be imagined: nor what he had done with the previous incumbent of the oblong box, the lid of which he removed with accompanying squeals and creaks, some of the wood and some from his own decrepit anatomy.

I examined Poe as a dresser might examine a Shakespearean actor before they step out on stage. At the outset, he was a facsimile of the Daguerrotype Reynolds, over twenty-five years on, to a tee. And resembled a dead man uncannily.

I had painted his face with zinc oxide for paleness, even pencilling fine blue lines to make his skin look translucent, and had used lead and antimony sulphide to darken the orbits of his eyes. Over the past weeks we had together devised—like a grotesque and indulgent hobby—every possible artifice to hide any remnant of a healthy glow. The gravedigger, at our explicit bidding, had even acquired a dead cat, which he now lodged at the foot of the coffin, to exude all the excesses of decay to the nose of any future beholder.

"A black one," said Poe, holding his nostrils. "How appropriate."

He dug into the greatcoat's pockets, knowing what he would find there. Turning to me, he decanted the contents of his right hand to my own: two half-cents, a Coronet cent dated 1848, a Liberty seated dime, and a double eagle. Upon those coins he placed a small book of poetry from the other pocket, its leather, embossed cover made brittle by age: *Sonnets from the Portuguese* by Elizabeth Barrett Browning.

His forefinger opened the cover to reveal an inscription in a woman's hand.

I read aloud: "*From AP to JJR, with fondest love.*"

He took it back and recited from memory:

"I love thee with a love I seemed to lose
With my lost saints. I love thee with the breath,
Smiles, tears, of all my life; and, if God choose,
I shall but love thee better after death."

With that, he walked over to the coffin and lay in it, hands crossed, palm upon palm over the book of poetry on his breast.

I knelt beside him, fighting the noxious stink of the dead feline, cradled his head, and administered a solution of chloral hydrate in ethanol, a narcotic that slows down the activity of the central nervous system. The dilution was crucial, as an overdose could lead to stupor, even coma. I was by no means an expert but I was no novice, having taken to imbibing certain substances of my own.

I told myself I acted in the tradition of Priestley, Hooke and Boyle as I pressed the brown syrup to his lips. I did not have an exact idea of how long it would sedate him, but I knew, if nothing else, that it would slow his heart rate and keep him calm. Which is not a wholly irrelevant objective when said person is about to be buried alive. The worst that could happen would be for him to become fully conscious, alert and—not unreasonably—panic, using up the available air much more rapidly and putting himself in danger of suffering a respiratory attack, with dire, possibly fatal, consequences. I tried to put such a possibility to the back of my mind, but my hands were shaking.

I stood back and brushed the mud from my knees as the gravedigger re-sealed the coffin lid using the original, rusted nails. When the time came, I was well aware it would be my job to ensure Ezra Dugdale didn't put an ear to Poe's chest or stab a pin in the back of his hand. Otherwise . . .

"Should we—you know—say something?" The old man tottered back, his chest heaving.

"No," I said.

"I feel we should."

I sighed, but did not answer, beating my arms to get life back in them. Or perhaps to reassure myself there was life in me, in that domain of death.

Undeterred, he made the sign of the cross with gnarled, root-like hands and murmured the ancient words of the pre-Carolingian liturgy for the dead, known as the *Subvenite*: "Come, saints of God, come, angels of the Lord, take his soul and carry it unto the sight of the Almighty. Amen."

"Amen," I found myself repeating.

A high voice from inside the coffin slurred as if from too much grog: "May God have mercy on my soul."

I caught my laugh in my teeth, lest it erupt into weeping.

Without delay, the gravedigger and I lifted the four cords he'd fed through the coffin handles and let them run through our hands as we struggled to lower the weight into the grave, careful that it didn't up-end itself. Far more difficult than it sounds. At times, the box hit the earthen walls as might a lifeboat against the side of a ship, causing me to inwardly apologise to Poe for the inconvenience, ridiculously like some train guard eager to placate an upset passenger. But the entire situation, as Poe accepted, *was* ridiculous. "*Sublimely, terrifyingly so.*" (I admit, the "sublime" was lost on me.)

Soil pitter-pattered on the lid of the coffin, then, once it was covered, landed in silent, thick clodges. With the monotony of every spadeful I could not help but imagine Poe lying down there in the darkness, his breathing flat and slow—*thump!*—his eyes closed—*thump!*—the chloral hopefully taking effect—*thump!* But in time, between the two of us, the grave was filled, and, for our sins, it was done.

⌒⌒

I was never so grateful to return to *l'esprit de Paris* as that night. The busy boulevards. The street lights. The gabbling and braying at

café tables in busy squares. It revived me, as I stepped back, mud-
died and muddled, into the real world from the realm of ghosts.
On arrival home I could not disrobe fast enough, and asked Le
Bon to run me a piping hot bath. I could not, of course, tell him
how badly I needed to scrub the clotted scent of putrefaction from
my skin.

Earlier that day, according to the plan I had concocted with
Poe, I'd left a carefully-composed letter for Dugdale at the Hôtel
de Laâge, urging him to come and meet me at eight o'clock sharp
that evening. I'd made it clear that our inquiries had borne fruit
and that we had important information to divulge.

Until then I had time to kill, over an hour in fact, so once
I had dried myself and dressed in fresh clothes, I attempted to
divert my anxious thoughts by reading Belot's novel *Mademoiselle
Giraud, Ma Femme*, which had caused quite a stir of recent moral
outrage. Quickly, though, I realised the depicted disintegration of
a marriage and a mental state did nothing for my peace of mind,
however much Poe told me subversive literature was a necessary
purgative. If anything, it made me appreciably more jittery.

I took a jorum of hot rum and egg and wrapped myself in
all the blankets I could find. Even so, I found I could not sit still,
so circumnavigated the apartment time and again, pausing to un-
crick my neck or stretch out the tension in my spine.

Our library, ever over-spilling, opened into Poe's inner sanc-
tum, his scientific collection, which filled the densely-packed
shelves: dozens upon dozens of bottles of evidence and oddities,
making the spacious room resemble nothing so much as a museum
of anatomy—or curiosity. *Tales of Oddity and Curiosity*, I thought,
as I hesitated at a pair of conjoined twin lambs, suspended in for-
maldehyde, whom Poe had dubbed "Roderick and Madeleine." I
sometimes longed to have a simple peasant's admiration of God's
miracles, of Life, rather than always having to examine mortality
and the monstrous.

Tales of Mortality and the Monstrous . . .

Returning to the fireside, I sat staring at the Daguerrotype of Reynolds, pondering his poor son's intolerable loss.

How could we justify what we were doing? Did we not uphold the idea of justice, law, fairness? What was *fair* about this, to a young man in Baltimore whose only wish was to know the truth about his father?

And yet, would it do any good to tell him his father died drunk and broke on the cobbles behind a tavern? Where was the justice, or kindness, in that? Then my thoughts ended up where they always ended up—with Poe in that fetid subterranean box.

⌒✖

Never in my life had I known a clock to move more slowly.

Eight o'clock came—and went.

I waited.

Fifteen minutes later I went to the door and looked down the stone stairs of the atrium. I saw no sign of a soul.

I returned, slamming the doors, and lit a fumbling cigarette.

Then, when it was spent, a second.

"Dugdale. Where are you?"

I cursed the air through gritted teeth, like a youth waiting on a street corner, stood up by his sweetheart.

I took to the needle. It calmed me, but not enough. Not nearly enough.

I paced back and forth even faster, checking my watch every ten seconds.

Every five.

Unavoidably, I thought of Poe's shallow breathing within his casket.

I thought of his panic. But the panic was mine—and the *fear*, like a roiling sea inside me.

What if this delay were interminable? What if I was wrong about the dose? What if he were to fully *wake up?* What if something should *prevent me from getting there in time?* Causing him to die the most horrifying death imaginable—locked, with mute screams unheard by any living soul, in that stinking, Stygian blackness?

"May God have mercy on my soul."

Dear Lord, what if those had been his *last* last words—so similar to his first?

That we had planned it together did nothing to diminish the all-pervasive self-accusation I now felt. I had made this happen, this madness, and no one else. It had been my *idea*, and mine alone.

The clock struck nine.

I could bear it no longer.

I ran full-pelt, dodging cabs and horse-drawn omnibuses along the way, to the Hôtel de Laâge. I must have looked like a dishevelled madman as I ran in and approached the desk, ringing the bell frantically.

I composed myself as best I could as the *concierge*—a worn beauty with a noble forehead—emerged from *la loge*, her apartment on the ground floor, brushing crumbs from the shawl around her *décolletage*.

"My name is Sherlock Holmes. Please let Monsieur Dugdale know immediately that I am downstairs waiting for him."

She replied with her nose in the air that she was quite able to remember my name from that morning. "But I'm afraid Monsieur Dugdale has been out all day. As you can see behind me, your letter is still in his room's pigeon-hole, exactly where I left it."

My heart hit the immaculately-swept floor.

I felt light-headed. I told myself not to faint. I asked if she had any idea where Monsieur Dugdale had gone, or when he was likely to return? She said she did not, on both counts. I asked her what she *did* know. She told me she did not like my tone of voice. That did not concern me in the least, I mumbled.

Turning away, I gathered what paltry thoughts and decorum I could, then spun back and apologised profusely, offering that it was a matter of grave importance.

"I can see that," she said, but reasserted that she still knew nothing. I'm not sure what she said after that. I was busy thinking of that bleak, deserted cemetery—that *occupied coffin.* I was thinking how I might live with being the man who killed Edgar Allan Poe . . .

The next thing I knew, a cuckoo poked out its stupid head, sounding its mocking gong of half past the hour.

Nine thirty!

How much air?—how much *time?*—

Why was I even debating it? I couldn't waste another second. I had to get to that grave and save him: to blazes with the plan—we would have to think of *another* plan. The fact was, I might *already* be too late! I ran for the door and stopped in my tracks.

"Dugdale!"

He acknowledged me with perfect calmness, then a smile, and, after stroking each side of his moustache, an outstretched hand. "Holmes. What a surprise. What are you doing here?"

"Where have you been?" I blurted.

My demeanour must have given him pause. He frowned, laughing. "Why, pursuing my investigations. As a matter of fact, I have a strong lead, up in . . ."

"Never mind that now! You must accompany me—"

"Whoah! Hold your horses!" He placed a small package tied with a bow of pink ribbon in front of the *concierge.* "Keep this behind the desk 'til I return, will you, please? My wife'd have my guts for garters if I came back from *gay Paree* empty-handed."

I dragged him by the sleeve out into the street.

Hailing a *fiacre,* I told the driver to take us to the St-Lazare *embarcadère,* where we boarded the Ouest Company's *Ligne d'Auteuil* to the western outskirts of the city, via Pont-Cardinet, Courcelles, Neuilly, Avenue de l'Impératrice and Passy, into the 16th arrondissement and to the final stop on the line.

The journey afforded me time, highly-strung though I was, to apprise Dugdale of our researches: that is to say, the entirely fictitious line of breadcrumbs which, I needed to convince him, had led us to Julius Jack Reynolds's grave. Dupin's stroke of genius, I explained, took us to a bookshop named 'Queequeg and Yoji', which specialised in selling American novels, poetry, and magazines. Dupin had been positive that an American abroad, however much in exile, would still hanker after keeping cultural ties with the nation of his birth. "And so it proved," I lied. "The bookshop owner, when shown the Daguerrotype, recognised Reynolds instantly as a regular customer over the years who called himself James Quaperlake." All of this was completely bogus information, yet I watched Dugdale absorb it gravely, without interruption. I continued to describe, as rehearsed, how we had followed the trail of this 'Quaperlake' from address to address . . .

"Did he marry? Does he have children?"

"No," I said. Then added nuance to the blunt statement to say we could find no record of such. Reynolds, I said, seemed to have lived a solitary, perilous and frugal existence, from what we could understand (i.e. invent), dealing sporadically in antiques, losing money as often as he made it, lurching from financial feast to famine due to his inveterate vice. Gambling.

"So, where are we headed?" Dugdale's eyes shone with expectation. "Have you found where he lives? Arranged a meeting?"

"Regrettably not." I unfolded a sheet of paper from my inside pocket. "He died in Emmaus a month ago. In circumstances where there is no will or mortgage but a lease involved, the *Bureau des Hypothèques* is invaluable." I handed it him. "When the death of a lessor is reported, all children and surviving spouses are recorded in the register called the *Mutation par*

Décès. This includes the full name—James Quaperlake—and the date of death—March 18th, 1878."

He pored over the lines of writing. I handed him another piece of paper. A death certificate with that very date, which Poe and I had procured weeks beforehand. (Hence our necessary use of the peculiar name upon it: "James Quaperlake".)

"He suffered from underlying *angina pectoris,*" I embellished. "But the cause of death was Bright's Disease, a form of disease of the kidneys, characterised by albumin in the urine and especially acute and chronic nephritis. Luckily for us, he didn't end up sewn into a cheap *serpillière* and deposited into a pauper's mass grave without the grace of a coffin, but benefitted from the charitable work of a local fraternity who take it upon themselves to bury the poor, and those without family or friends, with some kind of dignity."

Dugdale looked up.

"This is mere paperwork. I need proof."

"You shall have it."

The hands of the *clocher du village* showed midnight as Dugdale and I raided the shed at the gates of the cemetery of the Église Jésus-le-Roi, finding two long-handled spades there, as I knew we would. Of the gravedigger there was no sign. That again was pre-arranged. I did not want even the faintest risk of him letting the cat out of the bag.

Bad metaphor.

I thrust the shovel into the Pinkerton's hands, assuring him the attendant had been paid off for turning a blind eye, while explaining that getting legal permission for exhumation from a magistrate was a long-winded process and by no means a *fait accompli.* I then led him swiftly to the relevant plot, where I saw that the old man had covered our excavations with stone slabs. No mean feat for the two of us to shift. How that wiry bag of bones had done so without assistance was beyond me.

Our blades cut in deep. It had rained earlier, an advantage in lessening the possibility of Dugdale finding the softness of the loam suspicious.

As we dug with vigour, I couldn't help feeling sick with fear. I had told Dugdale we would find a dead man, but would that prove to be a hideous self-fulfilling prophecy?

How many hours and minutes has he gone without air? I asked myself as my heart thudded louder and louder in my chest.

What unspeakable horror may we find when we lift the coffin lid?

"Slow down."

I attempted to explicate my nervous frenzy between gulps of air, and another lie mattered little. "I don't fancy being arrested as a grave robber."

"If it comes to it, I have my badge to show."

"Let's hope it doesn't come to it."

Our shovels scraped the last remnants of soil away from the aged wood of the narrow box. Dugdale dropped to the head of the coffin and begin to lift it. I did the same at the foot. A combination of wetness and decay oozed out as we hauled it up. The nails were so rotten that we did not need a claw hammer, many either snapped or fell out as we pinched them with our fingers. I lifted off the lid and it was like unscrewing a jar of putrid pond water.

Dugdale reeled back a step, his cuff to his mouth, coughed, then turned his cheek away. When he turned back I observed his reaction as he looked down at Julius Jack Reynolds in all his *post mortem* glory.

Poe, that was . . . with no more life in his grey cheeks than had the funerary carvings that stood gawping down at us.

My stomach turned over. The bleak question gnawed.

Is he dead?

I'd brought a lantern from the gravedigger's store. Now I lit it with trembling fingers. A flickering amber fell upon the stony features in the coffin.

They did not move. The repellent stench of the black cat
caused me to splutter and bite on my handkerchief to stop myself
spewing, but in fact the action also secretly stifled my sobs.

I handed Dugdale the Daguerrotype he had given me, of
Reynolds and his beloved.

"Proof positive," I affirmed, my teeth chattering.

The Pinkerton held it in his eye line, then moved it slightly
aside, as if placing the smiling immortality of the photograph and
the corporeal reality of the corpse side by side.

The comparison done, he thrust the Daguerrotype back at me
and moved closer, staring down at the body with great intensity,
his breathing a low, growling murmur. Before I could stop him,
he had swiftly bent down and extracted the book of poetry from
under Poe's cold hands.

He straightened up and opened its cover.

"From AP to JJR, with fondest love."

"JJR." I repeated. "Julius Jack Reynolds."

He grunted through his nostrils.

I thought it a strange, almost dismissive punctuation with
which to end his odyssey. And I wondered why he dropped the
book of poetry to the dirt, when it was quite clearly an item of
evidence his client in Baltimore might think of some worth. As it
was, I was thinking about the wrong thing. As it was, I had no time
to catch his arm, or prevent him in any way, before he had done the
very last thing I expected him to do at that precise moment.

He scraped the back of his throat and spat hard and viciously
into the dead man's face.

Only then, too late, did my fingers tighten on his arm. Not
that he moved in the slightest. I don't think a regiment could have
dislodged him.

In spite of my grip, Ezra Dugdale did not look at me. He
simply fixed his gaze upon the face of the cadaver with the gout of
phlegm trickling down its cheek, clearly relishing what he saw. As

an impulsive act it was loathsome; as a premeditated one, baffling. Frankly, I was lost as to what to do or say. Mercifully, I was saved from saying or doing anything.

"Bury him," he said, devoid of compassion.

And by the time I'd registered what had just happened—staring down at Poe, my heart pounding, wishing I could tell if he was *alive or dead*, watching the spit create a blemish on the chemicals I had applied, wondering if that had been pointless, wondering if the man I had lived with for years would *open his eyes*—wondering why Dugdale had done what he'd done, what emotions had erupted, or been kept in check— . . . I looked all around me, and the Pinkerton was gone.

～

"Lazarus, come forth!" The unmistakably musical accent caused a pang in my heart. "O Grave, where is thy victory, O Death, where is thy sting?" A graceful, almost feminine hand reached out of the coffin, like the Arthurian Lady of the Lake. I was grateful for the darkness, that he did not see the tears in my eyes when he opened his own.

I pulled Poe to his feet, very unsteady feet though they were. Not entirely unexpected, after the chloral. Almost immediately the strength in his legs seemed to go and he toppled, but I managed to keep him upright, using one of the spades as a crutch while I picked up the book of poetry, wiping it in his greatcoat, which was too slithery with mould and damp to notice the difference of an extra bit of mud. I chose not to encumber him with questions. I was too delirious, almost hysterical, that he was alive to care.

Before we left, he insisted on pausing at the grave edge. He held out his open palm. Instinctively sensing what he wanted to do, I handed him Reynolds's coins and he cast them with a gentle flourish into the deep rectangular hole.

"*Requiescat in Pace.*"

Whatever the symbolism, whatever the motive, he intoned these words without cynicism—a rare feat for him. That excluded, to my relief, he was as uncommunicative as I was. Hardly, in fact, had the energy to stand, let alone talk.

I let him lean his weight against me and carried him like a war veteran to the nearby hostelry, Le Mouton Blanc, in which we had booked a room. Once inside, the nausea hit him and he began retching. Again, the chloral. Again, not unexpected. I asked for a bucket. I asked for two buckets: one with water and a sponge. I peeled Reynolds's greatcoat off him—not sure it was fit for the laundry or the incinerator—and plied him with copious amounts of water to clear the drug from his system. The minute he was safe to leave alone I sped back to the cemetery and filled the grave (coffin, cat and all) though by the end of it I only had the strength to heft half the slabs back in place. I'd have to rely on the gravedigger to tidy up after me.

When I returned, utterly spent, I collapsed upon the bed where Poe already lay, I suspect with the room circling round him. The first hangover he had had in years. Whether he was sleeping, I could not tell: I had extinguished the candle before entering, and noticed only that his breathing was shallow.

The irony was not lost on me. Death and resurrection had become a habit for Poe. I pondered whether, lying in his premature grave as the clammy air ran out, there beckoned a peace unknown in life. I wondered if fear transformed into a kind of bliss, a final acceptance of the indifference of the universe—no more penance, guilt, terror, obligation to normality, repentance, faith, or lack of it: just the utter perfection of oblivion. And whether, as the coffin lid cracked open, and he felt the icy night air, that dream, that terrifying *comfort* of a dream, had vanished. After an hour of sleeplessness, I had to satisfy my curiosity.

"Poe? Your experience . . . of being buried alive," I whispered in the dark. "What . . . what did it feel like?"

I heard only silence. Then, in a measured slur, another side effect of his sedative, just three precise words:

"Read . . . my . . . story."

～≺

The landlord of the hostelry reported, as I rushed downstairs, that my father had already left. How my "father" had risen and performed his ablutions without me noticing, I had no idea—but then, I was out for the count. A herd of elephants could have danced the can-can at the foot of my bed and failed to rouse me.

I hurled myself into a train carriage, trying to ignore the reactions of passengers to an otherwise respectable-looking young man who stank to high heaven. But that was nothing compared to what was to come. When I arrived home I was greeted by a sight so strange it almost made the past few days seem a glowing picture of normality.

"Poe!"

Still cadaver-like and even more rancid than myself, he was down on all fours like a dog, tongue hanging out and his face red with exertion through the ghoulish make-up, running his hands over the floorboards as if searching for something quite invisible. Insanity, all this time the author's bedfellow, had finally consumed him. Of this I had not an iota of doubt. His experience in Emmaus had been far more dramatic than I'd thought.

"Holmes!"

"What is going on?"

"Why did Dugdale spit in the face of the person he thought was Reynolds?"

"Excuse me?"

"Have you been asking yourself that question? And if not, why not?"

"I . . ."

"Evidently, because he has despised his father all his life."

"What?" I blinked feverishly. "Are you telling me Ezra Dugdale is, in fact, the man he espoused to be working for? Reynolds's *son?*"

Poe sprang to his feet, dashed to his bureau and waved an Atlantic cable in the air like a signalman's flag.

"Not questioning for a second your ability to discern whether his credentials were genuine or not, the moment you told me of your first meeting I decided to check his authenticity for myself by contacting my old acquaintance, Nathan Bullhouse of the Pinkerton Agency in Philadelphia. I received this reply today. You'll find that Ezra Dugdale is indeed the name of a Pinkerton: but one who went missing during his investigation in Baltimore into the death of Annie Phelps, and three other women similarly butchered. I read of the crimes a few months ago, and simply filed them away as an intriguing case, but an unsolved one."

He extravagantly swept a newspaper from our rack and laid its swan wings before us.

"Wait. I don't understand." I could hardly focus on the print. "Are you saying this man, this imposter, stole Ezra Dugdale's identity? To what end?"

"To what end do you think?"

"You . . . you cannot mean he is responsible for those murders in Baltimore."

"I can. And more than that." He took the soggy and misbegotten book of Elizabeth Barrett Browning poetry from his great coat, and showed me once again the handwritten dedication inside.

"From AP to JJR." He expanded: "From *Annie Phelps* to Julius Jack Reynolds."

Now it was my turn to extract something from my pocket. The Daguerrotype. I looked at the smiling face of the pretty young woman therein.

"Annie Phelps," said Poe. "Murder victim."

I was shaken. "So Reynolds is his father, and Annie Phelps . . ."

"His mother. And that was only the beginning." Poe gestured towards the door, where he had been on his hands and knees. "If you look closely at the floor you will find tiny indentations left by Dugdale, or rather, Reynolds *fils* in all but name. From the various scuffs and blemishes I would attest he wore roper style boots with a smooth leather outsole, a wider than average toe box and a heel between half an inch and three quarters high, with a nail or piece of hard material embedded in it. Indentations identical to those detected in the floor at the premises in the Rue Beaugé."

"The House of Blood!"

"Precisely so. My dear Holmes, he is not merely a murderer but one compelled to do so repeatedly from insatiable lust. And has brought his foul trade from Baltimore to Paris."

I could hardly absorb the revelation. My head swam. "The cut on his cheek!—dear God, which I so foolishly deduced to be a shaving scar—in reality, the defensive claw mark of a woman's fingernail as she fought off her attacker!"

"Again, precisely so. We must stop him."

Poe reached for his hat and cane, but lost his balance and had to steady himself against the wall with his shoulder, then his forehead.

"You're weak from the chloral and you look like a corpse," I said, forcing him to a chair.

"Nonsense." He got to his feet.

"Stay here!" I was insistent. "If he sees you it will be like Banquo's ghost. And the very reason for all this deception will be blown asunder."

He saw the logic in what I said, which, for him, was a miracle on a par with the loaves and fishes. He sank back into the cushions, head lolling in his hand, as I headed for the street.

"Holmes." His croak made me turn. I don't know if the paleness was from the vinegar I'd applied or that some pernicious thought had drained the colour from his cheeks. His eyes were sunk in coal-dark pits, the irises coal-dark themselves. "This man is a beast. It is nothing to him to snuff another flame." This was his way of saying: *be careful.* Armed with my baby dragoon, I had every intention of doing so.

"And Holmes..." I looked back a second time, and Poe seemed even more forlorn. "Look in his suitcase."

I dashed from the building, thumped in the shoulder by a squat, bearded figure entering in such haste he didn't register me, though I recognised him instantly. The only Hebrew in the *Préfecture.* Four uniforms by his side. He blundered past without apology, but I grabbed his arm.

"Solomon Grotowski."

"I need to see Dupin."

"Tell me why." I saw his hesitation. He looked sickly. "Tell me, man."

"There's been another murder, same as the last. Nose cut off. Entrails out."

"Where?"

"Body found round the back of the Place de la Croix. Marie-Louise Desmet, known as Cléopâtre. A mulatto." Offensive word some imagine derived from the Spanish for a mule, but in fact from the Arabic *Muwaladeen,* meaning white mixed with Moor.

"Come with me." I was about to ask if the policemen had fire-arms, but I saw that they had. The rest I explained along the way.

Hearing that our quarry was due to check out upon the hour, Grotowski told the *concierge* to stay in her room. One of the flat-feet escorted her. I was already climbing the stairs.

I knew what room Reynolds was occupying because I'd seen in which pigeon-hole my letter had been placed. It wasn't hard to find. The hotel was tiny. Homely. Family run. I thought of the

other guests, secreted here for a quiet stay with lovers, wives, hus-
bands. All that about to be disrupted. Probably by gunfire. Possibly
by maiming, or death. Only one staircase. Good. No escape route.

I pressed my shoulders to the wall outside Room 9. The door
to Room 11 opened opposite. Seeing my pistol, the female guest
screamed. Grotowski's men exploded into action. A boot loosened
the door handle. A second sent it flying ajar.

A suitcase lay on the bed, packed and ready to go.

Beyond it, Reynolds—the upright young American I'd here-
tofore known as Ezra Dugdale—stood combing his hair in the
mirror, sarcastically whistling "The Marseillaise," as unruffled as if
a maid had arrived with the room service he'd ordered. He calmly
slid the comb into his breast pocket as three cold barrels of car-
bines pressed to the nape of his neck. The police, fingers on triggers, trembled far more than he did.

On the chest of drawers next to him I saw an apple with a
chunk bitten out of it, making a mental note to ensure it was taken
as evidence. Reynolds could see me via the mirror but did not turn
his head, simply raising his arms as if mildly inconvenienced while
Grotowski patted him down for weapons.

Look in his suitcase.

I turned my back, unclipped the fastenings, and lifted the lid.

It was packed neatly with clothes. Nestled in the centre under
a folded shirt was something wrapped in newspaper. I gave Reynolds a sideways glance, but he showed no interest.

I undid the bow of pink ribbon that held it together and gin-
gerly peeled away the outer layer, then the one under that. The
newsprint next confronting me seeped dark, glutinous stains. My
immediate thought was of meat purchased from a butcher's shop.
Grotowski must have come to my shoulder, for I heard his intake
of breath close to my ear as the shiny contents were unveiled and I
felt the gorge rise like lava in the back of my throat.

We beheld the disgusting offal of a human uterus and womb.

To think, whilst I had been waiting on tenterhooks for 'Dugdale' the night before, the man had in fact been removing the body parts of Marie-Louise Desmet; a foulness confirmed by our finding a set of butcher's knives in the self-same item of luggage—one of which was later proven to match the wounds on Fabienne Gagnon. It would seem he shared the trade of another notorious criminal, Dick Turpin, though with none of the attendant folk-heroism. And while I felt sick with guilt at Cléopâtre's tragically avoidable fate, this loathsome creature did not so much as even deny his actions.

"It was worth it," were the only words he said before Grotowski escorted him to the wagon.

The police got their confession, and some weeks later I visited Patrick Paul Reynolds in his cell. (Whether he liked it or not, his birth certificate had that as the surname of his father. And so it appeared on the arrest warrant.) He was confined in a narrow waistcoat, shackles on his ankles, bruises reducing his face to a distorted pulp. Whether the confession had been hard to come by, or his custodians wished to mete out their own kind of justice before a court did, I could not know. But he exhibited no glimmer of contrition, his face purely a mask of contempt. I wondered why he had agreed to answer my questions. Perhaps he wanted to be in the history books alongside Dick Turpin after all.

"Why pose as a Pinkerton?"

He sighed. "It opened doors. It accelerated the chase."

"You sailed close to the wind. It was your undoing."

He shrugged. "I had faith in my abilities."

"You didn't think we'd check you out?"

"I thought I was convincing enough."

"As a Pinkerton, or as a human being?"

He laughed sourly and his grin remained long after the sound had faded, as though the remark was entirely predictable and that he had expected better. "You're staring at me. Do I have flesh on my teeth? It's hard to get a toothpick in this establishment. I do like to look my best. For the ladies."

He was toying with me. I was dashed if I'd give him the satisfaction of showing my unease. In fact, I would disarm him back. "Annie, your mother."

"Oh—*her* . . ." He groaned. "It was her *insides,* see. Wanted to see what they looked like, all laid out in a row. When you've worked in a slaughter pen, you realise we are all made of the same filth, to wash down the drain when it comes to it. The joke is, we conspire to think ourselves angels."

I kept my composure.

"Why did you seek your father?"

"My dear old Pa? Why, to kill him, of course. Death cheated me of that pleasure."

"Why not simply live in ignorance? Why was he so important to you?"

"Do you deny what's in your breeches, Sherlock, like those other eunuchs out there? You live in darkness, but there's nothing I haven't seen. I was born and raised in a bordello—and that's the world, if you but knew it—one big whore house, one big engine of coupling, steaming and grinding away. As a child I ran and fetched like a black-as-pitch slave. And I ask you this: where was my father when the others had theirs to clip the ears of the bullies? To tell me right from wrong? To put hot food on the table every night? How could I answer the question of who I was, without asking first, who was he?"

"Did your mother not tell you?"

He grunted as he looked away, fixing dead eyes on the bricks of the wall.

"She said she never knew his name. She'd get angry, and drunk. Tell me to stop asking or get another whipping. So I got another whipping. Plenty, till I got a job in Mount Clare in one of the abattoirs near the railroad yards—the area known as 'Pigtown'. Learned pretty quick I enjoyed it more if an animal had a spark of life. No satisfaction in chopping up a dead thing. Thus I got apprenticed in heralding meat while my mother got the disease of her kind. Some would say God's will. Her nose rotted away. Not many paid to kiss her after that. Some did. The wrong kind. Beat her. Made her meaner." His face distorted with bitterness and pain. "Few months ago, death rattling in her lungs, she finally told me his name: Julius Jack Reynolds.

"She'd known it all that time. Showed me the photograph the day they got engaged. Handsome couple. At first, I thought she told it to make me happy, but she hadn't. Said the moment he heard she was pregnant carrying me, he flew into a rage and cancelled the wedding. Marriage meant everything to her. Escape from a dark life, safety, security, love. Now there was nothing and he was gone. And all because of me, she said. 'I could have had a *good* life if not for you coming along and spoiling everything.' So you see, her last act in life wasn't one of love, oh no—it was to vent her bile on her only son.

"And I guess I inculcated somewhat of a rage too, because I killed her and cut her up, and tore out the stinking part of her that produced me. Then ran. Then hid. Then prayed. Oh, I *prayed* in those days! Fancy! Other whores knew me and could point the finger, so I killed them too. They meant nothing to me, just like she didn't. Far as I was concerned, they didn't deserve to walk this earth. If I existed and they do not, it is unimportant to God and to me. Which of us sinned the more?"

I did not answer.

"I cared only about one thing," he continued. "And that was to find him, my father, but the Pinkerton came looking so I finished him too. Took his credentials and badge and cattle drover clothes. Traced the ship's manifest, just like I said, talked to the Purser, came to Paris. My quest got frustrating so I found a bar, tot-hunting, succumbed to a spoilt little dirty puzzle and played

Cupid's kettledrums to the wee hours, then strew her crinkum-crankum to the four winds."

I thought of "La Maison Sanglante" with its blood-dripping walls and the woman's corpse with its nose sliced off.

"Made me feel better for a while. Taking my hurt out on her all over again. Blood over the sheets like the very day she gave birth to me. Fatherless. The feeling went away. Not forever though. Always comes back. Like eating. You can only starve so long, then you need a real good steak."

"Perhaps your father didn't desert you," I suggested. "Perhaps he had other reasons. Perhaps he loved you."

He shook his head at the ridiculousness of the notion and held me with the reptilian eyes I had once perceived as attractive. "There is no love in the world, Sherlock. Just obtaining and suffering. The only choice in life is choosing which. Every man would rather make love with a knife than his lips. Just most won't admit it. Truth be told, you look at me and you envy me."

"I don't envy a man going to the guillotine," I said.

"Then you have a very poor imagination," said the murderer of many.

⟨ornament⟩

My meeting confirmed everything Poe surmised. That it was the killing of his mother that had been the catalyst for Patrick Paul Reynolds's trip to France, and that he chose, knowingly or not, his other victims as her surrogates, by way of re-enacting that one primal and all-consuming hatred. His motive, however, was to find the father who had rejected him. The one he blamed for all the ills of his life. If alive, he'd intended to kill him. As it turned out, when he reached Paris, the savage urge within him built up again and he was compelled to satiate it on innocent women.

"How did you know to look in the suitcase?" I asked.

Poe exuded pipe smoke, crossing his legs in the comfort of our rooms. "To a certain kind of murderer the homicidal act is akin to the high attained by a powerful drug, and the comedown just as precipitous. The taking of objects from the crime scene, biological or otherwise, is almost always part of such a person's *modus operandi*, as Vidocq would have it. Such deviants use them as fetishes to prolong the pleasure, or to keep as a sentimental memorial of the deed."

"I did not think him capable of sentiment."

"Criminals as a breed excel at it. But only as regards themselves, never others."

I smiled, but Poe grew silent and sank into a reverie that was not light. And I knew why.

Back in 1849 he could not, of course, have remotely known what was to come in that Paris spring of 1878, but he did know that he had left Reynolds, the father, gasping his last in a Baltimore backstreet. And if he had *not* done so—what? Would the bastard child of that man have grown up any differently? Would the poor women, and the Pinkerton, now dead, be alive? Poe had taken the circumstances before him, and tailored a new life for himself. Yet out of that same cloth, though no one could have predicted it, a monstrous son was made.

"Did I create him?"

I could only answer, as some insignificant recompense: "You created me."

I give thanks that Poe was spared, by death, the knowledge that Patrick Paul Reynolds would strike again, and this time create a whirlwind of hideous slaughter that would beguile and astonish the world.

Wanted for the murders in America, he never did reach the guillotine. The US government did a deal. In return for a French criminal incarcerated in New York being returned to face justice on his own home soil, Reynolds was deported to stand trial in Richmond. En route to Calais he escaped and was never seen again.

Except he was, of course. By the eyes of those he killed ten years later.

Their names toll like a funeral dirge in my mind, even now . . .

Mary Ann Nichols. Annie Chapman. Elizabeth Stride. Catherine Eddowes. Mary Jane Kelly . . .

Where he had been in the intervening years, and what he had been doing, I could not possibly know, but that he was in Whitechapel in 1888, and a fox amongst hens, I knew for absolute certain. The mutilations—his *modus operandi*, "as Vidocq would have it"—were identical to that of the Rue Beaugé. The unspeakable brutality as unique as a fingerprint. And as brazen as a name on a calling-card. The name the public had spoken in hushed tones then—*L'Anormale*, "The Abnormal One"—was horribly apt again.

It is the greatest regret of my life that I failed to catch him. The wolf eluded the hunter at every turn. I could only watch as blood ran in rivulets through London streets and fear held unfettered dominion even unto the limitless shores of history.

I knew who he was. I had his name. I knew his past. I knew his method. But I told none of this to the police. Or to Watson. I wanted to solve the case myself, without their help. Not through arrogance, or vanity, but a deep and unshakable sense of duty. He was mine in the most vile, possessory sense, and it was my job, mine alone, to bring him to justice.

It was personal. He had made it so. The carnage and wickedness divested upon the innocents of the East End, to him, was a mere spectacle for my benefit. To show that, even though I had unmasked him a decade earlier, he was the more powerful. That he was in the ascendant, and I was impotent to stop him. He revelled in that, I knew.

So long ago.

And yet he was the architect of a fear that endures. His name—or his acquired one—is still whispered by children's lips: a bogeyman, a spectre synonymous with ghastly murder. But fear, as

Poe once told me, is not all. It is only a fragment of Man, and the greater is Reason. And Reason is our champion, our guiding light against the encroachment of Chaos.

I knew this even as, weary and in my darkest hour, I took a package addressed to 221B Baker Street from the postman, and opened it alone while Mrs Hudson fetched me tea and fresh-baked scones to revive my spirits. The contents had the opposite effect.

Wrapped inside a double-page of the *Illustrated Police News* I found an apple with a bite taken out, accompanied by this note:

~~~

To Mr Sherlock Holmes

Well, well, "Boss!" They say I'm an American now because I use that word. How near and yet so far! I see I've got a new name too. Sells papers, eh? And my Daddy's name, too! Who'd credit it?

Apologies for the enclosed . . . I planned to send you a kidney like I did for Lusk. Then I thought I'd remind you of Paris. Of course, none of them is quite like my dear old Ma.

The writing on the wall, that wasn't me, by the way. Still it got Warren in a good old lather. Ha ha! The boys in blue will 'not get nowhere' chasing a schoolmaster and a Jew. Little do they know I was under lock and key once upon a time. But now I'm free. The autobiography of a knife continues. I'll be out tonight looking for a new sow to woo. Think of that as you sip your cocoa, detective.

Think of me in your dreams, always,

With fondest regards,

Jack

The Language of Terror

From the Journal of George Alban Lestrade (Mortlake, June 14ᵗʰ 1926):

I am haunted by him now. Every clatter of the letterbox makes my heart quicken. I recognise the handwriting on the latest package, and a hundred memories flit dustily through my mind. Those seventeen steps up to 221B. The fug of tobacco smoke that used to greet me, along with Mrs Hudson's pots of tea.

But those chairs are empty now. I'm told an advertising man rents the premises, and children play and chatter there. It brings a lump to my throat, the thought that scenes so vivid to me are invisible to others—while cases, invisible till now, come to light . . .

My curiosity deepens as each new document arrives. Even as I rock grandchildren on my knee, I secretly try to read between the lines. Once a plod, always a plod, I suppose. But what do I know? Only that he retired from the public gaze, imprecisely, to some hermitage on the Sussex Downs. I shall save the stamp and envelope with its half-distinct postmark. Examine it later. Apply what I remember of his techniques between lunch and tea time, before I walk the dogs.

But first—the new investigation itself . . .

The title—a scrawl clearly added after the writing was complete—is intriguing. Will it be as bizarre and shocking as the last? Only the reading of it will tell.

And so I begin . . . from the very first line hearing the unmistakable voice of the man I knew so many years ago, and so well. That of Mr Sherlock Holmes . . .

It was a full twelvemonth since I'd first met Edgar Allan Poe in the guise of "Dupin", and the year of my coming of age, traditionally a time when parents speak with pride of their offspring's achievements. In the company of Poe, however, no such praise was forthcoming. Nor did I expect it to be. He was too lost in his own concerns to be bothered with such fripperies.

The Vinogradov affair had depleted his intellectual reserves enormously, reaching its conclusion, as it did, with the successful prosecution of Édouard Isidore Buguet—the "spirit photographer"—after a raid on the charlatan's premises. It had nevertheless pained me to observe the residual impact upon my American friend. The tawdry use of "double-exposures" and "messages from the dead" for fraudulent purposes (a verbatim account of which can be found in Leymarie's *Procès des Spirites*) had caused his mood to darken perceptibly, and around the anniversary of his late wife's birthday in mid-August, his gloom grew deeper still, as I was to find it always would, with grim predictability. For days on end his presence sucked the air from the room, and I was forced to endure hours of silence as he lost himself in memories of his beloved Virginia, whose life had been cut short by the cruel hand of a God he now rejected.

I will tell you, and it gives me no pleasure to do so, that at certain times during that bleak summer of 1875, he contemplated *l'appel du vide*—the call of the void; that is, the urge to end it all—holding a revolver to his temple, coming close to the final act—invariably resisting at the very last moment and firing a shell into the wall. Over a period of weeks, the bullet holes spelled out his initials: "E.P."—which he variously claimed, after each event, stood for "Everlasting Purgatory!", "Ending Perfectly!" or "Endless Possibilities!".

You will understand, therefore, when I say I'd left him uncommunicative that September morning, longing to get out for a brief stroll to blow the cobwebs off, why, upon my return, the sudden crack of a gunshot galvanised me. Fearing the worst, either by awful accident or terrible design, I ran upstairs at full pelt—to be greeted, out of breath, by a freshly-made puncturation in the wallpaper of our salon.

"In the name of heaven ...!" I waved the strong smell of cordite from the air.

"Equidistant Pancakes!" Poe cried from his armchair, the pistol hanging limply from one hand.

"Ever Pathetic!" I snapped back angrily, opening a window a few inches to dispel the smoke, then glaring over at the final dot at the bottom of the P. "So this is for my instruction? Thank you!"

"Not at all. Self-murder is instructive only to a fool, and I don't consider you a fool. At least you have not yet proven yourself to be one. But there is still time."

"Well, if I *were* a fool, I'd certainly be learning from the master!"

A smile flickered like faltering sunshine behind grey clouds. "Ah, you know my *methods*, my dear Holmes, but do you know my *madness?*"

"I think that is one class I'll give a miss, if you don't mind." I slumped in the chair opposite, refusing to give him the satisfaction of knowing he'd riled me.

Poe tittered and beckoned his valet-cum-factotum Le Bon, a descendant of the Saint-Domingue free coloured delegation who visited the French Assembly prior to the Reign of Terror. The man had, not unnaturally, been alerted by the sound of gunfire, but Poe calmly ordered coffee to medicate my jangled nerves. I pointed out that the effects of coffee, according to its chemistry, would do nothing to calm me. Quite the reverse. Whereupon he giggled again, but it caught in his craw and he leaned his head back against the head-cushion and shut his eyes. I swear, at times it seemed as if his genius and his insanity chased each other round a track like a greyhound and a hare, and I was damned if I knew which would get the better of which. But the coffee was forthcoming, and so was the announcement of a visitor. Two, in fact.

We rose as a mature, stately woman in a pigeon grey coat entered with a younger one on her arm, equally well-dressed in turquoise. I noted immediately that the latter was approximately my own age, petite, more than averagely pretty, with jet black curls tucked under a straw bonnet with velvet ribbon and feathers (more New York fashion than Paris). Her innate fine features were augmented by a highly pleasing air of natural grace and modesty, so different from what I found in French women of her age, who were invariably curt, formidable, sometimes even self-possessed to the point of menacing.

"M. Dupin, I come to you on a matter of grave concern." The older woman spoke tremulously, in poor French, with an American drawl.

"I know that, madame, for a number of reasons," replied Poe, also in French. "Firstly, you come here with an ally, evidently because you lack the courage to come alone. Secondly, you keep your gloves on, perhaps ashamed to reveal that you bite your fingernails to the quick with worry. Lastly, you gave no card to my manservant, which tells me secrecy is vital. Rest assured, anything said within these walls is sacrosanct. You have my word on it."

"*Merci*," said the younger woman, also American, pronouncing it *mercy*. She had removed her gloves and Poe pressed his lips to the back of her bare hand. A rosy tint glowed in her cheeks as she downcast her eyes timidly. Neither guest seemed perturbed by the reek of my chemistry bench, our newly-acquired skeleton of a macaque, or the plaster imprints of various breeds of dog on the mantel shelf, arranged in size from fox terrier to Newfoundland.

"Now, let us speak in English, if you please." Poe adopted the French accent he had perfected over many years and flicked the tails of his frock coat before he sat.

"You speak our tongue?"

"After painstaking lessons, yes."

"Singular for a Frenchman."

"Well, M. Dupin is a singular Frenchman," I said. "Please take a seat, madame."

"May I ask how you know of my services?"

"Your reputation is unparalleled for success and discretion." The older woman sat beside her companion on the chaise longue, below a large framed print of a salamander from von Siebold's *Fauna Japonica*. "I was told, confidentially, of the mission you undertook to the salt-baths in Biarritz in '65, when Otto von Bismarck had possession of a letter he claimed would see the collapse of the French government overnight."

I was knocked for six. "Is this true?"

Poe settled in his chair like an old cat in its basket. "I simply told him it so happened I was in possession of another letter. One which would, if revealed to the world, see the political demise of Bismarck himself at a stroke. What he didn't know was that my letter was non-existent. My bargaining chip was that he had a guilty secret he'd rather keep hidden. And he did. We agreed to destroy both epistles in unison. Nothing is more powerful in negotiations than an empty envelope. I didn't stop the advent of the Franco-Prussian War, but I do like to think I delayed it somewhat. You move in diplomatic circles to know such a story, and can evade identification no longer, Mrs Adele Washburne."

"Wife of Elihu B. Washburne," I interjected. "United States Minister to France."

"Forgive my colleague. It is my business to know the details of every important man in Europe. Mr Holmes has been memorising my catalogue and wishes to impress."

I found myself blushing hideously. "I apologise."

"And you, my dear, are his daughter."

The young woman confirmed this with a nod and a delicate smile that did not come easily to her lips. "Annabel."

"Named after 'Annabel Lee,'" said her mother. "The poem?"

"Ah."

"You know of it?"

"I'm afraid not," said Poe, rising to fetch a cigarette box. I alone noticed the dark shadow cross his brow. It had, of course, been the title of the last verse he ever penned; the immortal love poem about himself and his doomed bride.

To my alarm the young lady piped up, cheerfully:

"I was a child and she was a child,
  In this kingdom by the sea:
But we loved with a love that was more than love—
  I and my Annabel Lee;
With a love that the wingèd seraphs of heaven
  Coveted her and me."

I couldn't help picturing that slender figure of Virginia, light of footfall, creeping up behind a younger Poe as he wrote at his desk in that chilly cottage at Fordham. The touch of her small hands over his eyes, perhaps, or the soft sound of her laughter the first signal of her presence. Childhood sweethearts, they had met when he—the down-at-heel poet brimming with self-belief— had moved into the home of his aunt in Baltimore. "Sis" and "Eddie" they'd called each other. She, thirteen when he proposed; he, twenty-seven. Clearly she idolised him, even in his wastrel moments, and he reciprocated, doting on her by teaching her algebra, languages, and the piano. But, as every student of literature knows, the romance was cut brutally short when, during a music recital to raise money for one of his publishing ventures, Virginia coughed up blood. The doctors diagnosed consumption—the "White Death" that had seen off Edgar's mother when he was an infant. And there he was, forced to relive the horror of the most precious person in his life, pale of skin and red of lips, wasting away before his eyes, as the pendulum of the clock ticked inexorably towards oblivion. He succumbed to a downward spiral after years of sobriety, his grip on life, slippery and erratic at best, leading fatefully to his encounter with his *doppelgänger* on election night 1849, his escape from self-destruction to Europe—and to me.

"It's so romantic," said Annabel's mother. "Have you ever heard anything so romantic, M. Dupin?"

"I am not vulnerable to the aesthetic blandishments of *doggerel*, I fear, Mrs Washburne. I have more sophisticated tastes." If his heart was a raging tempest, he hid it expertly. Perhaps too expertly.

"Oh." Her face fell. "Elihu wooed me with those lines."

"Then I cannot say they were ineffective. As the proof of that marital union sits before me." Poe manufactured a smile.

"Dupin. Your name. It is of course the same as . . ."

Poe headed her off at the pass, giving a supremely Gallic shrug. "A common surname in France." Which seemed, happily, to draw a line under the matter. "Now, please, without any more ado, share your concern as best you can."

"My concern is for my husband's life and his reason." Mrs Washburne no longer clung to the pretence of composure. "If you know anything about him, you will know he is a man of incomparable will and resolve, and not easily shaken."

"He stayed in Paris throughout the Siege, if I remember correctly," said Poe. "Serving his country at a tumultuous time. That he remained at his post, alone amongst the foreign dignitaries in the capital, is admirable. He was Secretary of State under Grant, am I right?"

"Briefly. Before this tenure. We came in the spring of '69. He expected the posting to be relatively undemanding."

"History has a way of thumbing its nose at our expectations."

"He weathered the Commune because US citizens needed his assistance," she continued. "He could never shirk the responsibility invested in him. You see, growing up working daily in the fields and with instruction from the Holy Book, feeling the birch rod and seeing his father reduced to penury, he sees no man above him and no man below. It's what makes him a fine diplomat. And the finest husband."

She took the handkerchief I offered and dabbed the corners of her eyes.

"Eli has been a lion for the thirty years we have been married. But, I tell you, of late he is a different man. Waking at night. Fretful. Thinking an intruder is in the building. He keeps saying he hears footsteps—uneven footsteps, as of someone lame in one leg. A person intent on killing him."

I asked the obvious; if she knew who might want him dead.

"Oh, he knows *exactly* who is responsible, Mr Holmes. This is not an unknown assailant. Would that it were!"

Annabel reached over to squeeze her mother's hand. "My father is convinced that he is being stalked by John Wilkes Booth, assassin of President Lincoln, dragging his wounded leg like Captain Ahab on the deck of *The Pequod*."

I looked at Poe, expecting a reaction. He remained resolutely silent.

"But Wilkes Booth is dead." Incredulity tugged a laugh from my throat. "Well and truly. And ghosts exist purely in the minds of the living." I was thinking again of the trickster Buguet.

"This is not a ghost, and my father is not superstitious, Mr Holmes."

"Nor is his mind amiss or 'untethered'," added her mother. "I swear on the Bible, there is not a man walking this earth with a mind *more* tethered."

"And yet," said Poe. "The dead do not walk."

"That is as may be, sir. But he is convinced Booth is *alive,* and bent on assassination once more."

"Minister Washburne was a supporter and adviser to Lincoln, isn't that so? Then it would be natural for a fear regarding his own safety to run deep."

"So deep as to create a demon of it?" I asked, rhetorically.

Mrs Washburne shook her head vigorously. "You do not know my husband."

"I do not," said Poe, rising to his feet. "But we must neverthe-less be attentive to the facts, otherwise what is the point of facts?" He drew down a book from a nearby shelf. "As part of his educa-tion, my apprentice has been studying the most notable criminals of the century. This gives him the perfect opportunity to share what he has gleaned on the subject." He proffered his open palm in my direction.

"Well . . ." I straightened my back and tried to recall the essen-tial information without stammering. For a second, every scintilla of it evaporated from my mind. "Well, I know that Booth came from a family of theatricals. In fact, he was extremely successful on the boards. I believe the adoring public flocked to the stage door when-ever he was performing. And he was an outstanding *Richard III.*"

Poe grunted. "I seriously doubt his thespian achievements, though impressive, interest our guests terribly much, dear boy."

"Quite. Quite . . ." I stuttered, doing my best to trawl my memory for what was pertinent. "From what I recall, coming from a slave-owning family, his vehemence for abolitionists knew no bounds, and he believed the movement's very existence tanta-mount to destroying all he held dear about his beloved country."

"He was an agent for the Confederacy," said Poe.

"Yes. I was coming to that," I snapped. "And on that fateful day in 1865—"

"Good Friday."

"Good Friday, yes—he shot and killed the President at Washington's Ford Theatre during a performance of *Our American Cousin*, shooting his victim behind the ear with a .44-calibre pistol, before catching his foot on the bunting decorating the box as he jumped to the stage, crying out the motto of the state of Virginia as he—"

"*Sic Semper Tyrannis! Thus always to tyrants!*" Poe shouted, shaking his fist dramatically to the heavens, as if in a theatre himself, then blew smoke from his cigarette as he handed me *The Southern Rebellion*, open at a specific page. The American Brutus stared up at me from a WANTED poster—as a historical note, the first ever to use a photograph. Distinguished features. Curly hair. Dark moustache. Not a thousand miles from the young Edgar, I thought, uncomfortably as well as unkindly.

"In spite of a broken shin-bone," I continued, "Booth nevertheless managed to mount his getaway horse, and with his accomplice, fled through the night, pausing only to get his leg splinted. Thereafter, the duo evaded a manhunt, lubricated by a $100,000 reward and a thousand Union soldiers, before being finally surrounded at Port Royal, Virginia, in a tobacco barn. They flushed him out by setting it alight, and Booth was finally shot in the neck, taking a full three hours to eventually die."

Poe murmured: "I daresay many Americans gave thanks to God that he suffered agonies for his crime before expiring."

"My husband disputes that fact," said Mrs Washburne.

"How do we know it, as a certainty?" echoed Annabel.

"The official record."

"Can official records be fabricated? Can the public be deliberately misled? Would it be impossible for officials to find it prudent to say the assassin was dead, when in fact he was alive, and had slipped from their grasp?"

"What would they have to gain?"

"Or, you might ask, what to lose, if their failure came under a spotlight?" I said, hesitant to contradict Poe's scepticism, but unable to stop myself. "In the aftermath of the crime there were serious doubts voiced in abundance. Questions about who exactly had been killed in the barn at Port Royal. Then there is the question of the photograph. The authorities wanted one taken of the corpse to verify his death and to stop him being held up as a martyr. Yet the photograph went missing. So there is no record at all. And, as Annabel said, those who apprehended him had every investment to declare they'd got their man. They wanted to be the heroes of the day, not fools."

If Poe considered that a possibility, he failed to voice it, and took a different tack entirely.

"Has your husband visited a doctor or alienist?"

"No. He has no need to do so. He is as strong as an ox. Several oxen."

"He takes no medication that might be altering his perception in any way? For sleeplessness, for instance? Such substances can have their side effects."

"Please. Afford my mother some intelligence," said Annabel. "Do you not think we have explored such thoughts ourselves? Why do you think we come to your door and ask for your services? We are not here to talk of 'side effects.'"

"Clearly," said Poe. "However, it was said that during the autopsy, Booth was identified by a tattoo of his initials on his wrist."

"*Said?* By whom? And under what coercion?" said Mrs Washburne.

"I am merely applying Occam's razor."

"Well, apply it to this, M. Dupin, with the greatest respect." The woman was beginning to earn my admiration. The more her superficial gentility peeled away, a fierce determination revealed itself. "I have risen sleepless myself, and explored the house when he has had his terrors. I have taken my candle and wrapped on my shawl and sought the heathen, that acrimonious shadow, and left my darling sobbing into his pillow, and walked those cold corridors in the dead of night, and though I have *seen* no man, I will tell you, as the Lord is my witness, that I have stood petrified as I heard those self-same *footsteps* he described . . ." She leaned forward and with a sudden bang hit the table hard with the fist of one hand, then trailed her fingernails across its polished surface.

Thump . . . Scrape . . .

"One solid thump, gentlemen. Then a slow dragging sound, for all the world as if hauling a lifeless limb behind him . . ."

Thump . . . Scrape . . .

At the second enactment a chill went through me, but Poe wasted not an instant in quizzing the other woman.

"Annabel, have you heard anything similar?"

"No, monsieur. But I am at the back of the house. And a heavy sleeper."

My master's frown of concentration told me he was increasingly intrigued, as he addressed the older woman again, slow to take his eyes from the younger. "Excuse me, but I must ask again, why do you come to me? I'm sure you have military protection in the diplomatic corps with expertise you could rely on to investigate this fully. Am I to conclude you distrust your own people?"

Mrs Washburne shook her head. "Not at all. Major Ward Hartigan is a decorated war hero and patriot."

"Then explain."

"The truth is, monsieur, I fear that, even with precautions, word might get out to those less loyal, and those with ambition in mind. Politics is a business that thrives on perceived weakness and fragility. If one isn't seen as a lion, one is seen as, I don't know—the prey."

"Furthermore, if my father were to find out that we had . . ."

"I understand completely," I said.

"It is often the most sane of us," said Poe, "who runs the risk of being labelled mad. One last question, and I am done. Tell me, do you have a cavalry unit posted at your official residence?"

"No, monsieur."

"Are there stables of any kind?"

"Stables? No, monsieur."

"Of course we shall help you." I tried to make up for Poe asking something so trivial and bafflingly irrelevant. "It is eminently sensible for you to employ outsiders to assess the situation. Which we shall—with the utmost discretion."

"And, I hope, the utmost *speed*." Mrs Washburne extracted a card from her purse. She handed it to Poe, who read it and passed it straight over to me. "My husband is convinced the assassin, Wilkes Booth, will strike his fatal blow this very evening."

"*What?*" I looked up from the printed invitation and shot a worried glance at Poe. He seemed intensely thoughtful, but incredibly, almost absurdly, unperturbed.

At his gesture, a circling finger, I turned the card over and looked down at the message on the other side, scrawled in black ink with a narrow brush, as crudely legible as it was dramatic:

SIC SEMPER TYRANNIS!

The three words struck me dumb with shock—but Poe's eyes sparkled with what I have endeavoured to define before, but can only describe as a kind of animal electricity.

"Someone knows their history as well as we do," he pronounced.

"Or someone was *part* of that history," said Annabel.

"Someone whose intent is terror, as well as murder."

"In the first part," said her mother, "I hate to admit, he has succeeded."

"When did these invitations go out?" I asked.

"Three weeks ago."

"By mail?"

"Mostly, but some by hand."

"And this was returned by hand, or by post?"

"My husband found the envelope lying on the front porch."

"Did you keep the envelope?"

"No, I'm afraid not."

"The guards at the gate noticed no-one deliver it?"

"I asked Major Hartigan to quiz them. And yes, no-one."

I looked back down at the invitation. The event was a fund-raising gala to raise money for a "GREAT AND IMPORTANT PROJECT" to promote Franco-American relations. With a dog-tooth border and the name of the printer bottom right, the design was over-populated with eagles, bugles and flags, a rendering of a bare-breasted Columbia, traditional personification of America, prominent. I couldn't help wondering if Elihu Washburne was a target for one whose true enemy was the country itself.

"Drinks at seven." I handed the card back to Poe. "Speeches at eight."

"I take it your husband would not be persuaded to cancel?"

"That would be tantamount to conceding defeat."

"Or living longer—but we shall be there—incognito, that is. We want no sniff of 'detectives' to give the game away."

"In that case, write your aliases here, if you'll be so kind." Mrs Washburne stood up and produced a small notebook and pencil from her bag. "I will make sure they are added to the guest list. A copy of which I have for you. Here."

"Anticipating my next request." Poe smiled. "Thank you." We knew precious little about our potential assassin except that he had used the invitation card to convey his threat. Enough to make the information of paramount importance. He squinted at it through a dusty magnifying glass.

"The great and the good of Paris society," I surmised.

"Or so they would have you think."

Mrs Washburne placed two invitation cards on the table while her daughter buttoned her turquoise coat. We escorted them to the vestibule, and shook their hands. Annabel's was feather-light. I felt a frisson as her eyes looked into mine, briefly.

"Thank you," she said.

"We offer no guarantee of success," I admitted. "Even though my friend is the most brilliant analytical mind in Paris."

Poe's mouth tightened in a *moue* of imperial disdain. "Europe."

"Thank you, nonetheless."

Her mother walked out onto the landing, paused, and turned back. "Oh, I should tell you. The theme is red, white and blue."

"I am partial to red," said Poe.

No sooner had they left than he dashed across the room, produced from his bureau two tickets for a matinee performance of Labiche's *The Italian Straw Hat* and suggested I make use of them, taking Annabel with me, as a welcome diversion from her anxieties. The tickets were a gift from a satisfied client, he said, but he found *imbroglio*-style plays noisome, and cripplingly formulaic. He'd be far too busy that afternoon putting the guest list under the proverbial microscope, and the ink of the *"Sic Semper"* message under an actual one. For that he needed absolute concentration and no distractions—meaning myself. Without arguing, I ran down to head off the carriage before it left. Pretending to myself that my interest in doing so was entirely professional.

⌖

"What did you think of the play?"

Annabel interrupted my several minutes of silence as we walked side by side along the Rue Julius Sewitsky afterwards. Silence never troubled me, but I was slowly learning that it peculiarly troubled others.

"I suspect the theatre is facing hard times. The gold cord on the curtain to the right of the proscenium arch has been replaced, but not the one on the left. The woman playing 'Hélène' is having an affair with a stage manager. She's late on her cues and he whistled her curtain call rather more energetically than a mere colleague. And 'Fadinard' has sights on a glittering career. His every speech was directed towards a well-dressed businessman in one of the boxes."

She let out a good-hearted laugh. "You really are a *very* strange fish!"

"Fish? I hope not."

"I was asking if you enjoyed the play."

"I'm sorry if I amuse you terribly."

"Oh, not terribly! Not *terribly* at all." She took my arm, perhaps thinking she'd upset me. Perhaps she had, a little. I didn't want to think myself odd. Nor did I want her to think me an oversensitive prig.

"It's my job. Deduction."

"And is that terribly interesting, or terribly boring?"

"A little of both, if I'm honest." And I felt I *could* be honest, with her. "I can tell a brand of cigarette paper by feeling it between my thumb and forefinger, but it won't win me a round of applause at a children's party."

She laughed again, and again it was beyond delightful.

"What else can you do?"

"I can walk along a boulevard with a beautiful woman on my arm. In fact, I'm rather fond of it."

"So I'm the latest in a long line of conquests?"

"Quite the contrary," I said. "You're the first."

"And not a conquest. Not yet anyway."

Blushing. That is one biological function that we have no control over: blushing, and sneezing. We are at their mercy. I was at hers, but she took pity on me and her arm tightened.

"Daddy doesn't let me go out to cafés. Let's go to this one. I'll buy you a coffee *au lait*."

"I won't hear of it for an instant. I'm a gentleman."

"Oh, I do hope you aren't."

Taking her teasing on the chin, I ordered two coffees from the waiter, who held a copy of *La Monde* over his head until he realised that the recent mild shower had stopped. Whilst we waited, I noticed Annabel watching an old beggar playing a trumpet version of Bach's "Sleepers Awake," crutch under one armpit, left leg missing below the knee. His rifleman's beret with black tassel and a number at the front told me he was a veteran of Waterloo, though I estimated he must have been a mere boy when battle was raging around him. I don't know if it was due to the dirge alone but my companion's mood darkened appreciably as she listened. It didn't take the skills of a detective to conclude that her fears for her father had resurfaced.

"Don't let it torment you as it torments him," I ventured, softly.

"I can't help it. I feel so inadequate. If I could only do something."

"You have. By coming to us. I swear, if anyone on God's earth can solve this crime, it's Auguste Dupin. It was he who unmasked Pascal Uzan, the double-murderer, after the fugitive hid in the guise of 'The Mechanical Turk' for four weeks. He is relentless."

"But what do *you* think?"

Me? Why should my thoughts matter to her? Anyway, my theories were nebulous. That is to say, non-existent as anything but groping in the dark. "Booth had accomplices all along his escape route; like-minded folk who gave him food and shelter. Some were arrested. But all? Unlikely. It would be silly to presume the web of conspiracy was limited to those who went to the gallows. Some accomplices are no doubt still at large."

"But say it *isn't* an accomplice," she said. "Say it's *him*. You said yourself there was talk at the time that the man shot outside the barn wasn't Booth."

"Yes. There were reports that the man killed that day had red hair, whereas Booth's was black as sin. But he was a professional actor, don't forget. Skilled at changing his appearance. The first thing I'd do if I were him, under the circumstances."

"Or couldn't he have switched with another man along the way?"

"Who in their right mind would swap with a man carrying a death warrant on his head?"

"Well," she stumbled, "someone who intended to walk out with his hands up and say, look, you've got the wrong man!"

"And still face the noose?"

"Perhaps he thought he'd outrun them. Perhaps Booth switched twice, or three times, like in a relay race? We don't know."

"That's right," I conceded, unhappily. "We don't."

"I *want* to think otherwise."

"I know you do."

"Don't you think I'd rather believe *anything* than consider my own father might be the quarry of the most heartless, lethal and single-minded murderer in my nation's history?"

Her hand was the colour of marble. I took it in mine.

"You're cold."

"And I thought you the cold one."

She attempted to tug it back, but I held it firm. As a way of saying, I suppose, that I was not about to abandon her to her sorrows. Or abandon *her*, full stop. But what if she neither expected nor wanted such attention? For fear of misinterpretation, I loosened my grip. However, no sooner had I done so than she tightened her fingers around mine.

"You see . . . but I don't expect you *can* see. How could you? When I was born my mother and father were expecting twins. He, my poor brother not-to-be, died in the womb." The words were spoken plainly, yet they veiled multitudes, and I felt honoured that she had enough trust in me to utter them. "I think he was sickly. Whatever was wrong with him, I fed on all the sustenance he could not. We slept, but only one of us awoke. I was born, and thrived. He never saw the light of day. He let me go. Sometimes I can almost feel his small hand bidding me farewell." Now she did take her hand away, to pick up a napkin, to wipe her cheeks. "You see, I have always felt that I have needed to be not only a daughter to my father but the son he . . ." She did not finish the sentence.

"I'm sure he never thinks that."

"Never?"

At that point, interrupting our intimate *tête-a-tête*, a toothless crone with a mouth like a punched cushion approached our table heaving a wicker basket full of kittens, fleas doing cartwheels around their ears. I told her in my most congenial French to go away, but Annabel could not hide her distress as she voiced the thought that the creatures would surely now be destined for the river. I jumped up, parted with twenty sous—enough for a pound and a half of bread—and Annabel fell in love with the marmalade-coloured ball of fluff as soon as it was cradled in her arms, purring away as if it had discovered a hitherto unknown world of bliss. It was only the ribbon from her hat dangled over its pink little nose that excited it so.

"It will keep me warm in bed at night."

"If it doesn't, the fleas will. I'm itching already, and the waiter will not be thanking us. Two tables have vacated in the previous minute and a half."

Annabel laughed, before the sadness returned, born of a wave of guilt that she had enjoyed herself for an instant under such dire circumstances. Then she leaned over and kissed my cheek.

"Thank you."

The softness of her lips on my skin lingered inexplicably and I could not look at her face.

I realised then, with some irritation, if not anger, that this was the longest conversation I'd had with another human being, other than Poe, in months. I had been in solitary confinement, no less so than if I'd been a convict sent to Devil's Island, completely cut off from the outside world. To what end, I asked myself, had I been denied all the joys of hearth and home, of affection and family? In exchange for what? A life of memory games, pipe-smoking and crime-solving?

Annabel had earlier made light of my coldness, but the quip had stung. Was that what I had become, now? A cold thing, refusing or refused any part of a life of pleasantries and normal social interaction? Was that what I wanted? I'd thought it was. Up till then I *believed* it was—but had I been seduced into that belief? Ever since the death of the flower seller that had brought us together, Poe had explicitly set out to eradicate my pain by teaching me how to devote myself to the science of *ratiocination*. It began to occur to me, during that afternoon with Annabel, that he had removed the hurt, but not the longing.

A perverse impulse goaded me to be impulsive, to fly with her to a new life, just as he had abandoned his old one in Baltimore without a second thought. But I knew I could no more abandon a man who had been kind to me, and in some ways salvaged my very soul, than I could sever my right arm. As an Englishman, my sense of duty and honour could not be shrugged off so lightly, and I dismissed the giddy fantasy I was harbouring as . . . well, just that—a fantasy.

Anyway, what should have been troubling me was not my own emotional state, but the fact that a good man was at the mercy of an assassin whose plans were coming frighteningly close to fruition.

"Will you do something for me?" I said to Annabel, whilst simultaneously hailing the waiter. "I really have no logical reason to ask, but . . ."

"You don't have to have a logical reason for everything." She stroked the kitten on her lap, even as she sniffed back fresh tears.

"Booth and his accomplices. Fighters for the cause. They have no reluctance in using weapons, and not as a last resort, as a first and only resort. If something occurs this evening, I fear there will be bullets flying, or worse. I would feel far better if you were not in the vicinity."

"You're serious."

"I am."

"You *look* extremely serious, I must say."

"Please, Annabel. For my own peace of mind, if nothing else.

There's no need to put yourself in harm's way. Once you get home, pack an overnight bag, take yourself to a hotel. Any hotel. Will you promise me? I only have your welfare at heart."

"Do you?" She lifted the kitten and kissed its neck. Her eyes shone.

"Absolutely."

She placed it on her shoulder, where it clung with passive contentment as she stroked the length of its back to the tip of its tail. "Then I shall."

I breathed a sigh of relief. *L'addition* arrived. I dropped the requisite coins onto the small metal tray. "I suggest you get the fleas a separate room."

She didn't laugh, or even smile. I was surprised at that. And more so at what she said next.

"Now it's my turn. I have something to ask you, Sherlock. A question. Do you think I need protection? In this room?"

I was confused. I supposed that, if she required a marine from the platoon in service under her father, she could ask for one.

"That's up to you."

"Is it?"

Looking back on the scene, it was crystal clear what she meant, but my timidity and rank inexperience conspired to make it opaque. Or maddeningly unacceptable.

Without answering, I fumblingly said I'd hail a carriage, and did. They were gliding past like ducks on a pond. I took her elbow, gently helping her as she mounted the step. She faded into the shadowy interior, shutting the door, before leaning forward from her seat and lightly touching my hand, which rested now upon the frame of the window.

"Be careful," Annabel said. With those two caring words, it was as if she had wrapped me in an embrace.

The ride to our destination that evening was as heavy with despond as Poe's mood. Whatever the cogs of his mind were turning over, I sensed melancholy had secured a foothold once more. His suicide pistol was secreted next to my heart, and that comforted me, even if the sullen torpor in the air between us didn't. Upon my return to our apartment, he'd been crotchety, hardly meeting my eyes as we donned the costumes Le Bon had hired. I had no idea what I'd done to deserve such petulance, other than cutting it fine with my lateness. Even so, when I'd reported my conversation with Annabel, his disinterest had been palpable. I assumed he thought it of no relevance to our case. He often called such details of mundane social interaction "clutter" but it struck me as immensely rude.

True to form, then.

As we approached, the former bullet factory on Rue Cedric Pallant took on the aspect of a bastion threatened by the heavens. Under fading light, the grounds were punctuated with the neo-classical statuary, pyramids and sphinxes beloved of Empire. Armed guards with square jaws confronted us at the steps to the entrance, its Greek revival columns reminiscent of Jefferson's Monticello, though built in the distinctive *calcaire lutécian* of Paris. I recognised the strains of "Soldier, Soldier Will You Marry Me?" wafting from inside.

A Warrant Officer asked our names as he ran a finger down the guest list. I wore the blue tunic of one of Dumas's *Mousquetaire de la maison du roi* embroidered with a white cross with fleur-de-lis caps. Poe's costume was a hooded cloak . . . in what other colour but a cardinal's scarlet?

"Prince Prospero," he said. "Of Metzengerstein." French accent to a tee. After so many years in the city, "Dupin" came across as a native, even to Frenchmen.

"Arthur Gordon," I said—a blatant tease to my friend. "Dante to his Virgil."

Poe gave barely a sideways glance, but his nostrils flared.

We walked towards the ballroom. Directly in front of us, framed by the twin sides of a grand staircase, hung a large oil portrait of Ulysses Grant, while paintings of past presidents adorned the other walls, looking down like stern, authoritarian fathers. The music changed to "Lavender's Blue" and I couldn't help thinking, if we'd slipped in so effortlessly under false identities, who else might have done likewise?

Poe gritted his teeth as the hum of conversation grew louder. "People often asked me, in my former life as the poet laureate of terror, what terrified *me*. I would always answer the same . . . *Small talk*."

 He had often told me that he loathed the type of philanthropists and do-gooders who swarmed to such events not because they believed in any worthy cause but because they wanted to be seen by their social caste as good people. They wrote their cheques, he insisted, only to salve their miserable consciences, rather than behave with compassion in their daily lives. And he'd forever had to grin and court them, while Virginia played her tunes and they applauded politely, knowing nothing of her suffering, or his, and caring even less.

There was, at least, a sense of spectacle about this. The American flag with its thirty-seven stars resplendent side-by-side with the French. No bad thing. Swathes of red, white and blue hung looped from each window frame. For a second, it reminded me of the bunting on the theatre box which had caused Booth's broken leg. I pushed that thought from my mind. Entertainers conformed to the theme. A harlequin in white make-up wore red and blue pom-poms. A juggler tossed balls of the same three colours. I even saw a man wearing the costume of the *Orang-Utan*, a red-haired ape, tweaking ladies' jewellery and acting the fool. The more soberly attired wore sashes over their suits or dresses, but somehow red, always red—the colour of blood—was dominant, making the scene before me resemble one of those *Bals des victims* during the Terror, organized by the relatives of those who had lost family members to the guillotine.

"Minister Washburne himself."

Poe drew my attention to a figure prominent amongst the crowd, glad-handing, dressed unmistakably as "Uncle Sam" in the distinctive red and white striped breeches, cornflower blue tail coat, effusive red cravat and white top hat. His snowy hair was swept back behind his ears and a false beard hung goatishly from his chin. My first impression was of a broad-shouldered man with grey eyes catching the light like metal rivets on an ironclad, but upon a second glance I could see that under his fancy dress he was skin and bone, his cheeks sunken, his eyes deep in their sockets. He laughed and chatted spiritedly, as a good host must, but was today as much an actor as his foe had been.

"I'm glad to see he's not drinking the punch."

"Our enemy is no Antoine Desrues," murmured Poe. "And multiple deaths are not his remit. Still, we all have our poisons. Kentuckians maintain that when mint julep is made properly, you can hear the angels sing."

He handed me one, and himself opted for a glass of switchel— a ghastly-looking non-alcoholic concoction of vinegar, molasses, sugar and water—then picked a jellied fruit from the lavish ornamentations. I thought of the poor and the homeless beyond the perimeter fence, like the one-legged trumpet-player I'd seen earlier, in marked contrast to the bountiful luxury laid out before us and the entitled people who enjoyed it.

"Thank you for coming." A voluminous Mrs Washburne greeted us with a curtsey, hair piled high as a small watchtower. Had no-one advised her that an apple cobbler version of Marie Antionette might be in atrocious bad taste to the French? Obviously not.

"A veritable masque," said Poe.

"Let's hope we unmask at least one tonight." She inwardly shuddered, lowering her voice to a whisper. "I pray our adversary *does* show his face, finally."

"Assassins rarely wish to be anonymous." Poe's eyes scanned from party guest to party guest. "They often, on a fundamental level, want to inherit the fame of the very person they wish to depose."

"And Booth?" I asked.

"Booth was an actor. A professional show-off. He *definitely* wanted to be noticed."

"Perhaps he still does," I said into my glass.

Across the room I caught sight of an unlikely duo of characters, one a real Davy Crockett, head-to-toe in buckskin, leaning on the barrel of an antiquated musket. "Hello. I see we have The Deerslayer in our presence," I said, using the sobriquet of Hawk-eye, from Fenimore Cooper's *Leatherstocking Tales*. "Not to mention Chingachgook." The other chap was naked to the waist, with a slatted wooden breastplate, a large, copiously-feathered war bonnet, and a tomahawk tucked into his belt.

"White Eagle signed the treaty of Bosque Redondo which freed the Navaho from Fort Sumner," Mrs Washburne said, catching the elbow of a man in uniform just passing. "Major Ward Hartigan." I immediately noted his left sleeve was empty and pinned to his breast in the style of Admiral Nelson. The brass of his cuff buttons glowed next to the gold of his medals.

"Prospero." Poe shook the major's good hand. *Correction.* His only hand.

"I don't believe we've met. Actor?"

"No, he's a writer," I interjected, playfully. "But too modest to say so."

Poe sipped his switchel, surveying the assemblage past Hartigan's shoulder. "I have been known to . . . dabble."

"Teller of tales, eh? What kind?"

"Tales of terror." I decided to have a little fun. "And imagination."

"Here's one," said the military man. "Tennessee reb took my arm off with a hatchet at the battle of Shiloh. Sometimes I dream he has it in a steel drum, the kind used for poaching salmon. Maybe that's a story gruesome enough for you, Mr Prospero?"

"I can see the narrative developing immediately," replied Poe. "The hand, par-boiled, reaches out, to strangle the malefactor."

"Malefactor!" Major Hartigan laughed. "You have got a way with words!"

"Yes, I have got away with several."

Hartigan laughed again. Poe completely ignored him, his gaze instead already fixed upon a distinguished, dark-skinned man on the far side of the room who was glaring with unbridled dismay at the page boys in blackface handing out trays of bonbons.

"Er . . . If you'll pardon me, then," blustered the major, shuffling away from us to whisper to a pair of armed guards flanking the door.

"The patriot," I concluded.

"Indeed."

"A lot of firearms," I further commented: I'd counted twenty-three rifles so far. Ten outside the building. Five in the hall. Eight around the perimeter of the room.

"Americans always feel safe with firearms around. They're more afraid of being surrounded by books than by bullets. Excuse me for a moment."

Mrs Washburne was beckoning him to a group of women. Left alone and stranded, I quickly deposited my empty glass on a tray floating past, snatched a fresh one, and knocked it back.

Within seconds a coy tittering erupted. There was no doubt Poe was a charmer. He'd told me he was celibate since planting his feet on French soil, but he had chased many women back in America before he married, and they had chased him, too. Nonetheless, I always imagined his seductions were verbal rather than physical. Intellectual rather than carnal. Sometimes I saw him as a romantic, true, but always rather as a child playing a dressing-up game or a sport at which it effortlessly excelled. Even so, I envied him his incredible ease with the opposite sex, though it wasn't hard to see why women fell at his feet. He listened attentively, making them feel like the most important person in the room. I could see it happening before my eyes, yet the talent eluded me, just as I could stand in front of a great painting and only see the clumsy, embarrassing daubs that were the best of my efforts. And for all the arts and sciences he taught me, he never taught me the one that perhaps mattered most. Even so, despite my jealousy of his aplomb, I knew he could no more give himself to another human being than he could sprout wings and fly to the Moon. Because to experience true love is to willingly submit to—no, to *lose oneself in*—the spell of another. And he was too hermetically sealed a creature, too impossible and exasperatingly *individual*—and, truth be told, too fragile a one—to do that.

"Forgive me." The scarlet cloak returned to my side. "I was nearly caught in the bear trap of the Mothers of the Republic. Observations?" He took every opportunity to test me in my craft.

"Louis Buffet, our glorious Prime Minister," I reported, "looking at his pocket watch, thinking he'd rather be home in bed. The grey mutton-chop whiskers belong to Decazes, Minister of Foreign Affairs, standing beside his wife, Séverine-Rosalie von Löwenthal, daughter of Baron Löwenthal. And over there, in front of the fake Audubon, I spy the unmistakable walrus moustache of the German Ambassador, Carl Viktor Chlodwig, Prince of Hohenlohe-Schillingsfürst. The elderly black man with the face like thunder, I have no idea."

"Ptolemy Vance," said Poe. "One of the first of his race to serve in Congress. For years he's refused to smile for photographs, or when seen in public, reasoning that the smiling black man is a symbol of minstrelsy and subservience. Do not mistake seriousness of purpose for dourness."

Suitably chastised, I accompanied him to the nearest table.

"I have kept an eye on American politics from afar, which is, by far, the best way to do so." Poe took a grape from its bunch and popped it in his mouth. "Peculiarly, he is the same age as me, to the day. We are both Maryland natives, and both writers, but our lives could not have been more different. Vance was born into slavery in Cordova. One day as a child he witnessed the appalling violation of his mother by a white overseer, which resulted in her early death. This experience he carried with him whilst I lived cheerily in the bosom of Aunt Muddy's hospitality. Mercifully, he discovered learning as a path to freedom, taught Sunday school, gave the gift of reading to his fellow slaves, was whipped regularly for doing so, but did not bow, and rose to prominence in the abolition movement in Massachusetts and New York, penning notable pieces in *The Liberator*—a blistering counter-strike on those who argued that those of African lineage lacked innate intelligence. His autobiography, *From That Wood Am I Hewn*, is a work of remarkable restraint and sagacity, describing how he escaped servitude, boarded a train—the notorious 'Underground Railroad'—crossed the Susquehanna River, and eventuated via steamboat in Philadelphia, where he joined a Methodist church before founding his own. Non-segregated."

"Washburne was an ardent abolitionist," I reminded him. "Instrumental in Grant's Republican goal of ending slavery."

"And Vance was involved in the post-war ratification of the 13th Amendment outlawing it."

"Then he too was on the side of Lincoln."

Poe's mouth turned down at the edges. "Lincoln was seen by some as the white man's president. Some criticised, with some justification, his slowness in joining the cause of emancipation. Some even claim that he shared the prejudice of his white fellow countrymen."

"That's absurd. He abhorred slavery."

"Absurd to us, perhaps. But we are white. And we have a habit of writing history as we know it and want it."

So there were axes to grind. Axes everywhere. Lincoln supporters. Lincoln enemies. Was Vance one of them? If so, why was he invited? His upbringing gave reasons, compelling ones, to despise America—but did that make him a suspect? I had no idea. His eyes scoured the room in as hawk-like a fashion as ours did. Was I reading too much into their baleful, uncompromising intensity? And was there more to deduce from Poe's regard for him than a superficial respect, even admiration? He'd grown up in Richmond, a hub of the despicable trade, but I knew of no evidence that he spent his time defending the cotton culture, or, on the other hand, rallying behind its opponents. In "Eureka" however, he talked of the "utter impossibility" of any one soul being inferior to another. "The intense, overwhelming dissatisfaction and rebellion at the thought." I therefore concluded he believed all races, *logic dictated,* should be united in democratic harmony; "federated along one keel" in the words of Melville—who, in his best-known work, tells us, you could say, how obsession with "whiteness" leads to self-destruction.

As the string quartet moved seamlessly from "Lady Margaret" to "Early One Morning" I saw the Indian and the trapper shaking hands. Without a word, the chief then left the room. I was half-minded to follow him, but watched as the frontiersman rested his crossed palms on the muzzle of his musket. I wondered if the slight gleam on the sharpshooter's cheek was a line of perspiration, or indicated that his beard was glued in position with gum.

He caught me looking at him.

I turned away, wondering if the barrel had been loaded with powder and shot. His expression was hidden between fur and hair, the one just as thick and bushy as the other. Mouth invisible, and a nose on its own gives nothing away. Who was he anyway, this grizzled and bear-like presence? A marksman from the marines?

Try as I might, I could only think of the fatal bullet in that Washington theatre. The pall of smoke. The screams of the audience. The leap to the stage. The cry of the assassin triumphant. The singular truth that chilled me to the marrow was that Booth, as an actor—and a good one—could be almost anybody. So which of those dozens present might again utter *"Sic Semper Tyrannis!"* before we had time to stop them?

"The question is not who," said Poe quietly: "... but *when.*"

I had no time to ask how he had read my mind, since we were interrupted by the sharp but insistent chinking of cutlery against a wine glass. As silence fell, all eyes turned to Minister Washburne, the man holding it.

"Ladies and gentlemen, thank you for coming tonight," said Uncle Sam, as a short, dapper man with a centre parting gave a simultaneous translation into French. "Ours has been quite a journey from Washington to France, hasn't it, my love?" He addressed his wife, whose hand he held. "I honestly didn't know what to expect. One person told me: 'You will get on well with the population of the French capital. I have nothing but good things to say about the Parisites!'" He grinned at the laughter he earned, and took a self-congratulatory quaff of punch. Nobody could have gleaned from his demeanour that he was a marked man in fear for his life.

Poe's countenance was completely inscrutable as he listened, but I was preoccupied with surveying the room and its occupants while Washburne talked of the "unbridled excitement" he felt when informed of a grand plan for Franco-American relations—an "ambitious and unparalleled" project for which it was essential to get public support on both sides of the Atlantic. Such a plan would not be easily or swiftly executed, he said gravely, but the result, if achieved, would be of almost incalculable importance.

"A beacon to greet the poor, the frightened, the hungry, the dispossessed—those fleeing persecution, or those simply looking to build a better life for themselves and their families. A figure to welcome them to America's bosom. Imagine if you will, New York Harbour . . . Dim the lights please."

My heart quickened, knowing as I did that criminals invariably take advantage of darkness. The illumination from the Rococo chandeliers faded. I slipped my hand inside my *casaque* and slid my fingers around the handle of the Colt.

"Ladies and gentlemen, *mesdames et messieurs*, I present to you for the first time—'Liberty Enlightening the World!'"

The man with the centre parting echoed, almost in unison: *"La Liberté éclairent le monde!"*

My head jerked with sudden alarm as a sheet was whipped off an object on a plinth. I almost pulled out my pistol, but held myself in check. A human figure—an extraordinary one—formerly crouched, now raised itself to its full height. A burst of phosphorus shone blindingly bright, bouncing off the walls, causing a forest of black shadows. Colours danced in my eyes and I had to look away, seeing many of the party guests recoil instinctively in the same fashion, forearms upraised and eyes wide with shock. When I blinked and saw the vision before me I might easily have gasped, and several did.

A tall, robed figure with a striking, outward-pointing crown stood before us, a living woman painted green from head to toe, skin and clothing alike, her strong, handsome face with every aspect of a classical goddess. In her right hand she held aloft a flaming torch fashioned in metal—that which emitted the searing glow—while on the crook of her left arm there rested a votive tablet in the style of ancient Rome.

The applause was deafening. Whether for the design, the sentiment, or the *coup de théâtre*, I wasn't quite sure.

The Minister, Mrs Washburne, and those in their immediate vicinity joined hands, taking their cue from the string quartet to give voice to 'The Liberty Song'—which was soon taken up by all in attendance. All who knew the words. Sadly I didn't, so opened and closed my mouth like an imbecilic schoolboy at prayers with no hymn sheet. Poe, typically, didn't even have the good grace to do that.

> *"Come, join hand in hand, brave Americans all,*
> *And rouse your bold hearts at fair Liberty's call;*
> *No tyrannous acts shall suppress your just claim,*
> *Or stain with dishonour America's name."*

I perused the guests for the hundredth time, trying to separate the suspects from the innocent, those who sang with fervour from those who only paid lip service to the concept of Liberty, but I was silly to expect such a simplistic test to cause our killer to reveal himself.

I looked back at the woman standing with her head held high. Torch-bearing arm higher. Crown a spiky halo. A broken chain coiled at her feet. I could make out now that the *tabula ansata* was inscribed with "JULY IV MDCCLXXVI"—the date of the Declaration of Independence. Of course it was.

> *"In Freedom we're born and in Freedom we'll live.*
> *Our purses are ready. Steady, friends, steady;*
> *Not as slaves, but as Freemen our money we'll give."*

Our money we'll give.

That sounded fairly appropriate, I thought. Intentional or not.

When the song was over, the musicians struck up the French national anthem, again with those knowing the words joining in spiritedly. But one cannot sing the French national anthem *except* spiritedly.

As the *gasoliers* were turned back up, I tugged Poe's sleeve and frowned my impatience. He placed his index finger to his lips.

I edged away from my companion and circumnavigated the room, catching sight of a trio of press men huddled together like the three witches in *Macbeth*. Beauclerc from *Le Figaro*, Onglas from *Le Temps*, and Timothée Launier from the gossip rag *Le Petit Journal*.

I had little time for any of them, or their torrid publications, all of which strived to lead on sensational tales of butchery or ravishment, as if their readers' appetites were those of dogs. *"Sang à la une!"* was their motto—put the blood on the front page. I dreaded that tonight their prayers might be answered . . .

A new ripple of applause made me turn.

The Minister had introduced Édouard René de Laboulaye, the prime mover and instigator of the scheme, a short man in a stovepipe hat of Isambard Kingdom Brunel proportions. Someone should really write a paper on short men and big hats.

The one hundred and fifty foot statue—"Double the height of Italy's Sancarlone, or Germany's statue of Arminius!"—would be built as a "unique and marvellous" gift to the United States, Laboulaye declared in piping French, to honour both the anniversary of independence and the USA's friendship with France. To that end he wished to hereby announce the formation of a "Franco-American Union" as a fundraising body. At that point Uncle Sam started clapping and nodding heartily, and others followed suit, including his wife—whether by obligation or by genuine enthusiasm was hard to tell.

Adopting the style of a preacher from a pulpit, Laboulaye conveyed his belief that any such monument should, by right, be a joint enterprise of both great nations. He had crossed the USA by rail numerous times, and was already working towards the formation of American committees in New York, Boston and Philadelphia to raise money for the foundation and pedestal.

I did not pay too much attention to the patter, but clearly he was a born salesman. A Frenchman with what the Irish call the "gift of the gab," he hardly took breath, except to unfurl several large and impressive drawings of the proposal as he introduced its creator, Frédéric Auguste Bartholdi, renowned for sculptures of unalloyed French patriotism like *The Lion of Belford*. The artist stepped forward and took a bow, telling the assembled that he had been working on designs since 1871, his inspiration being the Colossus of Rhodes, a statue of the Greek god Helios that similarly stood at a harbour entrance to guide ships. On a trip to New York to discuss the idea with influential Americans, he had seen Bedloe's Island and thought the location heaven sent. Though small, it would make *Liberty* visible to every ship entering the city, and was, without doubt, he said, "the gateway to America." To his further delight, the island was owned by the government, and President Ulysses Grant, no less, had assured him *in person* they could use the site for the monument.

I alone failed to applaud. My eyes were drawn to the Indian chief as he re-entered the room, moving silently around the circumference to position himself next to Hawkeye, leaning back against the wall with his muscular arms crossed.

I then searched out Ptolemy Vance—his patrician profile that of a Roman bust in black marble—then turned back as Laboulaye emphasised the need to show something at the upcoming Centennial Exposition in Philadelphia, to stop US interest waning: that was why fundraising tonight was so important.

"Please give your name and your support to the creation of this beautiful giantess in beaten copper! The very construction of which will be a miracle of engineering! The world, I guarantee, will be in awe of such an undertaking! Countries will gasp in envy and admiration as she is built on French soil, transported by sea across the vast Atlantic, then finally, after years of labour and expectation, re-erected on her pedestal. Imagine her! Towering over the largest ships in any Navy, both saluting the past and guiding to the future. Imagine, as the *tricoleur* that veils her face is finally allowed to fall, her timeless gaze of strength and opportunity revealed behind the thunder and smoke of a thousand cannon, the hooting of a thousand bullhorns, the whistles and cheers of a million Americans! *Mes Frères, mes amis—La Liberté éclairent le monde!*"

The ballroom filled with rapturous appreciation. Laboulaye had won their hearts, and, it seemed, their wallets. His job was done, and he was drowned by a wave of well-wishers.

My own gaze fell elsewhere—on the harlequin, who sat on a straight-backed chair by the bay window with his elbows on his knees, his conical hat on the floor beside him. The applause still echoed as he tore a nub of tobacco from his pocket and proceeded to chew it. The muscles in his painted cheek undulated. I could see clearly where the colouring ended. The bare skin on his neck was as black as the ace of spades.

He looked up, the whites of his eyes appearing bloodshot against the stark white of the make-up. I turned swiftly away.

I drank from my empty glass. Placed it down on the nearest table.

The theatrics were over. Except I feared, deep down, that they might be about to begin. My stomach was more knotted than ever.

"Why on earth doesn't he strike, if that's his plan?" I appealed to Poe for an answer, but none was forthcoming.

"My dear Holmes, you have *observed* everything, but *seen* nothing."

His features were impossible to read. My skill in doing so was rudimentary, but often I felt oceans were swelling and crashing within that cranium, the great calculating machine whirring towards its final answer. But under the gaslight of the Baccarat chandelier I saw nothing.

"If you see our assailant, for pity's sake—!"

"In a game of chess you await your opponent's next move. Excuse me. I am going to talk to my twin. Did I tell you we were born on the same day? 19th January, 1809. Remarkable . . ." So saying, he walked away in the direction of Congressman Vance across the ballroom floor. The red-haired ape, who had been playfully dancing around the poor fellow, edged away, allowing the two to shake hands. Poe bowed his head convivially. Vance tilted his, more wary than effusive.

At the sound of a woman's laughter, my concern for Washburne's daughter resurfaced, that is to say, her own laughter resurfaced from the warmth of memory, and I made a bee-line for Mrs Washburne at the punch bowl. I don't know how much she had supped, but it struck me the ruddiness in her cheeks was authentic, and not the Marie Antoinette rouge any more.

"Excuse me. How was Annabel when she returned this afternoon? I was remiss in not asking you earlier."

"That's kind. That's very kind. She was much better. Indeed. Much more settled. Almost calm. She needed her spirits lifted, Lord knows. I can't thank you enough."

"Not at all. It was my pleasure."

"Oh, it was hers too. I can assure you of that."

My cheeks attempted to match hers. "And she had no difficulty getting to a hotel?"

"Pardon me?"

A sick feeling began to curdle in my stomach. "I advised her to go to a place of safety."

"Oh, she'd never want to miss the party! She said she had the most wonderful costume, but wouldn't tell me what it was. Said she couldn't wait to show her daddy."

The sudden, inexplicable but all-consuming certainty that Annabel was in mortal danger almost made me pass out. "When did you last speak to her?"

"Why, in her bedroom."

"Where's her bedroom?" I gripped her by the shoulders. *"Where's her bedroom?"*

"Up the main staircase. Turn left at the first landing. The corridor straight in front of you. Fourth door on your right. But—"

The harlequin's chair was empty.

The worst might already have been done, while we were lifting our stupid glasses and listening to boring speeches by short men in big hats.

Ignoring the stupid woman, I discarded my floppy D'Artagnan hat and sped off, zigzagging through the crowd to get out of that accursed room, barging into shoulders, spilling drinks, navigating a dozen noses in the air and disgruntled looks.

"Sir, you are not allowed up there!"

I sidestepped the marine who blocked me at the foot of the stairs. He grabbed the back of my collar. I elbowed him off me. A second marine ran to his aid as the first staggered and fell back against the banisters.

"*Sir!*"

If either levelled their slant-breech Sharps as I sped up the stairs, I didn't see it—and, if either had pulled the trigger and sunk a shell into my back, I wouldn't have stopped, or even slowed. I hung onto the newel post at the top of the flight without pausing an instant, and paying no heed to whether military boots were now on my tail, sped to the fourth door on the right, skidding to a halt, twisting the handle, throwing it wide.

The cheval glass showed me only my own pale and stricken face as I tried to haul breath back into my lungs.

The room was empty.

The wardrobe door ajar, but nothing taken.

A suitcase on the bed—open, but unpacked.

And, as I stepped closer, upon that bed I was confronted by a revolting image—a furry shape, immobile, flung there like a discarded toy. Closer examination was entirely unnecessary in order to conclude that the tiny creature's neck had been wrung.

My blood boiling, instantly I knew, beyond any shadow of a doubt, that some demon in human form had snatched Annabel from her bed, and she had not gone willingly. I pictured men's arms entwining her struggling body. Their rough hands pawing her pale, unblemished skin. The kitten mewling. A ruffian silencing it with the casual twist of his meaty hands. I wanted to vomit.

She had been taken, but . . . *why?*

Unless—my guts twisted—was the entire concoction in the ballroom below nothing but a gigantic *ruse?* The historically-worded message from "Booth" merely a cunning *misdirection* which both I and Poe had fallen for like utter fools? Was the truth of the matter that *the real target was Annabel all along?* That assassination was not the aim of this whole enterprise at all—but *kidnap?*

I hardly had time to absorb the implication of such a discovery when, to my horror, I heard it. Even as my body stiffened and every ounce of my rationality rejected the fact as absurd and unlikely and wrong, I heard it.

Thump . . . Scrape . . .

No. Simply, no, I thought. My ears must be lying. My aural faculties are impaired in some way. The source unreliable. Poe had taught me that images and sounds can be projected from, as well as received by, the brain—but try as I might, there was no escape route for me: there were only two mutually-exclusive explanations—that the sounds were real, incontrovertibly real, or that I was mad.

Thump . . . Scrape . . .

Again!

The self-same sound that Mrs Washburne had demonstrated so vividly. The very music of her husband's night terrors. No less than the footfalls of dead John Wilkes Booth, assassin of Lincoln.

Coming from the corridor outside.

I ran out immediately, wheeling round in panic to fasten my eyes upon Major Ward Hartigan, the patriot, walking towards me, sleeve pinned to his chest, dragging the heaviness of a wooden leg as he came.

Thump . . .

The dead weight of his boot hit the floor. He froze, jaw raised, startled suddenly at the speed of the charge I made, seizing him by the front of his tunic with both fists and lifting him bodily back out to the landing. I don't know if he was silenced by my violence, my rage or the barrel of my Colt thrust up under his jaw, causing his neck to crane back even as my other hand held him firmly by the chest.

We stood entwined at the top of the stairs. My eyes bore into him. My finger trembled on the trigger.

Hartigan grunted, unable to part his teeth, and that was fine. I had him. Missing arm. Missing leg. *"You have observed everything and seen nothing."* Well, I'd seen something now—and I had the swine in my clutches.

"You devil!" I spat out, wild-eyed, as he blinked furiously in my grip. "What have you done? *Where have you taken her?*"

Hartigan tightened his lips, his one good arm flailing, I thought, for balance. Imagine my surprise when he drew his sabre from its scabbard and held its razor-sharp blade horizontally across my throat, forcing me backwards till my back struck against the full-height window. I heard a pane crack with a *ping* behind my skull.

"Hartigan!"

I recognised the voice.

So did he, releasing the pressure of his blade on my throat and stepping back several paces from the gun in my hand, which I continued to point at his face. Behind him, and below, I could see the scarlet, monkish blur of Poe at the foot of the stairs.

"She is gone!" My voice broke with anger. "This blackguard has taken her!"

"Major? Leash your hounds," said Poe.

"Stand down, gentlemen. Back to your posts. False alarm." To my amazement, Hartigan also sheathed his sabre, standing before me unarmed.

I ran downstairs to where my tutor in ratiocination stood.

"Annabel is missing," I panted.

"Our enemy's weapon is cocked."

"This whole plot was a subterfuge for abduction."

"Your logic is impeccable."

"Treat this man's orders as my own," said Hartigan, clearly meaning Poe, and I had no idea why.

The marines still surrounded us, their thirty-six-inch rifles pointed at the floor.

I shoved them aside and rushed to the door of the ballroom. I could see Eli Washburne's Uncle Sam locked in conversation with the French Prime Minister. The string quartet were strangling "Over the Hill and Far Away" before doing the same disservice to "Yankee Doodle" and the chatter, loosened up by copious alcohol, was flowing more easily, and more loudly. I scanned the crowd, but could see no sign of either the man in the 'coonskin hat or the Navaho, and it worried me. All manner of things worried me.

"What in heaven is going on?"

Swinging round to look back at Poe in hope of an answer, I saw a tall, slightly stooped figure down the hall examining one of the oil paintings through a pair of *pince-nez*.

"Congressman Vance."

"I come to look upon the mighty." He eschewed the need for undue inflection to make his point: "White faces, all."

"Hartigan—to the door to the alleyway next to the butler's pantry." Poe gave the order as if the major were his subordinate. "It may be locked, or it may not—but if our friend has confederates, that's the way they'll come."

"Quickly!" Hartigan addressed his men *sotto voce* but in a sharp, authoritative tone. "You two, with M. Dupin. The rest, follow me." The officer made off, limping as hurriedly as his affliction would allow, towards the corridor on the far side of the staircase, which I presumed led to the back of the building.

"The wine cellar! Not a sound!"

Poe's order was directed not only at myself but to the pair of marines at my shoulder, at the ready with the self-same weapons which, minutes previously, had been aimed at my head.

"Do not utter a breath until I have spoken first. Is that clear?"

We nodded, and he was off, scarlet robe billowing towards a door that so matched the wainscoting as to be practically invisible. How on earth did he know it was there?

The door opened onto a narrow stone staircase and Poe shut it after us, cutting out the last merry vestiges of music and frivolity. Our shoulders brushed against the crumbling surface of the walls. The atmosphere seemed unnaturally dank, as of a tomb or cave populated by early Man, not opened for a thousand years. With every tentative step we sank deeper into a realm of shadows, though I detected some dull flicker below.

At the bottom step, Poe stopped in his tracks, holding up a hand for us to do likewise. The dim light was his aura. Its amber painted the vaulted ceiling and picked out signs above the bottle racks . . . Claret, Rhenish, Sauternes, *Amontillado* . . . A fine place to wall up your lover's lover, Mr P.

I heard the marines pull their hammers to half-cock. They'd seen the figure ahead before I had. Now, that figure turned from the oil lamp that gave horrid definition to its purpose.

I saw a lamp and I saw a fuse and I saw a hand ready to light it. It belonged to a red-haired ape—the *Orang-Utan*—but its head was on the floor. The one it wore now was that of a human being whose lustrous, coal-black locks fell to mingle with the russet curls of its simian shoulders.

Annabel!

. . . you were a child and I was a child . . .

Half-woman, half-beast. Half-ape, half-angel.

I watched, slack-jawed, as slim, elegant fingers extended from bulky sleeves covered in fur. The phosphorescent ball of a Lucifer flared and she looked upon it as if it was the most delightful magic, then touched it to the fuse. The yellow flare became an intense white star.

"It is done," she said, blowing out the match as she stepped back from a pyramid of twenty or thirty barrels.

"No!"

I pulled down Poe's arm, the barrier between us, and darted over to yank her back from the deed, but a hand stopped me, flat against my breast.

Annabel stared down the length of her arm into my eyes.

Before I realised what was happening, she was kissing me on the lips and momentarily I was hideously transported. That kiss surely held me back even more firmly than her splayed fingers against the ribs that imprisoned my heart. The flickering fuse burned brightly behind her, a dancing firework, gloating in its *joie de vivre*. I wondered why nobody else was going as insane as I was.

"I'm sorry," she whispered, after her mouth separated from mine. Though I felt her hot breath still making my skin tingle, I was sure I heard in those words the same sense of glorious triumph I saw in her retreating smile.

Coming to my senses, I wrenched her aside, not caring where she fell, and could see that the stuttering flame of the fuse was already blackening the wood of the barrel. I launched forward too late. Under my fumbling fingers darkness came and the white star died. There only remained, in the next split-second, for the explosives to go up, for the entire room and building to be blown asunder in a sudden and calculated inferno.

I closed my eyes, prepared to meet my Maker. My limbs were about to be torn apart and the flesh ripped from my bones.

Except I didn't and they weren't. I felt no pain. I felt *nothing* ... except the gentle weight of Poe's hand on my shoulder. I blinked open my eyes.

The fuse was burnt to the stub, and yet we were alive.

"The apology should be ours." Poe stepped forward calmly and addressed Annabel, her pink hands and face attached like the parts of a doll to the *Orang-Utan* costume, frozen against the wall of the wine cellar, looking as perplexed as I was. "The absence of gunpowder tends to result in something of a damp squib." She attempted not to offer him the satisfaction of reaction, but I saw her eyebrows flinch. "The barrels are empty." He, hearing the marines clip their weapons to full-cock, stepped a pace closer still. "Child, give yourself up, peacefully."

"Peacefully?"

The reply was accompanied by a snort of derision. To an uncanny extent this being seemed to be *imitating* Annabel. I had thought John Wilkes Booth "The Fatal American," but no—it was, in fact, the very person I'd been foolish enough to imagine my—what? Lover? *Wife?* The idea was repugnant now beyond belief.

"You have lost," Poe told her gently.

"We will never lose." She reached for a nearby bottle of Cognac.

The two marines moved forward, trigger fingers hooked. One rifle was aimed at her chest, the other at her head. They could not have had an easier target since boot camp. But Poe had raised his hand again.

"Will you join me in a tot, gentlemen?" She removed the cork with her teeth and spat it out after a pleasing pop echoed from the stone.

"Annabel . . ."

The word came out of me unbidden, and I had nothing to follow it.

She made as if to raise the bottle to her lips, but instead lifted it high over her head, letting the alcohol run out over her hair and down her face, the golden liquid shimmering on her cheeks and neck, gathering like thick black molasses in the knotted fur of the Orang-Utan costume.

"*Vive les pétroleuses!*"

Before any of us could move, she had taken the chimney from the oil lamp and held the fiery wick to her breast. A pool of yellow flame enveloped her torso, the intense light of which flooded the wine cellar like the Burning Bush or the coming of the Angel Gabriel. I cried out and had the immediate impulse to throw myself at the conflagration, but Poe grabbed me by the sleeve and hurled me back into the arms of a corporal, the two chevrons on his sleeve searing into my eyes. Struggling, I saw the reflection of the fire on his cheeks and the shuddering yellow planets that shone in his pupils.

Annabel was consumed. I knew that—even as I broke from the corporal's hold and tore Poe's scarlet cloak from his shoulders, falling to my knees and spreading it over her, trying in those desperate moments to wrap her up in it, stifling what flames I could, the smoke coughing out of every fold as I tightened it. Out of the corner of my eye I intuited the other marine dropping his rifle and tearing down a white sheet pegged to the wall. He knelt next to me, making from it some poor excuse for a pillow to wedge under that poor excuse for a human head. The black, burned, human head that only minutes earlier had been adorned with perfection.

She was no longer breathing when I tried to clear her lungs, afraid to press too hard in case I cracked her ribs, the idea of hurting, harming her, her flesh, still foremost in my mind. It still felt sacrosanct, even as I saw blisters form like bubbles, and wiped away ash in smears from her cheeks.

"Water!" I yelled at Poe, who stood in the dark, ineffectually. "Get some water, damn you!" But he knew she was gone, and that her beautiful eyes saw nothing of me. The charred lips, slightly parted, would never again know mine.

My head sagged. My shoulders lurched. The passing of time was somehow irrelevant. Then, I remember, however much later it was, a black hand touching my cuff and I looked up through a wall of tears into the face of Ptolemy Vance. I saw everything in his eyes that I would never see, or expect to see, in Poe's. Vance had trod the labyrinth of unbelievable suffering, but rather than carry it in rancour or bitterness, he wore it with a kindness, a majesty of spirit and openness of the heart, that lifted me with its sheer humanity. Not because he demanded anything of me, but because he did not.

I thought, not with great wisdom, but with great certainty: *This is what a good man is.* I had met bad men, even evil men, but this one gave me something, if only a question, that I carried with me for the rest of my life.

The lightness of his fingertips closed Annabel's eyes with a quiet dignity so alien to the horror of the moment that I closed mine, and I confess, the words he spoke, as smoke clung thickly to the air and I cradled her body still, were comfort, even if Poe would undoubtedly say they were a lie.

> *"Lord Jesus Christ,*
> *By your own three days in the tomb,*
> *You hallowed the graves of all who believe in you*
> *And so made the grave a sign of hope*
> *That promises resurrection*
> *Even as it claims our mortal bodies.*
> *Grant that our sister may sleep here in peace*
> *Until you awaken her to glory,*
> *For you are the resurrection and the life.*
> *Then she will see you face to face*
> *And in your light will see light*
> *And know the splendour of God,*
> *For you live and reign forever and ever.*
> *Amen."*

The rest of that night was, and is, a hideous blur. Even as Vance uttered his prayer, Annabel's valedictory cry—*"Vive les pétro-*

leuses!"—rang shrilly in my ears, yet simultaneously I heard *"Sic Semper Tyrannis!"* from the lips of John Wilkes Booth as he leapt, mad and dark-eyed, from the theatre box. Applause and laughter rang out and I almost thought myself back in that theatre of assassination, before realising that it came from the ballroom directly above. The revellers in their finery could have had no knowledge of the ghastly drama acted out under their feet. And that was important to Hartigan, and to Poe—who was nowhere to be seen. Both knew it was imperative that the guests remained unaware at all costs, and it sickened me, but something else sickened me more.

Poe had known Annabel was the assassin, and yet had kept it secret. My scorched brain tried to absorb the fact I'd been lied to, and betrayed. Little did I know that it would not be the last time he'd wilfully keep me in the dark. I'd learn it was ingrained into his self-possessed nature to think nothing of deceit, if the end justified the means. The feelings of others were merely a distraction from the Great Work.

And was this—*this blackened corpse in my arms*—the Great Work?

I was desperate to feel clean air in my lungs. For wind to brush the soot from my clothes, the hopeful dreams from my broken soul. The guards did not stop me. Coaches reined in their horses as I ran past, smelling like a chimney-sweep.

I walked the streets, weaving directionlessly under the giddy stars. How long, I could not estimate. I must have hugged a thousand lamp posts, brooding on every moment of the previous day, a puzzle I couldn't work out for the life of me, and could hear Poe's admonishment that the solution was there for a blind man to see. His talons dug into my back. I wanted to shake him off, be rid of him—my louche *King Pest*—once and for all.

I knew one thing. I was damned if I was going to go home to that apartment we shared.

Instead I curled up like a vagabond, slept in a doorway, shivering under my upturned collar, thinking; is this my fate, then? To slip off the map of gentility and join the ranks of the *misérables*, the dispossessed? Those homeless unfortunates deemed unworthy of consideration by people who knew nothing of their lives, or how they got there? Was I to slide down that slope to become like the woman selling kittens, with her peg teeth from the pox? The thought, like the cold and damp, punished me, and I was glad of it. Then I thought, if I vanished from the face of the earth, why would *he* care? He would no doubt carry on, unperturbed, and forget me almost instantly. Well, I wouldn't allow him that privilege, after what he'd done. No criminal should go unpunished for their deeds.

Consequently, at daybreak I resolved to return to the Rue de la Femme-sans-Tête, not with my tail between my legs, but with a sudden determination to show Poe the rage and suffering that was the product of his mighty, unassailable cleverness. As I rounded the last corner briskly, however, a sight struck me, the strangeness of which convinced me I must be still asleep and dreaming.

The figure of Lady Liberty was descending our stairs and leaving the yard, lifting her hem as she delicately picked up her bare feet over the cobbles, a stars and stripes flag wrapped around her as she tiptoed out into sunlight, pointed crown askew. Too bamboozled by the vision to stop her, I observed the woman disappearing along the pavement beside the Seine, like a lover fleeing after an illicit assignation. Consequently, by the time I walked into our sunlit morning room, I had completely convinced myself that "Liberty" and Poe had been bedfellows. The fact that he had procured such services from a complete stranger after what had happened and summarily sent her packing was a new nadir, even for him.

"Your expression betrays that you think me fallen." Poe added sugar to a tiny cup, stirred it, and licked the spoon. "Only for her charms, dear fellow. Only for her charms. The guests dispersed happily. The staff were busy. All the carriages but mine were gone. Somebody had to look after Liberty, so it was me."

Edgar Allan Poe as knight in shining armour was even more disturbing a picture than his being a seducer.

"I'm touched that you worry for my chastity." He sipped his coffee, still not meeting my stare. "But, as you know, I have loved and lost. That territory is forbidden to me now." Moving to the window, he tugged back the drape with two fingers, ostensibly to look down into the street, but if he could not feel the anger radiating from me, then he was either unobservant or a fool—and he was neither.

"I have no words," he said, finally.

"The poet has no words?"

"The poet left me years ago. When Virginia left me."

"So must I make a friend of death? Why not life?"

"They are the same thing. As hatred and love are different faces of the same coin." He turned with a sigh, as if resigned to tedium. "Punch me if it helps. I can tell you want to."

"How perceptive," I growled, bunching my fists, about to take him up on his kind offer. My knuckles whitened as I took five paces closer. Without flinching, he pressed the rim of his coffee cup to his lips, returned it to the saucer, then saw the muscles of my hands slacken.

"Good. Control is good. You are improving."

"Improving?"

He turned back to the window, behaving as if there were something outside of intense interest. For an extraordinary few seconds it seemed the city was supernaturally quiet, the quotidian bustle halted, as though the baton of a conductor had commanded it.

> *"For the moon never beams without bringing me dreams*
> *Of the beautiful Annabel Lee;*
> *And the stars never rise, but I feel the bright eyes*

Of the beautiful Annabel Lee
And so, all the night-tide, I lie down by the side
Of my darling—my darling—my life and my bride,
   In her sepulchre there by the sea,
   In her tomb by the sounding sea."

I'd heard the work of Poe recited before . . . but never by the author in person. After all, he'd "died" before I was born. But hearing that voice, melodious and almost feminine, I almost felt myself privy, in the most trusted and intimate sense, to his bared and innermost soul. The beautiful, yet childish, simplicity of the verse tugged at something deep inside me and seemed to cut a cord that held a canvas tightly furled. I was compelled to sit down in the nearest chair, bent over in the terrible knowledge that the two of us were united by a shared bond.

"To quote Melville," Poe said—"the ancestry and posterity of grief goes further than the ancestry and posterity of joy." He took down another cup in order to fill it. "A man has only one soul mate in a lifetime."

"And who is mine?" I asked.

His back shielded from me any sign of emotion, blocking it, as he always did—if not with fierce argument, then with blunt dismissal. "Don't forget we *averted* a death too. A crime was thwarted. A life saved. Many lives."

"Why didn't you tell me?"

"I was thinking only of the case."

Really?

"You were the perfect decoy to distract her attention," he said. His defence, the logic. Always. Hideous, *abominable* logic! "If you'd have known the truth, how could I have been sure you wouldn't do something impulsive? Out of control?"

"Oh, so you wish to control me?"

"I wish to stop you doing something stupid—yes."

"If you take me for a moron, why am I here?"

"To learn."

"To learn what? Everything but love! Because love, above all, is what terrifies you."

"And that terror is not misplaced," said Poe. "Love is treacherous. It results in a single, irrefutable outcome. As you now know. You will be abandoned."

"Some *deserve* to be abandoned!" I flung back at him. No sooner had the word escaped my lips than I regretted it. I saw all colour drain from his complexion. "I meant . . ." I hid my eyes.

"I'm sure you did not intend to be cruel."

"Actually, I did."

He could chew on that, even if it choked him. But he had no intention of doing so. As it was, he headed straight to the coat stand.

"By the by, the Samsöe case. The boy is innocent. The word *sepia* is Greek for cuttlefish. Partake of the *petit dejeuner* or retire to your bed chamber. I shall be taking the air."

The reality struck me with the power of a thunderbolt. "You did it deliberately."

Poe turned back, one kid glove half on. "What?"

"It suited you completely to stay silent. To allow me to feel passion. *You let it happen.* To teach me the fallacy of love."

He laughed. "Now you are embarking on a voyage of the imagination beyond any I wrote in my prime."

How dare he laugh.

"What sort of creature are you?" I answered my own question. "One of incomparable sadness. One who denies the possibility of joy, and has to inflict his morbid certainty upon others."

"One who protects souls, where he can. And one who wishes others to educate themselves on how to do the same. *Should it be of interest.*"

—and if you don't like it . . . Well, I *didn't* like it. And I *would* get out, with the utmost pleasure, if that was what he wanted. The

man could stew in his own glorious solitude, for all I cared. Rot in his bejewelled coffin and *ratiocinate* to his heart's content, if he had one. I would be gone, but he beat me to it, and with a flourish of his aubergine frock coat, the door slammed after him.

⤳

Cognac. It seemed fitting, and its effect numbing: exactly what I required. During the first I thought of the most famous drunkard in literature, now tee-total and wise, as all tee-totallers believe themselves to be, a consequence of the swelling of the head. After the second, I shed my Musketeer *soubreveste* and took to my bed with an ache in the soul more all-consuming than any physician could hope to remedy. I slept fitfully, dreaming of the gust of fire singeing my ears, the hot cinders sucking back into my nostrils. When I woke I could smell smoke from the grate. It was impenetrably dark outside.

I emerged wrapped in a dressing-gown to find Poe sitting at the dining table with his back to a fire that peppered the air with the tang of charcoal dust. He was dressed in an ankle-length nightshirt, shades of Cruikshank's Scrooge, but with a plum coloured waistcoat over it. A plate at his elbow showed the remains of his supper: *andouillette braisée* with "silk worker's brain"—a recipe of *fromage blanc* flavoured with herbs and shallots. Madame L'Espanaye asked if I'd like something to eat. I answered that I wasn't hungry. The very thought of food made me want to heave.

"Angels are a deceit." Poe did not look up as he glued examples of Buguet's notorious spirit photographs in one of the albums he called his *dossiers criminels*. The real angel he referred to was obvious.

"When did you know?"

"Almost immediately." He screwed the top back on the jar of gum and wiped his hands in a cloth. "It is always assumed that a crime is solved at the final moment, but in this instance it was almost the first. To be specific, when I kissed her hand. The scent was unmistakable. Sharp, peppery, metallic. Gunpowder—in this case, my olfactory senses told me French war powder: 75% saltpetre, 12.5% charcoal, 12.5% flowers of sulphur." He stood up and put the album back in its precise place on the shelves. "You were puzzled by my question concerning stables. Horses' urine breaks down into nitrates, so the ground is a traditional source of such compounds. Her answer in the negative ruled out the possibility that she'd come into contact with the chemical by legitimate means." Poe's fingertips did a dance in the air. "I also detected the faint odour of vinegar, which indicated to me she had tried to remove all traces of it from her skin. Unsuccessfully."

He spoke like a wine connoisseur, as if describing a vintage from a sunlit slope in the Loire Valley. I'd forgotten he'd once told me that, in the years before I'd met him, he'd spent much of his time refining and educating his senses to a remarkable degree, achieving the meticulous recall and precision of the best sommelier or perfumer. I would see these talents put to the test in many a criminal investigation to come, but at that particular moment it struck me, perhaps because his deductions had caused me such hurt, that his powers were not so much admirable as eerie, even freakish. Like his own Roderick Usher, whose painfully highly-attuned senses resulted in a terrible affliction, Poe had made himself stand apart, but also stand hideously alone.

"Knowing gunpowder was the intended weapon, it was imperative to act quickly. I had no time to think of an option other than to use the materials at my disposal. It was clear you found Annabel attractive, so . . ."

"I'd never use a friend that callously."

"You have pinpointed the difference between us."

"Does that give you satisfaction?"

"Not in the slightest. Shall I go on?"

"Can I stop you?"

"The minute you left with Annabel on your arm, I hastened to Minister Washburne's official residence and I introduced myself to Major Ward Hartigan. Yes, we'd met before the fund-raising. He didn't cover it up very well, did he? I told him my observations proved Annabel was the assassin-in-waiting. He was incredulous at first, *quel surprise*, but I insisted a search be undertaken. He could disbelieve all he liked if we found nothing, but all the marines in the world wouldn't save Washburne's life if I was right. He showed me the ballroom. I asked what was below. The wine cellar: my favourite room in days of yore. With a stroke of my fingertip I detected two dozen barrels without dust on them. I demanded one be opened. We found what I expected; enough gunpowder to blow the place to Kingdom Come. Hartigan doubted me no longer, and ordered his men, under my instruction, to empty the barrels of their contents, then replace them, exactly as they had been before."

He lit candles either side of the fireplace.

"How had they arrived? One possibility existed. The trades-man's entrance—the only door not guarded at night. I discovered it locked. Where was the key kept? 'In the butler's pantry.' 'It would take seconds to take a wax imprint and forge a duplicate,' I said. 'And the Washburnes' bedroom is directly above this corridor?' The major looked at me flabbergasted and asked how I had come by a layout of the house. I said I had not, but the sound of a heavy wooden powder keg rocked from side to side as it was slid along this passageway in the dead of night could very feasibly be interpreted as a person's footfall accompanied by the drag of a gammy leg."

Thump . . . Scrape . . .

Poe hit the wall with the flat of his hand, then trailed the fingers of his other down the wallpaper beside it, replicating the sounds made by Mrs Washburne earlier. "Something that Annabel was more than happy for her father to believe—the lame footfall of dead John Wilkes Booth—rather than the truth. We agreed that we could not tell either the Minister or Mrs Washburne what was happening under their roof. First of all, the devastation that would be—"

"What about the devastation to me?"

To his credit, Poe paused, and took a breath before carrying on.

"This much was clear. Annabel's accomplices came to the back door and she let them in. If we took her into custody, they would run to ground. The major and I reasoned therefore that if we let their plan come to within an inch of manifestation, we might catch them all red-handed."

The rest didn't need elaboration. Poe had come back to our apartment to await my return, his surly demeanour at the time all too explicable now. He'd known Annabel had no intention of going to a hotel, and it was obvious now that, even as she made me think she cared for me, her only abiding thought was of patricide.

"But why?"

"If you plumb the depths, you enter darkness. You do not descend and find the sun on your face. As Goethe says, we are our own devils cast out of Eden."

"But what makes the mind of an assassin?"

Poe crossed the room and ran his long fingers over the plaster cast of a skull given to him as a gift by the family of Charles-Henri Sanson, the executioner, or Executor of High Works as he was called in the late 1700s: a neat euphemism for the operator of the guillotine.

"Could one predict from an examination of Charlotte Corday's *occipital fossa* that she would stab Marat in his bath? Do we think that there are 'born criminals' doomed to commit evil acts due to the lack of symmetry of the face, or a small forehead? Nonsense." He handed me the macabre object. "As you can see, dear Charlotte's cranium could not be more regular and harmonious. Crime is at most a temperament that flowers under certain adverse conditions during life's journey. Criminality is not God-given, or *lump*-given, as Lombroso purports—it's a seed in us all that flourishes if the soil is fertile."

"She loved her father. What turned that love to hate?"

"We can only guess." He sat down opposite me and crossed his white, scrawny legs. Blue veins decorated his shins like tattoos. "But let us not forget that she wasn't acting alone. I have no doubt in my mind that her head was turned by others who infected her with their own malicious ideals."

"*Vive les pétroleuses.*"

"Precisely. The female arsonists of the last days of the Commune. In reality, a myth. A piece of propaganda fabricated by Versaillais politicians to make Parisian women seem unnatural, destructive and barbaric. Yet Major Hartigan told me this afternoon that Washburne detested those 'rebellious furies' as he called them, who purportedly floated through the rich quarters of the city flinging their bottles into cellar windows. He completely believed the rumours they were paid ten francs for every private house they burned, and outspokenly declared the *pétroleuses* threatened to destroy Paris and bury everyone in ruins. Is it any wonder that his sworn enemies used that flag to fly under?"

"But that was years ago."

"Resentments fester. Especially political ones. America was unpopular in certain quarters for not coming to the aid of France during the Franco-Prussian War. In fairness, in the aftermath of a bloody Civil War there was no appetite for it, and why would they get involved in a war in Europe? Nevertheless, some Frenchmen felt betrayed, and when Washburne failed to show support to the Commune, he made himself an emblem of everything they despised."

"Are you saying they found Annabel and used her as a tool?"

"Or she them. They found each other. A match made in heaven. She was ripe to be persuaded that the ills of her father and the ills of America were as one inseparable whole. His pride and patriotism would have become a festering wound inside her. The natural love of a child for its parent warped into something dangerous and inescapable for both."

"But the way it was done." It still seemed inconceivable to me. "The message imitating Booth—knowing her father's personal connection to Lincoln . . ."

"Terror has a power. I, of all people, should know that." He took Corday's skull back to its resting place. "But to create terror tales on the page is one thing. To create terror in *life* is another. Terror in a story, what is that? A component in a well-designed machine. But to use that same base metal for political ends? That approximates what I can only call genius."

I gasped, appalled. "She lied to herself that her mission was noble, her innocent victim a brute unworthy of life. I see no 'genius' in that!"

"My dear Holmes. Remove emotion and judge the concept objectively. You must agree the idea is captivating."

"No, it's revolting. Abhorrent!"

"But *perfect!* Because terror needs only terror." He tapped his wide forehead. "Of course, the real terror was hers. Control masking loss of control. Moral certainty masking moral emptiness. She gave her rage a purpose, and was compelled by it."

I took a long, deep breath and shut my eyes.

"I keep thinking of those twins in the womb." His voice, disembodied, seemed both sad and distant. "The brother and sister. The bond broken before they even drew breath . . ." To my astonishment I found that he was now standing behind me, and felt his hands rest upon my shoulders. "The self broken," he whispered. "The longing for a lost half that never went away. The unquenchable desire, even lust, for something that can neither be consummated nor gratified. The stranger within, ever-present. Completeness denied. It is the decay within her . . . inchoate, desperate to find form. She cannot even give it a name, but she can give it a voice. It begs destruction. Only by destruction, or self destruction, can they merge, and finally be as one." He moved away again, as if even our brief physical contact had been too much.

My words, when they came, followed the prefix of a sob.

"Why did it have to happen?"

A stupid question, worthy of a child in a nursery, I knew—but for once Poe did not pull me up on it.

"America reveres the family—that is its curse. They worship the idea of the perfect family, but no family is perfect. Every family is rooted in self-destruction. Every palace haunted by the souls of those backs that were broken to build it. Even in the sturdiest fortress, cracks will appear and widen."

The Fall of the House of USA.

The pun struck me without mirth. But, listening to him speak, I saw Roderick Usher before me—skeleton-thin, persecuted by his sensitivities, savouring the microscopic scent of gunpowder on a woman's skin, yet recoiling from human touch as if in torment.

Poor Roderick. Poor Edgar. Perhaps it is you that is cursed.

"Whilst you were sleeping I went back to see Major Hartigan," he said, returning to his chair after lighting another candle. "He apprised me that Washburne and his wife had been told everything. We can be confident the death of their daughter will be hushed up by the French and American authorities. Neither country wants to announce, far less explain, a failed assassination of a US minister on French soil. The repercussions of such a diplomatic incident would be impossible to overestimate. I suggested a disclosure to the press in a few days' time to the effect that Annabel has died unexpectedly, of natural causes—ischemic heart disease, to be precise: a leading cause of sudden death that will not arouse suspicion."

"You always were good at fiction."

"Sometimes fiction comes as a service to unpalatable fact. It's often the steam that drives the engine called politics, too. Not figures or absolutes, but perceptions and speculation. Which is why soothsayers, idealists and snake oil salesmen are better at it than scientists."

"I'm sorry. I'm not in the mood for clever word play."

"Of course you aren't."

Poe almost never reprimanded himself, so hearing that was a novelty I wish I'd had the wherewithal to enjoy. So too was the spectacle of him speaking as though the very production of words was a discomfort.

"Her death..." He actually hesitated. He almost never hesitated. "Her death will be felt by those who loved her, in private. But, in time, with luck and forbearance, we can only hope anguished memories will be replaced by those of a beloved person yet to take that thorny, ill-lit path. A person whose step could easily have taken them in another direction. Take what comfort you can from that, Sherlock." He meant it. I do think he did. Even if his intelligence, and experience, would have told him that no palliative could have been enough. "I was once a frequenter of cemeteries," he added. "Now, less so. Now, it's the streets."

"Don't tell me time is a healer."

"It is not, dear boy. But life is." At that phrase his voice lightened in a way I had never heard before, and never did again. "Life being the only possible revenge against death. To live a purposeful life, in the days we are allotted. What else is there?"

Nothing. As he always reminded me.

Nothing.

I didn't leave, of course. Nor did the horror of that night leave me. As I recount the events now, fifty years later, it is as if I experienced them yesterday. Their clarity a persecution beyond measure.

Before I happily tear this leaf from my note book, and leave that final image of the two of us bathed in candlelight, I should add as a footnote that, in the fullness of time, "C. Auguste Dupin" was given the US Congress Gold Medal for (tactfully unspecific) "services to national defence." It was an irony not lost on Poe that he'd never earned such an honour, or anything like it, for his literary works. I was glad that he returned it to sender. A part of me hoped he'd done so because of my feelings about the case. A larger part of me doubted it.

Elihu Benjamin Washburne served as United States Minister to France for two more years, until the end of Grant's term in '77. He went on to be a contender for the Republican candidacy for the presidency, the "dark horse" delegates were seeking, but failed to build the necessary momentum to win the party's nomination. His published memoirs, full of military insight and homespun charm, liberally quoting Shakespeare and the Bible, make no mention of his daughter.

Soon after the fund-raising event we'd attended, craftsmen and artisans began constructing the Statue of Liberty in France under Bartholdi's direction. The right arm holding the torch aloft was completed first, and displayed in Philadelphia as planned. The great, crowned head followed in 1878 at the Paris World Fair. However, due to lack of funds from America, it was years before construction of the pedestal began within the star-shaped walls of Fort Wood. After the gift was officially presented to Levi P. Morton, the new US Minister to France, in Paris on July 4th 1884, it was deconstructed and shipped across the Atlantic, arriving at its destination to huge fanfare, then reassembled on the skeleton of Gustave Eiffel's iron framework with incredible speed by an intrepid construction crew made up almost entirely of immigrants. The last section to be hammered into place was the face of Lady Liberty herself, which remained veiled until the Statue's dedication by President Grover Cleveland. The cheeks of the colossus, it was said, glistened with rain as a ticker-tape parade on land and flotillas on sea honoured her. I'm sure they were not the only tears that day.

On the other side of the ocean, liberty had become a fragile, frightened thing.

We never identified Annabel's accomplices, but, by 1892, according to police figures, there were over two thousand anarchists operating in small groups in Paris. Groups that gave themselves bellicose-sounding names like *Revolver à la main* or the *Bande noir* of Montceau-les-Mines. Bombings and political assassinations swiftly became *de rigeur* to their disenfranchised perpetrators like Ravachol, whose followers saw him as a "violent Christ".

It was the attack on the Paris Stock Exchange that paved the way for acts of extreme violence to come. A bombing in Marseilles targeted General Voulgrenant, and a few months later an explosive contraption was placed outside the Printemps department store. As dusk fell on the day of February 12, 1894, Émile Henry bombed the Café Terminus at the Gare Saint-Lazare, proudly killing one "bourgeois scum" amongst the young Parisians listening to the orchestra, and injuring more than twenty others as his fireball erupted.

In Baker Street, as the new century dawned and the "message of bombs" spread to other parts of the world, I dolefully collected the newspaper cuttings of Spain, Italy, Germany and Argentina in my own *dossiers criminels*.

If the message was bombs, I knew, its language was terror.

Each time, the news took me back to that autumn of 1875 when I painfully discovered that Poe was no longer alone in his shell of grief, and the Washburne affair, with all its horrible tragedy, strangely brought us closer, almost as if by some grand design.

Those times with my elderly master would return to me, unbidden, in my lowest moments. Such as when I used my British Bulldog to make the letters "V.R." out of bullet holes in the wall. I lied to Watson that they meant "Victoria Regina"—but in fact they stood for "Virginia Requiescat". He, and she, were never far from my thoughts.

Nor was Annabel. Just as I never let dear old Watson know who was really *the* woman. For whom Irene Adler became merely a convenient cipher in my friend's published 'adventures.' And a good name to use to him on occasions when nostalgic despair took me in its grip.

All those lies seem fatuous now . . . Hurt upon hurt. But the past can never be undone, or put right. Only accepted. Lived with.

As my education in the art of deduction continued, I never admitted to Poe that I was haunted by her. By the tarnished beauty that was Annabel Washburne.

She would appear, like a fatal lady out of a tale by Poe, at my bedpost, or I might see her in a bustling crowd. I'd think her perhaps resurrected in another's body, as dead Ligeia was in the young Rowena. The features were different, but I knew it was her.

She was everywhere and nowhere. Her motive unknowable. Her resentments incalculable. The product of her time, her father, her country, her rage.

Hiding behind the masks of the multitude.

Ready to light the next fuse.

The Mercy
of the Night

LESTRADE'S JOURNAL, July 1926:

*I don't know what I was expecting as I scanned the faces of the
postmen lined up as if for military inspection. I had produced his like-
ness. The stupendous brow. The aquiline nose. The ubiquitous pipe. All
greeted by blank stares. What kind of fool was I to have thought otherwise? The man I sought was a wily fox, long forced to earth by a
relentless press and hero-worshippers alike. I'd told them I was pursuing
a heinous criminal: in fact, I was after a world-famous sleuth who'd
brought many such blighters to justice.*

*An examination of the postmark on that last envelope had revealed
"SU" within its lower perimeter and an indistinct "SE/" around its
upper. I had deduced Sussex to be the county in question and Seaford
the nearest town to where he must dwell. I had consequently travelled
down to its Post Office on a misguided errand to find the exact address.
Alas, it was a long shot at best. As it turned out, no shot at all.*

*Disappointed, I trudged to my overnight lodgings at the Esplanade
Hotel, a grand French château-like building next to the Assembly Rooms
and baths. The manageress seemed keen to divulge that famous visitors
included the old king, Edward VII, and the Duke and Duchess of Sparta,
later to become King Constantine and Queen Sophia of Greece. My room
was adequate but sparse, furnished with an old copy of* Horse & Hound
*which struck a match in my brain. I sped to the public library in Broad
Street, back in the direction I'd come from the station, and on my swift
return immediately availed myself of the hotel telephone.*

The operator put me through to the offices of The Bee-keeper's
Record and Advisor, *a weekly publication. Using my Metropolitan*

Police credentials for the second time that day, I asked for a list of sub-scribers in the vicinity of Seaford. A young lady, in the most melodious but forthright Scots twang, said the editor would not be in until the following morning, it being already half-past five, and that she did not herself have the authority to divulge such information, on pain of instant dismissal.

Frustrated as I was, there was nothing I could do but take a light dinner, pilchards on toast, and sleep well, awaiting her call at nine, after the office opened. I shot to my feet as the telephone rang and was given three names: Burgoyne, Jewry and Lestrade. The latter almost knocked me off my chair, then elicited a laugh so loud I had great trouble explaining it.

Lestrade . . . *The cheeky devil!*

I uncapped my fountain pen and wrote down the corresponding address. Bounding to the hotel desk, I asked the manageress if I could trouble her for a map. I—or rather, she—found the location on it imme-diately.

Minutes later, facing the shingle beach and taking a rich lungful of bladder wrack and brine, I turned left and set off along the seafront promenade, following the line of gas lamps past the Martello Tower, then veering up the cliff-top path, which I followed for some miles to Cuckmere Haven. The sky reflected the remarkable crystal blue of the sea, almost as if to announce that the day was a unique one, and I was rewarded with some of the most blissful scenery the British Isles have to offer. The pure white of the Seven Sisters alone was more than compen-sation for each lengthy pause to get my breath back, even if I had to take a two-mile detour inland to cross the river at Exceat.

I carried on uphill, through a gate and up steps to join the South Downs Way. I had been told to bear left at the three-armed signpost, which meant enduring three dips, three summits, and the punishments of Job.

A symphony of gulls bade me welcome to Birling Gap, whose buildings became visible. Glad of my hat when the sun reached its height, even if the wind ever threatened to snatch it, I passed through a kissing gate at the peak of Went Hill, then descended, aiming for the landward end of the short terrace of coastguard cottages where the path, and my journey, ended in a startling sight.

I entered a garden decorated with rows of strange white-painted wooden pagodas, their roofs like the onion domes of a Russian Orthodox Church I once saw in Kensington. The occupants of the hives dotted the air, but thankfully, whatever their allotted task, it was not to impede the progress of an intruder.

I found the door unlocked.

"Hallo?"

Silence greeted me. The small kitchen was empty. The kettle cold to my touch. A single cup sat inverted on the draining board. Yet the tea cloth on its hook was still damp.

On the plain table lay a small pile of paper. Upon it, weighted down with a pebble the size of a goose egg, sat a note torn from a pocket book.

It read: "What took you so long?"

Three things struck me immediately. The sheets of foolscap were discoloured with age; dry and yellowed, unlike any of the MSS I had received so far. Secondly—and most notably—the contents were written in a hand markedly different; jagged, full of curls, almost spirals at times, yet erratic, as if the paper had been occasionally stabbed, as well as splattered, by an ink-laden nib. Thirdly, there was no title this time. If it was to have one, I would have to provide it myself.

I sat in the wooden chair, and read.

My Dear Holmes—

It is the mark of the very poorest work of fiction to begin with that most tired of devices, to wit: "By the time you read this,

I shall be dead!" Nevertheless, I have calculated, from an analysis of my present circumstances, that such is the case. Further, it is not lost on me that there is a certain poetry in the final crime, the final *murder*, being my own.

That I know the killer's name is scant relief.

Before night falls, that person will remain and I shall be gone, as surely as my storm-tossed hand moves this pen, and as surely as you, my loyal Holmes, are reading these words in the close proximity of my stone-eyed corpse.

Did we not once ruminate by the fireside about the possibility of detecting a crime *before it were to happen?* To be in such possession of *all the facts* surrounding such an event that it would present itself to one's mind's eye as not only vivid, and real, but *inevitable?* Well, *voilà*—such a thing has come to pass!

You have questions . . . and I must answer them all, whilst I have the breath to do so. And describe the occurrences fully, and chronologically.

I do not have to remind you—you have the record of your own eyes—that my body has grown more frail in recent months, but my brain, even after such onslaughts as have rained upon me these past few years, is still as agile as that of a stripling.

Such is the real tragedy of age—that either the brain turns into a swamp of emptiness and the body endures; or else the physical wilts, withers, contorts, mutilates, confiscates, decays, whilst the *psyche* trapped within has the sharpness of a barber's razor. One is reduced to a prisoner of incapacity, immobility and pain in the most horrific fortress or asylum imaginable, while conscious—all too *vividly* conscious—of that imprisonment.

And so it began, as the strains of Bach's Sarabande in D Minor bade me face the unwelcome day, twisted and wracked as if I'd spent the night in a torture chamber. Your violin faded before I dared open my eyes. While they stayed closed, I could remain awash in that perfect balm of sound. Then your voice, from the next room, replaced it, telling someone in whispers that I had, at most, two hours a day—and those in chronic pain. "Though," I was gratified to hear, "in periods of wakefulness his mind is as alert as ever."

Thank you!

My health was your prime concern, of course. You would not disturb me, lest the reason be of extreme importance. The other man's mumbled disappointment was evident as you showed him the door. I reached for my walking stick and hammered it against the floor three times. I think you always presumed that any intrusion from the outside world might speed my decline, but I knew the reverse to be true. When an unsolved crime crossed the threshold, it carried with it a life-giving potion more powerful than any tonic a chemist could dispense.

The rasp of the curtain rail felt like a cut across my skin. I groaned, lifted my hand limply to cover my eyes and heard a *"Monsieur"* from our guest long before my one good eye focused on him.

Short but thick-set, dressed like a *croque-mort* pallbearer in a suit he only wore on Sundays, he seemed as reluctant to remove his cloth cap as he was to expose his lips, hidden as they were behind a thick black moustache. I saw him gaze around my *boudoir* with the awe of a child in a waxworks. Little wonder.

I'd taken to suspending a large, sharp knife from the ceiling as others might a lamp—I can't remember why. Possibly a reminder either of Damocles, or Dr Guillotin. As it swivelled in the draught from the open door, its blade caught the light, glinting like a Star of Bethlehem atop a Christmas tree. But the cause of the abrupt stiffening of his spine was the sight of a human doll made from tapestries and cushions—"Fillette" as we called her—nested in an armchair in the corner opposite the window, with berets for breasts. She recorded an absence for me. A last shudder. Perhaps a sigh. A joke in the bedroom; where all the best jokes occur.

And facing my bed, in all its glory? As you know, Gustav Courbet's *L'Origine du Monde*. Acquired after its previous owner, the Egyptian diplomat Khalil-Bey, was ruined by his gambling debts—one such debt owed to me, for services rendered. The painting itself was undoubtedly something to savour, but the *name*— Courbet, a corruption of the Old French *corbet*, a diminutive of *corb*, meaning "raven"—made it completely irresistible. Love at first sight, you could say, as it depicted my twin passions; fear of the unknown, and the foolishness of *bourgeois* civility. As anyone but a philistine knows, the purest aims of a work of art are to be beautiful, to show the truth, and to shock. The woman in the painting's raven-dark hair—*and not on her head*—certainly shocked our visitor. He clearly felt he had stepped from a *de rigeur* Paris reception room into a den of libertinism. And perhaps he had. Or perhaps he had stepped inside my shadowy skull.

You leant over to tidy the collar of my night shirt. I wrote down: *"Que déduis-tu ce que tu vois?"* My usual instruction for you to use your powers of ratiocination.

"My name is Enoc Locard." His heels knocked together.

You raised a forefinger, said the man had military bearing but lacked the social ease of an officer. You therefore concluded that he was presently, or had been at one time, an NCO. You said he had no servants. That he had spent some considerable time abroad, probably in the Congo, very likely in the Katanga province, but quite possibly in Ontario, Canada. That his work entailed the wearing of a uniform. That his job was that of an asylum attendant or prison warder. Almost certainly the latter.

The man's jaw hung open.

My row of ticks on the sheet of paper in front of me showed you I concurred.

"But, monsieur! I . . . Have we met before?"

"No indeed." You sat on the edge of the bed and straightened my blankets. "It is my business to see not only what is before me, M. Locard, but what is *behind* what is before me." The phrase sounded considerably less ugly in the French.

"I . . . I do not understand." The man's grip on his hat became tighter.

"I see boot black under your fingernails, so clearly you brush your own shoes and do not employ staff for such domestic tasks. Upon meeting you I noted immediately a blue tint in your hair, a distinct sign that you have spent time working at, or near, a cobalt mine; Africa and Canada were the French colonies that first sprang to mind. The Congolese industry produces almost half the world's output of that mineral, amongst others. I imagine they need over-seers not averse to using force when need be, and your soldiering would make you eminently qualified. Your skin is sun-burnished, except for a whitish band at your wrist, telling me you wear some-thing other than this suit, which you have long outgrown, in your daily toil. Moreover, as we shook hands, I noted various healed scars on the back of yours, not from military combat but from den-tition. The only people who get bitten on a regular basis are mad house orderlies or prison warders. A slight red weal on your neck tells me you wear a high, stiff collar, and an almost invisible line, like an equator, around your head, suggests a *kepi*."

The man went silent for a few seconds, before puffing air and saying he couldn't fault your logic.

"That is what logic is for," you replied with a thin smile. "Not being faulted." You sucked your pipe and pointed with its stem. "I can also see how you heard of us."

Locard looked at the copy of *Le Petit Journal* wedged under his arm. I knew the headline on page two without him needing to open it.

"CONVERSATION WITH A SEVERED HEAD"

Lurid, to be sure—but not entirely inaccurate.

Below it: *"Voice From Beyond the Grave: How the Murderer was Unmasked by Dupin."*

Vulgar in its brevity—but at least they spelled my name correctly.

It had been an interesting case, over a twelvemonth ago. An elderly woman had drowned whilst out boating with her daughter

and lodger. However, the post mortem showed she had been bludgeoned—struck by an oar. The lodger confessed, but the police were
convinced the culprit was left-handed. The lodger was not, but the
daughter was. No amount of persuasion could get the truth out of the
accused and, consequently, on the basis of a signed confession, the
judge sentenced him to death. The police knew it was the daughter
who'd killed her own mother, but with days ticking closer to the
execution date, could not fathom how to expose her complicity.

You will recall, I'm sure, our plan was simplicity itself. On that
chilly morning at 6.15 a.m. the dour figure of Deibler, the "executioner metropolitan" (having been Roch's deputy for years), having
been made aware of the necessity of our subterfuge, went about
preparing the ceremony of *guillotinage*. Posing as an esteemed
English scientist, "Dr Bartholomew", you, Holmes, readied your
contraption next to his. The prison governor explained to the puzzled young woman that "Dr Bartholomew" built his theories on
the shoulders of Galvani, who had made frogs' legs kick with the
application of electrical current, graduating thereafter to the severed heads of dogs, which twitched and growled, and even the
heads of executed criminals, which grimaced when their nerves
were stimulated. His exceptionally important work, she was
assured, was to prove beyond doubt that the brain is alive and sen-
tient for seconds, if not minutes, after death.

Wrapped in blankets, I observed from a basket chair amongst
the onlookers. The lodger emerged from his confinement, was laid
upon the *bascule*, and the wooden collar of the *lunette* slotted down
to keep his neck in position. The blade fell. I saw the woman's fists
tighten and her chest heave as the head was lifted from the basket
onto a small bench. Wasting not an instant, you attached the metal
pincers of an electrical battery to the flesh, clipping onto the left
eyebrow and the right side of the lower lip. The lodger's voice was
immediately heard to cry out: *"You are safe now, my darling. I told
them it was me. It was me!"*

You will remember how the woman almost fell into a faint, but then burst into anger, screaming over the sound of our machine: "Oh you fool! You *fool!* Now they know! They know!" Thus incriminating herself, and in a state of collapse, she determined her fate at a stroke.

The dead man's head had not spoken, of course. As both of us knew, electricity might produce spasmodic movements of the eyes or lips, but the notion of a talking head *post mortem* is the stuff of bugaboo tales. Taking my inspiration from Brown's *Weiland*—in which spectral voices that drove Theodore to slaughter were in fact created by a diabolical *ventriloquist*—I had enlisted one of that same profession, Anibal Beristain, to throw his voice. We all shook hands after the event. The daughter got the death cell, the lodger got the lime pit, and *Le Petit Journal* its story.

"Our names were in the paper thanks to that *crime sensationnel*," you said to the man. "But what brings you to ask for our expertise? Do sit, by the way."

Our guest remained standing. "It is pertaining to another *crime sensationnel*, monsieur. One in the past, but possibly one yet to come."

Prisoner? I wrote with scratchy nib; the power of speech having long been taken from me.

"M. Locard, is this regarding a person in your custody?"

"Indeed, M. Holmes. Yes, sir."

"And who might that be?"

"Josephine Rappaport, sir. Known as the 'Ogress of Lyon.' Maman Rappaport, they called her. And call her a lot worse now, I can tell you."

"The child murderer."

He nodded, shifting from foot to foot, as if the very mention of the name might incur some preternatural wrath. *Call the Devil and he shall appear*, simple folk believe, and names—especially those of murderers—have a power to dispel rational argument. *Murderesses* the more so.

"We are familiar with the case," you said.

We were indeed, having attended the trial in the last days I was still ambulatory, though in such intense pain I often came close to passing out. I nevertheless wanted to see the multiple killer with my own solitary eye, perhaps motivated by no less of an urge to see "evil personified" than was the general public.

Her appearance in the dock, in heavy chains and plain grey dress, had been formidable. An exceptionally large woman, well over six feet tall, and built like a navvy, she had shambled from the subterranean cells through a doorway barely wide enough to accommodate her, ascending the steps to a hushed audience, towering over the guards that flanked her. Her face, when not downcast, showed the patchy skin of a russet apple, her head fringed by sadly thinning hair. The bovine vacancy in her eyes reminded me of a story I once consigned to the waste basket called "The Rhineland Auroch," in which a farmer and his family were terrorised by a gigantic prehistoric bull. She had seemed the very incarnation of that same *Bos primigenius*—a species of wild ox extinct for millennia.

The crimes had occurred in Bourg-en-Bresse, a sleepy market town sixty miles west of Lyon, the capital of Ain. The Ardèche is well-known as a place of harsh beauty, with deep gorges, and the old ways hold firm there; locals still nail fern leaves over their doors to ward off the evil eye and cup their ears to the wall when neighbours raise their voices. So it was with the Rappaports. The couple were known to have fights that could be heard the length and breadth of the valley. Then Josephine's husband wasn't seen for days. Somebody remembered her once yelling that she would cut off his private parts and bury them in the garden and before long rumours soon fell on the ears of the *gendarmerie* that the husband himself might be lying in the vegetable patch or under the flagstones.

To the horror of the *département*, a search of the property led to the discovery of bones down a well. But not the bones of the husband . . . of eight infants, mainly babies and newborns, together with traces of phenol to disinfect the hole. Dental evidence had proven one child to be twelve years old; a boy, missing for years, identified only by his missing teeth. All the remains were hastened to Lyon's "floating morgue"—a makeshift set-up with waste seeping through floorboards, chained to a pier jutting out into the Rhône. Meanwhile, Josephine was spirited to the garrison at Bourg. Her husband reappeared, after an innocent sojourn at a friend's house to let his wife's temper cool, horrified to find crowds howling for her head on a spike. It became clear to everyone she would never get a fair trial in Lyon. Magistrates became so concerned for her safety (as well as the city residents' growing anger), they summarily packed her off to face trial in Paris, where the penny press, with their usual moral indignation combined with a salivating hunger for the obscene, wasted little time in awarding her the grand appellation of "The Ogress of Lyon".

Remarkably—and in this lay our fascination, as detectives—the evidence against her was surprisingly weak. An apron with brown stains had a portion removed and the Schönbein test applied; a drop of tincture of guaiacum followed by a few drops of turpentine. The sample turned sapphire blue as an indication of blood, but the apron transpired to not be owned by Josephine at all. Most incredibly, no motive or method could be ascribed to the deaths, or was forthcoming from the accused, who freely admitted the children were hers, except for the older boy, which she said she knew nothing about, other than to offer the explanation that perhaps he had been playing in the garden and had fallen into the well by accident. Her own offspring, she said, had died of natural causes.

Faced with such evidence—or lack of it—the judges had no choice *forensically* but to find Josephine Rappaport "not guilty" of murdering the young ones whose sorry skeletons had been hauled up piecemeal in sacks from her well. Failing to ascertain *cause of death*, in spite of all the diligent scientific tests, they could do no more than sentence her to life imprisonment for *neglect*.

"The Paris dailies called her Madame Barbe-Bleue." You gave yourself a halo of pipe smoke. "Which I always thought peculiar— to apply to a female killer of children the name of Perrault's noble- man with a habit of murdering his wives. Unless they meant the original Bluebeard, of course—the Breton lord Gilles de Rais, who rode beside Joan of Arc before falling from grace, being found with the bodies of hundreds of dead choirboys in his dungeons."

"We have caged a monster, of that I am certain," said the man before us, with quiet conviction.

A beard, naturally, serves the purpose of making any woman monstrous, by dint of ridding her of any vestige of femininity. Even if only in words, it flayed Rappaport of humanity. Deservedly so, in their eyes. She represented the opposing sisters of light and dark, motherhood and murder-hood, combined in one ghastly aberra- tion. A gargantuan, pale, *beyond-the-pale* Medea encompassing the two most contradictory of talents—that of producing life, and that of snuffing it out.

"My only certainty is that Dupin and I were called in to help the *Préfecture*, and failed, miserably, as did they, to solve the mys- tery of how she despatched those poor, tiny victims. It was mad- dening, to say the least."

A German publication, *The Hamburger Abendblatt*, had one answer. The motive for Josephine's *Blutrunst* was to bathe in blood as a cure for the blue beard. That is why she collected the children's blood in basins. As fanciful as it was untrue. Our own hope to shed light with a scientific conclusion proved to be equally fanciful.

"The organs having long decayed, we had no bronchial tubes or windpipes to examine for asphyxiation, or lungs on which we might see the light patches caused by the rupturing of air cells, indicative of manual strangulation. A particularly violent death by ligature might have left a signature on the bones, but there was no indication of breakage. Reaching a *cul-de-sac* and seeking inspiration elsewhere, we pored over the case of Helene Jegado, who killed thirty-six people with arsenic. The Marsh test was, of course, useless since the stomach contents were corrupted. We saturated ourselves with crimes attributed to morphine, potassium and hyocine. Even the wourali poison used by the Macoushi of British Guiana. With no clues whatever forthcoming."

Locard shook his head in despair. "However she did it, she's tricked the smartest doctors and detectives in the land. She's a clever one, all right! One might be forgiven for saying, a witch. That's the only answer I can think of. If you ask me, a few years ago she would have been burned at the stake."

"As was your glorious Saint Joan."

"Ah—but that was by the English!"

"I am English," you said calmly, standing. A blue haze followed you as you propped one elbow on the mantelpiece. "If proof were there to be found, we would have found it. Besides, this 'monster,' as you put it, is behind bars. She can do no harm either to you or the public at large. She can commit no more crimes . . . so why do you need a detective?"

"The plain fact, sir, is that I am not perturbed by the inmate so much as her visitor."

"Visitor?"

I felt a nagging twinge in my lower back and tried to suppress a groan. You walked over immediately, eased me forward, and rubbed my spinal column, but your focus on what you had heard did not diminish:

"Continue."

"Well, for more than a week now she has had the same caller. A priest. Which you may say is not unusual, but given we have a dedicated chapel on the premises, and the place is virtually run by the Soeurs de Marie-Joseph, spiritual help is never far from her door. You can't get away from them."

Saint-Lazare, I wrote down, and showed you.

"I can only think the old man is a friend of the family," Locard said. "Such family that she has, since they all seem to have deserted her. Perhaps he is truly a man of God who sees the possibility of offering redemption to a black sheep who has lost her way. You see, he brings her gifts. *Books.* Every time he comes. A book, every day."

What books? You saw what I'd written.

"What are their titles? Do you remember? I take it not *The Count of Monte Cristo* with a file hidden inside it, to apply to the bars."

Locard did not smile.

"I made a list, sir. If I may . . ." He took a crinkled slip of paper from his pocket and read it out like a nervous schoolboy reciting a difficult poem to a headmaster. "John Bunyan, *Pilgrim's Progress.* George Eliot; *Felix Holt, The Radical.* Charlotte Brontë; *Jane Eyre.* Charles Dickens, *Hard Times.* Daniel Defoe; *Robinson Crusoe.*" Blinking, he folded the scrap up neatly, the torture of recitation thankfully at an end.

"I still fail to grasp your cause for concern," you said.

"My concern is for the meaning, M. Holmes . . . the *meaning* of it all. The why and the wherefore and the possibility of an accomplice, of a *deed.* I don't know. Of something going on, of the preparation of something I am too stupid to see. I don't think I was worried at all before the message . . ."

"Message?"

Enoc Locard took a deep breath. "Naturally we search every visitor on entry to the prison, without exception. To be fair, he doesn't protest about it. Knows we have our job to do. Stands with his arms out, just like Jesus. Even said that, as a little joke. Never found a thing on him. No weapons. No possessions. Just the little chain with the crucifix around his neck and the Bible he walks in with. But I'd flick through the Bible, just to be on the safe side. Just in case anything was being passed in, or passed out. And one day I noticed something. Letters written on the inside back cover—just that, at first. So small I could easily have missed it. Maybe I was meant to."

You frowned severely. The interrogator gargoyle pose I knew so well. "What kind of mark? What kind of letters?"

I held my pen in mid-air with quivering fingers.

Locard took it from me gently and applied the nib to the ink pot, then the pen to the sheet of paper at the top of the pile on my tray.

BB

He stood back. "I would have sworn it wasn't there when he came in."

"Sworn on the Bible."

He didn't pick up on your irony. "And the thing is, the next day when he left, and I searched him again, I caught sight of a *second* line underneath the first."

You shot me a subtle glance.

I opened my hand, gesturing to the sheet in front of me. Locard bent over.

TAV.DUF

"And the following day?" you asked.

"The same."

"If you'll be so kind . . ."

The light from the window, the furnace of the day, behind him, our guest leaned forward and wrote again, clumsily, sticking out his tongue at the side of his mouth as he did so.

300N

He looked up, without the pen leaving the paper. "And the last line, the next day, appeared under that." He continued to scrawl, head down, in a hand plainly unused to holding a writing implement. More used to rope and manacles. The sliding of a peephole cover and the prospect of a daily kick in the teeth.

demO

Light fell on the sheet of paper as I turned it to face my halfclouded vision. I stared from under my one good eyelid at the four lines before me, conscious that you were doing the same.

"Our friend the Papist has permission to visit from the *Chef de Bureau?*"

"Yes, sir."

"You read it?"

"I, er—well, I saw the signature, sir."

"He comes to see Josephine every day?"

"Without fail."

"Specifically her?"

"Only her, yes."

"Giving no reason?"

"The reason, I would assume, sir, is to administer confession."

"At what time does he arrive?"

"Midday, sir."

"Always?"

"On the dot, sir."

I knew precisely what you were thinking, Holmes. Obviously our prison visitor eschews the twelve o'clock mass. Perhaps a colleague does that and he supervises the six o'clock Vigil? Perhaps he is not a practising priest at all?

"So, you see, messieurs, the mystery that pesters my brain as a hornet circles a rotten fruit on a hot day—Is it a code? If so, to what end? Perhaps it means nothing. Perhaps it means a great deal. Who is he? Why does he come? Has he known her all her life? Did he know about her past crimes? Was he involved in them?

Most important of all, what does he want? Are they collaborating on some devilish plan?"

"You do not think he is doing the Lord's work?"

"I fear not, sir. Why would someone disguise their dealings in such riddles, if not to obscure some nefarious intent?"

"Good point."

I had written: *Ask her?*

You clenched your pipe in your teeth. "You did not ask the prisoner outright?"

"No, sir. I was worried if I did, I would give the game away. Alert them to the fact that I'd noticed something. To be frank, I didn't know what to do. Until I remembered the story I'd read in *Le Petit Journal,* and decided to come to you."

"Not go to your superiors?"

"And get locked up myself? They would think me mad! What do I have? Some squiggled nonsense. And a priest's word against . . . what am I?"

"An honest man, I think."

"Thank you," Locard said, with tears brimming, and wiped his nose with his cuff. "Do you think I am being foolish, though? Wasting your time on something trivial?"

Non, I wrote.

"M. Locard, we shall be the judges of that. But answer, if you will, a few more questions. Firstly, describe this clergyman for me."

"Frail. Hunched. With a slight tremor in his hand as he rested it on my forearm. Bald, with a white goatee. Half-moon spectacles. And a wen on his forehead. I'd guess he's my father's age. About seventy, if not older."

Talk? I wrote and held it up for you to see.

"Have you overheard any of their conversations?"

"I listen intently. He reads extracts from the Bible. She says very little. I see her grasping her rosary beads, kneeling with her

head bowed. Sometimes she says the—what do you call them?—
Hail Marys, that's it."

"She is religious?"

"She is now." This didn't surprise me. Many convicts gravitate
to Christ upon incarceration. With the key in the lock comes the
dawning of the light. Precious little else to occupy your thoughts
but bed bugs. "She has written on each of her four walls the words:
BETHLEHEM + NAZARETH + JERUSALEM + ZION, along
with painted scenes from the Good Book—the Nativity, the Bap-
tism, Jesus before Pilate, the Day of Judgement." I wondered if she
added *putti* in her rendering of heaven, with doughy cheeks and
little wings. "She's allowed paints. Brushes. It brightens the dull
brickwork." And perhaps her dull mind.

"Pencils?"

"Sharpened instruments? No. But charcoal stubs, yes."

"These marks were in charcoal?"

Locard nodded. "I presume, sir."

"Why didn't you bring us the Bible itself, so that we could
examine it for ourselves?"

"As I say, sir. To not arouse suspicion on their part. Which it
would have, had I confiscated it."

"A very wise move. You are far wiser than you think, M.
Locard."

Our guest chuckled and tapped his temples with two index
fingers. "I memorized it instead. Line by line. Wrote it in my notebook the minute I'd left her cell."

"You say 'cell'—she is not held in the dormitories at *Saint-
Lazare*, with the other prisoners?"

"By God, no! In the *ménagerie?*" Locard choked on a laugh,
showing the hole of a missing canine. "With the birthing mothers
and the *enceinte?* Can you imagine? The Ogress of Lyon passing
the *crèche* every day? Resting her lump of a body in the garden with
the wet-nurses? They wouldn't have it! The *condamnées* have their

standards. The thieves may spit at the prostitutes, and *les gigolettes* look down their noses at the thieves—but a murderer of babes is hated by both. She would have had her throat cut from ear to ear the second she entered one of the workrooms or laundry. Someone would have worn the act as a badge of pride."

"Even of justice," you murmured. "Go on."

"They take their exercise walking in a circle in the *préau*. She walks alone, at night, with the moon in the sky and a shawl about her shoulders. The sound of her rattling chains rattles them. She's like a ghost, they say. Not human, anyhow." The hated, bred by bullies and slaps, themselves often seek someone to slap and bully in turn. *C'est la vie* . . . "Prayers every morning in front of the Virgin, all stooped with reverence, whether those prayers are sincere or not. She is absent, for her own good. Infanticide? The Virgin? No. Even if the twelve-year-olds rub shoulders with the most vicious old crones, *les filles* don't want to see her. And resent she doesn't have to suffer the regulations and discipline they do."

"Tell us her daily regimen, briefly."

"She rises at five in summer. Six, or half-past six, in winter. All go to bed at eight. She has a private cell *'de la pistole'* which usually costs seven francs a month and is paid by the families of elite prisoners to look after their 'black sheep.' Like the rest, Josephine has meat with her *bouillon* on Sundays. The nuns in their dark robes and white *cornettes* supervise her, but . . ."

"Keeping an eye on her, rather than lending spiritual succour."

"Correct. Speaking of succour, she should have got skinnier after being incarcerated, but she still looks like a lamprey dumpling. Scoffs every morsel put in front of her as if it's her last. Eats alone in her cell. Not a pretty sight."

"Describe it. The cell, I mean."

"Grey bed. White bolster. Stove. Bucket. Broken tiles. Cockroaches. A pool of water. If it is water. You know in the olden days the jail used to be a *leprosarium?* There are some corners where the taint of that disease still seems to ooze from the stone." In that early incarnation, Saint-Lazare sat outside the city gates—on the road from Paris to Saint-Denis—until the population of the city exploded and expanded in the 1820s and '30s, hemming the building in between the bustling boulevards of the 10th Arrondissement, and it became the city's notorious prison for women.

"She can't come out. She can't pray before the statues of the saints like the others. St Joseph or St Dismus, the patron saint of reformed thieves. So she lights candles. A little shrine. A vanity closet one of the *surveillantes* gave her for firewood. Mirror so she can see her lovely reflection." Locard grunted slightly. "She said to me once: 'To God we are all innocent children. To this world I am repulsive.' She wasn't wrong there."

"You feel no sympathy towards her?"

"Not an ounce," Locard said sharply, straightening his back. "After what she's done? No, sir. Sitting there playing with her rosary while her paperwork goes through the appeal court . . . praying the President of the Republic will grant clemency . . . while those poor murdered souls . . ." He shook the image from his head. "No. The public purse keeping her fed and watered, at more than a soldier's wage? And those alienists and so on, fighting in her corner as well? Those oh-so-learned men who can't see what's in front of their eyes. Getting bamboozled by a common peasant."

"You have no time for mind doctors?"

The man grimaced. "They say a crime without motive means you are mad, and if you are mad you should get a soft bed. To me, a crime is a crime and punishment punishment." His viewpoint, from under that dark moustache, was as common as it was simplistic. We had heard it a thousand times, and often by those with power over life and death. There is no upper level of society where stupidity, like oxygen, wears thin. "If you are bitten by a Nipponese viper you do not sit and listen to its reason for doing so."

"Your own opinion of her nature, then."

"Placid." He considered his words carefully for a moment. "Gentleness made manifold, but a head of pig-iron and the wit of a dead starfish." Not so much *un buffalo*, then, as a dunderhead? "She doesn't yap, as many do. That's to her credit. But you recall the trial? She said she had been nipped when young by a rabid dog. She'd fallen from a tree, and ever since had headaches. She was forever beaten by her mother. And the philanthropes lap it all up. One guard told me she goes into a trance when her hair is combed by a man, and in her home town they say she was a dowser and could sense earthquakes. I don't believe a word of it. Or the mutism. Or the mania."

"You think any apparent madness is a sham?"

"Sir, in my experience, a madman will do anything to prove he is sane. Only a sane person tries to convince others he is mad. Mark my words, I have spent more hours with her than anybody. She is cleverer than she makes out, by far. My diagnosis is cunning. Cunning or imbecility. Or both . . . Excuse me . . . Is your friend?—"

I had lapsed into a coughing fit. One which proved to be volcanic.

The room and frightened man revolved around me, agony clamping around my heart like the claw of Sindbad's roc. Shutting my eyes in a vain attempt to stave it off, I felt your hands on my shoulders, lifting me forward, then the flat of your warm palms rubbing my back.

The fatal heartburn, I used to jest, but not anymore. *Touch a part of me that is not in agony,* I thought. Then blackness took me, and I knew no more.

By way of elucidation—given that these words are not for your eyes *alone,* but also for those of another—you will agree, Holmes, that I was never the same after my near-fatal stabbing in '79 during the strange affair of the hysterical patient at Salpêtrière. You saw yourself how the doctors prescribed their drugs on a haphazard basis, mainly to help me sleep; the effects often more unpleasant than the agonies they were meant to alleviate.

Over the months that followed, I'd found it increasingly difficult to walk, and began to find a cane, or your arm, indispensible. Chins were stroked, diagnoses altered, pills changed, but the pain never diminished, only adding to the attendant anxiety—no, *terror*—of my worsening health, exacerbated as it was by a sudden fall, seemingly a faint, but ascribed to apoplexy.

As a result, I was paralysed down one side. I could move one hand—my *writing* hand, thank God—but speech deserted me. My other arm had turned into a dead weight, and remained so. The sight in my left eye like peering through a sea of milk.

Our walks had to be curtailed. Our restaurant visits, once regular, out of the question. The task of venturing into the outside world as impractical as it was undesirable. The sun became agony. Chatter, ditto. I could not bear company. Society. Pleasantries . . . It was truly a mark of your character that I could bear even you.

And so, I resigned myself to a life—if you can call it a *life*—of acute pain and extreme discomfort. *With brain horribly intact.*

Less of a rationalist might have ascribed it to punishment for past deeds, but I'd seen too many bad people remain sprightly to the end and good people struck down before their time. Mme L'Espanaye had died of influenza the previous winter. Le Bon was a poor cook, but I cared little—I had no stomach for anything other than cucumber sandwiches, thinly sliced, with copious amounts of vinegar. (Illogical, I know—but there it is.)

Our routine had changed, in part. Le Bon would bring my breakfast on a tray. You, Holmes, would read my letters and newspapers aloud. I would indicate anything worthy of inquiry. But while you were out investigating, I would be alone, and *very* alone—passing the hours dozing fitfully or gazing at the convex mirror arranged so that I could observe the street below.

At my bleakest, I remind myself I had—what did the doctors say?—"a degeneration of functions of the heart"—but that heart quickened, as did my mind, when you brought me a full inkwell every morning and fifty sheets of foolscap.

We continued, you and I, as best we could. Solving crimes. And so it was, that morning, only a handful of days ago, when the world turned on its axis, and the die was cast . . .

When I opened my eyes, I had no idea how much time had passed. Minutes? Hours?

Where is he?

"Gone." You leaned over the bed, your knuckles denting the mattress, which sighed, as I did. "How are you?"

I feel, I wrote, answering your whisper, *that I have reached the final gradient.*

You didn't insult my intelligence by disagreeing. We were beyond platitudes by then.

The toil of one sentence took its toll. I placed down the pen. Once I used to write a story in an afternoon, as long as Catterina stopped pestering me. A masterpiece between Virginia's kisses. My chest heaved at the memory.

"Shall I fetch the doctor?"

I shook my head vigorously. If a shell of a man can be vigorous. If an Egyptian *mummy* of a fellow can be vigorous. You placed the pen in my splayed fingers.

The doctors have finished with me, I scratched. *They told me there was nothing they can do.*

"Do you want me to pull the curtains?" You must have seen me cringe from the sunshine.

I nodded. The room dimmed, the sheets turned grey, all cooled around me. A cold bliss. Chill comfort as my body burned with the fever called living.

You asked if I wanted breakfast. I managed half a soft pear, with the skin removed, and a sip of water. I could only dream of pancakes and sour plums. Sauerkraut and biscuits a supreme act of imagination and mental indulgence. You dabbed my lips with your handkerchief. I never had a mother who mothered me like you. Though you never played Juliet like her.

You informed me that you had ushered Locard to the door, telling him we would give his case our utmost attention. I'm sure he had no desire to stay longer after witnessing the spectacle of a dying detective with saliva running down his chin and one functioning eyeball.

My pen asked what you thought of our visitor's tale.

You made a face.

"To be frank, it's the kind of puzzle that sticks between your teeth like a piece of gristle, but I see nothing in it worth our energies. You must agree, it's as inconsequential as a hundred cases we leave aside." I was surprised you pooh-poohed it so readily. Surprised all the more by your tetchiness. "I'm sorry to be blunt—but I won't have your health being taxed unnecessarily by cases with little or no merit."

I was touched. Even if the avoidance of your eyes reminded me of the obvious implication—*time was short.*

"The warder's imagination has run away with him," you suggested. "He sees secrecy even in a silly scrawl in the back of a Bible. Which could indicate a hymn number, for all we know. Or almost anything. It certainly doesn't mean it's important, let alone indicative of criminal activity. The reputation of his celebrated inmate, and even the whole *milieu* he works in, has made him see demons everywhere—even in the form of a visiting priest. The truth is, surely, the simplest possibility of all? That the old man goes there to give the prisoner what she craves most. Absolution."

I listened and pondered. By no means in agreement.

Firstly, the husband troubled me—and always had. Having reappeared after his wife's arrest, he'd vanished from the narrative completely. We hadn't seen him at the trial. He was never mentioned. He remained an enigma. Another of which was the problem of the books the priest brought. Why *those* specific volumes? Or indeed, those authors? Dickens? Defoe?

But what wormed away in my brain most of all was the message pencilled in the back cover of the Bible. An obscure code waiting to be broken. And, as Locard had said, why a code *at all* unless hiding something?

"You must rest. You have had far too much exertion for one day. Visitors are exhausting at the best of times . . ."

A child-murderer, I used the talon of my nib as swiftly as I could to commit my thoughts to paper . . . *Committed—or yet to come?* I gave the question mark a curve like an ear.

"You cannot mean . . ."

I saw you grow pale at the implication. Your eyes flickering, as if some corner of the room held answers. Even horrid ones.

From out in the *salon* I heard the Mathieu Lejeune—white marble and gilded bronze, flanked by two dolphins and sur-topp'd with a lyre—strike eleven. Ample time to get to Saint-Lazare for the priest's next visit.

"Midday." Your eyes narrowed as you read my mind. "You would have me confront him?"

I shook my head, frowning.

If I am wrong, I am wrong.

"But if you are right . . ."

Keep your distance. Powder dry. Don't let him see you. Be invisible. Observe. Nothing else. I underscored *Observe.*

You nodded.

Little did I know that from that moment, our lives would be changed forever. My assassin's plan was already in play, and there was nothing I could do to halt it.

～✦

Less than a minute after you'd gone, a lightning-bolt of *sciatica* shot down my leg and I convulsed with a wail. Any attempt to shake it only set off other contortions. I writhed, as I did five times daily and six times on Sunday.

Soon thereafter, thanks to our servant's diligent obedience to the timetable, my remedies rode me steadily into a fitful slumber.

Beyond the dusty glass, children laughed with their hoops and ducks.

My *somethingectomy* throbbed, that bit sliced by assassin and mended by another knife—that of the tailor-surgeon who had sewn me up. With my eyes tightly shut, I saw my protesting guts stuffed back in—quack, quack! Fingers touching my belly, now convex, bloated as a barrel but taut as a balloon fit to burst. Dreams, then as now, aided by Morpheus and his lurking demons . . .

A trolley rolled on the cobbles.

Into my imagination flew a moth—species *atropos*—large as an eagle, hovering above a disused bathing machine—or was it a shepherd's hut?—careering down a slope towards a cliff--top. I thought anxiously of the woman trapped inside, naked or clothed—I knew not which and it vexed me why she made no sound. Was it to deceive me? Or was she behind me, planning her attack?

My next vision—*stirred by the medicine*—was that of a cave on a shore whose sand was salt-white—voluminous, pregnant with emptiness, an inverted V the rim of its mouth formed of colossal, shapely boulders, not really stones at all, and not the colour of stones. I knew straight away it was the lair painted by Uccello that housed a dragon, but the beast was nowhere to be seen. The battle won—or lost.

The soil burned my toes. I could hear the monster's breathing from deep within, but found to my horror I could move neither forward nor back, my limbs so lacked strength or will. I knew not how I had arrived there, nor why I had been planted in such a predicament—an inescapable and *fatal* one. For was not the earth around me scattered with bones and skulls? Rather than look at them I kept resolutely staring into the Stygian void—hoping against hope that something might be revealed. Some dim shape. Some dim hope to grasp on.

Slowly, as a collodion image takes form on a tintype plate, that hope solidified. First a shadow amongst shadows, then emerging, its own pale self, candle-wan, oozing from the dimness as a sack might be pulled up from a well.

The figure of a woman, *yes!*—an uncommonly *large* woman with thin—so *thin*—strands of hair hanging from her scalp and udder-heavy breasts under the grey prison garb. She smiled with small, broken teeth and held out her arms.

"*Viens, mon enfant. Je ne te ferai pas de mal. Maman ne te fera jamais de mal.*"

"Come, child. I won't hurt you. Mama will never hurt you."

⟅⟆

I woke to the trilling of Merriwether's Tempest Prognosticator. Its twelve leeches were becoming agitated, their attempt to escape the glass tripping a hammer which rang its bell, the insistence of which told me a storm was imminent.

You entered my bedchamber, Holmes, still wearing your coat, its shoulders speckled with raindrops. You asked if I had been fed. Struggling to sit up, I said I needed nothing but the food of information. You punched the pillows behind me. I eased back into them, noticing that you were shaking. I hoped it was the cold of the rain that caused your hands to tremble. I placed my own on them to transfer some warmth. You almost recoiled. I suppose warmth from me came as a shock.

You fetched the lacquered tray with its inkwell and paper and laid it across my lap. I dunked the nib of the pen and waited.

You told me you had hailed a carriage, hastened directly to Saint-Lazare and had placed yourself under a canopy at the La Petite Arcadie café, the most suitable vantage point across the street from the prison gates. As noon approached, you'd noted a motley assortment of people arrive and enter—mainly of the lower classes, from their attire. Relatives of the accused and incarcerated. Nothing in their behaviour to arouse suspicion of any kind. As the minute hand of the church clock neared five past, however, you'd begun to fear the journey had been wasted. At which point a small, black-robed figure rounded the corner into the square and hurried to the door of the building before disappearing inside.

Description? I asked.

"Exactly as Enoc Locard told us."

While the priest stayed inside, you'd ordered a *baguette* and green olives. Forty minutes later the rag-tag visitors emerged, white-cheeked and glum. Prison visits are never occasions for joy. The ghastly ripples of servitude invariably spread wide into society—sometimes more wide than we know, until society feels the wounds. Lastly, our Catholic priest appeared, Bible in hand.

Appearance?

"Furtive. An urgency, but not panic. I abandoned my *baguette*, pulled my cloth cap over my eyes and followed him at a distance of a hundred paces or so, just as you taught me. He never looked over his shoulder. Cut through the Rue Papillon into the Rue de Montholon, turning right into the Rue de Rochechouart, then left to the Avenue Trudaine, past the Abattoir." I saw your features tense as you strained to remember every detail. "After that he upped his speed and covered some distance through alleyways unfamiliar to me, swathed in washing lines and populated by disagreeable tenants. I was worried I'd lose him, but emerged into a paved *carré*. Up ahead, he approached a church called Git-le-Coeur."

Here Lies the Heart.

"Then I'm afraid my eagerness got the better of me." You rubbed your forehead. "As he mounted the steps, I was right behind him. So much so that when he walked inside, he, in the dark, held open the door for me to follow. I was afraid if I let him go we would have nothing. And that was the thing, you see? I *did* have exactly that—*nothing*. I stepped into the nave, not a single candle to punctuate its gloom, and he was gone. I don't mean he had made his escape, unless he had a magic cloak to make him invisible, or had turned into a holy wafer and slipped through a crack in the floor. He had—what can I say?—*vanished*."

My face showed nothing but a musing concentration, but I *knew the reason why that was so*. My ratiocination had been all too elementary—and indisputable—yet I questioned it . . . *because I could not believe it to be true*.

"I . . . I could see no doors nearby. No alcoves. No curtains to hide behind. The only explanation I could conceive of was a supernatural one. *Witchcraft*," you whispered. "I walked the length of the aisle and back again. Then I saw it." You dug deep in your coat pocket. "Lying on the flagstones."

You placed the object on my tray. The black background set off the key's golden hue. Bronze, then, rather than cast iron. I picked it up. You lit the candle stick at my bedside and held it close.

I ran my fingers around a thick stem, simple collar and quat-refoil grip. Too large to fit a piece of furniture. A mortise, then. My first thought was Swedish, from the Island of Gotland—the Swedes have a long tradition of using keys in their marriage cer-emonies—but the entwined vines on the arabesque bow made me think of the loggia of the Vatican.

You appeared to be impatient for my conclusion, so I wrote: *Eskilstuna.*

The free artisan's town. Actually, two towns merged into one to form a community of smiths—an industrial city, in effect. My thumbnail pointed out to you the tiny *fabriks märke* of a capital E with a vertical key bisecting it. The "JW" within the elaborate curves of the grip indicating its maker to be Johan Walén & Co., *Eskilstuna*.

"But its usage? And origin?" You seemed genuinely disturbed by your experience, supernatural or otherwise, plucking at the hairs of one eyebrow. "The key to some part of a church would seem obvious."

Or prison cell. Or shackles.

"Shackles?"

Or marriage.

"What? Bluebeard?"

The murderer with the secret rooms where his wives were not allowed to peek. Or the nasty nick-name applied to Josephine Rappaport by the newspapers. *Madame Bluebeard.* The key was a key to—what? The Case of the Vanishing Priest? Or the Witch's Spell?

"I'm as baffled as you are."

But I wasn't baffled at all. Everything was steadily falling into place.

My mind was afire with dread and expectation, the cold hand of Fate hovering over my shoulder—and you saw nothing behind my mask.

"If it is even possible that Rappaport's crimes are not over, we must do something. The idea other poor innocents . . ."

My lids were heavy, but I made out they were heavier.

I must sleep, my hand wrote. It had to write something.

"You're tired. You are tired, but I am not."

I let go of the pen. It rolled down the tray leaving a smear of ink. I held up a hand. Enough. *Enough.* If you could have known the pain that coursed through me—one not of the body, but of the *soul* . . .

"I am going to investigate this key." You snatched it up and shook it in front of my face. "There is a door out there it fits. If I have to talk to every locksmith in Paris I'll find it. And when that door is opened our mystery shall be solved."

The candle-light painted golden dots on your pupils. They shone even as you trembled. I thought to myself, in my grave I shall miss those shining eyes.

My power spent, I slumped, the pillows cushioning my bleating head and squirming body.

"Shall I send in Le Bon?"

I nodded, dangling my hand in midair.

My half-dimmed vision. You. Whiter than the wax, backing away through an open door, coat skimming your ankles, hair swept back from the rain. A long-nosed corpse who'd done without too much sleep—thanks to me. *Edgar Poe: Robber of dreams.* Oh, my dear, dearest boy . . . What you had *endured.* And what was to come.

~~∽~~

I reached for the cane and banged the floor with it—*unnecessary.* Le Bon had arrived. Gracious Le Bon. Ardent Le Bon. Trusty Le Bon. And his trust was what I needed now.

But first—*urination.*

The cold floor soothed my bloated feet. I rose, tugged by his hands, knees shuddering, legs like jelly. The china below me. My *tiré torchon* unwrapped. Manhood exposed. Gulliver's hosepipe. Now a brackish trickle at best. Behold! Poe pees in the 'po'. Alliteration! Edgar evacuates eventually. We had long passed that other "E"—embarrassment.

All effort spent, my limbs gave and I received. The sitting position, that is. Hunched like a drunk on a log. Were *wheezing* a sport, I'd have had no rivals.

The spider in the ink danced.

I told Le Bon to abandon his household tasks immediately and take a train: Route 20 to the South East, the main line
Paris to Dijon (Mont Cenis), then on to Lyon. The journey was
approximately *316 miles* and would take between *14 and 16 ½
hrs by standard service; 8 ¾ by express*. I told him to go by express.
To stay at the Hôtel de l'Universel at the side of the station of
Perroche.

*You can dine at any of the cafés in the Place de Célestines. Be sure
to take a cup of chocolate before dinner. Only ½ a franc. The Lyonnaise
are bright & jocose, fond of name-calling & habitually stubborn, sometimes petty, being descended largely from Protestants. Do not engage on
a trivial basis. And be in your room by midnight. The standard train
arrives at 4.30 a.m. & on no account must you be seen by the person I
believe will be on board.*

To smooth his furrowed brow, I explained to him my deductive process regarding the code written in the priest's Bible.

*BB
TAV.DUF
300N
demO*

"300N" seemed to me, applying no great intelligence, to
almost certainly indicate *nord*, north—and a distance of 300
something. The line below would, by the same logic, imply that "O"
meant *ouest*—west—and the abbreviation "dem" might reasonably
be assumed to stand for *demi*, or half. Looking back at the top line,
therefore and knowing now that these are, in fact, directions, what
could the initials "BB" indicate? Surely *Bourg-en-Bresse*, the town
where Josephine Rappaport committed her crimes. So what did
we have? "TAV" could only mean *taverne*, so "DUF" presumably
indicated the rest of the name of the hostelry in question, such as
"Dufresne," "Du Fretay," or "Du Fromage".

Consequently I urged Le Bon to travel from Lyon to Bourg-en-Bresse as early as possible the following day. To seek out the Taverne Dufresne—or whatever similar name could be found. There could not be many.

Go at first light. Walk 300 metres north, then half a kilometre west.

I didn't know what was there, or why my murderer wanted to go there. But my life—or rather my *death*, depended on it.

You will see somebody, I scribbled. *If not that day, then the next. As soon as you have, return & come directly to me.*

Le Bon nodded.

I knew he would carry out my instructions precisely. Good *Le Bon.* True to his name—but, of course, it was the name I gave him. "Rue Morgue" has a lot to answer for. He'd played his role well over the years.

I told him that he would have to be my eyes and ears. I was sending him off to play detective, while the real detective rotted in his sheets, drained by the keel-hauling of a simple piss and a page of scribblings.

Exhausted, I let the embrace of sleep take me to its bosom.

The door shut, and I was alone in my tomb.

⌁

I had been a writhing bedbug for years, my mottled arms spindly as bone and my belly round and aching with gas. Yet in the dream I stood like a bridegroom and walked unaided, as lithe and fit as a man in his twenties.

Around me, all seemed lit by a pasty, unappetising candle-light, and I heard what I first took to be a lullaby, echoing sibilantly from the walls, accompanied by a *click, click, clicking* I imagined akin to the sound made by those knitting needles of the *tricoteuses* who sat beside the guillotine.

"Je vous salue Marie,
pleine de grâce
Le Seigneur est avec vous,
vous êtes bénie entre toutes les femmes
et Jésus, le fruit de vos entrailles, est béni . . .

The prayer seeped into the ears of the stones, the silence weighing heavily, as if to emphasise the last phrase, or to relish it.

L'heure de notre mort.

The hour of our death . . .

Beside a small pile of books, Josephine Rappaport sat on a simple wooden chair, most of it obscured by her immense and overflowing body, her grey garment, ragged but not filthy, touching the floor. The clacking of her rosary beads had stopped abruptly but her eyes remained closed, her smile one of infinite peace, if not infinite rapture.

Enoc Locard, the gaoler, stood behind her in his smart navy blue tunic and *kepi*, running his fingers firmly in a circular pattern through her sparse tufts of hair. Head tilted to one side, she gave every appearance of being transported by ecstasy; whether of the beatific or the carnal kind impossible to discern, but being witness to either made me intensely uncomfortable. Locard himself was so fixated in his work he not only failed to notice my presence but appeared to be locked in a trance himself.

"Ce qui t'a gardé si longtemps?" Josephine said, without opening her eyes. "What kept you so long?"

My gaze scanned the walls that hemmed me in, emblazoned, as Locard has reported: BETHLEHEM + NAZARETH + JERUSALEM . . . yet as I revolved a second time, new vistas emerged, rendered in the paint, if dimly, if crudely, with figures banal and brutal, ill-conceived, families, crimes—a bludgeoned man, a falling woman . . . FORDHAM + RICHMOND + PARIS . . .

I covered my eyes to steady my senses, but the sound of a weeping baby forced me to look upon the sight of Josephine cradling a tiny, naked form in a plaid shawl, rocking the newborn in her hefty arms with surprising gentleness and care.

"What does it have to live for, poor thing?" she said, fondly.

"Life," I answered, thinking it my job to do so.

"Exactly." She gazed down at the newborn and let it suck her finger. "He clings to it like the breast. Not knowing the one who loves him most will kill him."

Remembering her ghastly crimes, I was suddenly disgusted. "Stop it!"

She ignored me. Beyond her, on a gimcrack dresser-cum-altar made of peeling-painted wood, I saw a wilted daffodil in a jar decorated with a lamb carrying a flag—*Hee hee hee, it's the Agnus Dei!* Beside it an ornate, oval picture frame with nothing inside.

"Who is in the portrait?" I asked, troubled by such an absence.

"Who is always in the portrait?"

The Ogress smiled an enigmatic smile, her final uttering more enigmatic still, as she imparted two words, as if a secret —*only this, and nothing more*—shared like a nightly kiss from mother to child.

"Mammoth Cave."

I thought of the Cheshire Cat and my own Berenice, for the smile remained even as the earthquake came. The bricks shifted. Thunder roared.

The Ogress was impassive.

I hammered the door to be let out, but nobody came. Everybody had died and it was my fault. It was always my fault.

My cries for help were drowned. I had no voice again as the walls shook and great cracks opened from floor to ceiling in a huge V splitting the garrison from chin to groin, rending the oleaginous surfaces asunder, and loosening not the cries of freed prisoners dangling their broken chains, but the thick bushes of thorny plants and a choir of children, their stubby arms clambering from the bloody dark.

I woke—a-blubber, egg-eyed—to find my stick arms being shaken by Le Bon. I wondered if my shouts had reached the land of the living and he had feared for me, or my sanity, although I was used to that. I hadn't been "sane" since the age of six. Some might say earlier.

I held his cheeks. He had returned. He knew my questions. They were written in my face.

"*Oui. Oui. Tout ça, oui . . .*"

The back of his hand wiped his lips. I had caught the whiff of brandy and I knew why he had partaken. *What time was it?* If he had caught the morning train back from Lyon, I must have slept around the clock. The gloom outside said sunset—I could pin down the lamplighter's whistling to the minute.

He talked like a condemned man obliged to confess a crime. But did so, in French, from the chair he pulled nearer the bed.

"*Vous aviez raison.* The Taverne Dufour. Half-timbered, like many of the old buildings in Bourg. A mangy dog chained up outside, so I don't know how it attracted customers. *Specialites Regionales*, its awning read, which probably meant *poulardes de Bresse,* but I wouldn't eat there if you paid me. From its coach yard I took a narrow country lane north, skirting a field. After three hundred paces I found a footpath heading west, into the Forêt de Seillon, leaving red-crested chickens and those curious Saracen chimneys behind me. The tangled branches above were so dense they almost totally cut out the light, and at times the ferns so knotted I had to hack at them with my arms. I was glad to stretch my legs after the train but the crunch of pine cones underfoot soon grew tiring. After half a kilometre I was hoping for a landmark. What I found was a clearing where a few thin shafts of sunlight jutted down through the canopy. I thought my best bet would be to hide there—since there was a good deal of cover, bushes and fallen trees—rather than to wander about aimlessly and risk being seen by . . ."

Le Bon paused.

I patted my throat, indicating I needed water. While he was out of the room I wrote a single word on a sheet of paper and folded it in two. He came back in, pressed the glass to my lips and returned to his seat.

"The dog at the tavern started barking again in the distance. I ducked down near a badger sett, and presently the silhouette of a man appeared through the trees, by the same path I'd used, placing his feet with deliberation, as if counting every step. As he entered the clearing and circled it, I made out he held a Bible, which he inserted into a canvas gamekeeper's bag over one shoulder. His collar was turned up. It was only when, startled by the piping of a roe deer, he stepped into one of the shafts of light did I see his face."

Le Bon stopped dead and looked straight at me, as if he himself was about to deliver a fatal, murderous, blow.

I held out the piece of paper.

He took it and unfolded it. One word was written: *HOLMES*

Le Bon's intake of breath was audible as he forced himself to pass it back to me. And, with immense effort, nodded.

"*C'est vrai.* But this . . . *this* is the extraordinary thing, monsieur—because it makes no sense. He stopped, staring down at something covering the ground. All I could see were whitish knobs no bigger than my thumb, hundreds of them, scattered on the grass, surrounding the roots of an old, gnarled tree. He took a muslin bag from his pocket, knelt on one knee and began collecting them. *Oui,* it was Sherlock. *Oui,* he had followed the directions to the letter. But—*why?* To pick mushrooms?" Le Bon laughed incredulously. "That's what I watched him do. That's *all* I watched him do! Pluck those stalks with their little purple-grey heads. And when his muslin bag was full, he departed. *Je ne comprends—*"

I held up my palm. I had heard footsteps ascending to our apartment, and then—both of us this time—heard the sound of our main door opening and closing. Only one person other than us had the key.

"*Que se passe-t-il?*" Le Bon hissed, eyes wide.

I put a finger to my lips.

You had caught the standard service from Lyon. Le Bon had beat you back—but by far less time than I'd predicted. Had the *Train de Luxe* been delayed? It was of no consequence anymore.

"Hullo!" A voice, in English.

Go! I was already writing for Le Bon, calculating the time it would take for you to hang up your coat: *Take yourself out of town and stay there. 3 days, then return. Tell Holmes your sister is ill. But tell him nothing of what we have discussed or anything of what you know. If you do nothing more for me in my lifetime, do this—GO!*

The door opened a crack. I caught an inch of your cheek and worried eye before Le Bon quickly shut the door after him.

⌒⌐

"Je suis soulagé que vous soyez revenue, M. Holmes." I strained to observe if you detected any falsity in his tone, but luckily any nervousness could easily be read as concern. *"Il a eu une nuit troublée. Non, ne le reveille pas. Laisse le dormer s'il vous plaît."* I didn't hear your reply, but sensed both of you moving away from my bedroom door.

I tore the piece of paper with your name written on into strips and forced each bolus down my gullet. It tasted of Dolos, Apate and Alathea—trickery, deception and truth.

I had known it would be you that Le Bon would see in Bourg. You told me as much yourself—though not in words.

Your mistake had been in forgetting my lesson that that all criminals have a "tell". Any interrogator of merit knows this and, with experience, spots it. In your case, a rubbing of the forehead, and, *in extremis*, the plucking at an eyebrow with your fingers. A gesture you are quite unaware of, I'm sure—but once I'd seen it, everything fell into place. You were lying.

There was no priest.

Because you *were* the priest, Sherlock—and *always had been.*

Your description of assiduously following him to the church, therefore, and what happened there, disappeared in a puff of smoke.

You'd presented the key to me as an important clue, but in reality it was meaningless. You probably purchased it from a local *brocanteur*. It was nothing but a red herring designed to divert this hound from the scent. I used my assessment of its provenance in similar fashion to make you think you had been successful.

Your *reason* for doing so was similarly unavoidable. My conclusion, though far from pleasurable, an inevitability . . .

Back then, my mind had raced. What could have been your purpose in taking such measures to see the Ogress of Lyon? The books she acquired must have been part of a *quid pro quo* in return for some secret she passed on to you. You gained what you wanted; her directions to the forest near Bourg-en-Bresse—but why? . . . At that stage, I had no idea.

I knew you would waste no time in going there, but only when Le Bon returned did the scenario finally make sense. Then I had it, as a world *in toto*, within my grasp, my breath catching in my throat with as much delight as despair.

I laughed. Your purpose. Your method. Your *modus operandi.* All was clear!

You had gone there to find *the murder weapon*—with precise knowledge gained from the Ogress of what she had used to poison those infants *and yet had evaded detection*, even under the most fastidious eyes of both justice and criminology. Indeed, even our own. It was you, Holmes, who had gone to the murderess, gained her trust, bargained with her and extracted the esoteric knowledge only she possessed. The knowledge of *how to commit a murder.*

Under the pretext of investigating the key, you had travelled to Bourg-en-Bresse—to that special, perhaps *unique,* location where the *fungi* occur in abundance. I suspect the townsfolk know the danger of the local toadstool well and that Josephine, as a child, was told by her parents how to identify and avoid it. Some irony, then, that she subsequently utilised it to kill her own children.

I racked my brains to identify the species, having once made a comparative study of the subject.

Amanita verna, Destroying Angel, is a malignant *basidomycete* which causes liver failure if not treated, but its cap, *stipes* and gills are all white. Fly Agaric—red with white spots—is not poisonous *per se* but a very strong narcotic; even drinking water it has been cooked in can cause intoxication and vomiting. But Le Bon was specific in his description of a purple sheen. Death caps are generally greenish with a white *stipe* and gills. He made no mention of rings round the stem or of a *volva,* ruling out Fool's Mushroom, which grows in European woodlands and hardwood forests in springtime and has been instrumental in a number of fatal poisonings. Then I remembered his description of his feet crunching on pine cones. This told me the answer was the rarest of all deadly toadstools which forms *ectomycormizas* with, exclusively, pine.

Jean-Baptiste Lamarck gave it distinct species status in his *Encyclopédie Méthodique, Botanique—Misericordia Noctis* in Latin. In French, *La Miséricorde de la Nuit.* In English, *Mercy of the Night.*

I recalled my research indicated no negative symptoms. No violent cramps or diarrhoea that other species kindly facilitate. Merely a slight unease due to the heart quickening, sometimes misinterpreted as a sign of recovery, but most of the time simply a herald of the final onset of a dull, luxurious slumber.

You will have asked the Ogress if it was painless. She will have confirmed that it was. I am certain this would have been important to you. Important enough for you to seek it out, when you could have chosen other options.

I close my eyes and picture you resting the tray across my lap. I recall that its toxins are heat stable, so their effect is by no means reduced by cooking.

You will feed me and may even encourage me to eat more than I wish, because it is good for me. *Good for me.* That will be a very good touch, for a poisoner.

And you will disguise the feelings in your countenance as expertly as the putty, theatrical powder and false beard covered your features when you played the wizened priest. Oh, my boy—you always were an excellent actor! I shall enjoy that performance, as you will think back to my own when you read these words, which you will discover tucked under my pillow.

Within an hour after ingestion I shall be sleepy, and before dawn I will be dead. You might sit with me and listen to my laboured breathing as it grows shallow, but more likely I will ask you, in a weak scrawl of my pen, to leave the room so that I may rest.

I hope, for a short time at least, you will have held my hand. And that yours, come light of morning, after drawing back the curtains to let in the sun, will be the one that is first to touch me when I am cold.

～

The assassin's tread is near. The nightingale chirps its glissando. You press a glass of water to my cardboard lips. You administer my holy communion in the form of wafer thin slices of cucumber, cold on my tongue.

"Time for your bath."

Two washcloths and sponges, three towels, two water basins—one viscid with soap, the other pure, for rinsing.

The ritual.

You roll me to and fro to place a towel under me. You slide my nightshirt off over my head. I am thankful I don't have to behold this sack of gruel, these hanging paps, this blotched and blighted landscape of woe. Of Poe.

You move around me, tender as a ghost. Shoulders, upper body, arm, hand ... Was Christ himself bathed in frankincense thus on his bier? Were Martha's hands so sensitive and giving? Is the lavender of Provence the fragrance of the tomb?

At any point I could ask for the pen and tell you what I had deduced, but that would disrupt you from carrying out your plan. I do not want that and neither do you.

The Ravages, you well know, are endless now, and unendurable. I want to weep when I go to sleep and want to scream when I wake. I wish I were a plaster saint to enjoy my torment, but I was only ever an amateur martyr. It's the one thing writers do well.

When you are done, you cover me with the last towel to keep me warm, patting it down all over. You take away one bowl and return silently for the other.

"I bought mushrooms from the market. I've made a soup. I think it'll be delicious."

My eyes are closed.

"When you are ready," you whisper.

I nod.

"I'll leave you now." The silence remains as you walk to the door. "I'll warm it up in no time."

"Thank you." My lips shape the syllables, but there is no sound.

⌒⌇⌒

You have tended an undiminished intelligence trapped within an ailing body wracked by pain—but *your* pain, too, has not gone unnoticed. Do you seriously think I, who observes everything, have not observed the turmoil within as you watched me deteriorate? My arms thinning to the bone. The whites of my eyes turning a buttery hue: clear indication, as well you have *deduced*, that my constitution is faltering. So, I shall be gratified when it is over; when that duty which you have taken upon your shoulders will be lifted.

When we are young, with supple frames and irrepressible hopes, we are puzzled why the old do not rail against death, howling in indignation to the last. The truth is that, by then, we *want* to go. Our ineffectual bodies have long since betrayed us. The burden of the world has become too heavy. The endless ticking of the *pendule* too much to bear.

But shed no tears.

Or, *shed a few* ... that our time on earth together has not been in vain.

Sentimentality is for buffoons, I know—but what am I, if not a buffoon? A solver of crimes? Hoping to make the world a safer place? What could be more idiotic or arrogant? We leave the world as we enter it—neither improved nor worsened much. We pass the time in the illusion that we matter.

Above all—do not burden yourself *with guilt*.

Wall me up with a cat for company! Put me under the floorboards and nail them down! But do *not* be a troubled murderer, haunted by my all-seeing eye or the beating of my unfeeling heart!

Believe me, it is a kindness to end my suffering.

I do not blame you.

Far from it ...

I commend you! For your diligence. For your courage. For your deception. What you are doing is a heroic act.

You were always much more the hero than me.

My words are gone. My body is gone. My sight is near gone. I am a Half-Man at most, reduced to lying in the gloom, a bag of frayed nerves and tangled spasms. My mind barely tethered to the pier, constantly beaten by a squall which can only turn to a hurricane. This vessel shall never be becalmed, nor its crew reach shore.

In the face of which, your logic has been faultless. You applied the science of *ratiocination* and have decided to do what was unerringly *right*.

In short, monsieur—*I am proud of you.*

Moreover, do you not see that you have succeeded magnificently where I have failed? All my life, whether in fact or fiction, I have tried to fathom the criminal mind, but you have *in this one simple act* done so at a stroke. For what more complete way is there to understand the criminal brain than to become *yourself* a criminal?

I'd even say it is fitting that the final lesson of a detective's education is to commit a crime and get away with it. And a murder at that!

An act so often committed for the base motives of greed, gain, lust, or by dint of the onset of madness—yet seldom, *if ever,* have I seen it done in the name of *friendship.* Which brings a smile to these weary lips.

Je souris.

I could never have planned it thus, but I have no doubt you will pass the last test with flying colours, and your transformation will be complete.

Tomorrow, with the new dawn, you shall understand the criminal as you have never done—*could* never have done—before. Because, by the time you read these words, you will be more than a detective examining crime; you will be Crime itself.

My task, your education, Sherlock, is complete.

You are a murderer, and a good one.

You have nothing more to learn.

⤙✦

My will and testament is in the bureau, together with other legal documents, all in the name "C. Auguste Dupin" (as you would expect). I have bequeathed to you any objects you wish to possess. I know you have always coveted my Persian slippers, even though they are two sizes too small, but you might find another purpose for them.

I have arranged for Le Bon to be taken on by Ptolemy Vance, the United States congressman, as his personal secretary. Small repayment for the years of loyalty my beloved servant has shown me, but I am confident the New World, with all its vigour and optimism, will offer opportunities denied him here. You will find a personal letter to him amongst my aforementioned effects. My one request is that he visits a certain grave in Baltimore on my birthday to raise a glass to me and perhaps leave it there, in the manner of an offering of sherry to Santa Claus. A vainglorious wish, I know, but it would please me for Poe to export a final mystery to the land of his birth.

Our dear departed "Mme L'Espanaye" left instruction for the apartment, after I passed away, to be used as a dancing school. Those wishes will be adhered to. It would have amused my old friend Degas, and it amuses me to think of tiny ballerinas twirling on the very floorboards where you and I stood as we tried to unknot our *conundra*. Perhaps the joy and laughter of children might blow the cobwebs away from our fusty delvings into dark lives.

That leaves you homeless. I have no doubt you will wish to return to England. To fly the coop and to be alone will be a sorry prospect, but I have endeavoured to soften the blow. Due to my work in rescuing the reputations of some exceedingly well-off clients over the years, an annual dispensation will transfer to your name upon my death and enable you to follow your studies in detection unencumbered by financial concerns. The executor of this arrangement is Osric Sleet of Mondesir, Bynum & Sleet in Grey's Inn Road. He is the other person for whom I am writing this manuscript in such fastidious detail.

Show it him as soon as possible after your arrival. He will need to know the full and true nature of my demise, not to mention my feelings on the subject. I have associated with many disreputable types over the years, and my handwriting and signature will demonstrate these pages are not forgeries. For reasons I shall not bore you with, he will carry out my wish, thusly expressed, that he turn a blind eye to my murder and I can assure you he is to be trusted with our secrets implicitly.

I ask the same of you—while those who are still alive might be hurt or horrified by the knowledge I did not die when the history books say.

It would not gall me if my reputation were to be scorched to oblivion by the scandal, however I do have a dim fondness for my literary accomplishments and would like them to survive untrammelled by the viciousness of public discourse. That said, I have a feeling, given the crime you will have committed, you'll be only too happy to keep quiet about our association.

Get at least one suit from Solon & Sanger in Mayfair, and beware of Stoke Newington, where the *mauvais garçons* of the underworld are more dangerous than the Paris Apaches. It will be a jolt to find yourself in London with its drabness, fog and stunted passions, after the dandified urban perversity of Paris. There was, sadly, no revolution in England and so no revolutionary thought. Desire is an unwelcome agitation to the English and so fuels everything all the more.

As far as my mortal remains are concerned, I request a vein to be opened in my neck by the doctor pronouncing death: you know my fear of premature burial cannot be said to be inconsiderable. I further specify cremation. No ceremony. No flowers. No headstone. Scatter my ashes in the Seine, from the Pont Neuf. I hear that lovers gather there nowadays. If you are asked, it will be easy to pretend you are dispersing the ashes of someone for whom you cared deeply.

Rest assured, my dear Holmes, I die with nothing unfulfilled. No wishes hanging in the air. And only one regret—concerning that poor wretch in Baltimore who stood in for me as the curtain came down on the first act of my life.

Perhaps the truth is that what we all want is not for crimes to be detected, but for them to be *prevented,* and if I had my time again, I would apply myself to that science—the one of the mind, filtrating the nascent impulses and causes of such phenomena, striving to eradicate their occurrence rather than standing witness to the incessant cycle of violence, prison, and punishment.

That is the final mystery, perhaps. How to make it so that *all* people live good lives, instead of striving for selfish ends. Perhaps an unattainable ideal, but I was a poet after all. And I can think of no finer Utopia to try to build. One of kindness instead of destruction and suffering. We all aspire towards such a goal, do we not?

That is why Josephine Rappaport needed her books so desperately. Even she, now, harbours the urge to discover humanity. The books a last ditch attempt to civilise herself before her final judgement in heaven.

My last request of you, then—inevitably—is to take the Ogress of Lyon a copy of one of my own volumes.

It seems only fitting. The Wiley & Putnam *Tales* of 1845, I suggest.

Let her read the indignation of Hop-Frog as he is humiliated and of the brick-laying madness of Montresor. Let her be gripped, if she will, by the trajectory of a clever detective and a razor-wielding ape on the streets of Paris. Let Circe's lips mouth the words from a haunted palace and those of countless lost loves, buried and exhumed. Let *yarns,* if nothing else, transport her for a while. Let them offer a glimpse of the dark and blessed hues of what it means to be human.

A small gift in return for the gift she has given me.

⌒

Presently I shall rap the floor with my stick.

You will open the door and I will detect—*detect*—the aroma of the soup. The agaric tang of aniseed and almond, with an after-taste of Indian ink and the Conqueror Worm.

Thereafter I shall be only the pages I have written and the crimes I have solved. Wrongs righted, once in a while, are no bad legacy. That, and a passing fondness for the tallest of tales.

I do not think any of us truly fear dying. We fear only suffer-ing. In ourselves and those we leave behind.

I shall know nothing of it. I shall be in a state as insignificant as I was before I was born. I knew nothing before I entered this life and shall know nothing after it. I take comfort in that design.

Ah! I hear your violin playing Schubert's "Swan Song Serenade". *Un geste très approprié!*

Soon I will have reached the end of my *Chemin du Crépuscule*, with, thankfully, no sanctimonious saint to greet me and deliver the roll call of my worldly sins. Speaking of which, on no account let anybody tell you that I bought that goldfinch because its red feathers were symbolic of the blood of Christ. Its song reminded me only of the sweetness of life. Though I will be the fool if, in the somnolent darkness, I hear a voice cry: "Halt! Who goes there?"

As I drift on the broken raft of my corpse-to-be, I think of the words whispered to me by the Ogress in my dream:

"Mammoth Cave."

The three syllables ring like the clamour of the Angelus.

You see, *I know of such a place* . . .

A subterranean network of passageways and chambers in Louisville, Kentucky—the world's most extensive cave system—purchased in 1839 for $10,000 by Dr John Croghan, a sufferer of phthisis who had the bold and unique vision to develop it as a sanatorium.

Croghan had heard extraordinary reports that visitors felt exhilarated after spending time in the cave. Even a walk of five hours caused them little fatigue. Furthermore, both timber and animals seemed impervious to decay, which the doctor could only conclude to mean the environment was both therapeutic and restorative in nature.

He wasted little time in establishing an experimental hospital below ground, and fifteen patients suffering from various stages of the white plague took up his offer of residence, unperturbed by smoke and ash from oil lanterns and the less than salubrious living conditions presented to them by two stone cabins with canvas roofs. Meals were prepared outside and a horn blown to call this company of skeletons to dinner, after which said unfortunates seemed unafraid to yet again cross the aptly-named River Styx and succumb to near darkness.

They endured it, I am sure, because it represented hope, when little else did.

Mammoth Cave.

Virginia and I had talked of travelling there.

As I'd read Clark Bullitt's *Rambles* aloud, I'd pictured hospital gowns and the echo of hollow coughing, but she brightened considerably at the idea, listening intently with her hand on my knee. My wife showed no terror of the prospect of touching walls surrounding the "grand and gloomy" Bottomless Pit where "not much was known, but all peculiar," or standing within a cave as big as an amphitheatre—it was, as to a child, an adventure, you see. When I spoke about a stone they called The Altar, where some foolish folk were married once upon a time, I remember her chuckling at that like a six-year-old.

The writer, compensating for hideous grammar with flowery verbosity, described crystallizations on the rock ceilings—stalactites—while others rose from the ground, often joining them, "as if one lover reaching to unite with its soul mate."

One of the great cruelties of *spes phthisica* was that Virginia reacted to this with a light heart and indomitably hopeful spirit. Nobody could perceive from her euphoric joy and beatific softness of touch that she carried disease in her lungs, or that the blood vessels in her chest were steadily and irrevocably disintegrating. Behind the wan smiles, ours was a world of dismal sweats and scarlet flecks on the pillow.

I hoped—yes, *hoped,* against all reason, all the way to madness and back again; (how d'you think I know that dancing partner so well?)—but all our hopes and plans were as wisps in the breeze.

We never reached Mammoth Cave.

Virginia was never well enough to leave her home and hearth, or even her bed. The blood, sputum and fever got the better of her. She took the last hope we kindled to her grave.

But I am not a fool. The two words cannot have been uttered by the Ogress. The dream was my own. And yet ... When I sink into sleep now, wishing for nothing but respite, I find myself uncontrollably pulled back there.

This time, though, Josephine Rappaport does not stand at the mouth of that gaping cavern. Her place is occupied by another. An altogether thinner woman. Too thin. With her arms open wide to welcome me. And I find myself dreaming of stepping into the dark and feeling the peace and succour of Virginia's perpetual embrace.

I have often said; there cannot be true beauty without true sorrow, but if death is a dream, and my dream is this ... I will not be displeased.

So I say this, before my inkwell runs dry ...

Beware of cutting yourself off, as I have done.

Apply my methods coldly, yes—but that coldness serves no purpose if you have no warmth for your fellow man. Our vocation is not a game or puzzle. Our duty is to others in their time of need, not to our own vanity. Says vanity personified.

Carry goodness in your heart, Sherlock. As I know you will. It was ever your nature, even if it was lacking in mine.

"The author lives on." Poe, reprobate, provocateur, liar, sham—while my other life, this shadow, this after-life—fades to nothing. All that will be left of me is a gold-leafed name on a Maroquin-bound spine. While Holmes the detective is newborn. Kicked from the nest, he discovers wings as he falls.

Now I shall call you with rappings, like a discarnate spirit, and ask you to read to me one last time.

We've been enjoying Flaubert again, in honour of his recent death, but I wonder if today I can have one of my favourites? Maupassant's "Boule de Suif". Those ten passengers on a stagecoach travelling from Rouen to Le Havre. Its precision and message never fail to delight me. The representatives of Virtue shown as they are to be hollow and selfish, while the individual, whose morals they disdain, is shown to be braver and stronger than any of them.

Afterwards you will ask if I am ready for my soup.

I will nod my head, smelling the earthy, almost metallic tang as it fills the room.

You will lift the spoon to my lips. Blow the steam from each mouthful.

How near *morsis* is to *mors*. The bite and death. *Morsel vincit omnia.* Words, words, words.

Is that the last lesson of all, Sherlock? In the end, all human beings really want to do is connect? And art is the only way we have of doing so? The nearest we can come to holding maps of the soul?

Perhaps that is what Josephine Rappaport knows. Or even feels, if she feels nothing else, as our snow-white cats, Ampersand and Apostrophe, sought comfort in the cradle of our arms. That

Science, when all is said and done, fails as our driftwood to cling to. That language in its opaque incalculability, in its shifting shadows, in its alphabet of fears, surmounts the light of cold Reason.

That, at the last gasp, or sigh, or smile, it is all we have.

The words of a madman, naturally.

Soon the mirror will be broken, but the world remains, all in its pretty place . . .

On the morrow you will see from the window the inscription on the sundial opposite. That familiar line from Horace that has greeted every morn—PULVIS ET UMBRA SUMUS—"We are but dust and shadows."

Thus it is and always has been. The night sky reminds us, starlit as we are, insignificance is all. Mysteries are everywhere, but there is no greater mystery than the peculiar magnetism between two souls.

So I entreat thee, Sherlock, let go my hand and, like the raven, fly.

Yr. eminent (and eminently ridiculous) friend,

Edgar A. Poe

⌒⤙

Lestrade's Journal, July 1926:

The last page of the manuscript shook in my hands. I was unable to comprehend it, at first, as anything other than a morbid and reprehensible fiction. Then it dawned on me, this was the very reason I had been sent the whole series of missives over the past several months.

Holmes had lived with the knowledge of this awful deed his entire life. Shackled by a promise to divulge nothing, he had kept silent, even to those closest to him. No wonder, with every package, the urge to secrecy was repeated . . . and yet the compulsion to set the record straight over-whelming.

I knew instinctively his abiding sense of justice meant he could not go to his grave without—

My stomach turned over.

I swivelled on my heel and looked back at the shoes by the door. Tan Grecian slippers, a pair of gunmetal Balmorals. Neither suitable for walking. In the rack beside them—an umbrella. No walking stick.

As I ran from the house the scent of wild thyme almost snatched the breath from me. Throwing open the gate, I squinted at the mud on the path, seeing my own footprints, yes—but also those of another, deep and ridged. Those of walking boots, and a line of indentations a stick had made at regular intervals.

Compelled to follow them, I climbed the steps behind the Coast-guard Cottages straight onto the downs, where the wind in the grasses and yellow gorse was shrill. At the top I halted, swaying, lest my heart peg out, then hurried, wheezing, across the chalk heath.

The path in the direction of Beachy Head pointed to the Belle Tout Lighthouse, that bold sentinel, whose rotating lamps had scoured many a rolling tide.

Having reached the edge of the cliff, I reeled back. The footsteps ended. Or, if they continued, did so in thin air. No sooner did I fear the worst than had it horribly confirmed.

I picked up the walking stick at my feet. A salty gale kicked at my raincoat.

I howled a curse. The thunder of brutal waves, three or four hundred feet below, drowned it out.

In a state of numbness, I staggered back to my hotel at Seaford, then returned home, too sodden with dismay to even contemplate informing the local police. I think, in retrospect, I was refusing to believe that someone as brave and indefatigable as Holmes could have taken his own life.

Over the following days and weeks my heaviness of heart seg-regated me from my family as I secluded myself in my study, beset by *troubled thoughts. Above all, weighing my duty to Holmes, who had committed himself to the sea, his mind in unspeakable turmoil, against my duty as a policeman—albeit retired—to report the truth to the authorities. Of what had happened at Beachy Head, at least. But, if I did, would it be pronounced an accident, death by misadventure, or suicide? What if they investigated further, and found the packages I had consigned to the Black Museum, and discovered that the world's most celebrated detective was guilty of murder? The murder of one of the greatest literary figures in history?*

Finally I could bear it no longer, and found myself putting on my hat and coat with the intent to reveal all to my colleagues at Scotland Yard. To my amazement, at that very moment, an envelope fell through the letter box. Written in a familiar hand, and postmarked Paris.

My dear Lestrade,

I could not let a toothless old bulldog suffer any longer in the misapprehension that I took my own life. My ruse was a rash act, and a regretful one. Foolish and impulsive. I can only offer these feeble words as any kind of recompense—and explanation. Do read on, I beg you, even if, within seconds after reading, you commit the contents to your fire.

At Seaford, I had made a longstanding arrangement with the local postmaster to hold any correspondence addressed to me, which I collected periodically in person, utilising a modicum of disguise on each visit. In view of my fame, I also bade him inform me of any enquiries by strangers. Consequently, I was primed by a hand-written note to expect you within hours of your arrival.

Ironically, I had been on the point of sending you my final manuscript—the one written by Poe—but the news that you were in close proximity filled me with unexpected and overwhelming horror. The idea that the crime I had kept hidden since I returned to these shores would shortly be exposed was suddenly terrifying in the extreme. My emotions, normally under check, as you know, surged to the surface. I could only picture the next few hours leading to arrest, trial, prison, and utter disgrace. Until then, you see, I had thought myself unburdened by taking you into my confidence, but now—now the result bearing down on me struck me as—yes—*unbearable*. Literally so.

I first considered burning the manuscript, but that, in another way, seemed to sully the value of everything Poe and I had experienced together. It would have been an awful and inexcusable betrayal, the notion of which repelled me. I could not bring it upon myself to destroy the one piece of evidence that proved what I knew to be the truth.

The only option, then, was to flee.

Thinking swiftly—if irrationally—I devised a means by which I would leave the stage in a manner that would, hopefully, be convincing.

Afterwards I cursed myself, sure you would spot the same technique I used at the Reichenbach Falls, and documented by Watson in print—that of walking backwards in my own footprints, then removing my boots and treading the remaining way through the grass in my socks. And leaving my stick at the cliff edge? Dear me! Looking back, that was so dashed convenient as to be absurd! But no . . . You drew the exact conclusion I had planned. It worked. All of it worked—hideously well.

I know, you see, because I watched you come to the cottage and watched you leave. Had you glanced down towards the beach, my friend, you may have seen an old fisherman in a sou'wester sitting on a stone bench, gazing out to sea. That fisherman was soon bound for Paris on a ferry from Dover.

It was not my first "escape" there, however. I had visited the city twice since Poe had passed away.

The first time, drawn to the capital by an inconsolable sense of loss regarding my old mentor, I ended up in a café seeking solace in bad wine and worse decor, where painters and poets drank absinthe from golden bowls. The owner, Rodolphe Salis, larger than life in his floral doublet, coppery beard and hair dyed vermillion, noticed my mood and endeavoured to lift it. His humour was biting and sarcastic, which reminded me of Poe at his most exuberant, so, without furnishing him with the reason why, I persuaded him to call the dive *Le Chat Noir*. As you will know, it later became the most famous cabaret in the city, with patrons famously painted by Toulouse-Lautrec. Edgar would have been at home there, but at that time his absence at my table only deepened my gloom.

My second visit you will recall from another of the exploits recorded by Watson. In "The Empty House," I told him I'd spent time in Montpelier after my tussle with Moriarty. This was a white lie. In fact, I was again drawn back to Paris. At my nadir, half-broken in spirit, I walked again those streets I'd trodden with my friend and tutor. Through copious tears, memories of those days with "Dupin" gave me the mettle to face London and to root out the last of the Moriarty gang.

And so I find myself in France again ... under a fig tree in a courtyard of a humble abode. A large black bird squawks on a branch overlooking me.

My dear, dear friend, I am sorry to cheat you of apprehending the murderer of E. A. Poe—that exasperating wizard who astonishes all, but none more than he astonished me. Furthermore, I can see why you would be inclined to give chase like the good old bloodhound you always were.

On the other hand, I trust that, having read the manuscript, you may understand the motive for my crime—which was done for love—and will judge for yourself whether I warrant the brutal punishment the law would exact.

The choice is yours. I leave it in your hands whether the world has heard the last of Sherlock Holmes.

Should you pursue me, however, do not seek a person answering to that name. As you would expect, under the circumstances, I have created a new identity for myself, as Poe did before me.

Being fluent in the language, I have blended in with little effort. Black coffee and *Tabac Semois* my sustenance, I now spend my hours writing up some of the other cases solved by C. Auguste Dupin and his eager, if stumbling, pupil, such as the hair-clipping fiend and "The Graveyard Mole", the strange affair of *Les Ombres Chinoises* and "The Sugar Barons' Duel to the Death".

I am grateful, now, that a thoughtful friend from Grenoble, who helped me after Reichenbach, has sent his grandson to look after me in my dotage. The lad takes my arm when we go for walks. An uncommonly bright, inquisitive boy. I cannot entirely resist the notion he has the making of an apprentice.

I plan to try out on him the old test Poe gave me soon after we first met. A still life of a bowl of fruit, arranged not to paint, but to elucidate what can be deduced from it by sheer observation. Sheer *ratiocination*.

The snow melts on my roof, my eyes grow dim, I've not many years left, but as long as the sun still rises and sets, I may as well put this old brain to use while I can.

You never know. I might make a detective of him yet.

Your erstwhile colleague,
and eternal friend,

Sherlock Holmes

STORY NOTES & ACKNOWLEDGEMENTS

"Edgar Allan Poe, who, in his carelessly prodigal fashion,
threw out the seeds from which so many of our present forms
of literature have sprung, was the father of the detective tale,
and covered its limits so completely that I fail to see how
his followers can find any fresh ground which they can
confidently call their own . . . On this narrow path the
writer must walk, and he sees the footmarks of Poe always
in front of him."
Sir Arthur Conan Doyle
Preface to *The Adventures of Sherlock Holmes* (1902)

MANY WRITERS, not least Doyle himself (as the quote above testifies), have said that Sherlock Holmes owes his creation in no small measure to the "first detective" in fiction—that master of ratiocination, Monsieur C. Auguste Dupin—who appears in Edgar Allan Poe's three immortal conundrums "The Murders in the Rue Morgue", "The Purloined Letter", and "The Mystery of Marie Rogêt". I became intrigued by the idea of dramatising that indebtedness in story form.

It all began when editors Charles Prepolec and Jeff Campbell asked me for a Sherlock Holmes story to appear in their anthology *Gaslight Arcanum: Uncanny Tales of Sherlock Holmes*. In response to which I wrote "The Comfort of the Seine," introducing Dupin (i.e. Poe himself) and a callow young Englishman named Sherlock visiting Paris for the first time. An early draft greatly benefited from the feedback of novelist Simon Kurt Unsworth and my fellow "Poe freak" Christopher Lloyd King (a director with whom I'd collaborated on a screenplay based on the life of Poe). I received tweaks on the French from Sasha Wardell and Jonathan Romney, and Vadim Cosmos pointed me to the illuminating *Spectacular Realities: Early Mass Culture in Fin-de-Siècle Paris* by Vanessa R. Schwartz, which reassured me that the inspiration for this tale—the scene of Laurent visiting the Paris morgue in Zola's *Thérèse Raquin*—was more than justified. For those who want to extend their macabre interest in the locale, I'd recommend an article at *messynessychic.com*, queasily called "That Time When Parisians Used to Hang Out at the Morgue for Fun".

However, I was soon to find out that this wasn't the one-off story I thought it was, but rather the first of several featuring the same duo.

At the end of "Comfort," I'd mischievously dropped, Doyle-fashion, a hint that Poe and Sherlock had been involved in the investigation of other crimes: notably the "true story" of the Phantom of the Opera. So when Charles and co-editor Paul Kane requested a story for their *Beyond Rue Morgue: Further Tales of Edgar Allan Poe's 1ˢᵗ Detective* anthology with the request going out to writers to concoct new Dupin exploits, I felt duty-bound to pick up the gauntlet I'd thrown down for myself. The result was my second story: "The Purloined Face". My friends Christopher Gillett and Lucy Schaufer, both opera singers, happily shed light on many aspects of their craft, as well as its traditions and superstitions, opening the door to my exploring parallels between Poe's tragic life and *La Traviata*. Again, Simon Unsworth gave splendid, detailed comments on the work in progress. (I should also give a salute here to the eerie cinematic masterpiece *Don't Look Now*, directed by Nic Roeg, the climactic reveal of which I shamelessly reversed.)

When editor Simon Clark sent me the brief for *The Mammoth Book of Sherlock Holmes Abroad*, another in my putative series, set as they are in Paris, seemed like a perfect fit. As in the case above, the catalyst for "The Lunacy of Celestine Blot" was my throwaway mention of Charcot's "mysterious patient" in the previous story. Thereafter, inspiration came from Georges Didi-Huberman's *Invention of Hysteria: Charcot and the Photographic Iconography of Salpêtrière* and my acute memories of the play *Augustine (Big Hysteria)* by Anna Furse. *Jules Verne* by Jean Jules-Verne and *The Sphinx of the Ice Realm*, edited by Frederick Paul Walter, proved vital. I must also thank Bill Boyes for a helpful discussion on ballooning logic, Piers Bizony for notes on the history of scientific ideas about the Moon, and John Llewellyn Probert for medical technicalities regarding stabbing.

Though set earlier, the fourth adventure of my Dupin and Holmes to be committed to paper was "The Three Hunchbacks," written for inclusion in the small companion volume to my story collection *The Parts We Play*, entitled *Supporting Roles*. This one came about when Paul Kane (see above) half-jokingly suggested I do a Poe/Dupin story about Quasimodo. This was, of course, impossible, since Hugo's character was set in medieval Paris, not the Paris of the 1870s. However, an article in the pages of *Fortean Times* by Theo Paijmans about the so-called monster makers of Hugo's *L'Homme Qui Rit* gave me an unexpected way to rise to the challenge. John Probert again helped on medical matters, and Charles Prepolec, a trusted Sherlockian eye, gave me the reassurance of reading a draft (as did Paul and his wife, Marie O'Regan).

Gaslight Gothic: Strange Tales of Sherlock Holmes was to be Charles and Jeff's next Holmes anthology. Delightfully, the brief was encapsulated in the title. Once again they requested that I contribute, and I was overjoyed to do so, since for at least two years I'd been pondering about "Father of the Man"—(a suitably Poe-esque title, I thought)—the story of the bizarre unintended consequences of the writer's 1849 encounter with "Reynolds". Their call to action spurred me to finally start committing it to paper. I must also not forget to thank Anne Billson for her help in naming both "The House of Blood" and "*L'Anormale*".

For "The Language of Terror" (helped towards its final form by Charles, again, and my good friend the novelist/editor Mark Morris), I gleaned useful information on America's involvement in the Franco-Prussian War from Babs Nienhuis and Gary Fry. *Elihu Washburne: The Diary and Letters of America's Minister to France During the Siege and Commune of Paris* by Michael Hill might prove interesting to those readers intrigued by the factual background to this case. However, one word of warning: my Washburne family is entirely fictitious. Information on the spirit photographer Buguet can be found in *The Perfect Medium: Photography and the Occult* by Clément Chéroux. Other sources I turned to on this one include "Pétroleuses, Witches and Fairy Tales" by Wren Awry (Fifth Estate); "Blood, Rage and History" by Johann Hari in *The Independent*; *The History of Terrorism* by Gérard Chaliand and Arnaud Blin; and "Love and Woe Nevermore: The Women in Edgar Allan Poe's Life" by Magdelana Salata (*Diabolique* magazine). Because of the subject matter, I should also draw attention to "Did John Wilkes Booth Get Away with Murdering President Abraham Lincoln?"—a fascinating piece by Edward Colimore in *The Philadelphia Inquirer* (www.inquirer.com).

I first had the idea for "The Mercy of the Night" in July 2014, when it occurred to me these stories were all about the passing on of the baton. Poe's letters, extensively reproduced in Arthur Hobson Quinn's *Edgar Allan Poe: A Critical Biography* (1941) were indispensible in furnishing me with the kind of prose EAP used *outside* of stories. I thank Douglas Starr for his short (but vivid) description of Lyon's floating morgue in *The Killer of Little Shepherds*, an excellent book on the early days of French forensic science, while some remarkable "severed head" tales can be found in Jan Bondeson's *The Lion Boy and Other Curiosities*. More on the role of Mammoth Cave in the early treatment of consumptives can be found at www.nps.gov ("Hidden History: Tuberculosis in Mammoth Cave"). As some readers will know, the "Poe toaster" appeared annually for years, leaving a glass of cognac on the poet's grave, a tribute that continued until 2009, the identity of the imbiber shrouded in mystery. In 2015, however, the Maryland Historical Association decided to carry on the tradition, albeit in a modified, tourist-friendly form (See: "Who was the Poe Toaster? We Still have No Idea" by Kat Eschner at www.smithsonianmag. com). By strange coincidence, Josephine Rappaport's selection of books mirrors *exactly* those read by Vincent Van Gogh on his visit to England in 1873. Lastly, the notion that "true sorrow is connected to true beauty" may sound like quintessential Poe, but in fact comes from the artist Yun Hyong-keun (1988).

Needless to say, countless Sherlock Holmes books have accompanied me on this journey, such as *The Life and Times of Sherlock Holmes* by Philip Weller and Christopher Roden, as well as many biographies of Poe; notably David Sinclair's *Edgar Allan Poe*, Wolf Mankowitz's *The Extraordinary Mr Poe*, *The Haunted Man* by Philip Lindsay, not to mention *The Annotated Edgar Allan Poe* edited by Stephen Peithman, and the seminal Marie Bonaparte opus *Edgar Poe: Étude Psychoanalytique* (1933). My influences, however, are never exclusively literary, and the catalyst to create this series was probably as much my watching *The Murders in the Rue Morgue*, adapted by James MacTaggart for BBC television in 1968 under the *Detective* umbrella, directed by James Cellan Jones and produced by Verity Lambert, starring Edward Woodward as Dupin and Bernard Kay as Poe. Kim Newman informs me that the episode is tragically "M.B.W." (Missing Believed Wiped). Nevertheless it remains vivid in my memory, down to the indelible final shot of an Orangutan at the zoo.

I also have to acknowledge the many great screen actors who have made Holmes incarnate over the years; and the legendary Roger Corman (whom I met, briefly, with regard to the ill-fated

Poe biopic mentioned earlier). The stories herein would never have been dreamt of had his cinematic adaptations of Poe not burned brightly in my young imagination. And, indeed, do so in my adult imagination to this day.

The indefatigable Peter and Nicky Crowther, Mike, Tamsin, and all at PS Publishing, have been unflinching in their support and enthusiasm, and I cannot express enough gratitude to Charles Prepolec for his humbling introduction, penned during the first COVID-19 lockdown, which none of us found particularly conducive to writing. With King Pest at his elbow, he came up trumps, and, for me, one of the most valuable outcomes of writing these stories over a period of time, though we live on different continents, has been our friendship. I must also give all due credit to my wife Patricia Volk, who continues to put up with me—possibly the most inexplicable mystery alluded to in these pages.

Every one of these excellent people has helped in their different ways, and this book would not exist without them, but most of all I am eternally indebted to E.A. Poe and A.C. Doyle, those titans of literature to whom no act of gratitude can possibly be enough.

Finally, if there are inaccuracies, inconsistencies or plain old mistakes within these covers, I must of course lay the blame at the feet of my elderly narrator. The great detective's recollections may be faulty, even if his memory is phenomenal.

Stephen Volk
Bradford on Avon
January 2021